CHOSEN

D1396069

An original novel based on the hit television series
by Joss Whedon

POCKET BOOKS

NEW YORK LONDON TORONTO SYDNEY SINGAPORE

Historian's Note: This novelization is based on the shooting scripts of the entire seventh season of *Buffy the Vampire Slayer*. Certain scenes and dialogue exchanges were cut from final telecast due to length.

First Pocket Books edition January 2003

™ and © 2003 Twentieth Century Fox FilmCorporation.
All rights reserved.

POCKET BOOKS
An imprint of Simon & Schuster
Africa House
64-78 Kingsway
London, WC2B 6AH

www.simonsays.co.uk

The text of this book was set in Times.
Printed in the United States of America
2 4 6 8 10 9 7 5 3 1
A CIP catalogue record for this book is available from the British Library
ISBN 0-7434-7824-X

For Joss

Acknowledgments

My sincerest thanks to Joss Whedon, Marti Noxon, and the cast, crew, and staff of *Buffy*. You opened your doors to me many times, and I am grateful for the opportunity to have worked with you. To my editor, Lisa Clancy, thank you for this brill gig, and thank you to the other Simon & Schusterians past and present, who've worked so hard on the publishing program, long may it continue to wave: Liz Shiflett, Micol Ostow, and Lisa Gribbin. Debbie Olshan at Fox, thank you for your generosity and expertise. To my angelic agent, Howard Morhaim, his daughter, Rebecca, and his assistants, past and present, Lindsay Sagnette and Ryan Blitstein, you rock my world. To my friends, Debbie and Scott Viguié, Brenda and Scott Van De Ven, Kym Rademacher, Karen Hackett, Barbara Nierman, Linda Wilcox, Allie Costa, Angela and Patmom Riesnstra, Katherine Ramsland, Elizabeth Engstrom Cratty, and Dal and Steve Perry—and

ACKNOWLEDGMENTS

of course the Bronzers and the PBP'ers—here's looking at you. To my sister, Elise Jones, and to Cap'n Hank Chase, *mahalo* with one kiss always. And of course, to my daughter, Belle . . . my little darling, you make it all worthwhile. Thank you for blessing my life.

Angel ™

Available from POCKET BOOKS

Buffy the Vampire Slayer™

Available from POCKET BOOKS

Chapter One: "Lessons"

Istanbul

I *can't die!*

The beautiful Turkish Potential had raced through the entire city, from the modern high-rises to the old quarter, and the assassins were still gaining. She had no idea how long they had been chasing her, but she knew what they wanted: her death.

As she glanced over her shoulder, panting from her exertion, her momentum threw her down an embankment. Two of the many robed figures saw her, and came after.

A door opened, then was quickly shut. No one was going to help her. No one had helped her Watcher, either, and he was dead.

This alley, then that: She was trapped in a dead

end. Her breath came in shallow, panicky gasps. Then she saw a drain pipe and grabbed at it, using it to clamber up the side of the whitewashed building.

One of the assassins grabbed her foot, but she shook him off and made her way to the top of the building. She got to the roof.

I'm going to live through this, she thought exultantly.

But another one was waiting for her. Before she had a chance to elude him, he rushed forward and pushed her off the building.

Screaming, she tumbled to the ground, landing on her back. Still alive.

But only for one moment longer.

Two held her down; she fought, but the third raised his curved dagger into the air; it flashed like the crescent moon.

And then it cut the life from her, and another one was dead.

Sunnydale, a cemetery

The night was damp, and there was a chill in the air. An owl hooted, and tree branches rustled.

Other sisters watch TV.

The Summers sisters strolled in graveyards.

Tonight, the newly rising vampire that was Dawn's assigned practice target was middle-aged and in his burial suit . . . and bursting halfway out of his grave.

"It's about power," Buffy said to Dawn as they

watched him. "Who's got it. Who knows how to use it."

She tossed a stake to Dawn, and Dawn caught it, swallowing. Buffy reminded herself that Dawn had acquitted herself well when they had been stuck in the pit with all the root monsters. She had a streak in her, some fighter's blood. She had wanted this training, and Buffy had agreed that she should have it.

"So who's got the power, Dawn?" she demanded.

"Well, I've got the stake," Dawn said tentatively, raising it a tad for emphasis.

"The stake is not the power," Buffy shot back.

"But he's new," Dawn argued. "He doesn't know his strength. He might not know all the fancy martial arts they inevitably seem to pick up." She was less sure now, a little more frightened. Exactly how Buffy wanted her to be.

"Who's got the power?" Buffy pressed.

"He does." Dawn was grumpy.

"Never forget that," Buffy said, going to her. "No matter how well prepped you are, how well armed you are, you're still a little girl."

"Woman." Dawn straightened her shoulders.

"You're a little woman," Buffy amended patiently.

Dawn added, "I'm taller than you."

"*He's a vampire,*" Buffy reminded her, putting the focus back where it belonged. "Okay? A demon. Preternaturally strong, skilled, with powers no human can ever—"

"Excuse me," the vampire said. "I think I'm stuck."

Buffy and Dawn both glanced over at him. His

smile was pleasant as he indicated his predicament: he was still only waist level out of his grave.

"You're stuck," Buffy deadpanned. *Why couldn't a slightly more intimidating vampire rise tonight, to help me prove my point?*

"My foot's caught on a root or something," he continued, a bit sheepish. "I don't even know how I got down there. If you girls could just give me a hand . . ."

Dawn couldn't resist a . . . well, dig. "So he's got the power."

"Zip it," Buffy snapped as she crossed to the evil demon of evilness-lite.

"I really appreciate it," the vamp prattled. "It's just so dark, and I don't know what I'm doing here—"

While he yammered on, Buffy yanked him up by the collar of his jacket and set him on his feet.

"Whoa, thanks. That was a help." He grinned evilly. "Unfortunately it was the last—"

Bored now, Buffy thought. She clamped her hand around his throat and gave it a big hug.

"—thing you'll ever do," he concluded in a rasp that sounded eerily like Donald Duck on helium.

"Listen up," Buffy instructed him. "I'm the Slayer. You don't want to get into it with me. You want blood. You can have hers." She gestured to Dawn. "She's not the Slayer. She's the one to go after. Not me."

"I was thinking along those lines," Vampire Donald croaked.

"Okay, then."

Buffy let him go and stepped back, essentially

quitting the field so Dawn could have a shot. The vampire lurched forward toward her and Dawn got ready to rumble, although her bravado had evaporated. She was scared, and good thing, too.

"Power," Buffy reminded her. "He's got it, he's gonna use it. You don't have it."

The demon rushed Dawn—who ducked, and Donald smacked directly into a tombstone.

"So you use that!" Buffy said. "Perfect!"

Flush with her momentary success, Dawn scrambled for her stake, leaped at the vamp, and staked the sucker.

He did not dust. Solidly still there, he backhanded her. Like a stuntwoman hooked up to a wire, she flew backward. Blood dotted her lip, and then the vamp was on her.

Buffy held back, making Dawn fight, making her see that this wasn't about executing a few clever moves and then figuring you were gonna get the trophy and the best lines, too. Dawn slid forward to get free of him, and showed the bad guy the stake.

He jerked back and hissed . . . then promptly grabbed her arm and twisted it until she dropped the stake, wincing with pain.

He came in for the bite, and still Buffy held back. Dawnie had to see that this was reality, this was what death looked like when it rose from the grave and traded jokes for a while. Those fangs, that saliva; the sharp first prick on one's neck . . .

"Buffy!" she screamed.

Just in time, Buffy grabbed his suit jacket from

behind. He dropped Dawn, and she went into her moves, kung-fu-Slayer, giving far better than he gave. Then she grabbed the sword from her weapons bag and whacked off his fangy, drooly head.

Dawn lay sprawled on the ground, her hand to her neck. There was blood; the vampire had started his bite. She looked stunned . . . and accusatory.

"It's real," Buffy said evenly. "That's the only lesson, Dawn. It's always real."

She held out her hand, and Dawn took it. As Buffy helped her up, she moved to examine Dawn's neck.

"Let me see."

"It's nothing. Just a scrape." Dawn was trying to be brave. Her face was ashen. "Plus, I had a plan the whole time," she added.

"Really?" *Gotta admire her pluck.*

"Yeah. I planned to get killed, come back as a vampire, and bite you." Her voice carried an undertone of embarrassment. Buffy knew that feeling well. But that was not where to put the power, and she couldn't let Dawn leave it there.

"You wanted to be trained," she reminded her sister.

"Well, the next time you're gonna disappear—"

"You did pretty well," Buffy cut in.

"I did?" Dawn asked, all attempts at machisma dropped. Now she was Buffy's little sister, eager for her big sister's approval.

"Yeah," Buffy said.

Dawn brightened. "'Cause with the rolling thing, I

was using his strength. It got very tai chi, plus I nearly got the heart."

As Buffy moved to gather up the weapons, she said, "My first time out, I missed the heart, too."

Dawn's eyes got huge. "No way."

"Just the once," Buffy fibbed, basking in the hero-worship.

"Well, the next vampire I meet—"

"The next vampire you meet, you run away," Buffy ordered her.

Then she thought about what was to come, and pitied her poor little sister. Something far worse . . . far, far worse . . . something from which Dawn could not run away, could never hope escape: her first day at the brand new version of Sunnydale High. Different stucco, new principal . . . and same old Hellmouth.

"Then we'll never know what's coming next," Buffy murmured.

But what was coming was inevitable. The morning dawned a beautiful day, perfect weather for the ribbon-cutting ceremony—reporters, grandstand with city officials—all focused on Robin Wood, new to Sunnydale, and here on business.

"It is my great pleasure and privilege to announce the official opening—on the very ground it first stood upon—of the brand new, state-of-the-art, Sunnydale High!" he announced.

Then Principal Wood cut the large red ribbon with an oversized pair of scissors.

Let the games begin, he thought wryly.

England

England was a land of rolling green hills and Druid groves, villages and medieval graveyards. It was a place Willow had come to understand, and to regard as her safe haven. Now, as she urged a Paraguayan flower to take root, to sprout, and to blossom, she felt a connection to the universe that had not been with her for a long, long time.

The first time I ever felt like this . . . was the first time I held hands with Tara, back when the Gentlemen arrived in Sunnydale and stole all our voices. When Tara was murdered, it was like my goodness was stolen . . . like all that was left was a connection with evil. But that's gone now, or lurking . . . and hey, growing things. That's good, right?

She became aware of a shadow. Giles stood beside her, gazing intently at the flower. It was not a native English plant; he knew that, and he was intrigued that she had chosen to bring it to this place, this time. And that she could.

"That doesn't belong here," he ventured.

She was pleased with herself. "No, it doesn't."

"The *flora kua alaya*. A native of Paraguay, if my botany serves," he added.

She glanced up at him and smiled. "Is there anything you don't know about?"

"Synchronized swimming. Complete mystery to me," he confessed. He drew closer, studying the flower. "Yes. Paraguay." He looked at her. "Where did it come from?"

"Paraguay," she said breathlessly.

"You brought it through the earth," he commented.

"It's all connected," she told him. "The root systems, the molecules, the energy. Everything's connected."

"You sound like Mrs. Harkness," he observed, referring to Willow's Coven Mistress. She realized he'd been sent to find her, that the Coven had been concerned that she hadn't shown up at her lesson. Afraid, more like.

"The Coven is . . . they're the most amazing women I've ever met," Willow told him. "But there's this look they get, like I'm gonna turn them into bangers and mash or something. Which I'm not even really sure what that is."

"They're cautious," Giles said gently. "I trust you can understand that."

"I don't have that much power," Willow murmured. "I don't think."

"But everything's connected," Giles reminded her, gesturing to the flower, using her own words back on her. "You're connected to great power, whether you feel it or not."

"You should just take it from me," Willow ventured, rising, crossing toward the place where she lived.

As they walked, he said, "You know we can't. This isn't a hobby, or an addiction. It's inside you now. It's magic. You're responsible for it."

"Will they always be afraid of me?" she asked him.

He considered. "Maybe. Can you handle it?"

She felt a little lost. A lot lost. She had no idea how to answer him.

"I deserve a lot worse. I killed people, Giles."

They stopped walking and regarded one another.

"I've not forgotten," he said soberly.

"When you brought me here," she confessed, "I thought it was to kill me. Or lock me in some mystical dungeon for all eternity, or with the torture . . . instead, you go all Dumbledore on me. I'm learning about magic, and energy and Gaia and root systems . . ."

"Do you want to be punished?" Giles asked.

She felt terrible guilt and pain, and still some anger, too. *I killed Warren . . . but he killed Tara.*

"I want to be Willow," she answered.

"You are." Giles voice was still calm, still gentle. "In the end, we are all who we are . . . no matter how much we may appear to have changed."

Does he mean to comfort me with that? she wondered.

Sunnydale

It was Dawn's first day at the new and completely rebuilt Sunnydale High.

"Dawn! Xander's here!" Buffy bellowed.

"Just a minute!" Dawn bellowed back.

"You're going to be late."

"I'm comfortable with that!"

She opened the front door to let Xander in.

"Good morning," he said warmly. He was carrying rolled-up blueprints in a tube.

Buffy gave him a nod then yelled to her sister, "Well, you have to eat something. I made cereal."

"Okay!" Dawn sang back.

Buffy said to Xander, "You're unconscionably spiffy."

They walked into the kitchen. Xander had come to pick them up, dressed up now that he was a general contractor.

"Client meeting," he told her, glancing around the kitchen. "How exactly do you *make* cereal?"

She flushed a little, shrugged, gestured. "You put the box near the milk. I saw it on the food channel. Want something?"

"I ate. I'm good." He cocked his head. "How are you?"

She shrugged. "My sister's about to go to the same high school that tried to kill me for three years. I can't change districts, I can't afford private school, and I can't begin to prepare for what could possibly come out of there." She put on a smile. "So, peachy with a side of keen, that would be me."

"Well, here's a little something for what ails ya," he told her. He gestured to the tube.

They went into the living room.

He unrolled the blueprints and said, "Take a look."

Dawn sailed past, saying, "Hey, check out double-O Xander."

"Go," Buffy ordered her. "Talk with your mouth full."

"I've got two crews working on this diabolical yet lucrative new campus," he told her. "One here, finishing the science building. And one here, reinforcing the gym. There are no pentagrams, no secret passageways. Everything's up to code and safe as houses."

"Nothing creepy? Strange? From beyond?"

Dawn appeared, and said with her mouth full, "Maybe you're just paranoid."

"Well, there is one interesting detail," Xander conceded. "I managed to scare up the plan from the old high school. You remember the very center of Sunnydale's own Hellmouth?"

He took both sets of plans over to the window, putting one set over the other so they could make comparisons.

"Under the library," Buffy said.

"Right." Xander nodded. "So I lined up the plans, new and old. And right exactly where the library was, we now have . . ." He looked to her to fill in the blanks.

"Principal's office," she said.

Dawn was intrigued. "So the principal's evil?"

"Or in a boatload of danger," Buffy said.

"Well, the last two principals were eaten," Xander pointed out. "Who would even apply for that job?"

"Guess we'll see," Buffy said. She checked the time. "Oooh, we have to leave, though." She turned to Dawn. "You have everything? Books, lunch, stakes?"

"Checked thrice."

Buffy gave Dawn a present—a cell phone—and Xander dropped them off. After Buffy warned Dawn to stay away from hyena people, lizardy-type athletes, and especially invisible people—to which Dawn retorted that it was pretty safe to say she was not going to be seeing any invisible people to stay away from— Buffy concluded her cautionary lecture by saying, "This place is evil" just in time for the new principal to overhear her.

Whoops.

"Tough to let 'em go, huh?" he asked her.

She was still flustered. Plus, all the old feelings about being an extreme geek in high school. Both of them. She got kicked out of Hemery, in L.A., for burning down the gym.

"I'm Robin Wood," he said. "New principal."

Whose office sits over the Hellmouth . . .

"Oh, uh, Buffy Summers," Buffy said. She gestured to her sister. "This is Dawn."

"Nice to meet you," he said to Dawn.

"Hi," she replied,

"So you're the new principal," Buffy went on. "I expected you to be more . . . aged." He was young and . . . wow, kinda hot.

"Huh. You seem a bit young to have such a grown-up daughter.

She was wounded to the core. "Oh. Uh, uh, no. Sister."

"Oh, right, um, of course," he said.

"You didn't really think she's my . . ." She turned to Dawn, stricken. "It's my hair. I have mom hair."

"No," Dawn assured her.

Principal Wood smiled. "I actually have heard of you, Miss Summers. Graduated from the old high school, am I right?"

Taken aback, she gazed at him and said, "Uh, yeah. How did you . . . ?"

"Well, I better get back to work. Gotta start deadening young minds. It's really nice to meet you. You have fun," he said to Dawn.

"That was suspicious," Buffy murmured as he walked away.

"You betcha. Bye." Dawn practically ran.

"I know," Dawn called over her shoulder. "You never see it coming, the stake is not the power, *To Serve Man* is a cookbook. I love you. Go away."

So Buffy . . . went.

And where she went was back in the bathroom to check on her hair, wondering if made her look older. Not Mom hair, she decided.

Then she noticed some weird chicken-bone thing tied together with string and picked it up . . .

. . . and what looked back at her over her shoulder was a very dead girl, looking the way the decomposing dead look in real life and not on TV, who said eerily, "You can't protect her. You couldn't protect me."

Then an equally dead janitor appeared and bellowed, "GET OUT! GET OUT! GET OUT!"

Then they both disappeared. Buffy stayed in the corner, trying to process what had just happened.

Home schooling, she thought anxiously as she did just that. *It's not just for crazy religious people any more. I am so getting Dawn out of here. . . . Expulsion works. . . . It always worked for me. . . .*

* * *

Dawn was up for the count—facing the class halfway through her intro to the world of Dawn Summers' faves and raves—which included Britney Spears' early work, history, and dancing. And never having to do an intro again. People were smiling, chuckling at her wit—*I can do this! I can fit in!*—and then—

BLAM!

The Slayer flung herself into the room, shouting, "Dawn! We gotta go! It's not safe!"

Dawn could feel herself melting into nothingness . . . or wishing she could, but now everyone was staring at Buffy as if she were completely out of her mind.

Perhaps actually realizing how badly she was ruining Dawn's life as the class stared at her in amazement, Buffy took it down a couple million notches.

"I, uh, Dawn, I just thought you were in danger of um . . . smoking." Dawn winced at Buffy's lame attempt to save her social life. "I'll be around."

Then she ducked back out, leaving Dawn to deal with the wreckage.

"I also have a sister," Dawn announced unnecessarily.

It was girl-time at the café, but a human couple were singing to each other, some dippy song about eternal love and blah, blah, blah. It was positively sickening.

"Six weeks, tops," Anya muttered to Halfrek, her

best vengeance-demon girlfriend, "and she's calling on me for vengeance."

"Oooh, he'd better run for cover," Hallie jibed, chuckling.

"What's that supposed to mean?" Anya demanded.

"Oh, sweetie, you know exactly what it means," Halfrek said, not without tenderness.

"Excuse me?"

And it all came out: The other vengeance demons were gossiping about her behind her back. Saying she'd lost it, calling her Ms. Soft Serve.

"You've lost your powers," Hallie concluded. "It happens. And you fell for this Xander guy."

Anya was stunned. "It was a glitch!" she insisted. "A summer thing! I am so back into the vengeance fold."

Hallie enumerated Anya's sins of omission. "No deaths, no eviscerations—you're not goading women into anything inventive and you're not delivering when it is." Hallie softened a little, leaning forward, getting conspiratorial.

"Anyway, if it was just me—"

Anya was alarmed. "What do you mean 'if it was just you'?"

"D'Hoffryn, the lower beings, they're all feeling the heat. Something's rising. Something older than the old ones, and everybody's tail is twitching. This is a bad time to be a good guy."

"Well, what is this, an intervention?" Anya asked, hurt and a little afraid. "Shouldn't all my demon friends be here?"

Halfrek picked up her coffee, looked sad, and said, "Sweetie, they are."

At the school construction site, Buffy sought out Xander.

"So how's it looking?" he asked her. "Does the place pass inspection?"

"Oh, it's great," she said sarcastically ". . . if you're a zombie-ghost thing!"

They looked at each other, concerned . . . and perhaps not too surprised.

"So school's back in session, huh?" he asked.

She sighed. "Seems like old times."

They moved away from Xander's construction guys; Xander asked her, "So, zombies or ghosts?"

"I'm not sure," she told him. "They were in the mirror, but they disappeared. But they touched me. I think." She frowned. "Well, let's just start with dead and pissed."

"They were after you personally?" he asked.

"They talked about protecting people," she replied. "Told me to leave."

"No damage, though," he said leadingly.

"I think I may have destroyed Dawn's social life in all of about thirty seconds," she said sadly, "but apart from that, no."

He shrugged dismissively. "Ah, being popular isn't so great. Or so I've read in books."

She was not a happy big sister . . . or a happy Slayer. "This isn't a coincidence, you know, the school being rebuilt. It means something. . . ."

Dawn's class got over her sister's weirdness, and she began to have a little hope again. An okay boy, maybe a little nerdy, asked to borrow a pencil. She got one out of her pencil case and handed it to him . . . and the fingers that took it from her were blue and white and peeling and hideous and very, very dead.

Before she could react, the nerd attached to the hand—who was also very, very dead, just one decomposing layer of skin after another—said, "Thanks a lot" and tried to stab her in the eye.

She screamed, clutching her face, and fell out of her chair . . . and by the time she realized nothing had really happened, everyone was staring at her as if she were even crazier than her sister.

Fighting for composure, she made up a lame excuse about a bee and a bee allergy, and escaped into the bathroom.

I know from evil weirdness, she reminded herself, but just the same, she sat in a stall and shook, sweating and trying to compose herself.

Yeah, right . . .

She became aware that farther down the row of stalls, someone was sobbing. Really crying hard, having edged past hysteria and into the kind of crying she herself had done when things had been unbelievably bad . . . such as when she had discovered that she wasn't really a human being.

And she had not been the ninth caller to get the Justin Timberlake tickets. . . .

Taking her own terror into her hands, she crept out of the stall. Her footsteps rang on the tile, just in case there was a monster around listening for young girls making foolish moves.

Stall door by stall door, she listened, and then bingo: Huddled on top of the seat in one of the last ones in the row was a tough-looking Goth girl, practically catatonic with fear.

"There's someone in here," she told Dawn.

I have a bad feeling she doesn't mean just us chickens, Dawn thought.

"Saw something pretty creepy, huh?" Dawn asked sympathetically as she helped the other girl out of the stall. "Was there a pencil involved in any—?"

She turned and glanced in the mirror.

Dawn's dead nerd stared back at her. A dead girl and an older man, also very dead, had joined him, and as they lurched forward, a shower of sparks exploded from the overhead fluorescent lights.

As the two girls screamed, three pairs of dead hands smashed through the tile floor and grabbed at their ankles. A whole chunk of floor crumbled beneath them, and down, down, down they slammed, to the lower level of Sunnydale High.

Hellmouth level . . .

Buffy hard returned to the main building to continue investigating the zombie ghosts, when she literally bumped into Principal Wood in the hall.

"Whoa," he said.

"Ooh, sorry."

"Miss Summers," he said affably. "I didn't know you were still about."

"Uh. Yeah." She glanced around. "I was just looking for . . ."

"I thought in general it was customary for a person to, um, you know . . . go somewhere else."

"Well, it's a new campus. I'm just getting to know it. You know, to make sure it's safe for my sister," she said brightly.

He looked confused.

The school basement was not a pleasant place to be. Nor was it user-friendly in terms of exits. And it also seemed that the walls might be moving.

Dawn said to the other girl, whose name was Kit, "What did you see when I found you in the stall?"

"A girl," Kit told her. "She said she died here, and that everybody dies here, and that we would too."

"And here I was worried about not fitting in," Dawn muttered.

Then they made another turn . . . and a guy appeared. All three screamed.

His name was Carlos, he was not a dead guy, and he was just as scared as they were.

"I just came downstairs for a smoke, you know, and I saw . . . It was the janitor, yelling at me. I thought he was just pissed, but I saw him in the light . . ."

"Wait. You came downstairs," Dawn prodded. *"Where?"*

He shook his head. "Man, I got no clue. I ran away like a girl. I don't know this place at all."

Dawn realized with a jolt that she was in charge. The other two were too frightened for the honor.

I have the power.

"Okay, so," she began. "We can run around in circles, or—"

"You really think you can run away?" asked the dead janitor as he moved from the darkness into the dim light.

"It's not real," Kit begged, pleaded.

But Dawn remembered the session in the graveyard with the vampire. She understood what Buffy had been trying to teach her.

"Lesson one," she said grimly. "It's always real."

"Go ahead and scream all you want," Dead Bathroom Girl taunted as the three moved in for the kill. "No one's going to hear you."

Hear us! Yes!

Because Buffy had gifted Dawn with a cell phone, and orders to call her whenever she needed help.

Anxiously she demon-dialed—*weak ha, ha*—and wondered about the reception this far down.

Please, please, please, Buffy, she mentally called out to the Slayer.

"You know, I, um, have to be honest," Principal Wood was saying to Buffy, still out in the hall. "I actually know more about you than I let on before."

She went on alert, said, "Isn't that interesting."

He gazed at her. "Oh, it really is. The school board recommended I spend a little time reading your record. It's, ah, quite a page-turner. Kind of a checkered past . . ."

"Huh." She laughed nervously. "More like a plaid.

Kind of a clan tartan of badness, really. You know, there were factors."

Then her cell phone went off.

She answered immediately, heard about the three dead people in the basement, and extricated herself from her discussion with the admittedly handsome, yet far too inquisitive, Wood with a bogus excuse concerning dead dogs or dead dog walkers or a dog tragedy of some sort. *Not for nothing do we skip having pets, you should have seen the zombie cat we had for, oh, five minutes.* She raced as fast as she could to the bathroom, where she had seen the dead girl.

There was a hole, big enough for a most beloved little sister to fall through. Buffy leaped and landed . . . and ran into Mr. Dead Janitor and his two friends, Dead Nerd and Dead Bathroom Girl.

"This place is ours now," the Dead Bathroom Girl said spookily. "It's built on our graves. We rested easy until we felt your return."

"Leave," the janitor chimed in. "Leave and never come back."

"I'd love to. Really," Buffy soothed, but of course there was Dawn to find and save.

And then she realized they were trying to keep her from noticing a particular door. As she moved to open it, they flew at her. Moving into Fighty McFight mode—Nerd went first; and she grabbed him single-handedly (in the literally sense), swinging him back into the janitor. They both went flying and screaming, and then the girl jumped on Buffy, trying to bite her—shades of dead weirdness.

Buffy jumped up and back, flying through the air and landing as hard as she could on the girl, wrestler style.

For a moment she thought she'd best them, but they reassembled in front of the door like bowling pins.

"If at first you don't succeed . . . ," Buffy said, running at them. They charged her—and she leaped over them, flipping in midair, and landing on her feet with a clear shot at the door.

". . . cheat," she finished.

They tried one more time—the lock slowed her down—but she yanked that sucker open; metal groaning, locks snapping—and there stood

Spike?!

What the hell . . . ?

It was Spike, looking gaunt and horrible, his hair a mess and his eyes bloodshot. He was trembling. She drew back. The last time she had seen him had been in the bathroom of her home as he had tried to rape her to make her "feel" for him. . . . As he had savaged her, brutalized her.

He was giggling hysterically. She couldn't believe she was actually seeing him, and wondered if he were actually one of the zombie ghosts.

Then he stopped laughing and tenderly touched her face.

"Buffy, duck," he told her.

"What? Duck? There's a duck?"

And the evil janitor smacked her over the head with a pipe.

He kept hitting her, but Buffy fought him off, smacking him on the head with the door. She went in the closet, Spike too. Then she latched the door.

"He'll probably show up in a sec," she said.

"Nobody comes in here," Spike assured her, and she saw that he was . . . crazy. Spike had lost his mind.

She was barely able to process that.

What happened? Where's he been?

"It's just the three of us," he continued.

"Spike, have you seen Dawn? she asked.

That upset him. He started yelling, "Don't you think I'm trying? I'm not a quick study." Then he burst into tears. "I dropped my board in the water and the chalk all ran. Sure to be caned." He laughed. "Should have seen that coming."

He moved away from her into a corner. She followed. He leaned against the wall and pulled his loose shirt over his chest.

Cautiously she pulled it back to see what he was hiding. He was gravely wounded, his torso a mass of cuts and welts.

"I tried, I tried to cut it out . . ." he wept, and she was completely bewildered.

But no time for that now: the phone rang. It was Dawn again, terrified. They debriefed, and the Slayer told her sister she was on her way and damage-bound. But what were they fighting? Ghosts? Zombies?

"Manifest spirits," Spike filled in, "controlled by a talisman and raised to seek vengeance."

"A talisman," Buffy echoed. *That bone thing in the bathroom*, she realized.

She called Xander, hoping he was still on campus, and asked him to look for the talisman.

Then she set off in search of her sister.

School. It never changes.

Buffy's coming, but until she shows, it's up to me to get these guys out of here, Dawn resolutely told herself.

So they kept creeping through the basement, edgy and scared and Dawn wishing with all her might for a return to middle-school days. Carlos found some bricks, and Dawn had the idea to load up Kit's shoulder bag. It was hard for her to pick up.

I should work out more.

They crept through the frightening maze that was the lower level of Sunnydale High. And the deadly trio reappeared, stinking of death, leering with bad teeth and worse intentions.

Dawn knew she wasn't ready for them, and she knew that didn't matter. She swung the brick-loaded bag at the dead girl, who fell against the janitor, while Kit screamed and screamed.

Dawn was not powerful enough to follow through with the swing. A wave of despair rushed through her; these things were going to kill Kit, Carlos, and her, and she wasn't going to be able to stop them.

Then Buffy appeared almost as if by magic, all shiny and grim purpose like Daredevil, and Dawn's heart soared. The janitor attacked, then the nerd, with a big pipe, and Dawn shouted at Buffy, "The bag!"

Buffy grabbed it and began swinging with ease. It was bag-fu time as she swung it into the faces of the evil dead, then overhead heard, around her back—wow—around the pipe, headkicking the dead girl, wiping out the nerd—it was one huge Jackie Chan ballet, and Dawn was in awe.

Then Buffy finally let the bag go, and it flew into the janitor's face and sent him rocketing back.

Dawn couldn't lead, but she could help. She tossed her sister the big pipe the nerd had tried to hit her with. Buffy caught it without looking and twirled it like a big huge dream majorette baton of death . . .

"You really wanna keep this up?" Buffy demanded.

The janitor mocked her. "What are you going to do, kill us?"

He has a point, Dawn thought anxiously as the three evil beings began to converge on the good guys . Her heart was slamming against her ribs; adrenaline was coursing through her body with no conversion—as yet—into action. *They can fight for, like, ever. Not even Buffy can fight that long. What* are *we gonna do?*

And then *pop!* went the weasel, and the bad dead guys completely and totally vanished.

Upstairs in the girls' bathroom, Xander gazed at the broken bits of talisman in his hands. The dead girl who had been riding his back as if he were a mechanical bull while trying to stop him, vanished into thin air.

The halls—and basement—of Sunnydale High were cleansed of evil manifest spirits with the snapping of the bone.

Xander enjoyed his accomplishment, and then he

set off to complete his appointed rounds as sidekick to the Slayer—making sure she and her sister were okay.

My work here, nearly done.

The deeper recesses of Spike's mind processed the victory.

But Spike's own victory had eluded him. Buffy's abrupt arrival had caught him unawares; and though he had planned their reunion, played it out in his mind a thousand times. He had botched it.

". . . I had a speech, I learned it all," he keened to himself, ". . . Oh, God, she won't understand, she won't understand. . . ."

"Of course she won't understand, Sparky," a voice answered calmly. "I'm beyond her understanding."

A mind clearer than Spike's would have recognized the speaker as Warren, the evil scientist/member of the evil threesome who had shot and killed Tara, and who had been flayed alive for his crime. Flayed by the red witch, back in England, and Warren should not be here—*cuz, dead*—but he was, with his dark eyes and brown hair and his smirk.

"She's a girl," Warren continued, dripping with contempt. "Sugar and spice and everything *useless,* unless you're baking. I'm more than that. More than flesh."

He morphed into Glory the Hellgod, the being who had caused Buffy's second death as she had swan dived into a sea of mystical energy.

"More than blood," she exulted. "I'm . . . you know, I honestly don't think there's a human word fabulous enough for me." She strutted, enormously pleased with herself. "Oh, my name will be on everyone's lips, assuming their lips haven't been torn off—but not just yet. That's all right, though."

Glory morphed into Adam, the part-demon, part-metallic-construct created by Riley Finn's superior, Dr. Maggie Walsh.

"I can be patient," Adam assured Spike. "Everything is well within parameters. She's right where I want her. And so are you, number seventeen. You're where you belong."

Number seventeen . . . my prison ID code, when the Initiative got me, chipped me . . . this monster knows all my secrets . . .

Adam morphed next into Mayor Wilkins, who had adopted the dark Slayer, Faith, and tried to devour Buffy's graduating class on Ascension Day . . .

The Mayor squatted opposite Spike, all affable intimidation, as he had been in life.

"So what'd you think, you'd get your soul back and everything would be Jim Dandy? A soul's slipperier than a greased weasel. Why do you think I sold mine?"

He added pleasantly, "Well, you probably thought you'd be your own man and I respect that. But you never will."

And as he reached for Spike's face, he morphed again.

"You'll always be mine," Drusilla the vampire murmured. She was his beautiful sire, and he had loved her for centuries. Burned for her, until she'd left him . . . and he'd been so ridiculous as to fall in love with the Slayer.

"You'll always be in the dark with me, singing our li'l songs. You like our little songs, don't you?"

He couldn't force away her touch, didn't want to; she wasn't there, she wasn't, and yet . . . her touch was real. Her voice, real.

I am utterly mad. I'm mad as a . . . weasel.

"You always liked them, right from the beginning. And that's where we're going."

She stood, and gone was his Dru. And in her place . . . The vampire who had sired Darla, who had in turn sired Angelus, who had in turn sired Dru, who had in turn sired . . . Spike.

The Master.

A vampire so old he was more batlike than human, him in his leathers and his monstrous fangs and fingers . . . the creature responsible for Buffy's first death.

"Right back to the beginning," the Master proclaimed evilly. "Not the 'Bang,' not the 'Word,' the true beginning."

Not there, not there, Spike told himself, rocking back and forth.

"The next few months are going to be quite a ride," the Master added, "and I think we're all going to learn something about ourselves in the process. You'll learn you're a pathetic schmuck, if it hasn't sunk in already."

He towered over Spike's hunched figure, magnificent in his contempt.

"Look at you," he spat. "Tried to do what's right.

Just like her. You still don't get it. It's not about right. It's not about wrong."

The most terrifying transformation had been saved for last, as the Master morphed into the one being in all the world who had consumed Spike body, heart, and soul . . . who could spell his end . . .

Buffy.

With a quiet smile, she said, "It's about power."

Chapter Two: "Beneath You"

Frankfurt, Germany

Tattoo Nachtlocal was the Potential's hangout. It had been easy to find her there, with her hot pink hair and her black bangs, her nose ring and metal collar.

She raced across the breezeway of the technoclub and jumped down a level; then she dashed into an exterior door and scaled down the building.

Ja. She was safe, back outside with some of the other club patrons . . . until her robed pursuers pushed her back inside and shut the door.

She fought back, but there were too many. Then one of them pulled a long curved dagger. She blocked his swing.

She missed the other one.

It went so deep inside her the assassin's wrist was soaked with blood.

Her dead face stared out. Flecks of blood freckled her cheeks and her eyes glazed. Then her mouth opened, and an inhuman voice rumbled out of her:

"From beneath you, it devours . . ."

Buffy screamed.

And woke up.

Her sheets were bunched around her, sweat dripped off her brow, and Dawn's were hands on her shoulders as her sister tried to rouse her.

"I heard screaming," she told Dawn. "And there was a girl . . ." She processed some more nightmare, recalled the unnatural voice.

"'From beneath you, it devours.' That's what she said, and then they . . ." She took a breath, seeing the death again. "There's more like her, Dawn. Out there somewhere."

Buffy rose and looked out her window, at the uneasy somnolence of Sunnydale.

"And they're gonna die."

England

And Willow snapped out of her vision, sprawled on the lawn before the old stone house, while Giles urged her to breathe.

She had collapsed. She was lying on the ground with her hands in the grass. She looked up at Giles, stunned by what she had seen and felt . . . by what she *knew* . . .

"We were talking," she told him. "And I felt . . ."

She jerked her hands away from the grass.

"I felt the earth."

She looked at Giles uneasily. "It's all connected, it is, only it's not all good and pure and rootsy . . . there's deep, deep black, there's . . . I saw the earth, Giles. I saw its teeth."

He understood at once.

"The Hellmouth," he said.

"It's going to open." She was terrified, swaying with what she knew. Sick from it. "It's going to swallow us all."

Sunnydale

A rat. Just a wee beady-eyed one, but bloody mammal all the same. Spike was on it, a wee bit of smackerel, rather like a scrambling kipper, blood and whiskers and a small heart to beat it all . . .

Then rumbling blasted through like a train, like a hellish California earthquake, pervading his basement. The rat felt it, too, and took off; the rumbling jittered Spike's fingers and his fangs and his brains; until it shook him hard like an angry, drunken uncle. He screamed in agony for it to stop. Begged the monsters, begged his mum . . .

But it did not.

Dawn was perky for someone who had slept very little, but then, she was young. She was very excited that Buffy was going to be working at her school.

"You understand you cannot talk to me, look at me, or hang out with any of my friends, right?" she continued.

Buffy understood.

Principal Wood was there to greet her on her first day as a member of the faculty. He had personally offered Buffy her part-time job as liaison to the world of troubled teens. It seemed rather convenient, she being the Slayer with a sister to protect, he having his office directly atop the Hellmouth. Maybe it really did have something to do with her being young enough to remember what a special hell high school could be . . . even in a normal town.

She hoped to God it had nothing to do with mom hair.

"Just remember that while you're here to help," he advised her as he led her to her brand spanking new office, "you're not their friend. Trust me, open that door, these students will eat you alive."

She took a breath. "You heard about Principal Flutie, right?"

She couldn't be sure what he'd heard about. But he seemed to be up on his discipline. "There's only three things these kids understand: the boot, the bat, and the bastinada. Bad joke," he added, seeing her blank stare. "It's the 'bastinada.' No one ever knows what that thing is."

Without hesitation, Buffy replied, "Wooden rod they use to smack the soles of your feet with in Turkish prisons, but if you use the right wood, they make an awesome Billy club."

Following this revelation, there was a long pause as Principal Wood stared at her as if she'd grown a second head. Then he smiled.

"Think you're going to fit in just fine," he said.

Then he left her alone, leaving her to sneak off to the basement to see how Spike was doing.

But of the bleached-blond vampire, there was no trace.

The streets of Sunnydale were dark and deserted, but Nancy didn't mind. Alone was good. Alone was . . . free. It was far more pleasant to walk Rocky, her little Yorkie, even though the stubborn little creature had yet to pee, than it had ever been to toe the line with her psycho ex-boyfriend, Ronnie.

"Come on, baby," she urged the pup, a little bored.

Rocky trailed behind, sniffing at everything. Nancy groused, "Could have gotten a cat, but nooo . . ."

She waited.

There was a small, almost imperceptible jerk on the leash line, followed by a tiny yip.

Frowning Nancy turned around . . . and there was no more Rocky. Just the leash, and then . . . a hole in the ground. Just a hole.

She took a moment to process the odd tableau.

It was a moment too long.

For suddenly and violently she was jerked off her feet by a mighty tug on the end of the leash; she hit the sidewalk in a full-body dive, hard. Dragged along, she realized that the leash was being sucked into the hole, and she was being pulled toward it, that there was nothing stopping her progress as she was reeled in like a helpless fish . . .

Then something roared and burst out of the ground; it was hideous, unbelievable. Screaming Nancy managed to crawl back as fast as she could, untangling her bloodied hand from the leash just in time. She screamed, ran and ran into the broad chest of a dark-haired guy, who said, "Hello."

I meet women in the oddest ways, Xander thought.

He had brought the hottie in distress, whose name was Nancy, to Buffy's house. Nancy was telling them what had happened, in the words of someone who was not so used to the dark side as they were.

"You hear things in this town, living in Sunnydale," Nancy was saying, "but no one actually believes them. You have to be crazy and . . ." She took a breath and looked at Buffy, Dawn, and Xander. "You all think I'm crazy, don't you?"

"I don't," Xander assured her.

"We've seen things too, Nancy," Buffy chimed in.

"And we're gonna do something about this," Xander said manfully. "It's your lucky night. Considering, you know, your dog just got all ate up and stuff." *Oh, smooth, Harris*, he chided himself. "Can I fresh up that tea for ya?"

"So you say this thing just came up out of the ground without any warnings or anything?"

"Just this kind of rumbling, you know, like just before an earthquake?"

Uh-oh, Xander thought, as Buffy gave voice to his thinking.

"'From beneath you it devours.'"

Nancy was puzzled. "What?"

"Nothing," Buffy murmured.

"Nothing good," Dawn added softly.

"It's sounding monsterific, all right," Xander observed.

"Round up the gang?" Dawn suggested.

"Good thinking. Except . . ." Xander was glum. "This is the gang."

Buffy turned to Nancy. "We're going to get into this," she informed her. "And if your dog's alive, we'll find him. I promise. The only thing we need . . ."

"What you need is help," said a suave, deep, and vaguely familiar voice. "Fortunately you've got me."

If someone had slapped Xander with an electric eel, he wouldn't have been more shocked.

Spike stood before them, cool, calm, collected. Well dressed—blue was a good color on him—and looking rather studly, not that Xander noticed.

Totally together, like the last time Xander had seen him, when he wasn't trying to rape Buffy. . . .

He's different. He's not crazy anymore, Buffy thought, perplexed. She felt terribly anxious having him in the house, and confused about the one-eighty that seemed to have taken place since she saw him in the basement.

What's going on with him?

* * *

Then Buffy was talking to Spike, while Dawn and Xander tried to explain to Nancy that Spike was Buffy's ex, only more so, and Xander's shockometer soared when it came out that Buffy had recently seen the former object of her twisted obsessions—and guess where: in the mucho mojo basement of Sunnydale High.

And Spike wanted to *help*?!

"Help me what?" Buffy demanded, and Xander was right there with her.

"I was kinda hoping you'd tell me. You're the Slayer. Connected to the visions, the long line of worthies. Right? And I'm just a guy with his ear to the ground, but even *I* can feel it. Something's coming. Don't know what, exactly," Spike continued. "But something's brewing and it's so big, ugly and damned, it makes you and me look like little bitty puzzle pieces."

It's like Casablanca, only not, Xander thought.

"Ball's in your court, Slayer," Spike concluded.

And Xander thought, *Man. Bastard waltzes right in here after what he did. Talk about balls . . .*

England

Coat on, bags packed. Willow sat in the old stone house that had become her refuge. In the drive, the taxi idled, ready and willing.

Willow was not so much. She wasn't ready to leave her safe heaven.

"What exactly are you afraid of?" Giles asked her.

"How about the Hellmouth's getting all rumbly

again and now I know it's got teeth. And those are literal teeth, 'cause I don't know if I can handle it. And what if I *can* handle it? Does that mean I have to be a bigger, badder badass than the source of all badness? What if I have to give up all this control stuff and go all veiny and homicidal again? And what if—"

"They won't take you back?" Giles asked gently.

And of course that was very high on her list.

"I would offer some guarantee you'll be welcomed back in Sunnydale with open arms. But I can't," he admitted, his face so kind, yet honest. "You may not be wanted. But you will be needed."

Sunnydale

I don't want him every again, Buffy thought, as she and Spike patrolled, coming up on the hold that had swallowed Rocky, *and I need to let him know that.*

So she told him. She delivered the words harshly, aware that they fell on him like blows, and he took them, seemingly more interested in finding the monster they were after than in finding his way back into her good graces.

"I can't say 'sorry' and I can't use 'forgive me.' All I can tell you, Buffy, is I've changed."

"I just know what you've changed into," Buffy said frankly, as she shone the flashlight in the hole. Spike crouched examining the darkness. "You come back to town, you make with the big surprises— twice—and I don't know what your game is, Spike, but I know there's something you're not telling me."

"You're right. But we're not best friends anymore, so too bad for me," he said. "I'm not sharing."

Then he rose, wiped the dirt off his hands . . . and whatever moment they had, whatever closure they had achieved, was done.

We're having a moment, Xander thought, even if it was all about walking Nancy home to make sure she could there in one piece . . . or at all.

Even better, she was opening the front door to her apartment complex. When Xander was in high school, this kind of thing never happened . . . unless the female in question was a some kind of demon.

She was talking to him, saying, "Boy, I still can't believe this is happening. I mean, even with this town's reputation for, you know, unexplained weirdness."

"Right," Xander riffed. 'Sunnydale: come for the food, stay for the dismemberment.'"

She smiled. "There's good food?"

Not only was it a moment, but a moment with sparkage, as they went back and forth with talk about phone numbers, and her coming right out and announcing that she was hitting on him.

And then—*of course*—the lights flickered and the glass in the door shattered as rumbling more intense than any thunderstorm or sonic boom took over the air waves. The wood of the doorframe splintered and the floor beneath them buckled, furrowing in a deadly way straight line heading their way . . .

Something is plowing through the ground, Xander realized. *Chasing us.*

He grabbed her hand and together they raced the length of the floor, then took the stairs. The burrowing thing followed. Tiles cracked and scattered as it pursued them.

He got her up the first few steps before it burst from the hallway floor—demonic, a giant eyeless worm creature that was mouth and teeth and little else, and in his panic did he register the teeth. It lunged, with the teeth, perilously close to Nancy . . . but it couldn't get to her no matter how hard it tried.

With a roar of fury, maybe some desperation, it disappeared back into the floor.

Once it was obviously over, Xander ventured, "Two attacks in one night. I'm thinking this is more than just coincidence."

"Ronnie would love this," she said mournfully. And as she started talking about her psycho ex-boyfriend who had been, like, her stalker, never letting up on her, never leaving her alone, and how she had wished it would all stop . . .

Xander caught an earful of that all-important word: *wish*.

And then he had another moment.

An "oh, great" moment.

Buffy led the way to where Anya was seated in the Bronze with an earnest and upset woman. Xander's ex-fiancée was not pleased to see the Slayer, her sister Dawn, her former kinky sex toy Spike, and the creep himself, Mr. Xander Harris, all accompanying a former client.

She asked her current client to get herself a drink, then she and the others skipped the formalities. They asked a lot of questions and she gave answers. Why, yes, she had turned Nancy's ex-boyfriend into a giant worm. A Sluggoth demon, to be precise, same phylum as worm, just a bit of tweaking with the wish there.

"I had a quota, the guy had it coming, what's the big?" she asked, already bored and more than a little defensive.

And then, as Spike ordered her to cancel the spell, she stared at him "What are you staring at?" he demanded.

"Oh, my God!" she said again.

"Right. Let's go." He tried to walk away, but she grabbed his arm.

"How did you do it?" she insisted.

"Spike, what is she talking about?" Buffy asked suspiciously.

Anya was gaping at him. "I can see you."

"Nothing. Let's go. Got some worm hunting to do."

Spike tried to walk away again, but Anya kept prodding. At last he lost his temper and punched her in the face. She fell to the floor, then she kicked him across the room. He landed with a crash on the pool table.

She rose with her full demon face on as Spike got off the pool table. He vamped. They began to fight in earnest, and Buffy tried to intervene.

She rained blows on him, and he began to goad her. "Working out some personal issue, are we?" Buffy punched and kicked him. "I guess this would be first contact since, uh, you know when. Up for another round up on the balcony, then?"

She hit him again, and he landed on the floor, laughing.

"Right you are, love. I haven't changed, not a lick." He was in her face, sneering at her. "And watching your face trying to figure me out was absolutely delicious."

"Buffy! Nancy. She's gone," Xander interrupted. "And out there all alone, she's worm bait."

"I'll go find her," Buffy told him. "Stay with Anya. Get her to reverse that spell."

The worm had turned up by the time Buffy caught up with Nancy. Problem was, it had turned on Nancy.

She was halfway up the ladder outside a building when Buffy located her—the hideous Ronnie-sluggoth shaking her loose from her moorings, getting ready to rumble, as only Anya had made it possible for him to do . . .

While Xander, tried his best to get her to change back the spell. She was not eager to cooperate.

"I'm in enough trouble as it is," she said. "D'Hoffryn is not pleased with my work."

He tried another tack. "Buffy's the Slayer. You're a demon. You kill people. How long do you think it's gonna be before she has to do her job?"

That gave Anya pause. "Buffy wouldn't slay . . . me."

"Not if you stop now," Xander asserted.

Xander's words worked, and Anya hurried out into

the night, watching from afar as Buffy swung down from a rooftop on the end of a rope and grabbed Nancy as the Sluggoth—Anya's creation—burst from the pavement. Rows and rows of teeth loomed wide— *What was I thinking? Well, what I was thinking of D'Hoffryn, of course, and saving my butt*—and then Spike was at Buffy's side, with a big pipe—*how symbolic*—yelling, "That's right! Big bad's back, and looking for a little *death*—" He rammed the pipe into the demonic snake just as Anya reversed the spell—*oh God*—and Sluggoth became naked, filthy Ronnie, with a pipe through his shoulder. He screamed as Spike screamed too.

Has to be the chip.

And then the vampire said the most incredible thing: "I'm sorry."

The ambulance came and loaded up Ronnie while Spike carried on like a crazy man, moaning and sobbing and completely insane.

"A warm-up act. The real headliner's coming, and when that band hits the stage, all of this . . . all this . . . will come tumbling down in death and screaming, horror and bloodshed. From beneath you, it devours! From beneath . . ." And then he sobbed, "Poor Rocky."

Spike ran away. Anya wished she could, too.

"I know this is bad," Xander said gently to her, meaning, of course that because of her, Spike had nearly killed a human being. "But it could be worse."

"Oh," Anya assured him, churning with resignation, "it will be."

Once she was sure that Ronnie was safe in the ambulance, Buffy trailed after Spike.

In a cemetery, one of the twelve within Sunnydale city limits, she found a chapel on the hallowed ground, and in it, a single light glowing like a tentative searchlight.

The twin doors were heavy; no matter for someone with Slayer strength. Nor for a vampire.

Once inside, Buffy found a religious picture of Jesus and his Mother hung on the wall and stained-glass windows. It was a place that reminded her—painfully—of her mother's funeral. Her heart fluttered at the memory. Steadily, she walked toward the plain stone-and-metal crucifix, startling when Spike spoke to her from the darkness.

"Hello," he said simply.

She whirred around. "What the hell are you—?"

The vampire was naked from the waist up; the terrible wounds on his torso had begun to heal. But from his demeanor, she sensed that other wounds . . . deeper ones, hadn't even started to get better.

His shirt was in his hand. He held it out to her in a pathetic gesture very much like surrendering as he said, "It didn't work. Costume. Didn't help. Couldn't hide."

She kept her voice firm and almost cruel as she replied, "No more mind games, Spike."

Even though he stood directly in front of her, he kept his gaze trained on the ground in a submissive posture. It was frightening her a little.

"No more mind games. No more mind."

She had it in herself to be kind to him, even if she didn't trust him. Tentatively she reached out her hand, nearly grazing his injuries, as she said, "Tell me what happened to you."

He flinched, jerking away, and frowned at her. "Hey, hey, hey! No touching. Am I flesh? Am I flesh to you?" He began to calm, to re-adopt his whipped-dog eagerness to please her. "Feed on flesh. My flesh. Nothing else. Not a spark."

As if she had reacted in some way, indicated her wish, he nodded. "Oh, fine. Flesh then. Solid through." He began to unzip his pants. "Get it hard. Service."

Shocked, disgusted, embarrassed—*I slept with him, this sad, pathetic, terrifying . . . thing*—Buffy smacked his hand. "Stop it!

Reacting instinctively to her violence, Spike caught her by the throat; in turn, Buffy grabbed his shoulder and hurled him across the room. Wood splintered and split as he crashed on top a row of pews.

His madness undaunted, he half-sat up, propped on his elbows, and said, "Right. Girl doesn't want to be serviced. Because there's no spark. Ain't we in a soddin' engine?"

Buffy came toward him.

"Spike, have you completely lost your mind?"

And then, in that lucid way crazy people have of snapping out of the scramble for an instant or two, he blinked at her and said disdainfully, "Well, yes. Where've you been all night?"

She was still struggling, still confused. "You thought you would just come back here and . . . *be* with me?"

He shrugged. "First time for everything."

"This is all you get," she said quickly. "I'm listening." And then, more earnestly, more carefully, "Tell me what happened."

He remained matter of fact, but she saw terrible disappointment in his eyes. "I tried to find it, of course."

"Find what?

"The spark. The missing . . . the piece that fit. That would make me fit. Because you didn't want . . ." Spike started to cry and looked away. "God, I can't . . . Not with you looking."

He rose and walked away from her to one of the beautiful windows. Shaded and shadowed, his injured body directed away from her, he dared to look at her from over his shoulder.

"I dreamed of killing you."

The Slayer went on alert.

Keeping him in her sights, Buffy bent down to pick up a large splinter from the broken pews at her feet. She had a stake now—*but it's not the power. It's not. I can't forget that. He's still a vampire. He's always been a vampire.*

He began to pace, highly agitated now. Warily she watched him unwind as he spoke in a jumble . . . but one that began to make sense.

"I think they were dreams. So weak. Did you make me weak, thinking of you, holding myself, and spilling useless buckets of salt over your . . . ending?"

My death. He's cried before. He thinks he loves me. He's crazy.

"Angel—he should've warned me. He makes a good show of forgetting, but it's here, in me, all the time."

He walked around her from behind. She kept herself on alert, kept focused. He could turn on her at any moment, become a target at any time.

"The spark. I wanted to give you what you deserve, and I got it. They put the spark in me and now all it does is burn."

Oh, my God.

"Your soul," she said slowly.

His laugh was hollow. Joke was on him. "Bit worse for lack of use."

Buffy turns to face him.

She said it again, because it was so hard to believe. "You got your soul back." A beat. "How?"

He looked at the ceiling. "It's what you wanted, right? Looked up. What He wanted?" Pressing his fingers to his temples he walked toward the cross.

"And . . . and now everybody's in here, talking. Everything I did . . . everyone I . . . and him . . . and it . . . the other, the thing beneath—beneath you. It's here too. Everybody. They all just tell me go . . . go . . ." He gazed at her. ". . . to hell."

"Why? Why would you do that?" she asked, her voice rising.

He had enough dignity to snap, "Buffy, shame on you." And then, more brokenly, "Why does a man do what he mustn't? For her. To be hers. To be the kind of man who would nev . . ." Again, he looked away, awash in shame and self-loathing. ". . . to be a kind of man."

He continued toward the cross. He murmured, a chant of sorts, perhaps a quotation from an ancient book of comfort.

"She shall look on him with forgiveness, and everybody will forgive and love. He will be loved."

He stopped directly in front of the cross and stared mournfully at it.

"So everything's okay, right?"

He sighed. Slowly, deliberately, he slung one arm over each side of the cross bar, and laid his head in the corner of the intersection, an angle of repose, in the arms of the angels. His body sizzled from the contact; smoke rose from his flesh.

Oh, Spike . . . He had sacrificed himself; he had gained his soul only to lose his hope.

"Can . . . can we rest now?" he asked. "Buffy . . . can we rest?

Exhausted, the man who loved her . . . burned.

Chapter Three: "Same Time, Same Place"

Sunnydale Airport Terminal

It was 9:24 P.M., and Willow's plane was about to touch down.

My buddy's coming back, Xander thought as he, Buffy, and Dawn waited in the terminal. Around him, humanity swirled—the passengers deplaned, some guy bent down to pick up his kid's sweater, *ah, life . . .*

"Giles wouldn't let her leave unless she completed whatever recovery course," he added, having been in mid-conversation with Buffy and Dawn about the very weirdness of this welcome. He had made a WELCOME HOME sign with a yellow crayon to remind Willow of how he had literally stopped her from destroying the planet with his very own words. Its very yellowness belied the fact that she had flayed Warren alive and tried to kill Dawnie as well.

Dawnie, who piped up, "Right."

Then both of them noticed that Buffy was not so on board with the joy.

Dawn repeated, "Right?"

"She kinda didn't finish," Buffy admitted.

"She didn't finish?" Dawn's voice rose, and why not? "She didn't finish being not evil?"

"Guys, I just noticed something," Xander said. "Everyone's off the plane . . . so where's Willow?"

It was 9:24 P.M. Willow's plane had landed exactly on time.

Where is everybody? she thought as she deplaned. The passengers moved into the terminal, the dad in front of her picking up his daughter's sweater.

They didn't show, she realized. *No open arms for the black-haired murderess . . . I worried about this all the way over here. Worried that we wouldn't connect.*

"Welcome home, me," she murmured.

She caught a cab to Buffy's house and knocked politely—I used to just walk right in . . . and eventually, when no one answered, she got the key under the rock and . . . walked right in. By then it was almost eleven, and she was exhausted. She wondered hopefully if she'd missed them at the airport—they might have gotten a late start, gotten mixed up about the schedule . . . there were so many reasons why they might not have been there.

There was some new furniture downstairs, but the

bigger changes had taken place upstairs. Buffy had moved into her and Tara's room. There were pictures of Dawn and Xander, other friends . . . but none of Willow.

In Buffy's day planner, there was contact info for Xander and Dawn.

It's like I stopped existing.

She heard a dog bark, a door opening, and brightened. "Dawn?" she called.

No one came into the house. No one at all.

Confused, hurt, she curled up on the couch.

Giles was wrong, Buffy thought, worried, as she, Dawn and Xander returned home. *She wasn't ready to come back.*

Since it was nearly eleven at night in Sunnydale, it was a decent hour in the morning London time; not that that would have stopped Buffy. Meanwhile Dawn and Xander scoured the house.

Of Giles, Xander asked, "Is he throwing a tasteful British wiggins?"

They all sat down on the couch.

"Oh, with extra wig. He's blaming himself pretty hard, like he should've known she wasn't ready to come back. I—I kept telling him, you know, it wasn't his fault. Maybe there's something about us she couldn't face," Buffy said.

Xander said, not without some extra sauce, "Like she didn't think we were ready to forgive her? I get that."

Dawn was irritated. "So Giles is blaming Giles,

and we're blaming us. Is anyone gonna blame Willow? Oh, don't give me shock face. I mean, will anyone around here ever start asking for help when they need it?"

Buffy knew her sister had a point. "Look, if Willow flipped out, it's her bad. We can only be here for her so much if she won't be, you know, here."

They sat together on the couch, and tried to process.

Willow woke up, fuzzy-headed, until she realized she had fallen asleep on Buffy's couch.

And Buffy and Dawn were nowhere to be found.

She called Giles in London, but he was in a day-long meeting with the Watchers Council, probably about the looming apocalypse, so that would be good. So she wandered around, bewildered.

Did they move in the middle of the night?

After awhile she left the house in search of them. Though other people were walking on Main Street, she felt completely alone.

Then she saw the Magic Box, burned and boarded up.

Oh, my God. That's my doing.

Then Anya bustled out, a box in her arms. Thrilled, Willow ran toward her, crying "Anya!"

Anya was not thrilled. Stepping back defensively, she said, "What are you doing here? I thought you were with Giles studying how to not kill people."

Willow tried to stay upbeat. "I just got back."

Anya stayed downbeat. "Just got back, as in you're

all better, or just got back to bring about a fiery apocalypse of death?" she asked suspiciously.

"Neither, but I—I have been studying, working real hard, and I—I'm gonna be fine," Willow assured her.

"Oh. Good. 'Cause I remember the last time you said that." Anya indicated the box in her arms. "I've spent a lot of time since then cleaning the debris out of my ex-livelihood. Stuff like that.

Willow winced inwardly, but she worked hard to stay direct and honest. "Well, yeah, I wanna help any way I can with that. I—I feel really responsible."

Now she'd pissed Anya. She walked toward Willow, brows lifted, and said, "You feel really responsible? You *are* really responsible!"

"I—I know I hurt you and . . . and everyone. I'm sorry," Willow tried again.

"Here's something you should know about vengeance demons," Anya informed her. "We don't go with the 'sorry.' We prefer 'Oh, God, please stop hitting me with my own rib bones.'"

"Go on. Say whatever you want," Willow replied. She knew she had to take the blows. "Rib bones and so forth. I—I deserve it."

"Then you won't mind?" When Willow shook her head, Anya's face fell. "Well, then, that's no fun."

"Sorry." And she truly was.

Willow sat down on the curb. After a beat, Anya set down her box—it was filled with items she had salvaged from the store—and joined her. Willow toyed idly with a tri-horned demon skull—*probably a Darthberg*—grateful for some company.

She said, "So, um, where is everyone these days?"

Anya settled in for a long chat. "Well, I'm back in my own apartment. And, of course, vengeance takes me all over the world. I was in Brazil yesterday. They love their soccer."

"And the others? Dawn? And, um, Xander? Buffy?" As she spoke she accidentally broke off one of the horns—*whoops*—and quickly put it back in the box.

Anya looked surprised. "You haven't seen them?"

"Not so much," Willow admitted.

"Huh. I guess they're still mad at you," Anya ventured. "They've been a little temperamental lately, just between you and me. We had this little mix-up a few days ago, and —"

"That sounds great," Willow interrupted her. "So, um, where do you think they'd be?"

Anya waved her hand. "Oh, at the new high school, probably. Everyone's all about the high school. Buffy's got some kind of job there helping junior deviants, Spike's insane in the basement, Xander's there doing construction on the new gym—"

That caught Willow's attention. "Wait, Spike's what in the whatment?"

"Insane," Anya filled in. "Base. Xander does construction. He likes to start early, so he's probably there by now."

Oh, please, oh, please, Willow thought.

She took her leave of Anya and headed for the school. There was a large pit filled with the things of construction—machines, big piles of dirt, rebars—but as far as she could see, no Xander.

There was, however, someone else there.

Willow gasped, sickened. Lying on the ground was a dead guy. At least she thought it was . . . had been . . . a guy. The corpse was ghastly, all red muscle, eyes, and bone. He had been flayed . . . just as she had flayed Warren.

I did not do this, she told herself. *I did not.*

There was a guy who had died horribly in the bottom of Xander's construction pit.

Buffy said, "No skin."

"Tough to look at," Xander said.

"And yet my eyes refuse to look away," Buffy said grimly. "Stupid eyes."

"I found it first thing this morning. I gave my crew the day off, and I called you right away."

"I got to get a job where I don't get called right away for this stuff."

Xander wiped his mouth as he turned around to check on a noise—seemed like the ladder—but there was nothing there.

Buffy was churning inside.

"Yeah, I know exactly what you're thinking," Xander said, sharing her wiggins. "Maybe Willow *is* back."

After she scrambled up the ladder in terror, Willow made her way through the halls of the new high school. Finally she located the access to the basement and headed down.

It was dark. There were spare bookshelves and

other classroom equipment just like in her day.

Then Spike jumped out of the shadows and shouted, "Out! This is my place. You need permission to be here. You need a special slip with a stamp."

"Spike!" she cried. "My God . . . I—"

He paced, agitated. "You go off and try to wall up the bad parts and put your heart back in where it fell out. You call yourself finished, but you're not. Worse than ever, you are . . ."

He froze, looking rather sad, and turned away from her. He grew calmer, somehow . . . held in; he said, "You went away. You've been gone since . . ."

"I needed to go," she ventured, seeing that he really was pretty crazy in the basement . . . or the head. "But I'm back now. And I found . . ." She didn't know how to put it. "There's a body."

"Tragedy," he offered. Then, facing her, asked more hopefully, "Is there blood?"

Ewww. "Uh, I, yeah, and I can't find Buffy or Xander or Dawn. And there's this thing killing people. And the victim was . . . skinned. What could do that?"

"You did it once. I heard about it."

She had to let that go for now. "Anything other . . . other than me?"

Then he was off again, looking elsewhere, talking as if he were addressing someone else. Willow didn't follow it all, but she wondered anxiously, *Could Spike have done the killing?*

"Everyone's talking to me. No one's talking to one another," Spike told Buffy, as she and Xander arrived.

As with the witch, they tried to talk to him about the tragedy. He was confused about why they were ignoring his guest, who remained in the room.

And then he realized . . .

They don't see her!

"Someone isn't here," he said aloud. "Button, button . . . who's got the button? My money's on . . ." He turned and looked straight at Willow ". . . the witch."

That got the Slayer's attention. She and Xander turned around to face him.

"Red's a bad girl," he explained.

"He's talking about Willow," Buffy said.

Xander murmured, "And that means something because he's chock-full-o-sanity."

Spike said to Willow, "They think you did it. The Slayer and her boy. They think you took the skin."

And Buffy asked him, "Is there something here? Something that killed?"

Xander said, "Her boy? I'm her *boy*?"

Spike walked up to them and announced, "I have to go. There are things here without permission. I have to check their slips. Make sure they have authorization."

He took his leave, and went about his business.

Willow hurried to Anya's.

"Something horrible killed a boy," she told the vengeance demon, sweeping in the front door. "Took his skin right off."

Simultaneously each asked the other, "Was it you?" And then, shocked, "No!"

Willow managed to persuade Anya to help her find out

who did. They prepared Anya's apartment for the same demon-locating spell Willow had done long ago with Tara.

As if she could read her mind, Anya asked her suspiciously, "This isn't going to get all sexy, is it?"

It didn't. As they sat facing each other on the floor, they blew demon-finding power on the map of Sunnydale between them. Dots showed up, including one for Anya, who chirruped, "Hey, that's me!"

There was a very bright clump at the high school. "It's all Hellmouthy underneath," Willow observed.

The high school clumped burned brighter, and brighter still, until smoke rose and the map burst into flames. Willow and Anya jumped up, Willow stomping out the fire.

"This could be it," she said, studying the lights that were left. "It's strong, it's near the body, and it's all by itself, hiding in the woods or maybe a cave. There are a couple of good caves around there."

Willow assumed Anya would be able to teleport them on over to the cave area, but it turned out that Anya had lost her teleportation privileges for doing something that had pissed D'Hoffryn off.

"Causing pain *sounds* really cool, I know, but it turns out, it's really upsetting," she confided in the nearest person who had tortured someone to death. "It didn't used to be, but now it is."

Willow considered. "Is it like you're scared of losing that feeling again, and having it be okay to hurt people, and then you're not in charge of the power anymore because it's in charge of you?"

"Wow, that was really overdramatically stated, but

yeah, that's it," Anya said, impressed by Willow's insight.

And Willow way got that . . . on her way out the door to catch herself an entirely different pain-causing demon altogether.

Dawn, Buffy, and Xander sat around the dining room table at the Summers house doing the research. Buffy was grazing books while Dawn surfed the net.

"Okay, so I looked up demons that skin their victims and demons that flay their victims 'cause, you know, same thing. There's a ton of prospects. Anything else gone? Uh, eyeballs, toenails or viscera? That's guts," she added, puffing up a little.

"She knows about viscera. Makes you proud," Buffy drawled.

But privately, she wasn't proud. She had a terrible feeling in her gut—*my viscera*—that Willow was the one who had—

"Oh, guys!" Dawn cried, gesturing. "Here's a good one. A demon called Gnarl. He's a parasite with these nasty long fingernails. He secretes something through them and uses that to paralyze his victims. He then cuts strips of their skin while they're still alive. It takes hours."

Xander made shuddering noises and Buffy asked more questions . . . and it turned out that Gnarl accompanied his skin meals with blood, which was "like his natural beverage."

Blood lapping leaving blood specks, making . . . Spike a natural candidate to track Gnarl down.

"Should have put a leash on him," Xander muttered, as the three of them listened to Spike's bizarre ramblings while they wandered through the woods.

Buffy said, "Yes, let's tie ourselves to the crazy vampire."

Then Spike stopped. He stood still and stared through the bushes at a rock cliff as the others joined him.

"That's it," he announced. "End of the line. Everyone off."

"That's a rock cliff," Buffy said disappointed with Spike.

"Well, give him a break, Buffy," Xander offered. "Maybe it's a vicious skin-eating rock cliff."

"There's a cave in it," Spike ground out. "Look." He moved the foliage out of the way to reveal a narrow cave opening. "I'm insane. What's Xander's excuse?"

I'm scared, Willow thought, as she stood near the cave entrance.

Nevertheless she squeezed through to discover that the passage opened into a cavern. There was a bit of light from a fire. And some noises.

And a voice.

"All alone. Look at the shorn lamb. See how he trembles. Is it the cold wind? Or is it that the flock is nowhere to be seen?

"Poor little lamb, all alone."

"You guys hear that, right?" Dawn asked, as she stood with Xander and Buffy inside the cavern. They had just squeezed through the passage.

Then something jumped from the shadows and slashed Dawn. She cried out in terrible pain. She immediately began to stiffen up.

"Dawn! Are you okay?" her sister cried.

But it was obvious that Dawn was not so much.

"Okay we need to get her out of here," Buffy told Xander. "We'll deal with him later. Seal him in."

Someone is sealing me in here! Willow thought, panicking as she watched rocks covering up the entrance.

"What's going on?" she shouted, racing toward the passage entrance. "Who's there? No! Stop!"

"No way out now. No way out," came a voice from the shadows. "Your friends left you here." He sang with evil delight. "No one comes to save you." Then he added, "They wanted me to have you."

"Were they here? Were my friends really here? I heard something," she said, looking around.

The creature swooped at her like a great bat. A sharp pain slashed her stomach. As she writhed in agony, the monster's shadow rose on the wall. And then it came for her.

It was a frog-colored monster with protruding ribs and leathery skin. It looked almost elfin with pointy ears, a long hooked nose, and yellow eyes. As it admired its quarry, it clicked its long black nails together, making a ticking noise that marked out a high counterrhythm to Willow's pounding heart beat.

Then he moved her blouse away from her wound to enjoy his feast.

* * *

Dawn was lying horizontal, like a rolled-up carpet, by the time they got her into the house. The Gnarl-induced paralysis had set in to the extent that she could no longer move any part of her body, including her mouth.

They put her down on the sofa, and she rolled over onto her face. Without moving her mouth, she protested, "Face up! Face up!" like the Tin Woodsman asking for the oil can in *The Wizard of Oz*.

Buffy went to use the laptop in the dining room to see if she could find the same listing Dawn had found for the Gnarl, and figure out an antidote for the paralysis.

"Oh, got it," she announced. "It says the paralysis is permanent."

Dawn squeaked.

"No. Oh, wait, my bad," she said, reading further. "Permanent until the creature dies. Sorry."

"Guess we have to go back," she said to Xander as she walked into the living room.

Xander frowned. "We can't just leave her here like this. What if she vomits?"

Dawn mumbled, "Ew. I won't vomt."

Buffy was concerned. "Do you think she'll vomit?

"Stp tking abt vomt!" Dawn said.

"I'll call Anya," Buffy told Xander. "She can watch her."

Xander was doubtful. "Right, she'll love being called for vomit watch."

Buffy picked up the phone as Dawn ground out, "Plees, stp tking abt vmt!"

* * *

Anya did show. She also showed Buffy and Xander that Dawn was "poseable," and sat her upright on the couch. Then, as she popped open a can of Brazil nuts, she said airily, "No need to thank me, by the way, for sitting with her. I'm feeling very benevolent today. Helping Willow. Helping you. You might even call it even for that whole worm thing last week."

Buffy was mildly incensed. "Yeah, I don't think we could call—" Then she processed what Anya had just said. "Wait. *You saw Willow?*"

"Umhmm." She chomped away. "Oh, she's looking for you, by the way. Decided you might be out in some cave."

Buffy looked at Xander. "Xander, she could be there right now. Willow could be trapped with the Gnarl."

"It's not 'the' Gnarl," Anya corrected. "Just 'Gnarl.'"

And once Buffy realized that Anya knew about 'just Gnarl,' she drafted her into this Slayer's army and armed her with a battle axe. Then she put the remote in Dawn's hand and she, Anya, and Xander left for the cave.

And when they got there, Gnarl screeched and ran for cover.

"Where's Willow?" Buffy demanded.

"She's right here," Anya said, perplexed. "Can't you see her? She's hurt!"

"What? Where?" Xander felt around with his hand. "There's nothing here."

But the revelation that Anya could see her and

Buffy and Xander couldn't, would have to wait.

Gnarl was attacking.

Buffy had a dagger, Gnarl had a sword. They fought hard, lunging at each other, while Anya called out, "Get him in the eyes!"

Then the vengeance demon said to Willow, "Buffy's fighting the demon over there. See?"

But Willow didn't see. She didn't see Xander or Buffy.

"They came? They didn't leave me?"

"No, they didn't leave you," Anya explained. "They can't see you."

Buffy battled Gnarl. The creature leaped over her head and landed behind her. She whirled around and slammed her dagger into his foot, pinning him to the earth. The pain made him shriek. While he was distracted, she grabbed his hand and plunged both her hands into his eyes.

It was extremely gross, but it did the job.

Then Buffy ran to where Anya was, and Willow slowly came into focus. They finally saw each other.

Finally connected.

She was very, very badly hurt.

Buffy tried to be reassuring. "It's going to be okay, Willow. You're going to be okay."

"I know," Willow said gratefully. "You're here."

They took Willow home, where she belonged.

A few days later, Buffy hovered in the doorway, watching her meditate. She started to turn away when Willow opened her eyes and urged her to stay.

"I'm healing," she explained. "Growing new skin."

"Wow," Buffy said. "That's magic, right? I mean, when most people meditate, they don't get extra skin. Right. 'Cause Clem should, like, cut back."

They both smiled, and talked about magic for a while, Willow confessing that she had accidentally cast the spell that had made them invisible to each other. And Buffy confessed in turn that she had been afraid that Willow had flayed the dead boy in the construction pit.

Willow knew that. She tried to meditate some more, even though she was very tired.

"I got so much strength, I'm giving it away," Buffy offered.

The Slayer sat cross-legged across from the Wicca and took her hands. They mediated together, Buffy murmuring, "Good."

And it was.

Chapter Four: "Help"

Sunnydale

Willow was back, and it was time to say hello to her darling.

Willow and Xander walked among the headstones, talking about what was happening. What might happen.

Willow told him about her vision back in England only to discover that the same message was being received here in Sunnydale.

"From beneath you, it devours," Xander mused. "It's not the friendliest jingle, is it? It's no 'I like Ike' or 'Milk: It does a body good.'"

"It's going to be bad," Willow told him. "And I wonder . . . will I be able to help? I don't know what I can do. And frankly, I'm scared of *what* I can do."

"I get that," Xander told her. "Figuring out how to control your magic seems a lot like hammering a nail." When she obviously didn't get where he was going, he added, "Well, at the end of the hammer, you have the power, but no control . . . so you could hit your thumb."

"Ouch," said Willow. "So you choke up. Power, control. It's a trade off."

They stopped talking for a minute. "That's actually not a bad analogy," Willow mused. "Except . . . I'm less worried about hitting my thumb and more worried about going all black-eyed baddy and bewitching that hammer into cracking my friends' skulls open like coconuts."

"Right. Ouch," Xander said.

"Sorry." She hesitated. "Xander, being back here . . . I don't know."

"It'll take time." He sighed. "Are you sure you're ready for this?"

Willow nodded, and walked on alone. A blue sky above, and grass as green as the rolling hills of England, Willow made her way to Tara's grave.

She put stones on the headstone, mindful of her Jewish heritage, and said, "Hey. It's me."

Wistfully she traced the lettering:

Tara Maclay
Oct. 16, 1980—May 7, 2002

Buffy, Xander, and Dawn lay in closed caskets in the mortuary for over half an hour to kill one vampire the night before Buffy faced a far greater evil: a high school full of high school students.

The next day it was time to start her guidance counseling job, and she was petrified.

She did okay with the hostile guy who turned out to be scared, and the guy looking to hit on her by pretending to be worried about being gay, and the girl who kicked some guy's butt in the parking lot because she was tired of being picked on.

All in all, she was doing much better at high school the second time around.

And then . . . Cassie Newton came into her office.

And Cassie told Buffy that she was going to be dead by Friday . . . almost as if it was no big deal. And no, she wasn't talking about suicide.

Buffy was alarmed. "Are you saying you know someone wants to hurt you? Has someone threatened you?"

Cassie shrugged. "No. I just know next Friday I'm going to die. Some things I just know. I don't know how. I just do." She took a moment, then added, "Like I know there will be coins.

"And I know that you'll go someplace dark underground."

"What do you mean, underground?" Buffy persisted.

"And I know you'll try to help. But you can't, okay?"

And then she told Buffy to be put on a sweater so she wouldn't stain her blouse, and left Buffy's office.

Extremely troubled Buffy told Principal Wood, who tried to assure her that kids said awful things, thought awful things. That didn't always translate into doing awful things, like committing suicide.

"Every time there's a threat like this, we do the same dance," he told her. "Inform teachers, search lockers, but we can't know what's going to happen. We can't search their brains. We just do what we can."

"It's not enough. I need to fix this," Buffy insisted. "I don't usually get a head's-up before somebody dies."

That caught his attention.

Then Buffy spilled coffee on her blouse, staining it . . . and thought of Cassie, who seemed to know too much about the future.

So while she sent Dawn to spy on Cassie, she, Xander, and Willow did the research. Cassie Newton had done well in school, had been fine . . . and then, there was a sudden drop in her GPA, absenteeism, and comments about apathy and depression.

"It's hard to do homework if you think you're about to die," Buffy observed.

Her medical reports yielded nothing substantive.

And then Willow asked, "Have you Googled her?"

And that was when they hit the mother lode. Cassie had her Web site . . . and her own very sad, very death-oriented poetry:

Xander said, "Poem. Always a sign of pretentious inner turmoil."

Willow began to read aloud:

"The sheets above me
cool my skin

like dirt
on a madwoman's grave
I rise into
the moonlight white
and watch
the mirror stare
pale fish looks
back at me
pale fish that will
never swim
my skin is milk
for no man to drink
my thighs unused
unclenched
this body is
not ready yet
but dirt waits for no
woman
and coins will
buy no time
I hear the chatter
of the bugs. It's they alone who
will feast."

Dawn had walked in while Willow was reading, and reacted when Xander said, "Okay, death is really on her brain."

She said, "We all deal with death."

Xander shook his head. "This girl isn't just dealing, she's giving death a long, sloppy word-kiss. She has a yen for the big dirt-nap."

"I don't know," Willow said thoughtfully. "I mean, a lot of teens post some pretty angsty poetry on the Web. I mean, I even posted a melodramatic love poem or two back in the day."

Xander perked up. "Love poems?"

"I'm over you now, sweetie," Willow said gently. "Look, all I'm saying is that this is normal teen stuff. You join chat rooms, you write poetry, you post Doogie Howser fan-fic. It's all normal, right? Let's see what other sites there are."

And that was when they located Cassie's father's police record. He had a record of violence and drinking.

Not so good for Cassie, Buffy thought. *But it may be what we've been looking for.*

Dawn had a different idea.

"I've got this case cracked wide open. I got the perp fingered. I told you about Mike Helgenburg, right? The one that keeps asking her to the dance. I'm thinking, who likes to be rejected?"

She thought of her spying mission, where Cassie and Mike had been quite together, talking about tattoos and stuff. Mike had really pushed her to go to the Winter Formal, but she wouldn't do it.

The spying mission had turned into her own personal getting-acquainted mission, when she had discovered that she liked Cassie very much.

Mike hid it well, but I'm sure he's pissed off at her, Dawn thought. *Homicidally so.*

But Buffy and Xander were already out the door and on their way to Cassie's dad's house.

* * *

When the reached the front door, Buffy rang the bell and muttered, "Buffy the Vampire Slayer would break down the door."

"And Buffy the Counselor?" Xander asked.

"Waits," Buffy said impatiently.

Phil Newton didn't want to let them in. But when Buffy mentioned Cassie, he do so grudgingly . . . and The First words out of his mouth about Cassie did not endear him to Buffy.

"So is she screwing up her grades again? Because she's not the sharpest apple in the barrel."

He had been drinking; his words were slurred. Buffy saw the open bottles and pressed her case.

"Frankly we were worried that you might drink too much and hurt Cassie."

He was outraged. "You come in here in the middle of the night, into my home, and start accusing me of beating on my daughter? Did Cassie's mother put you up to this? 'Cause I pay my support, okay? She just wants to take away the one weekend a month I get to be with my girl."

"Which is when?" Buffy asked.

"What?" He was confused.

"Which weekend is it?"

"I . . . I just had her last weekend." He took a breath. "Look, I may not be the greatest dad in the world, but I don't beat up my daughter."

"So, you won't be seeing her this Friday, then?"

"Not unless my ex-wife gets a personality transplant."

That's crosses him off our list then, Buffy thought.

They left shortly thereafter . . . to find Cassie in the driveway. She used her car security remote, which let out a little beep. Buffy and Xander both looked at her as she approached them.

"It's not him," Cassie told them. "He's not the one who does it. Thank you for trying, but I probably shouldn't have told you anything. You're making such a big deal out of it, and I want it all to just go away."

Xander asked bluntly, "Are you talking about killing yourself?"

"No, of course not," Cassie replied.

"Then fight. Try," the Slayer told her.

"There's no point." Cassie sounded patient, almost detached. "I told you."

"This doesn't sound like someone who really wants to live," Buffy accused her.

"You think I want this? You think I don't care?" Cassie began to cry. "Believe me, I want to be here, do things. I want to graduate from high school, and I want to go to the stupid Winter Formal." She sniffed, smiling sadly, looking scared.

"I have this friend, and it would be fun to go with him. Just to dance and hear lame music and wear a silly dress and laugh and stuff." She sniffed again. "I'd like to go. There's a lot of stuff I'd like to do. I'd love to ice skate at Rockefeller Center. And I'd love to see my cousins grow up and see how they turn out 'cause they're really mean and I think they're going to be fat. I'd love to backpack across the country, or, I don't know, fall in love. But I won't. I just never will.'"

Buffy said firmly, "You will. Cassie, you will. You just have to tell us what you know. You have to tell us everything. Please, help us."

"I can't," the other girl replied, just as firmly. "I don't know why and I don't know how, but something out there is going to kill me."

Not on my watch, Buffy thought, as she read every piece of Cassie's poetry that she could find, looking for clues. Xander helped, and Willow and Dawn, everyone reading her work, absorbing her cadence, reading of her pain.

And speaking of pain . . .

She went to see Spike, who sat in the basement, immobile, trying to keep out the voices. He was lost to her in madness, out of his mind with penance for hurting her. Buffy was the only girl he could think of.

And so she left him, as he struggled to find his peace.

Principal Wood had the lockers searched. And Buffy grilled Mike Helgenburg, who happened to be walking by her. Turned out he wasn't very pissed about much except getting a "B" in Egyptian history . . . and that he was thinking of asking Dawn to go the dance.

Buffy was offended. "You're asking my sister, and she's your *second choice*?"

Then behind her, as Principal Wood and the security guard opened another locker, coins rained from the locker onto the floor.

Lots of weird coins, which Cassie had mentioned to her . . .

. . . so she took the locker's owner into her office.

"I want you to tell me what this is, and what this has to do with Cassie Newton."

At first he protested his innocence.

At first.

Dawn and Cassie left for the day with the hordes of other students. And Dawn fessed up that she had started out befriending Cassie to help Buffy find out more about her.

"And look, she was worried and now I'm worried and I'm not pretending at all," Dawn told her. "I really wanted to be your friend."

Cassie chuckled. "You are my friend." And then she touched Dawn's shoulder and said, "Listen, Dawn, whatever happens now, it's not your fault, okay?"

Then Dawn got distracted by a big dork named Peter who pretended he was asking her to the dance, only to make fun of her . . . and the next thing she knew, Cassie was gone.

The followers of Avilas gathered that night in the school library and began the rite that would bring them riches. In their red robes, their sacred coins ringing their ritual fire, the red-robed figures were giddy and up. Keith had set up a cool booby trap. No one was coming in . . . and nobody was getting out.

Then Peter dragged in their sacrifice to Avilas . . . the girl Cassie Newton, bound, gagged, and terrified.

"It's nothing personal," Peter told her as her eyes

bulged above her gag. "It's just that you have this death-chick suicide vibe going."

On his cue, the brothers extinguished their candles . . . and Peter brought a huge cleaver up against Cassie's throat. As he intoned the ritual, one of the followers jumped to her feet and unfastened her robe.

It was Buffy.

"Okay," she told Peter. "That is going on your permanent record."

He came at her, and she dropped him hard. As he lay writhing on the floor in agony, she shook her head at the lot of them.

"Do you know how lame this is? Bored teenage boys trying to raise up a demon? Sorry it didn't show. I'll bet it's because you forgot the boom box playing some heavy metal thing, like Blue Clam Cult. I think that's the key to raising lame demons."

Despite his pain, Peter smiled triumphantly and said, "That lame demon?"

Buffy turned.

The demon, Avilas, towered over her. He was actually quite impressive, with scaly brown demon skin, muscles, horns, and fins, and a strange, circular indentation in his stomach.

Buffy grabbed up the cleaver and threw it at Avilas. It cut into his chest, but he didn't even grunt. Then he threw Buffy across the room and yanked the cleaver from his body, tossing it on the ground.

Peter grabbed it and went after Cassie. Buffy kept the volume up, but the demon was getting the better of her. It had her down. . . .

. . . and then Spike appeared, a torch in his grasp. He pressed it against the demon's back, and it roared in fury and pain.

"Here to help," Spike said. "No hurting the girl.'"

"Untie her," Buffy told him, taking over the demon battle. The other followers began to scatter and flee, sensing that the battle was going against them, as Spike crossed to Peter and hit him. The chip jolted him with pain. He did it again and again, each punch forcing him to hold his aching head. But he kept on.

"Who are you?" Peter demanded, bloody and reeling.

"I'm a bad man," Spike replied.

Then he knocked the bastard out.

Buffy rammed the torch into the hollow in Avilas' abdomen, and the demon went up in flames.

With the sacrificial knife Spike cut Cassie's hands free and yanked the duct tape off her mouth. She was crying, but she forced herself into composure long enough to say, "She'll tell you. Someday she'll tell you."

The other demon worshippers had run away. Buffy and Spike had no more work here. They prepared to leave as Peter crawled toward the charred remains of his demon god. "You can't be dead," he groaned. "Where are my infinite riches?"

As if to say, "bite me," the demon did just that: it reared up and chomped Peter on his shoulder. The it collapse, shattering into so many charcoal briquettes.

"Help me! Please! I'm bleeding!" he shrieked.

"Sorry," Buffy said coldly. "My office hours are ten to four."

Triumphantly Buffy walked Cassie toward the main exit doors of the library.

"It's all okay now," she told Cassie, add wryly, and with great kindness, "I hope you're not too disappointed."

Then she opened the door . . . triggering the cool booby trap of demon-worshipper Keith. It was a cross-bow, and it let a bolt fly . . . but Buffy caught the bolt just in time to prevent it from shooting Cassie in the forehead, which would definitely have killed her.

"See?" Buffy broke the bolt in her fist. "You can make a difference."

With great tenderness Cassie pushed a strand of hair out of Buffy's face.

"And you will," she said.

Then she took one sharp breath and collapsed to the floor.

Dead.

Memento mori.

The Summers home was once more a place of grieving. Buffy, Dawn, Willow, and Xander sat in the living room in silence, until Willow finally spoke.

"How's her mom?"

"Okay," Buffy replied. "As okay as . . . she told me that her family had a history of heart irregularities. But she never told Cassie."

"Cassie didn't know?" Willow repeated. "Then it was fate."

"I think she was going to die, no matter what, wasn't she?" Xander observed quietly. "Didn't matter what you did."

Racked with guilt, Buffy murmured, "She just knew. She was special. I failed her."

Tears rolled down Dawn's face. Poor Dawn, who was so young, and had suffered so many losses. "Uh-uh, no, you didn't," she managed through her sobs. "You listened and you tried. She died because of her heart, not because of you. She was my friend because of you." She added brokenly, "I guess sometimes you can't help."

"So what then?" Buffy asked her friends, asked the walls, asked her own heart. "What do you do when you know that? When you know that maybe you can't help?"

In the morning, Buffy got up, got dressed, and went to her office at the high school.

It didn't matter if you knew that you couldn't help. You had to keep trying.

Chapter Five: "Selfless"

U.C. Sunnydale

Death had come to over a dozen young men, bloody death, and excruciating.

Anya's work here was done.

She had wreaked terrible vengeance at the fraternity house on the U.C. Sunnydale campus. Corpses were strewn everywhere, their hearts torn out.

Just as thher client had wished.

Now she sat in shock, unable to comprehend that it had been she who had made this massacre happen. So much blood. So much death.

"What have I done?" she murmured.

How had she come to this?

Sjornjost, 880

It was a beautiful day in the village of Sjornjost. Aud's beloved Olaf, he of the red hair and large body, had just returned to their hut, smelling of blood and musk. She set down the bunny she had been cuddling to tend to him, a bit concerned about the odor of blood and musk that hung around him. He had been battling trolls again, and she thrilled as he boasted, "It takes more than a band of minor trolls to bring down the mighty Olaf!"

He wanted mead more than fussing, and breeding almost as much as mead. She bustled around him, slightly disappointed as he mocked her thoughts of sharing the bounty of her rabbit-breeding program out of simple altruism.

He mocked her, saying, "Sweet Aud! Your logic is insane and happenstance, like that of a troll. It is no wonder the bar matrons talk of you."

"You've been to the bar," she murmured.

"Oh, Aud," he said with total condescension. "Forget it and please me now."

"I do not like you going there," she said.

He shrugged. "It is not my fault they don't take kindly to you. You've always been most aggressive in your not-fitting-in with people. You speak your mind, and you are annoying." He added, smiling, "It's one of the things I love most about you."

She had to ask. "Was Rannveig there?"

He scoffed. "Bah! I've told you a thousand times: I have no interest in this Rannveig. Her hips are large and load-bearing, like a Baltic woman."

He cuddled her and stroked her face. "You are much more to my liking. Your hips are small, like a Baltic woman from a slightly more arid region."

"I am sorry," she said, nestling in as he held her. "I simply love you so much . . . I feel as though I could burst at times. I could not live without you."

"You are my perfect Aud. I could never want for another. Fear not, sweet Aud. You will always be my beautiful girl."

But he lied.

How he lied.

And a fortnight later, she had transformed Olaf into a troll. She watched on as they chased him down, grimly satisfied.

"Hide your babies and your beadwork!" someone cried.

Another bellowed, "Hit him with fruits and various meats!"

"Impressive," said a voice beside her.

He was some sort of stately personage, demonic in appearance, and she thanked him faintly as her former beloved, Olaf, raced through the village, trying to tell the others that it was he, Olaf, and not a troll intent on causing havoc.

"What is that, a Woodlow Transmogrific Spell?" he queried.

"Thorton's Hope," she told him.

"Thorton's Hope," he mused. "But how did you get the troll element?"

"Eelsbane," she murmured, still watching Olaf as he contended with the villagers.

Then they exchanged introductions. He was named D'Hoffryn.

"I'm the patron of a . . . family of sorts. We're vengeance demons. I'm sure you've heard of us."

"No, I'm sorry," Aud confessed, barely listening to him, distracted and pensive.

"Oh, well, that's quite—"

"Don't feel bad," Aud told him. "I don't talk to people much. I mean, I talk to them, but they don't talk to me. Except to say, 'Your questions are irksome' and 'Perhaps you should take your furs and your literal interpretations to the other side of the river.'" A beat, and then, "I'm sure your group is quite well-known."

Then, though she told him she was called Aud, he insisted that her true name was Anyanka.

Then he invited her to join his family of vengeance demons.

"What would I have to do?" she asked.

"What you do best," he told her. "Help wronged women. Punish evil men . . . but only those that deserve it."

"They all deserve it," she said bitterly.

U.C. Sunnydale

They deserved it, she thought now, as she washed the blood off her hands. But there was so much of it. *That girl wished for this. I simply complied with her desires.*

In a daze she stumbled out of the frat house.

It seemed odd that the day would be so bright, that there should be clouds and rain. Then she ran into

Willow, who was excited about resuming her studies, and that, too, seemed odd. Willow, who had also killed humans, was happy and enthused about life . . . whereas she, Anya . . .

. . . lied to Willow about what she had been doing in the frat house.

"I have a new boyfriend," she told the Wicca. "We just had lots and lots of sex."

"Oh, okay," Willow said. But it was not okay. She saw blood on Anya's hand, and the vengeance demon was acting so strangely.

After Anya walked off, Willow went to the frat house.

She was stunned. There was blood everywhere— on the walls, on the floor. It had been a slaughter. A massacre.

Then she heard a high-pitched whimper from another room, and hurried to investigate. It was coming from a closet. Inside, Willow found a young woman curled up into ball. She was rocking and crying. Blood smeared her clothes, and she was weeping hysterically, "I take it back. I take it back. I take it back."

She realized Willow was there and said, "'S gonna be a party. Everyone's gonna be there. Everyone's bringing a date. But it was just me. And he broke up with me in front of them. I was a game.

"They laughed and they laughed and I yelled, 'Just once, I wish you could feel what it's like to have your hearts ripped out. Just once, I wish.'" She sobbed. "And it came."

"Okay," Willow said, rising, bringing the girl with her. "Come on, what came? What did this?"

"A spider."

Demonic, Willow realized, as she asked carefully, "Where did it go?"

The other girl's eyes went wide and glazed. Willow whipped around, looking up, just as an enormous spider demon launched itself at her.

"Protégé!" Willow shouted, which meant, "Shield!"

A magic force shield appeared just as the spider crashed into it. It ricocheted off the force field and smashed against the wall.

Then it reared back again, giving Willow a better look at it. It was a black widow from hell, about the size of a large Rottweiler. It attacked again. Willow kept the shield up with great effort, feeling the magics churn and swirl inside her, gathering force, beginning to take over.

The spider attacked again and bounced off again . . . this time through a window.

"For God's sake, shut your whimpering mouth," she snapped at the frightened girl.

She heard the coldness and the evilness in her own voice and broke her own concentration. As the shield disappeared, she said to the girl, "I'm sorry."

Buffy the Vampire Slayer spun slowly, lazily, in her office chair at Sunnydale High, a cup of pencils on her forehead. There wasn't much else to do—no troubled students wandering in looking for advice from someone who was young and with-it and possessed no strand of mom hair.

When the phone rang, it startled her. Pencils came crashing down as she grabbed the phone.

"Hello? Willow?" she said by way of greeting, for it was the Wicca on the other end of the line. "Is everything all right?"

It wasn't.

Willow told her about some horrible spider demon that was ripping out people's hearts. She had come across it while on campus. It had eviscerated an entire fraternity, then bounded away, probably to commit more unsavory fatalities.

That message delivered, she made a halfhearted offer to help deal with it, but Buffy knew Willow was tired out and still trying to figure out how to use her magics now that she was no longer veiny and brunette.

So Buffy said, "Don't worry I'll get Xander. . . . Wow, ripped out their hearts, my God. . . . Hey, did you get that physics class you wanted?"

It was horrible being mad, and bloody good to talk to Buffy about it. She listened patiently as he tried to put his mind jumble into words:

"I don't trust what I see anymore. I don't know how to explain it, exactly. It's like I've been seeing things. Dru used to see things, you know? She'd always be staring up at the sky, watching cherubs burn or the heavens bleed or some nonsense. I used to stare at her and think she'd gone completely sack of hammers."

He sighed heavily, remembering happier days.

"But she'd see the sky when we were inside and it'd make her so happy. She'd see showers. She'd see stars. Now I see . . . her," he confessed, his voice catching.

"Spike," she began.

"I'm in trouble, Buffy." He looked away, afraid of what was inside his mind, afraid of her scorn.

"I can help you," Buffy said.

Her generosity was almost too much to bear. "I could never ask. Not after . . ."

"It's different. You're different."

Spike said again, "I could never ask."

"Spike, it's me," she said clearly, obviously in her own right mind, since, well, she knew that much. "It's you and it's me, and we'll get through this."

He scratched behind his ear, still nervous, not even daring to hope.

"Never . . ."

"We'll get through this," she insisted. Her eyes were clear and steady. She meant it.

And just when he had begun to relax . . . and to hope . . . Buffy walked up. The real one, in a different blouse and wearing a bit of a scowl—that was how he knew she was real, and that the one he had been speaking to was a figment of his addled brain.

He began to lose it, realizing that the Buffy who had been kind to him, the one who had offered him support, was part of his madness.

Should've known it, shouldn't have trusted it, shouldn't've . . .

"Spike," the real Buffy said with asperity. "This basement is killing you. This is the Hellmouth. There is something bad down here, possibly everything bad."

He shut her out, struggling to hold on, to bear it . . . "Can't hear you. Can't hear you."

She said coldly, "You have a soul? Fine. Show me."

He retorted, "Scream montresor all you like, pet."

"Get up and get out of this basement," she demanded.

Filled with self-loathing, and self-pity, truly nearly at the end, he looked up at his love and revealed to her the sum total of his nadir: "I don't have anywhere else to go."

Willow hung up, fully aware that she had successfully managed to avoid telling Buffy about Anya. With determination, she headed for Anya's apartment . . . and heard her on the other side of the closed door, debriefing with her demon buddy, Halfrek.

"There was just so much screaming. So much blood. I had forgotten how much damage a Grimslaw demon could do," she admitted. "I didn't think it would hit me like this."

Halfrek's reply was warm and supportive, but the words she spoke sickened Willow. "Oh, sweetie. This is perfectly normal. It's a reflex. You'll get over it in time. Trust me."

She's talking about becoming used to the carnage again. Deadening everything inside Anya that could stop her from killing more people . . .

Willow barged in, straight-backed and angry. "Get out," she ordered Halfrek.

Halfrek was affronted. "Lemon Drop, if you think I'm gonna—"

"Get out," she said again.

The two vengeance demons obviously sensed that she meant business. After a nod from Anya, Halfrek teleported away, leaving Anya alone with Willow.

Willow cut to the chase. "Anya, you have to stop this."

Anya picked up her and Halfrek's tea cups from the coffee table and took them into the kitchen. "Do you know what they did to her? Do you?"

Willow would not be distracted. "Anya, listen to me. You're in trouble. You know it. I'm here to help you."

Anya actually chuckled. "Well, that's great, Willow. Flayed anybody lately? Have you? How quickly they forget."

"I haven't forgotten one second of it," Willow replied evenly.

"I am a vengeance demon," Anya reminded her. "They got what they deserved." But it was clear from her expression that she wasn't sure of that.

Not sure at all.

Buffy and Xander went spider hunting. It left a boy heart-free in the woods and gooey, sticky, icky webbing in the trees, but they weren't sure where it was, exactly. The treetops above them were rustling; and they both went on alert.

Then a gooey piece of webbing shot down on Xander's shoulder. Xander dove out of the way . . . and the horned monster-spider came crashing down on Buffy, knocked her onto her back, and pushed out its inner mouth, fanged and sharp-toothed and hideous. It was trying to bite Buffy's face, but she managed to push it off. It bounded away.

"You okay?" she asked Xander, who nodded.

"Buffy, where'd it go?" he asked, as she stared up at the tree. "I think we need more swords."

She watched the foliage moving. "Uh-huh."

"I say we go home, pick up more swords, and some sort of spidery demon protection amulet. We come back, and—"

She hurled her battle axe up into the treetop. The spider plummeted, her axe in its thorax.

The spider's talons had cut deep red marks in Buffy's back and arm. But what Willow told them about the spider's creator—Anya—upon her arrival home cut even deeper.

Xander was livid as he said to Willow, "How could you not have told me?"

But Buffy got it. She understood Willow's reticence and her reluctance to deal with it even now.

"She didn't tell us for a reason," Buffy explained to Xander. "She didn't tell us because she knows what I have to do." As Xander looked from Willow to Buffy, the Slayer said, "I have to kill Anya."

She added quickly, "She's not the Anya you knew, Xander. She's a demon."

"That doesn't mean you have to kill her," Xander insisted. He added angrily, "Took you all of ten seconds to decide to kill one of your best friends."

"The thought that it might come to this has occurred to me before." She paused, then added, "It's occurred to you too."

She had him there. Hadn't he said exactly that to Anya on Worm Boy night?

"This isn't new ground for us," he pointed out. "When our friends go all crazy and start killing people, we help them."

"Willow was different," Buffy shot back. "She's a human. Anya's a demon."

"And you're the Slayer," he said bitterly. "You have no idea what she's going through."

Buffy stood up. "I don't care what she's going through!"

"No. Of course not. You think we haven't seen all this before? The part where you just cut us all out? Just step away from everything human and act like you're the law. If you knew what I felt—"

"I killed Angel!" she yelled at him. "Do you even remember that? I would have given up everything I had to be with . . . I loved him more than I will ever love anything in this life. And I put a sword through his heart because I had to.

"Do you remember cheering me on?" she continued shouting. "Both of you? Do you remember giving me Willow's message? 'Kick his ass'?"

Willow frowned. "I never said that."

"At some point someone has to draw the line, and

that is always going to be me," Buffy continued heatedly. "You get down on me for cutting myself off, but in the end the Slayer is always cut off. There's no mystical guidebook. No all-knowing council. Human rules don't apply. There's only me. I am the law."

Xander left. And Buffy armed herself.

She looked to Willow to come with her, but Willow shook her head.

After the Slayer left, Willow summoned up D'Hoffryn. The demon appeared . . . and took time out from their meeting to compliment her on the flaying of Warren.

Willow would not be deflected. She said to him, "We need to talk about Anya."

I started the Russian Revolution without blinking, Anya thought vaguely as she touched the blood splatters on the walls of the frat house. *Men on fire rushed past me and I chatted on about the rise of the State with Hallie. She was so impressed with me. Those were such glory days . . .*

Then Xander was there, Xander who had, essentially, ripped her own heart out of her own chest . . . to warn her that the Slayer was coming.

Of course she is. Sooner or later, it was going to come to this.

Then there she was, the Slayer, barking at Xander to get out of her way. He wouldn't.

So Anya backhanded him and got him out of the way.

They began to fight. It was fairly even. Anya thought she might even have a slight upper hand. In fact she was fairly certain of it, as she threw Buffy to the floor.

Slayer's not such a great fighter after all, Anya thought. *Maybe her heart's not really in this . . . ha, ha . . .*

Then Buffy got to her feet and said, "Anya, I'm sorry."

Anya scoffed. "You're apologizing to me? What fight are you watching?"

That was when Buffy pressed her against the wall and rammed her sword through Anya's heart.

Life with Xander . . . it's a song again, a wonderful musical . . . I am singing about marrying him. . . .

"Mrs. Xander Harris . . ."

Anyanka.

My two identities. Without them, I may as well be . . .

. . . dead . . .

Anyanka revived, pulling the sword from her chest. It hurt, but she was still back in the game.

"You know it takes more than that to kill a vengeance demon," she remonstrated the Slayer.

"Oh, I'm just getting started," Buffy retorted.

They resumed their battle, Xander gallantly intervening, getting in the way and then—

D'Hoffryn appeared with his standard lightning bolt show. He said, "Continue with whatever you were doing," and glided to look into the room where she had done the maximum carnage. He was so pleased.

"Oh, breathtaking. It's like somebody slaughtered an Abercrombie & Fitch catalog." Then he reminded Buffy, who was about to pounce, "I'd be gone before you could swing."

"I've been talking to your friend, Ms. Rosenberg," D'Hoffryn told Buffy. "She's a firebrand. I have high hopes for her."

He went on. "Ms. Rosenberg seems to think Anyanka would be better suited outside the vengeance fold. I think we already know what Lady Hacks-away wants." He made air quotes and gave Buffy a cool look.

"And the young man . . . he sees with the eyeballs of love. But I'm not sure if anyone's bothered to find out what Anyanka herself really wants."

"I want to take it back," she murmured softly.

"I'm sorry. What was that?" He was going to make her claim her words.

And when she did, it was clear that she had broken his heart. Then quickly regained his composure.

"Must be twelve bodies in there. Such a thing, not easily done. But not impossible."

He looked hard at his former protégée. "You're a big girl, Anyanka. You understand how this works. The proverbial scales must balance. In order to restore the lives of the victims, the fates require a sacrifice." He hesitated for effect. "The life and soul of a vengeance demon."

"Do it," Anya said without hesitating.

Xander's eyes went wide.

"Wait!" He tried to argue, to find a loophole, an alternate price. "Something that involves grueling, hard labor. At fair market value, taking into account your project's special needs."

"Xander," Anya said, "you can't help me. I'm not even sure there's a 'me' to help."

She turned back to D'Hoffryn and told him clearly, "I understand the price. This is my wish. Undo what I did."

"Very well," D'Hoffryn said. He clapped his hands together.

Anya braced herself; Xander rushed forward, and—

Halfrek appeared.

She sang out gaily, "Anya!"

—Just before she burst into flames and died an agonizing death.

Anya was in shock. Betrayed, desolate . . . guilty beyond bearing.

D'Hoffryn laughed and said, "Did you think it would be that easy to get away? Haven't I taught you anything, *Anya*? Never go for the pain when you can go for the kill."

"You should have killed me," Anya said wretchedly.

"Oh, I wouldn't worry about that," D'Hoffryn flung at her. "'From beneath you, it devours.' Be patient. All good things in time."

And then he teleported away.

The frat boys started reviving, and Buffy went to check on them.

Battle-scarred, bloodstained, and shell-shocked,

Anya hurried out of the building and down the front path. Xander followed after, calling to her. Wearily, she turned.

"Whatever's between us, it doesn't matter," he told her. "You shouldn't be alone in this."

She looked at him gratefully, but she was resolved.

"Yes, I should. My whole life, I've just clung to . . . whatever came along."

He half-raised his hand. "Well, speaking as a clingy, kinda didn't mind."

And he was wonderful in that moment, but she wasn't Anyanka, and she wasn't Mrs. Xander Harris . . . and she had to find out who she was, alone.

"What if I'm really nobody?" she asked brokenly.

His smile was gentle, kind. "Don't be a dope."

"I'm a dope?" she echoed. "Well, that's a start."

The campus lawn was dark, and deep. Anya started walking.

She had miles to go before she could sleep.

Miles and years and hopes.

Chapter Six: "Him"

Xander was not loving the fact that Buffy had forced him to let Spike move in.

"You're going to live in that small room over there," he informed the vampire. "I know it looks like a closet, but it's a room now."

Buffy and Dawn followed him into the apartment. Spike stayed in the hall.

"You're not going to touch my food," Xander continued. "I take The First shower in the morning, and if I use up all the hot water, that's your tough noogies." He said to Buffy, "I hate this plan." And then, to Spike, "Are you keeping up, or do you need some kind of English-to-constant-pain-in-my-ass translation?"

Spike just stood there. Buffy leaned forward. "Invitation," she reminded Xander.

"Is there something more emphatic than hate?"

Xander asked her. "Can I revile the plan? Fine." He said to Spike. "I invite you in. Nimrod."

"Don't want your soddin' food anyway," Spike huffed.

"I just don't understand when his problems became your problems . . . more specifically mine."

"The school basement is making him crazy," she said. "We can't just leave him there."

"Why not? Crazy-Basement-Guy is better than Stalking-Buffy-Guy."

Spike protested, and made noises about the plan not working, and about how he should leave.

"You've been out of the basement for half an hour and you've already stopped talking to invisible people," Buffy countered. "Okay, so there was that one episode in the car, but—"

"I don't need your mollycoddling," Spike protested.

"It's not coddling," Buffy insisted. "Now go to your closet."

"I just don't think it's the school basement that's making people crazy," Dawn told Buffy. They were sitting together on the bleachers and it was a pretty, sunny day . . . and Dawn was trying to figure out why love made people go so wacky.

"I don't see why people bother. I mean, you put all this energy into the chase and the having and the brooding and—I just don't understand these relationships where you all do insane things."

She ranted on about what a waste of time it all was,

when people could be doing things like painting murals and—*there he was*.

The quarterback, noble leader of his team, putting on his letterman jacket after practice. Tall and blond and amazing and gorgeous . . . so gorgeous she leaned over to watch him as he walked away, the leaning tower of Dawnie, and she fell right off the bleachers and landed as hard as she had just fallen . . . for *him*.

Buffy was killing the demon while Anya crawled away from it on the floor, desperately suggesting, "Maybe I'm not even the right Anyanka. Ever think about that? There's tons of Anyanka's out there. Maybe one of them pissed off this . . . what did you say his name was? D'Hoffryneffer?"

Oh, lame, Buffy thought, but she continued the battle until she hurled her battle axe at the demon. It landed in his chest, and he died.

"Good thing I stopped by and heard screaming," Buffy said, helping her up. "So, I guess D'Hoffryn decided to take you out after all?"

"He's not head of vengeance for nothing," Anya murmured. She got some ice and made an ice pack for some of her many injuries, thanking Buffy for helping her and asking her to leave.

"I don't need anyone's help, so stop helping."

Buffy essentially refused. "Something bad is happening. I don't want my friends out there alone right now, okay?"

* * *

I go to this school, so I'm part of the gang, Dawn told herself, trying to psych herself up to actually speak to her one true love. She paced the school hall, her heart pounding: *He* was there, talking to some of the other football players and cheerleaders, one of whom was on crutches. They were talking about tryouts for new cheerleaders, and . . .

    . . . and his name is R. J. What a beautiful name. It's just perfect . . . like he is . . .

    "Hey, R. J.," she began, as she walked up to the group.

    "Hey, Summers," he replied.

    He knows my name!

    "You had Mr. Gurin for English back at your old school, right?" she asked.

    "We all did," R. J. replied.

    "I have him this year." She paused and got no reaction, so she added, "What a drag."

    "I actually kind of liked him," R. J. said.

    "Right!" she cried. "Right. No, no, I like him. It's just, I meant drag in a good, fun way."

    The conversation went even lower after that, with R. J. and his friends pretty much ignoring her and walking away.

    So the next day she showed up in the gym for tryouts in Buffy's old cheerleading uniform, ready to wow the judges and show R. J. her school spirit. She was not the only one in cheer attire, but she knew the uniform was old-fashioned compared to the midriff-baring outfits of the other girls. But it was the best she could do on short notice.

She began her routine, acutely aware of R. J.'s presence:

"Razorbacks, razorbacks, we're gonna play!
We got a secret weapon and his name is R. J.
Hear us cheer, hear us yell, listen to what we say:
Razorbacks, razorbacks, go R. J.!"

Then she did a cartwheel—or tried to—and fell smack on her butt.

In front of *him.*

Disaster city, she was so embarrassed, and Buffy did not listen to her pain. All Buffy cared about was that Dawn had shredded her cheerleading outfit. She had no idea what true love was.

But Dawn had a chance to prove her love the next day at school when one of R. J.'s so-called friends got in R. J.'s face and told him that he, not R. J., was going to start the game.

"It isn't fair," Dawn told the guy. "He works so hard."

"What do you care?" he sneered at her as they both stood on the stairs. "I mean, this is how the game is played. It's dog eat dog, may the best man win."

"But nobody's better than R. J.," she insisted.

The guy laughed. "Yeah, well, that's not really up to you, is it?"

Before she could stop herself, she pushed him down the stairs without so much as a blink.

She got sent to Principal Wood's office. Buffy was there, too, but neither of them could believe that Dawn would actually push someone down the stairs, no matter what the guy said, so she was allowed to leave.

Then even better, R. J. caught up with her . . . and asked her to hook up after school.

She dressed really hot—stretchy top and no bra, hiked up to *here*, and belly pants; lots of makeup and her hair all curled and feathery. She was kickin', if she did say so.

They connected at the Bronze. She was getting into her groove, dancing with him, hips swaying, body in motion, when someone grabbed her

It was Buffy, and she was way, way pissed off.

"So, do you have plans later, or are you just gonna go down to the docks and wait for the fleet to come in?" she demanded. "Where do I start with the bad? First, you told me you were going to the library. Second, you do not go out on a date without informing me first. Third, Anna Nicole Smith thinks you look tacky."

Buffy kept it up, and Dawn grabbed her coat and stormed off.

That was when R. J.'s cheerleader *ex*-girlfriend jumped out of the shadows and picked a fight with Dawn over him.

They had fallen to the ground when Buffy arrived to break up the fight.

"Okay, first with the lap dance, now with the cat fight," she said. "Hey, you wanna get drunk and barf next?"

"Let go of me," Dawn said to Buffy. And to her rival, "This isn't finished."

"I'll never let you have him, bitch." She kicked Buffy in the shin and took off. "R. J. is mine. I mean it! Stay away from him!"

Buffy said, "Well, at least someone agrees you shouldn't be dating this guy."

And as for that guy . . .

The next day at school, Buffy overheard Principal Wood chastising R. J. for getting girls to do his homework. He took it well, his letterman jacket slung casually over his shoulder.

After the principal was finished, it was Buffy's turn.

"I see how you get along," she said, pacing while she built up a head of steam. "Oh, look at me, I'm Mr. Quarterback, I crush little girls and all their feelings. All I have to do is . . ." She turned and faced him. He was wearing his letterman jacket and wow, was he *hot*.

". . . lead a team of high school athletes trying their best to do a good job," she said in a pleasant tone, "Everyone depending on me . . ."

He is incredibly hot.

"You know, I just realized that I'm basically the same age as you. I'm not really older at all, actually. Just like you, but with the sexual experience and stuff."

I want him. Here. Now.

Then another faculty member came into the office lobby area, and Buffy pulled herself together.

"I'm really glad we had this talk. So . . . I think you'd better get back to class."

When Dawn got home from school, Buffy nipped her sister's pathetic little crush in the bud.

"He said that you came on a little strong," Buffy plaintively informed her.

"Oh my God! I'm the pushy queen of slut town," Dawn moaned.

"No, honey. not at all. It's just . . . you know . . . lay back a little. Let him come to you."

With her sister eased out of the way, Buffy came on as strong as possible the next day at school, pulling R. J. out of algebra class and straight into an unused classroom.

"I've always been fascinated by football," she gushed. "So, what's it like to lead a team?"

"The thing of it is the time," he told her. "Nobody gets how much time goes into it, with practices and games."

"I totally get it," she said, loving the bond between them. "I was kind of juggling some stuff when I was in high school, which was also very recently. Principal Snyder was always on me."

"I still say Wood's the worst," R. J. told her. "You haven't seen the way that guy rides me. I wish somebody'd get him off my back."

"Yeah, that would be cool."

"And sometimes, I didn't even do anything wrong . . ."

Buffy grabbed him by the collar and kissed him. He pulled back a little—although it was obvious he didn't want to—*how could he not want to, he was her soul mate*—and said, "You're . . . like a teacher."

"Not really," she purred. "But I mean, does it bother you?"

His eyes gleamed. "Not so much."

They started kissing passionately . . . oh, he was fabulous . . . and then they moved on to other things . . .

It wouldn't be stalking him just to see how his day was going, Dawn decided.

She meandered her way over to his math class and peered in for the second time . . . no R. J., but his books were there.

Did something bad happen to him?

So she glanced into nearby classrooms, and then she saw . . . him . . . and them . . .

Oh my God!

Buffy and R. J. were having sex!

She ran out of the school and flung herself down on the edge of a planter, sobbing as though her broken heart would break all over again. Then she looked down in her distress to see Xander's workboots. She looked up at him in utter misery. Concerned, he sat down next to her.

"Dawn? What's wrong? Is this—did that guy in the jacket . . . ?"

"Ugh!" she screamed. "I don't even want to hear his name anymore!"

Xander raised a brow. "I just called him 'that guy in the jacket.'"

"That's what I used to call him in my head before I knew his real name!"

"Dawnie, honey, you seem extremely perturbed. Maybe I should go get Buffy . . ."

"No!" Her voice could have cracked windows. "I don't ever want to see her again!"

"I thought this was about that guy in the . . . the guy with the thing . . ."

"No. It's about both of them!" And she cried harder.

It was so hot. He was so great. And, oh, yeah, it was going fantastic as she straddled this incredible hunk of man, loving him with all her . . . self . . . until Xander showed up and ruined the moment.

"Xander, hi," Buffy said happily. "This is R. J."

"Hey, guy," R. J. said to Xander, "it's called knocking."

"I'm sorry," Xander said to R. J. "It's just checkout time was an hour ago. We were hoping to make up the bed. Also, it's a classroom, you chowderhead!" Then he said to Buffy, "Now get off the boy, Buffy. We're going home."

At home poor Dawnie had to at last confront the truth about R. J.'s love for Buffy.

"Crying isn't going to make his love for me go away," Buffy said sympathetically.

"Listen," Xander said, "you're under a love spell. That's what this has to be."

"You're right," Buffy said to Xander. Then, to her sister, "You're under a spell. Oh, poor little Dawnie."

The sisters eventually left the room, while Xander, Anya, and Willow did the research on how to break the spell.

"Love spells," Willow murmured. "People forget how dangerous they can be."

Xander said, "Hey, been there . . ." And remembered five years before, when every woman in Sunnydale—except Cordelia, for whom the spell had been intended—had fallen in love with him. Madly, truly, completely . . .

"Good times," he said wistfully.

Then as they searched the Web they discovered that Xander had known R. J.'s brother back in school—he used to stick chewing gum in Xander's hair.

He made Spike go with him to the Brooks residence, and Xander gave Spike a head's-up lecture.

"I'm just saying, we're—we're tangling with a powerful spell here. We don't know what the deal is so . . . so keep an eye out if this guy looks twitchy. And don't let this guy charm you, either. He had everyone around him practically kissing his ring back in high school."

Then he rang the door . . . and a paunchy guy in a pizza delivery uniform opened the door.

It was Lance Brooks, the former BMOC of Sunnydale High, and Xander was stunned.

"You might not know it now, looking at me with a couple of extra pounds, but back then, I was quite the guy," Lance announced.

Then as Spike glared at all the dozens and dozens

of angels on shelves and turned their backs to him, he came across a picture of R. J. and his brother.

"He's wearing your jacket," Spike noted.

"That jacket was with me all the way through high school. Gave it to him when I graduated." And his father, it turned out, had worn it before him. Lance's mom was a former Miss Arkansas. . . .

It's the jacket, Xander and Spike realized, and abruptly left.

It's him, Anya and Willow thought dreamily.

Wearing his jacket, R. J. had come to the Summers home and rung the bell. And now he was ringing chimes . . . even Willow's.

"A. J. is my best friend and my dearest darling," Anya insisted.

"It's R. J. And what you were picking up on was his deep caring and devotion to me."

Then Buffy and Dawn came back downstairs, overheard their conversation . . . and Buffy finally realized what was going on.

"Clearly, you've both been affected by the same spell that got Dawn."

Willow said, "There's a simple answer to this. Just think about who loves him the most. Clearly I do, since I'm willing to look past the whole orientation thing."

Dawn yowled, "I need him."

Anya scoffed. "Well, you're going to have to do better than that. I'd kill for him."

Willow glared at her. "You'd kill for a chocolate bar."

"Yes! Kill for him!" Buffy proclaimed. "I'm the Slayer. Slayer means kill. Oh, I'll kill the principal."

Anya looked daunted. "Ooh, that is hard to top."

"Yeah? Well, I have skills," Willow interjected. "I can prove my love with magic."

"Yeah, right, what're you going to do, use magic to make him into a girl?" Anya flung at her. When Willow's eyes widened, Anya muttered, "Damn." Then she brightened. "Oh, I know what he'll like."

The three older loves of R. J. went on their separate ways, Buffy managed to be generous as she faced victory. She said to Dawn, "Sorry, Dawnie. You're never going to get him."

"No, never," Dawn grieved.

They hopped to it.

Willow was halfway through her supplication to Hecate, to change a son into a daughter, when Xander and Spike stopped her . . . and she spilled the beans about the others.

They decided to start with Buffy first, since murdering the principal, not a good thing.

They got there in time, and managed to wrestle the rocket launcher from her just in time.

Then Willow, whom they had brought with them, did a locator spell . . .

. . .and they found Dawn, lying on the train tracks, waiting for the train.

Buffy jumped onto another oncoming train and leaped onto the tracks, gathering up her sister and rolling her away just as the train bore down at them.

"This is the plan? You're going to steal R. J. by being trisected?" Buffy demanded of her weeping sister.

"What am I?" Dawn asked, sobbing. "Going to compete with you? You're older and hotter and have sex that's rough, and you kill people. I don't have any of that stuff. But if I did this then his whole life he'd know there was someone that loved him so much they'd give up their life."

"No guy is worth your life, ever . . ." Buffy insisted.

That was when Buffy realized that, well, maybe she was under a spell . . .

The girls went home . . . and Xander and Spike concocted a brilliant, strategic plan to steal R. J.'s jacket—namely they swooped down on R. J., who was window-shopping with a cheerleader, and while Xander tackled him, Spike yanked that evil leather garment clean off the quarterback.

They burned it in Buffy's fireplace to dulcet tones on the radio.

"That, my friend, is the smell of sweet, sweet victory," Xander announced.

"Also, burning cotton poly-blend," Anya added.

Buffy smiled at her old friend. "Xander, be honest. You didn't, you know, think about slipping that jacket on, just for a little bit?"

Xander said, "I refuse to answer that on the grounds that it didn't fit."

Anya groused, "Man, this fool gets his jacket from

his brother, who got it from their father, and we'll never know where he got it. That bites."

"Yeah, welcome to the Hellmouth," Xander said, "where even outerwear isn't safe."

Then Willow, Buffy, and Dawn agonized over how stupid they had been, what terrible things they had almost done . . . powerless to stop themselves over a stupid curse.

But powerless was the operative word.

"I feel so stupid. All over a spell," Dawn said, sighing.

"Get ready to feel even stupider when it's not," Buffy told her.

"Hey, Anya," Willow piped up. "You never told us what you can't believe you almost."

"I, uh, wrote an epic poem comparing him to a daisy and a tower and a lake," she said, lying through her teeth

But as she stood there the radio announcer said: ". . . *with the latest on Sunnydale's late-night bandit, who is still at large. A masked thief held up a number of businesses, including . . .*"

Anya snapped off the radio.

"Okay, who wants ice cream?" she burbled.

Chapter Seven: "Conversations with Dead People"

Secrets have power. Share them, and they weaken . . .

Not going to be alone tonight much longer, Buffy thought, as she squatted beside a fresh grave.

As if on cue, a hand shot up through the earth. The rest of the vampire soon followed, faster than Buffy had anticipated and catching her a little off guard. It should have been easy to dust him, but he was surprisingly strong. Or was she just not up for it tonight?

They got into a clinch, and he was starting to beat down on her when he stopped and looked at her . . . and said, in surprise, "Buffy?" He laughed. "Buffy Summers?"

* * *

It was dark. Dawn let herself into the house and found
the twenty and the note:

> *Will and I are out*
> *until late.*
> *Here's money for*
> *the store.*
> *NO PIZZA!*
> *Love you,*
> *Buffy*

A night alone, Dawn thought, flopping onto the couch.
Cool.

She ordered pizza; whoops, got it on one of
Buffy's blouses while she was trying it on; and
danced around to Mexican ranchera music on the
radio. Then she watched marshmallows expand in the
microwave and exchanged TV viewing comments on
the phone with Kit, her bud from the basement adventure.

"There it is again," she said into the phone. It was
a thump, and it had been going on intermittently for
most of the evening. She had thought maybe it was a
tree branch scraping on a window, something like that,
but so far nothing.

Or maybe it was someone at the door . . .

Dawn got up from the couch and opened the door.
It flew open on its own accord, a wind blowing violently. She managed to get it shut, crying, "Kit? Is
there a storm? Are you there?"

The door blew open again, more insistent, more

violent. This time it hit Dawn, making her drop the phone.

Suddenly the TV started blaring. And the CD player . . . and the radio . . .

Dawn raced to the TV and tried to turn it off . . . then she pulled the plug . . . and it stayed on.

She got Buffy's battle axe and slammed it down on the TV screen, and it finally went dark. Then she swung the axe and smashed the CD player, and it went silent.

Hoisting the axe, she headed into the kitchen, intent on smashing the radio, which was blaring a crazed *banda* tune. But before she could get to it, the microwave began to hum . . . and hum..

It exploded, the door blasting outward in fragments of glass. Dawn yelped and ran for the back door, stepping on the glass. Her feet were being sliced into ribbons.

On the way, as she passed near the radio, the music dissolved into static, and through that static, she heard . . .

"Dawn?"

It was her mom.

She froze, staring in astonishment. Had she really heard that? Had she?

"Mom?" she whispered.

She didn't recognize him, not even after a few prompts—history essay, lightboard accident during the school production of *Pippin*. He was hurt. It took her so long to realize who he was. She tried to cheer him up a little.

"No, I just—I didn't recognize you, you know, your face, all demon, and I think you've filled out a lot."

They chatted a bit more—he'd been a psych major, took a year off to do an internship—then his face demorphed, and he said excitedly, "So, I'm a vampire! How weird is that?"

"I'm sorry," Buffy murmured.

"No," he assured her. "It feels okay. Strong, and I feel like I'm connected to a powerful all-consuming evil that's gonna suck the world into fiery oblivion. What about you?"

"Not so much connected," she said. Then she told him about being the Slayer, which way surprised him.

"Lotta kids thought you were dating some really old guy, or like, you were heavy religious. Scott Hope said you were gay."

"What?"

"So all that time, you were a Slayer."

"'The,'" she corrected him.

"'The.' Like as in, the only one?"

"Pretty much," she murmured.

"Ah. So when you said not connected, that was kind of a telling statement, wasn't it?"

She put her hands on her hips and gave him a look. "Ah. Psych 101 alert. I really need emotional therapy from the Evil Dead."

"Hey, it was *your* phrase," he said.

"I'm connected," she insisted. "I'm connected to a lot of people, okay?"

Unaware that on the ground, her cell phone was ringing . . .

* * *

The lights were on the Summers home. Dawn was sitting on the living room floor, picking glass out of her foot and wrapping cloth around it. The phone was pressed against her ear.

On the floor, the radio remained silent.

Her mother said nothing, and Buffy wasn't answering the phone.

She gave up and hung up, rising and shaking the radio.

"Do it again! I heard you!" she cried.

The lights went out and the room fell into darkness . . . but only for an instant. Then the lights flared back on.

The room had been altered: the weapon's chest stood on end, the chairs were piled on the table, and the wall was splashed with the bloody words MOTHER'S MILK IS RED TODAY.

The lights went off again. In the darkness Dawn heard her own panicked breathing . . . and a slow, steady thump that shook the house on its foundations.

The lights came back on. Everything was back in its place. No chairs in a tower, no disarray.

No blood.

The thumping resumed, even louder, more insistent, *thumpthumpthumpthump*.

"Stop it," Dawn pleaded.

THUMPTHUMPTHUMP

"Stop it, please!"

THUMPTHUMPTHUMPTHUMP

"STOP IT!" she shrieked.

Silence.

Surprised, Dawn looked around. The silence reigned.

"Hello?" she called.

THUMP.

She lowered her voice and whispered, "Mom?"

THUMPTHUMPTHUMPTHUMPTHUMP.

"Wait. Wait! Wait! I don't—"

THUMPTHUMPTHUMPTHUMP.

"Slow down!" She thought to herself for a moment. "Once for yes . . . okay, once for yes . . . and twice for no."

To the silence she called, "Mom?"

THUMP.

Her voice broke. "Mom, it's you?"

THUMP.

"Are you okay?"

THUMPTHUMP.

"You're not. Mom . . . Mommy . . . are you alone?"

The house shook violently, earthquake levels. The lights strobed on and off, blinding Dawn in flashes as everything tumbled to the floor—vases, pictures, lamps, her house tumbling down around her ears, as she screamed.

Then a sound raged through the house, like a frenzied, growling animal, and she tried hard to stand her ground.

"I hear you," she called. "I hear you breathing. Are you hurting my mother? Are you keeping her from coming back to me?"

A brilliant flash of blue light revealed her mother

lying on the couch, her eyes milky and dead. Dawn hurried toward her.

"Mom? I see you. I'm coming toward you, okay?"

There was another flash. A strange, dark figure loomed over Joyce, choking her as she helplessly reached out toward Dawn. It was choking her mom, hurting her!

Dawn screamed. "She's trying to talk to me! Get off her and let her talk to me!"

She got down on the floor, groping through the wreckage for her battle axe. Another flash of light revealed that the figure had it, and was swinging it straight at Dawn's head. Dawn screamed and ducked . . . and the figure missed.

Then it said in a low, gravelly voice, "Get out!"

Dawn ran toward the front door, which had swung open. Wind blew at a gale force. She was almost across the threshold, but she stopped and turned on her heel, resolutely staying inside the house.

"No!" she shouted, and shut the door. "She's my mother. I'm staying."

On the couch, her mother's eyes flashed open.

Buffy was lying on a sarcophagus, using a carved stone book as a pillow. Holden sat in the analyst's chair, in this case a headstone, and probed gently.

"So, you meet someone, you form a bond . . ."

"But it never lasts."

"I just target the impossible ones with deadly accuracy," Buffy said, frustrated.

"You think you do that on purpose? Maybe you're trying to protect yourself?"

"Protecting myself? From heartbreak, misery, sexual violence, and possible death? Not so much."

"From committing," he said patiently.

She sat up, and retorted heatedly, "I commit. I'm committed. I'm a committee."

"So it's them? You're reaching out, they're not coming through?"

She shifted uncomfortably. "It's different. I think you're confusing me because you're evil."

"I just think you're in some pain here—which I do kind of enjoy 'cause I'm evil now—but you should ease up on yourself. It's not exactly like you have the patent on bad relationships."

"Wouldn't it be cool if I did?" she asked mournfully.

"And what are you, supposed to be settling down already? At . . . twenty-one? You know, my girlfriend at college, she's sweet, but that doesn't mean I'm gonna go vampify her just so we can be together forever."

"Sire," Buffy told him. "When you turn a human into a vampire, you 'sire' them."

He stood and leaned on another headstone. "Oh, I have so much to learn. Come on, isn't this insane? I mean, I was afraid to talk to you in high school, and here we are mortal enemies." He paused. "We're gonna have to fight to the death, aren't we?"

"It's the time-honored custom," she said, and she felt a twinge of sadness.

"Wow, reality just shows up sometimes, doesn't it? You know, I've got the bloodlust pumping, but you don't seem as thrilled. Is it because we're going to fight?"

"It's because I'm going to win," she replied, with another twinge.

He chuckled. "Do the words 'superiority complex' mean anything to you?" Before she could argue with him, he said, "All Chosen. All destiny. Who could live with that for seven years and *not* feel superior?"

He continued. "Is it possible, even a little bit, that the reason you have trouble connecting to guys is because you think maybe they're not worth it? Maybe you think you're better than them?"

She glared at him. "Say, there's that bloodlust I was looking for."

And they fought, she grinding out at him, "I think I'm gonna kill you just a little bit more than usual."

She kicked him, her momentum carrying the two of them through a stained glass window in a nearby crypt.

She whipped out a stake and got ready to pay her bill to the bloodsucking wannabe shrink, when he said, "Okay, are you killing me because I'm evil or because you opened up?"

"What is wrong with you!" she yelled. She got to her feet. When he tried to do the same, she kicked him in the face.

He laughed. "Nothing. I got no worries. Biggest thing on my mind is whether or not Tricia Waldman came to my funeral or not. Do you remember her? Ooh . . . bite-able."

"See, this is what I hate about you vampires! Sex and death and love and pain . . . it's all the same damn thing to you."

He walked around her, looking curious, interested. He said, "Let me ask you this. Your last relationship . . . was it with a vampire?"

A night alone, studying in the library. Willow could barely contain her sorrow, remembering how much she and Tara had enjoyed talking about their classes and trading theories about life, the universe, and everything.

Maybe she dozed, or maybe it was just time for something weird to happen. At any rate, someone started speaking to her from the stacks.

"So, this is the U.C. library, huh? It's so big."

The figure came out from the stacks, and Willow startled, her eyes widening. Though she had never met Cassie, the girl who knew she was going to die on a Friday, she had stared at her face for hours on Cassie's Web site, as she had tried to find a way to save her.

"Did I fall asleep?" Willow asked.

"No, no, I'm here," Cassie assured her. "It's kind of complicated." Then she sat down and added, "I knew this would completely freak you out."

Not so much, Willow thought. *Ghosts . . . seen 'em before.* But she was puzzled why Cassie was here.

"It's just . . . she asked that I come talk to you." She smiled sadly. "She says she still sings."

"What?" Willow was stricken. Cassie was talking about Tara. She had a message from Tara!

Cassie nodded slightly. "Remember that time on the bridge, when you sang to each other? Well, she says even though you can't hear her it, she still sings to you."

"Tara?" Willow cried, looking around, fingers twisting, heart clutching. "Is it you?"

"She's sorry she couldn't come herself. She just can't," Cassie continued forlornly, "because of what you did. You killed people. So you can't see her."

Willow nearly choked on her grief and remorse. "But she's talking to you? And she can hear me? Tara, Tara, I miss you. I miss you so much."

"She's crying," Cassie told her. "She misses you. She wishes she could touch you."

"Me, too. Oh, me, too. Oh, God, Tara, it hurts so much. Every day, it's like this giant hole, and it's not getting better. After Warren shot you, it was horrible. I was horrible. I—I lost myself. The regular me." Tears streamed down her face.

"Well, you were grieving," Cassie replied, and Willow didn't know if she was speaking for Tara or for herself.

"A lot of people grieve," Willow argued. "They don't make with the flaying. They don't kill people."

"It was the power," Cassie said.

"I am the power. It's in me," Willow said. "Did I mention the random destruction of property? The Magic Box—"

"The power is bigger than you are," Cassie cut in.

"I know, but—"

"Things are more clear where Tara is, where we

are. We can see your path, and you have to stop. You can't use magic again, ever."

Willow was confused. "Black magic, of course. But Giles says it isn't as simple as quitting it all cold-turkey—"

"It's too dangerous," Cassie told her. "You can't take the chance that you'll lose control."

"I—I don't want to. I can't." Willow was distraught. "I never want to cause that kind of pain."

"Of course you don't," Cassie assured her.

"So, I won't," Willow finished. "I'm gonna be okay."

Cassie listened a moment. "She says . . ." She looked straight at Willow. "You're not gonna be okay. You're going to kill everybody. But if you stop completely . . ."

"Right," Willow said quickly, but she was still incredibly confused. "W-What about Giles? He made it seem like it's just as dangerous for me to quit completely, like I'll go off the deep end again—"

Cassie was adamant. "If you do so much as another spell . . ."

"I tried to stop. I—I tried. What if I can't do this?" Willow demanded, distraught.

"Don't think that way," Cassie said calmly.

"Well, how can I not? You're telling me I'm going to murder all my friends. I'm not strong. I'm not an Amazon. I'm just me."

"Well, there is one thing you could do to stop it."

"What? Anything," Willow begged.

"And you could see her. You wouldn't have to talk through me."

"Tara?" Willow asked softly.

"So go. Be with her. Everybody will be safe, and you'll be together again. It's not that bad. Really. It's just like going to sleep."

Willow stared at her.

Cassie was trying to get her to kill herself. Commit suicide.

This is wrong. Something is wrong. Tara was all about life. Our Wicca tradition is about the power to heal. . . .

"Who are you?" Willow coldly asked Cassie.

Still seated Cassie—or whatever entity was masquerading as the dead girl—made a little face and said, "Suicide thing was too far, huh. Hmm. You seemed so ripe."

She mocked Willow. "'Oh, baby, you left such a big hole. It hurt so bad.'" She leaned in all serious and cold evil. "You don't know hurt. This last year's gonna seem like cake after what I put you and your friends through, and I am no fan of easy death. Believe me, I'm going for a big finish."

In horror Willow murmured, "From beneath you, it devours."

Cassie leaned back in her chair, grinning at Willow. "Oh, not it. *Me*."

Her grin grew until her mouth became her entire face, her jaws engulfing her head as she turned inside out, becoming a floating sphere of flesh. Just as Willow managed to understand what she was seeing, the sphere disappeared.

Buffy, she thought, horrified.

* * *

"Wish we'd stayed in Mexico," Jonathan muttered.

He and Andrew were in their El Camino, which they had boosted in Mexico and which was decorated like a border gift shop. Dingle balls bobbed and danced as they sped toward the city limits of Sunnydale. Jonathan had never dreamed he would see this town again.

"I didn't like it there," Andrew contended. "Everyone spoke Mexico-an."

"You could've learned it. You learned the Klingon dictionary in two and a half weeks."

"That had much clearer transitive and intransitive rules." He hesitated. "And besides . . . I can't keep having those nightmares."

Jonathan shuddered. "Right. Me neither." He took a breath and intoned, *"Desde abajo te devora."*

"'It eats you, starting with your bottom,'" Andrew translated.

"We're gonna make it right," Jonathan muttered to himself.

Andrew nodded, growing misty-eyed. "We're outlaws. With hearts of gold."

Then da-da, da-da-da-da, just like in *Mission Impossible*, they cut a hole in the window and rappelled down, their equipment stowed in two large black backpacks. Flashlights, map, check, check; walkie-talkies, check-check-check-check-check-check . . . and they had successfully infiltrated the brand-new Sunnydale High School.

"Maybe we should just go get Buffy," Jonathan

murmured. "We'll just tell her what we know about the Seal of Danzalthar—"

"Think, McFly! Why would she believe us without any proof?" Andrew insisted. "Think of it as a trial by fire. A quest."

In search of the library Andrew sent Jonathan off in one direction while he took the other.

Then Warren finally appeared to him.

"There you are," Andrew said. "I'm scared out of my friggin' gourd here?"

Warren laughed. "Take it easy. Take it easy."

Andrew was not amused. "One time you left me, and I ended up a Mexican."

"We've been over this. Now, this death thing is part of the master plan. Short Round holds up his end of the bargain, we'll both become gods."

Andrew got that. He got it all the way down to the basement, as Warren led him to the Seal while Jonathan, unable to see Warren, consulted the map.

They finally got there and began digging. Jonathan was in a chatty mood, reminiscing about Sunnydale High, even though his days there had sucked so totally that at one time he'd tried to kill himself.

So what I'm about to do, not so bad, Andrew thought. *He's been partway down this road by himself . . . I'm just helping him make it to the end of his questa . . .*

They dug, Jonathan rammering about caring about his old "friends" and that being why he was doing this.

Finally they uncovered the Seal, and Andrew had

to catch his breath. It was like something Indiana Jones would collect—a circular metal object with a diameter of six feet—making the circumference nearly nineteen feet, molded into the shape of an upside-down pentagram embossed with the likeness of a horned goat.

Mission accomplasido.

While Jonathan busily packed up his equipment bag, Andrew got out the dagger. Then, as Jonathan registered Warren's presence behind his other live friend, Andrew did just as Warren had told him, and sliced Jonathan in the abdomen.

Shock . . . theater!

Then Jonathan collapsed onto the disc. He bled—*a lot*, Andrew thought nervously. It just ran out of him, and there was more than Andrew would have expected. It was . . . gross.

But Warren looked pleased. And, as he had told Andrew it would, the Seal drank Jonathan's blood, and began to glow.

Power on, Warren thought dazedly.

Dawn had lived with witches and she knew a little bit about the power of magic.

Now she sat cross-legged on the floor, surrounded by white candles and spell books.

"I know you're there," she said boldly, listening to the terrifying breathing that reverberated through the house. "I will cast you out. My mother needs to talk to me."

She was holding a bowl of powder and she sprinkled some on the floor. For her troubles she was slammed backward against the wall. She held tight to the bowl.

"I cast you from this place!" she shouted, sprinkling more dust. "It is your poison and your bane!"

Invisible fingers raked her cheek.

She screamed again, but sprinkled more dust. "It is the skin that is cut from your flesh!" she cried.

Then the hellwind rose and blew out all the candles. The living room window imploded, and shards of glass showered down on her like bombs.

She didn't know how much time passed, but eventually she got her breathing under control. Shellshocked, terrified, she sat in the middle of the living room, trying to absorb what had happened.

Then . . . glowing, white, transcendent, her mother appeared.

Joyce Summers was robed all in white. She glowed like an angel, and her smile was sweet and gentle, belying the message she had for her daughter.

"Things are coming, Dawn. Listen. Things are on their way. I love you, and I love Buffy, but she won't be there for you."

Dawn was thunderstruck. Her eyes widened as she said, "What? Why are you—?"

"When it's bad, Buffy won't choose you. She'll be against you."

The glowing image of Dawn's mother began to fade.

Dawn cried, "No! No, don't go! Please, don't go!"

As her mother vanished, Dawn sobbed uncontrollably, amid the ruins of her home.

* * *

Holden had hit the mother lode of her issues, and Buffy couldn't hold back. They sat together on the steps of the crypt, Holden practicing the reflective listening he must have learned as psych major.

"He loved me," she told him. "I mean, in his own sick, soulless way, he really did care for me. But I—I didn't want to be in love."

"Didn't you?" he asked gently.

"I have all this power," she continued. "I didn't ask for it. I don't deserve it. It's like. I wanted to be punished. I wanted to hurt like I thought I deserved. Um, this is sort of complicated. If you'd rather fight."

He leaned back and said, "Tell me."

It all rushed out. "I feel like I'm worse than anyone. Honestly, I'm beneath them. My friends, my boyfriends. I feel like I'm not worthy of their love. 'Cause even though they love me, it doesn't mean anything 'cause their opinions don't matter. They don't know. They're not the Slayer. I am. Sometimes I feel . . ."She sighed heavily, burdened down by her guilts and confusions ". . . like I'm better than them. Superior."

Holden smiled kindly. "So you can't win."

She looked down.

"And I thought *I* was diabolical," he said. "Or, I plan to be. You do have a superiority complex, and you've got an inferiority complex about it. Kudos."

"It doesn't make any sense," Buffy murmured.

"It makes every kind of sense," Holder shot back. "It just adds up to you feeling alone. And, Buffy . . .

everyone feels alone. Everybody is, till they die."

He rose.

"Speaking of which . . . you ready for our little death match?"

She stood slowly. "I suppose. Thanks for listening."

They moved to opposite corners in preparation for their face-off.

"There's some things you can only tell a stranger," Holder told her.

"You're not a stranger," she said. "But that stuff with Spike is pretty—"

"Hold it," Holden said.

"What?" she asked.

"Did you say Spike?"

"Yeah, why?"

He chuckled expansively. "He was the guy that um, oh, what's the word?"

Buffy felt herself go hollow and numb. "Sired?"

"Yeah." Holden nodded happily, as if to say, *small strange world*. "He was the guy that sired me."

Buffy stared at him in utter disbelief.

Spike sat in the Bronze drinking whiskey and listening to the singer, taking in her words.

And where were you?
Warm skin, wolf grin, where were you?
I fell into the moon and it covered you in blue.
I fell into the moon, can I make it right?
The air is dew and where were you?

> *I died, and where were you?*
> *High tide inside . . .*

Nice bird in fake fur came in, plopped a pack of cigs in front of Spike, and took the set next to him. Pretty. Interested.

> *Can I spend the night?*
> *High tide inside.*

After he chatted her up she suggested they leave. It was his idea, but he allowed her to lay claim to it.

They strolled together, talking, smiling. Got to her apartment building—looked a bit like Rupert's old digs—and she invited him up.

> *I crawled out of the world and you said*
> *I shouldn't stay.*
> *I crawled out of the world. Can I make it right?*

He demurred, glancing at the picture window behind him. Drapes were closed, no one to see, as she descended, to see what he was about. She moved in closer to tempt him. . . .

> *I fell into the moon and it covered you in blue.*

They were hip to hip, and the bloodlust was upon him. Firmly he grabbed her, held her, and tore out her throat. Drank lustily, drank deeply.

Then he threw her corpse away, which sprawled at

his feet. Brimming with satisfaction, he wiped his mouth with the back of his hands. If he'd been a were-wolf he would have howled with joy.

I fell into the moon.

Buffy thrust her stake into the unbeating heart of Holden "Webs" Webster, former psych major, former vampire, and he exploded . . . just as he had known he would, the moment that he rose.

Rest in peace, and thanks for the analysis, she thought mournfully. *You actually helped me quite a bit.*

The ashes of fear were dry in the Slayer's mouth.

Spike sired him.

It has to be a mistake.

It has to be.

He can't do that and he wouldn't now, even if he could. He has a soul. He wants to be good.

The Slayer stared down at the pile of dust, and disconnected on so many levels that part of her power was, for a moment, shut off—it was the power to feel, to move, to think. She stood in the graveyard like another monument to the inevitability of death, stunned.

Can I make it right? Can I spend the night?
Alone?

Part Two: Ordeal

Chapter Eight: "Sleeper"

Who's that knockin' at my door? Xander thought groggily as he staggered from his bedroom toward the front door of his apartment. "At 4:30 in the morning," he grumbled. "Sweet mamalooshin. Who is it?"

"Me," Buffy said. "Where's Spike?"

He unlatched the door and opened it. She sailed past toward Spike's bedroom, peering in only to find it empty.

"He's out. I think," Xander said, yawning. "Least he was when I got home."

Buffy not loving that news. "Any idea where he went?"

"I don't know," Xander replied, shrugging. "Creature of the night, Buffy. He's probably out . . . creaturing." He looked at her intently. "Why? What's happened?"

Buffy was loathe to answer. She walked away to the window.

"He in trouble?" Xander asked.

She hesitated and peered out the window.

"I hope not," she murmured to herself.

Early one morning . . .

Spike hummed the tune as he dug a hole in the cellar. Nice of the old place to come with a dirt floor.

Nice of him to have someone to bury in it.

Bird was still wearing her faux-fur jacket, which he was tempted to take, mostly on principle, because it was definitely a woman's piece of clothing. His leather duster, now, that'd been a trophy, too—taken right off the back of a dead Slayer back in New York.

This one's eyes were open and blood caked her bite wounds, rather like frosting on a sweet. He picked her up, gave her a cursory look-see, then tossed her body into the shallow, unmarked grave.

Early one morning . . .

The Watcher named Robson was still reading his book when he let himself into his flat. It was a venerable old tome written by the Venerable Bede, actually, and it had some nice bits about the nature of mystical power.

He looked up from his reading and froze for just one instant.

lo?

proceeded straight into alarm mode. The

furniture was tipped over; a broken vase lay in shards—signs of a struggle, and he with a Potential to protect.

"Nora? *Nora*?" he called, searching the place for signs of her.

He crossed into the next room and what he saw stunned him for a moment into inaction.

No, he thought, *please, God, no.*

Her dark braid like a hangman's nose draped over her neck, Nora lay unmoving on the floor. She had been stabbed in the back. There was blood, and no signs of life.

My Slayer, he thought, grieving, disregarding for the moment that she had not been Chosen.

A rushing sound alerted him that he was not alone; he turned around as a hooded figure in a black robe rushed him, a scimitar-shaped dagger in his hand. Robson blocked the attack with his valise, the dagger sliding deeply into the side. Then the Watcher palmed the figure in the face and pushed him backward. The figure stumbled.

Taking advantage of the moment, Robson reached for one of the wall-mounted swords, just as another black-robed figure emerged from the shadows and stabbed him in the back.

He collapsed beside Nora, whose life he had sworn to protect, and thought, *Just as well . . . it's what I deserve for failing her . . .*

. . . as his lifeblood streamed out of him.

* * *

I have to tell Buffy about seeing Cassie in the library, Willow thought anxiously, as she pushed opened the door to the Summers home. *Or, not Cassie, just the thing that's threatening to devour us, and it devoured itself!—It was so hideous . . .*

"Buffy?" she called.

She had just started up the stairs when she heard Dawn say flatly, "She's not here."

Silhouetted in darkness, Dawn was sitting on the floor hugging a cushion. The room looked exactly as if a bomb had gone off, everything shredded into hundreds and hundreds of tiny shards and pieces.

"Dawn? Oh, my God," Willow breathed. She ran to her side. "Dawn, what happened here? You're cut."

Dawn turned her face for Willow to inspect. Her face was earnest, troubled . . . and tinged with a strange joy. "I saw Mom. She was here, Willow. I saw her. She was here and she spoke to me."

Willow's narrowed with understanding. There had been more than one "visitation" tonight, then. She said sadly, "Oh, sweetie. It wasn't her. At least, I don't think. I—I saw something, too, and it looked like . . . someone else, but it wasn't."

Dawn frowned. "I don't understand."

"It's the Big Bad, Dawn. The one we knew was coming."

"But that's what she said. Mom said that things were on their way, and that she loves . . . us. So it had to be her, right? I mean, her warning was true." Her eyes were luminous with tears, her voice breaking with emotion. She had been through hell, but she was convinced that she had seen an angel.

And I thought I was communicating with Tara . . .

Willow shook her head. "I don't know. I just don't think we can trust anything right now."

Xander was making caffeine while Buffy paced. She was very wigged about the possibility that Spike had sired someone, and he was doing his best to be rational Xander.

"Spike can't be doing this, Xander. He couldn't even if he wanted to," Buffy protested.

"Why not?" he asked.

"Well, for one thing, pain chip, remember? He can't hurt anyone."

"Didn't stop him from hurting you," Xander pointed out.

Buffy looked away. She knew they were talking about many kinds of pain, and she just didn't want to go into it with him.

"It's working," Buffy asserted. "I've seen it."

"Is it? Or is that what Spike wants you to think?" Xander pressed.

The were still discussing it when Spike came in through the front door, saw Buffy and Xander staring at him, and froze.

"Well, this can't be good. You here at this hour. Is there trouble?"

They mooked around and he muttered, "Right, none of my business. No worries."

"How was your night?" she asked him.

"S'alright," he allowed, shrugging.

There was a beat, and then he shyly attempted to enjoin her in conversation.

"And . . . yours? Bag any baddies?"

"One. Vampire. Uh, someone I used to know, actually, a little. Holden." She waited for a reaction. "Holden Webster."

She tensed, waiting for him to betray a hint of name recognition.

But Spike was only sympathetic. "You knew him, huh?" He walked closer to her. "That must have been a picnic."

"Yeah," she said awkwardly.

Then he went in his room and Buffy left for home. It was nearly sunrise. Spike would sleep now and nothing else, at least not in the daylight hours.

If there's even been an anything else . . .

"We need to keep an eye on Spike," she told Xander as she prepared to go.

Xander help up his hands. "Whoa, whoa, whoa,. By 'we,' you mean 'me' and me's gotta go to work. I got a big client meeting in a couple of hours."

"Xander, this is serious," Buffy insisted. "We cannot let him leave this house until we know if he's killing again. We need to find someone that can watch him."

Anya got volunteered, and she was not loving what she was hearing.

"Come on, Anya," Xander said impatiently as he opened all the blinds in the living room. "You said you'd do it on the phone."

"Yes, but that was before you told me Spike's killing again, and now you want me to be alone with him?"

Xander muttered something she couldn't quite catch. Then he told her that all she had to do is let Buffy know if Spike left the apartment. That was the complete mission, and thanks to all the sunshine pouring into the living room, she was going to be just fine.

"Better be, because if I get vamped, I'm gonna bite your ass," Anya threatened him.

As Xander walked out the door he murmured something else that she didn't catch.

Just as Willow quietly closed the door to Dawn's room, Buffy raced up the stairs yelling, "Dawn? Dawn!"

"Buffy, it's okay," Willow said softly. "She's okay. Not hurt. She's just exhausted. Finally fell off to sleep."

Buffy took that in. "What the hell happened? Downstairs looks like . . ."

". . . Hell happened?" Willow finished for her. "This big evil that's been promising to devour us? Well, I think it's started chomping."

"Oh my God." Buff looked in the direction of her sister's room. "And it started with Dawn."

"Both of us," Willow told her. "Buffy, this thing knows us. It made us think that we were talking to people we knew. Mine said it came with a message from Tara. But Dawn actually saw . . . your mother."

Buffy reacted strongly, and Willow continued.

"This thing . . . it had me for a while . . . I mean,

before it started letting loose with the pulse-pounding terror. But before that, the lies were very convincing."

"Lies," Buffy interjected. "Vampire I killed last night told me Spike sired him two nights ago."

"Well, that's impossible right?" Willow asked. "So maybe it wasn't a real one. A fake-out. You got one, too."

"It dusted real enough," Buffy said, a bit mournfully.

I gotta know what's going on with him, Anya thought anxiously as she glanced at the door to Spike's room. *It's getting late and I'm running out of sunlight.*

She had been sitting in Xander's living room all day, and she had run out of magazines long ago. Now she was repaging back through *Wired* and considering that pretty soon, she was going to have to turn on a light to read.

Call Buffy? she wondered. But not for nothing had she chosen to become a vengeance demon twice. Anya, if nothing else, was a woman of action.

So she crept into Spike's room with a stake in her hand, searching for evidence of his killing spree— teeth, scalps, ears, matchbooks.

Of course the door went *creeeak* . . .

This was the final resting place of Xander's junk— drafting table, old workout equipment . . . and the roommate Xander just could quite get rid of. *He had an easier time getting rid—and staying rid—of me*, she thought.

But this wasn't about Xander. This was about

Spike. He lay asleep—*I'm thinking naked*!—under a thin sheet . . . or pretending to be asleep, before he pounced for the kill . . .

She poked around in his dresser drawers, then decided to go for his real drawers. Anxious she slowly and carefully rooted around his pants, and then his shirt . . . and this his vampire-strong grip was around her wrist, and he was saying, "Anya, do be specific and tell a fellow just exactly what you're doing here."

Oh God, he's gonna kill me, she thought. Her mind raced into overdrive looking for a "Well . . . Spike, I . . . am here, obviously, for . . . um . . . sex."

He let go of her as he sat up. "Beg pardon?"

She knelt beside the bed, a loaded with anxiety. "You and me. Here and now. Let's go. Let's . . . get it on, you big bad boy." She groped him urgently.

He was flummoxed. "Wait, wait. Anya. Just a minute . . . is that a stake?"

"Yes. Kinky." She rambled on. "No questions. No talking. Why else would I be here? It's not like I'm snooping around looking for proof that you're some sort of whacked-out serial killer."

It sure didn't go uphill after that . . . and Spike actually did not respond her advances. Not that she was disappointed, but she was awfully hurt.

"It's not that I'm not tempted," he said kindly. "Obviously, if things were different, you're a right catch."

"I got it. No problem. You think I'm fat. Or the haircut . . ."

He couldn't win. She wouldn't let him and she went out and pouted in the living room, flipping back through *Wired* again—why the heck didn't Xander subscribe to *Vogue*?—and then Spike came out fully dressed.

He tried to apologize, Anya didn't buy it, and he left.

So, as instructed, she called the Slayer and so informed her.

Buffy kept far enough from Spike to stay off his radar, but close enough to keep up with him. He went to the Sunnydale Promenade, which reminded her a lot of the Santa Monica Promenade back in Los Angeles. People were bustling down the streets; it was noisy and busy. A street musician played the blues.

And Spike wandered over to a young woman waiting in line to get into a club. He smiled, whispered in her ear, and she walked off with him, hand in hand.

And then, shortly after that, Buffy lost track of him.

The busker with the mouth organ was playing Spike's song.

"Early one morning . . ."

"So what kind of name is Spike?" the girl asked silkily, as Spike led her into an alley. She went, willingly, murmuring, "What, are you going to make me guess?" She giggled. "I'll guess you're a little bit bad, huh?" She kissed him. "Am I right? Are you a bad boy?"

And she let him know she didn't mind bad; bad was good.

There was her neck, ah, and there the vein . . .

And there was Buffy, walking right up to him.

His eyes widened. Buffy's smile was eager, her eyes bright.

"You know you want it," she told him. Then her expression grew more lusty. "You know I want it."

Yeah, I do.

He vamped; the girl screamed; he bit her.

Human blood, oh, God, so much of it, so warm . . .

Buffy's smile grew. "There's my guy," she said lustily. "Now, doesn't that feel better?"

What have I done? What . . . who . . . ?

Spike dropped the corpse, shuddering, and raced off in a panic.

Then Buffy smiled . . . and morphed into a perfect likeness of Spike.

"'How could you use a poor maiden so?'" he drawled.

Buffy lost track of Spike at the Promenade; thwarted, furious, she stomped back to Xander's apartment, found him in bed, and yanked him onto the floor.

"Did you kill her?" she demanded.

Spike was slowly rousing. "What?"

"The girl. Last night," Buffy flung at him. "I caught The First act. I missed the curtain call. Did you kill her? Did you turn her? Is she one of your kind now?"

"Are you following me?" he asked, taken aback.

"Answer the question. Where is she?"

He stood. "Who knows? I certainly didn't off her. Where are you getting this? You know I can't."

"Right. The chip," she replied.

"No, not the chip!" he said, frustrated. He lowered his voice. "Not the chip, damn it. Do you honestly think I'd go to the end of the underworld to get my soul back and then . . ." He sighed, shaking his head. "Buffy, I can barely live with what I did. It haunts me. All of it. If you think that I would add to the body count now, you're crazy."

She would not be mollified. "So, what, you just troll the Promenade looking for drunk co-eds because you're hungry for conversation?"

Spike laughed. "You're jealous!" As he began to put on his shirt he added, "Yeah, you saw me chatting up another bird, giving the eye to somebody else. Touched a nerve, didn't it?"

Buffy huffed. "Don't flatter yourself."

"As daft a notion as 'Soulful Spike the Killer' is, it is nothing compared to the idea that another girl could mean anything to me. The chip, they gave to me. But the soul, I got on my own . . . for you."

"I know," she replied, soberly reminded. She took a beat. "Spike, this vampire told me you sired him."

"And you believe him?" Spike queried.

"I did follow you last night," she said, "and you know, you didn't look lonely or casual to me. You looked like you were on the prowl."

"We talked," he insisted, then added, "That's all I remember."

Buffy looked at him sharply. "All you *remember*?"

"I don't know," he said, sounding less emphatic. "I go out. I talk to people. Or I don't. It's boring. It all bleeds together."

Buffy said leadingly, "Well, if you seem to forget so much . . ."

"Not that," Spike insisted. "The taste of human blood? That I'd remember."

Buffy jumped back in. "You were camped on the Hellmouth talking to invisible people. Recently. How can you be so sure what you've been—"

He cut off her. "No. You are wrong. You've got an accusation from a pile of dust . . . and not a shred of proof."

"So I'll get some," Buffy told him.

Then she left the room.

At Buffy's house the group debriefed as Buffy set Willow and Dawn into research mode. Dawn stood near her sister, looking on.

Dawn said, "You only think Spike is turning people 'cause that vampire told you so, right? But that night we were all told things that weren't true . . ." She trailed off and glanced down. *At least, I hope they weren't true . . . because Mom . . . or whoever that was . . . told me that Buffy was going to let me down . . .*

Willow looked up from the laptop with a strange look on her face. "Well, just because those weren't the spirits of, you know, our people, just because it was some evil thing, it doesn't mean what they said can't be true."

Dawn looked anxiously at Buffy as Anya nodded in agreement. "I used to tell the truth all the time when I was evil."

"We can't assume anything. We need hard facts," Buffy piped up.

"Missing people," Willow announced, gesturing with her head toward the computer screen. "Maybe eight. Oh, ten of 'em. No bodies. They're just . . . missing. Mostly young, lots of girls."

Dawn's heart skipped a beat.

So the ghosts are telling us the truth.

"It still doesn't prove it's Spike," Buffy insisted.

Right bitch, Spike railed, as he put on his coat. *Comes in here, accuses me of bitin' girls . . .*

He stuffed his hand into his duster as he walked toward the door. There was something in his pocket, pack of cigs . . .

Cigs, sumpin' about cigs . . .

Early one morning . . .

Flash. Bird with the fur collar, placing the cigs in front of him.

Flash. Chatting her up, leaning in close.

Flash. Her limp, on the ground . . .

Shaken, he put the cigs back in his pocket and hurried out of his room.

Xander was eating a frozen dinner in front of the TV. Spike headed for the door.

"No, no," Xander admonished him. "You're not going out."

Spike was irritated. "I know what the Slayer told

you," Spike said, as Xander blocked his way. "It's not true. Let me go and I'll find a way to prove it."

"Okay, I'm gonna list the reasons that won't happen," Xander said. "One . . ."

Spike punched Xander and the chip gave him what-for. As Xander went down the count, Spike grabbed his coat and walked out the door.

Then he headed to the Bronze, looking for something that would prove his innocence.

Strange word, applied to me, he thought.

Aimee Mann was singing, which was a bit of an all right. "Pavlov's Bells," one of his favorites. Her dusky voice provided a nice counterpoint as he wove among the patrons and waitresses, asking about the blonde. No luck on the ground floor, so he hit the balcony.

He was up there on the catwalk, drinking from his flask, when a fetching young woman sauntered up to him, scanning along with him, and finally saying, "One of them take your wallet?"

"What's that?" he asked, distracted.

"The way you're scanning that crowd. You look like you're out for blood."

He winced inwardly at her choice of words and muttered, "I'm just looking for a certain bird I met here the other night."

"Hmmm." She smiled languidly and touched his shoulders. "Was it me?"

"Sorry, love. Don't think so."

She kept smiling. "Not even if I ask nice? Or are you the type that has to be convinced?" She took the liberty of sitting next to him, even though he hadn't invited her.

"Friendly warning, pet. I'm the type best left alone."

"Huh, I get it. You'd rather I slip into something . . . more comfortable."

She vamped.

Spike went on alert.

"Should we pick the crowd off one-by-one, or block the exits and ravish the place?" she asked, her voice eager and evil as she curled around him.

"Get away from me!" he spat at her.

"What's with the wallflower act?" she demanded. "You didn't seem so shy when you were *biting* me." At his look of horror, she added, "I'm not asking if ya wanna be soul mates, just figured you'd wanna have some fun." She looked down at the crowd. "I take him, you take her. Or the other way around. Whatever."

Spike grabbed her. "No, you're lying!" he shouted. She punched him and he threw her to the ground.

"Is that all I was to you, a one-bite stand?" she asked, living.

They went at it, fighting on the catwalk. She grabbed a vase and tried to stake him with it, but he wrestled it away from her and staked her with it instead.

Then she tumbled off the catwalk, landing hard and dusting in the middle of the crowd. Everyone froze for a moment . . . and then the music started up again.

Spike hurried to the back of the bar to the pay phones. He dialed Buffy's cell phone number. Sweat rolled off him. His hand was trembling.

Then she answered, and he was unbelievably grateful.

"It's me," he told her. "I'm seeing . . . I think I'm remembering. I think I've done some very bad things."

Buffy's voice came through clearly. "Where are you?"

"I need . . . I need to see you. There's a house. Six-thirty-four Hoffman Terrace."

"I'll meet you."

They both disconnected. Relieved Spike turned around . . . only to be confronted by his own image.

His mind went numb. *Don't understand . . .*

"You shouldn't have done that," his double said. "It's not time yet. Not nearly. You're going against the plan." It smiled. "But we can make it work."

The rendezvous house was a large brick building that reminded Buffy of the old Tudor-style homes of Pasadena. Spike let her in; they headed for the brick basement, Spike in the lead, as he went down the stairs, Buffy hesitated at the top.

"I understand," he said, indicating her unwillingness. "It's a risky proposition."

Then Spike's double blocked his way and said, "There's an order. The Slayer's not in order. But it can't hurt to play. Get your claws in the mouse, you know?"

Spike said carefully, "You are not here."

Just then Buffy came down the stairs, pulling his attention back to their reality, and he said in a rush, "I've been remembering. The girl. I walked her home. The one you saw. And the one before that. And I think I killed her. And I think . . . I think I killed the lady who lived here. And there might be others."

Buffy stared at him and said, "Oh my God."

He walked to the center of the room, and Buffy followed. "Here. I—I think I buried them here."

"Spike, why?" she asked, her voice filled with emotion.

He felt as if his insides were on fire. He was terrified. "Well, I don't know, do I? I don't even know how. Shouldn't be able—"

He was distracted by the appearance of his double gliding past the stairs. He was humming.

And he was then singing, as he lounged on an old ice box with a smirk on his face.

"'Early one morning, just as the sun was rising, I heard the fair maid sing in the valley down below. Oh, don't deceive me. Oh, never leave me.'" He rolled his eyes with mock innocence. "'How could you use a poor maid so?'"

Spike was mesmerized. *It is my song*, he thought vaguely. *My order . . . in the order . . . claws . . .*

Then he vamped out, and it was glorious! Wonderful! He was all fire and fury, and there was the Slayer, meant for killing.

He attacked her. She had a stake, but he yanked it out of her hand and threw it away. A glass bottle shattered. His blood sang.

The Slayer threw him across the room.

"What are you doing?" she demanded.

He grabbed a shard of glass and went for her, slicing her shoulder. They fought, and she pushed him to the ground.

"Spike, listen to me. You don't want to do this!"

He shoved her away . . . and then his double said, "And it's just about to get fun."

A fist shot through the earthen floor. The ground shifted and cracked as others burst through, fanged faces cauled with dirt through like demonic children struggling into the world. Vampires, all of them . . . murder victims.

They gathered in a ring. They were the stupid, raving kind of vamp, the worst kind, decaying extras from Michael Jackson's *Thriller*. They took turns hissing at Buffy and attacking her. Then one of them found a spade and started after her with it. Buffy grabbed and punched him in the face with it. "You know what I want you to do," Spike's double said to him.

But one vamp grabbed her arm and another grabbed the spade, using it as a pinioning weapon, and even though she fought that off, the second vampire grabbed her arm. She was being held between two vampires, and they held her fast.

"They're waiting for you," Spike's double told him. "Take her, taste her. Make her weak."

He stood and walked toward her. She struggled.

"Spike, no!" she cried.

Spike put his face near hers, savoring her, wanting her blood. In a dream he leaned toward her cut shoulder, smelling the fear, the steam from her wound.

He tasted.

Slayer's blood.

Buffy's blood.

Flash: Killing the bird.

Flash: Killing others. Carry a corpse through town. Burying two men. Killing the lady whose house this was . . .

"I remember," he said, as he recoiled from her sight and staggered back through the brick arch of the basement.

Buffy's vampire captors were distracted. She took advantage of the situation and grabbed up the spade, using it rather like a *kendo* sword, taking a strong stance, jabbing, thrusting, lunging, dusting vampires with order and precision. Then she swiped three of the vamps' feet out from underneath them.

Spike's double crouched near him, talking to him in a sibilant, low voice.

"You failed them. Now she's going to kill you. You lose, mate."

A single hand tentatively pushed through the earth; Buffy grabbed it and hoisted the elderly female vampire up. As she staked her, she said, "Sorry, ma'am, but it's my job."

Spike was jammed behind the brick archway, utterly defeated. Buffy carried the spade with her and stood in front of him. He gazed up at her with misery and resignation, as he scooted out of his hidey-hole, and very purposefully opened his shirt. He was not without dignity; he was crying.

"Do it fast, okay?" And when she didn't move, he added, almost angrily, "He said you'd do it."

Buffy asked, "Who said?"

He didn't have the words. "Me. It was . . . me. I

saw it. I was here the whole time, talking and singing." He let out a heavy sob. "There was a song."

"I don't know," Spike confessed. "Please, I don't remember. Don't make me remember." Then he turned his head and said to the air, "Make it so I forget again! I did what you wanted!"

Buffy stiffened, looked around. "There's something here." Resolutely she threw away the spade.

"Oh, God, no, please," he begged, realizing that she was sparing him. "I need that. I can't cry the soul out of me. It won't come. I killed, and I can feel 'em. I can feel every one of 'em."

She knelt beside him, trying to get his attention. "There's something playing with us. All of us."

"What is it?" he asked her wretchedly. "Why is it doing this to me?"

"I don't know." She felt sorry for him, but she did not lose her edge.

Spike looked at her with wet eyes.

"Will you . . . help me?" he asked her. "Can you help me?"

His double watched from the stairs, sneering as Buffy said, "I'll help you."

Spike was wrapped in a blanket like a shock victim while the others talked. Buffy had just finished telling them about what had happened.

"And you believe him?" Anya asked incredulously.

"You didn't see him down there." Buffy glanced in Spike's direction. "He really didn't know what he'd done. It wasn't in his control."

"Oh, an out-of-control serial killer," Xander said, dripping with sarcasm. "You're right, that is a great houseguest."

"Wait . . . is he staying here?" Dawn asked worriedly.

"I don't know," Buffy admitted. "But I'm not letting him out of my sight. That's for sure."

Willow was not so sure. "Buff, he's been feeding. On human blood. That's gotta do stuff."

Buffy said, "I'm not keeping him around just to help him. I think there was something there, talking to him. Making him do things."

Willow considered. "Something like what was talking to us?"

Buffy nodded. "Maybe. But if it was, it's been screwing with Spike big time."

Xander still needed leading. "So, you want him around because . . . ?"

Buffy's gaze took in all of them. "Look. There's something evil working us, and if we are ever going to have a chance to fight it, we need to learn everything we can about it. This thing has been closer to Spike than any of us."

"And if you want to understand it," Willow said.

Buffy glanced Spike's way. "I'm going to have to get close to Spike."

"Nah, it's too dangerous," Xander argued. Not for nothing had he been called "gallant" by D'Hoffryn, who, as a rule, held the male species in contempt.

"I don't have a choice," Buffy said. "Whatever this

thing is, from beneath us, it's bad, and it's only getting worse."

London

Robson had not shown for the scheduled meeting of the Council of Watchers, nor had he answered his phone. So Giles was sent to see if anything was amiss . . .

And it was: There was Nora, Robson's Potential, lying on the floor. Her blood was pooled beneath her. Giles knelt beside her and checked for signs of life. There were none.

"Oh, dear God! Robson, are you here?"

Giles got up and searched for his colleague and friend. He hadn't far to look: Robson was half-propped up near a chair in the next room.

"You too?" Giles took off his glasses, tears filling his eyes.

Robson's eyes flashed open. "Gather them," he said with great difficulty. "It's started."

A wave of ice washed over Giles, and then he composed himself.

"It's all right. I understand. I'll take care of it," he assured the dying man.

Then a robed figure snuck up behind Giles, a weighty battle axe in its grip.

It swung at Giles. . . .

Chapter Nine: "Never Leave Me"

Aftermath.

The gang was trying to put Buffy and Dawn's home back together after the fury of the haunting Dawn had managed to exorcise. In the living room of the Summers' home, Xander was measuring the picture window, having just covered the empty square with plastic. Anya was dusting candles and knick-knacks, while Willow swept wreckage off a table. Dawn stood beside her, debriefing about Spike.

"So the basement was filled with dead bodies?" she asked, referring to Spike and Buffy's visit to the Hoffman Terrace.

"Apparently," Willow said.

"And Spike couldn't have sired countless others and buried them around town? And we're waiting for him to do what, exactly? Do something crazy?"

Willow sighed and said, "It's not that simple."

From her place beside the mantel, Anya looked up from her dusting . . . of candles, not Spike, and asked, "Shouldn't we stake him through the chest? Isn't that what we do when these things happen?"

"Look," Willow said loyally. "Buffy knows what she's doing."

Not getting comfort from that, Anya looked over at Xander. "Well, Xander, you know what we're all talking about. I mean, you've always been part of the 'Spike is evil' faction."

Xander let that slide by saying, "I've got a house to put back together."

"Fine. You guys keep your heads buried in the sand, but I think we should prepare ourselves for the possibility that William the Bloody is back."

Kicker boots.

Long, dark coat.

Hair.

And the most evil-looking human on the planet award goes to . . . Andrew, master of all darkness, the man who had killed his best friend.

Master of all darkness, that is, except for Warren, who was über-master of all darkness. Now he appeared beside Warren and gave him a bit of applause. "Looking good," he said appreciatively. "We've got work to do."

"I have to do work right now?" Andrew whined. "Can't I just walk around awhile in my coat?"

"Don't go soft on me now," Warren chided him. "We're right in the trench. The exhaust port's in sight."

"I thought that was it," Andrew argued. "I did what you told me. It's not my fault it didn't work. Why do *I* have to do all the wet work?"

Warren halted. "Hey. You know the rules. I can't take corporeal form."

He gestured for Andrew to try to touch him, easing his shirt lapels aside. Andrew's hand went straight through his chest.

"Pretty bitchin', right?" Warren crowed. "I'm like Obi Wan."

"Or Patrick Swayze," Andrew said dreamily. Then, "I just don't think I can kill anybody else."

Warren turned into Jonathan, and Andrew said, "I didn't want to kill you. Warren made me."

Jonathan replied earnestly, "Hey, I'm glad he did." He chuckled. "This is the best thing that ever happened to me. It wasn't that bad. It's kinda like when I used to get ulcers in high school, only at the end I became one with light and hope."

"It's my fault the ritual didn't work," Jonathan added generously. "I'm little, and I probably should have told someone I was anemic. Don't worry. We're going to fix it. You've got to trust us. We know what we're doing."

Robin Wood regarded the two incessant troublemakers—Grimes and Hoffman—in his office.

"Now, we can settle this one of two ways," he told them. "You can help repaint the walls, or I can suspend you and report the incident on your private record."

"Fine," Hoffman deadpanned. "Do that."

Robin uncrossed his arms. "Okay, I was bluffing. I hadn't really thought that through." He looked at them. "The whole 'permanent record' thing is a myth anyway. Colleges never ask for anything past your SAT scores and it's not like employers are ever gonna check how many days you missed of high school."

He stood up and walked around to the front of his desk.

"I could suspend you, but that would mean calling your parents, alerting your teachers, filling out paperwork, and possibly talking to the school board. All of which sounds positively exhausting to me."

He paused. "No, I think it would be much easier if I just called the police and let them deal with it. "

The boys looked at each other, unsure what to make of him as he stared them down. "In case you're wondering, now's the part where I'm not bluffing."

The boys did a buddy-check with each other, then nodded. "

"We'll repaint it," Grimes said.

"Good," Robin told him.

There was a knock on the door, and he was mildly perturbed by the disruption.

"Excuse me," he said.

He walked to the door and opened it. Dawn Summers stood on the other side.

"Miss Summers," he said.

"Hi. Sorry to interrupt."

"I'm with students," he informed her.

"I just wanted to tell you that Buffy won't be coming in today," Dawn said. "She's really sick."

Robin was concerned. "Oh, no . . ."

"Yeah," Dawn continued. "Last night she was vomiting and then this morning she was vomiting some more and then just when we thought she was done, she started vomiting again."

He nodded. "We've got stomach flu going around."

"Her exact words were, 'I've got stuff coming out both ends.'"

Pause.

"Thank you," Robin said. "That's very helpful."

"Sure, no problem," Dawn said to him. She looked around him to the boys. "Hey, how's it going?"

"Pretty good," Grimes said.

"Tell your sister not to worry," Robin said to Dawn. "We'll solider on without her. She should just concentrate on getting better."

"Yeah, she'll be fine," Dawn said. "She just needs to get some stuff out of her system."

The Slayer had called Watcher Headquarters, and Quentin Travers, as Council head, was the man to speak with her. As the rest of the Council looked on, he listened to her speaking from across the puddle, in Sunnydale.

She told him that she was looking for Giles.

"He's not answering any of his numbers," she explained.

Quentin remained polite, if aloof, as he said, "Miss

Summers, ever since Mr. Giles pulled up his stake in Sunnydale, we've not made it our business to follow his every move. I suppose if you feel the matter's urgent, we can look into it."

He could tell that she was aware that he was simply trying to mollify her. After he hung up, he looked down the expanse of the polished wooden table at the other Watchers and informed them, "The girl knows nothing."

He rose. "And we need to find Rupert Giles as soon as possible."

Power.

Addictions scream with unbelievable power for satisfaction. Base, primal hungers wreak havoc on the system when denied, make sane men mad, and make madmen madder still.

In her bedroom, Buffy had tied Spike to a chair, and she was watching him shiver and shake as he withdrew from drinking human blood. Buffy sat on her fern-green-and-cranberry bedspread, her heart breaking for him. It was agonizing to watch.

Once her back was to him, he vamped yet again, raging at her, chomping and clacking like a mindless feeding machine, fighting his restraints.

Upset, she went into the hall. Willow was there, and they conferred.

"I think we need to get him some blood."

"Do you want me to kill Anya?" Willow asked helpfully.

It was decided that Willow should go the

butcher's—Buffy had done the same when Angel had come back from hell—and get some animal blood. The Wicca was almost as eager to run the errand as she had been to kill Anya.

"Xander's installing the new windows," she explained, "and he keeps giving lectures on proper tool maintenance."

I've got the power, Andrew thought, hunting knife in hand. He stared down at his victim in the basement of Sunnydale High. *But I just can't use it.*

"*Babe 2: Pig in the City* was really underrated," he said weakly.

His victim was an adorable little piglet, heir to the mantel of school mascot, which, okay, she knew the job was dangerous when she, um, got picked from the litter for it. One of her predecessors had been a pig named Herbert, who, legend claimed, had been eaten up by Xander Harris.

"You're Conan. You're the Destroyer," Warren silkily reminded him. "Everyone knows you. You play by your own rules. It's kill or be killed."

"That'll do, pig!" Andrew cried desperately.

He lunged at the little pink piggy; it squealed and ran. Andrew charged after it, missed again; charged, missed. He was sliding all over the basement floor.

Finally the pig clicked on its little trotters down the hall.

"Isn't there some other way we can get blood?" he asked Warren.

* * *

And there was. Soon Andrew was number 87 at the butcher shop, and he had a list for the grouchy butcher man waiting to take his order. Andrew had on his coat, his boots, and his cool hair, and he felt very out of place among the mundanes in the shop.

The butcher prepared to write his order, and Andrew moved to Step 2 of Plan B.

He said anxiously, "I'd like twelve pork chops, two pounds of sausage, eightquartsofpigsblood, three steaks, a halibut . . . some toothpaste . . ."

The butcher looked at Andrew as if he were an idiot. "This is a butcher shop, Neo," he said, referring, no doubt, to Andrew's outfit. *Erg. How embarrassing. I thought it looked cool.* "We don't sell toothpaste."

"Oh, okay," Andrew said, loaded to the gills with anxiety—*no toothpaste,* but *does he have the halibut?*—and while the butcher went into action to fulfill the order, Andrew kind of snuck to the back of the store to admire the steak sauce away from the eyes of common men.

The bag was enormous; he picked it up and lumbered out of the store, colliding with someone as he crossed the threshold.

Chops and sausages and several clear packages of blood went flying all over the place.

But that wasn't the bad part.

The bad part was Willow Rosenberg had been on her way into the store. Willow, who had flayed Warren alive!

She was staring at him, wide-eyed and obviously very, very clear on who he was.

He ran down the street and into an alley.

So did she.

He begged her, "Don't kill me! Don't torture me and send me to an eternal pain dimension! Warren killed Tara. I didn't do it. And he was aiming for Buffy anyway."

Willow glared at him. "Not making it better."

"And you got your revenge. You killed my best friend. We're even."

She looked shocked. "*Even*? You think I get satisfaction from what I did?"

"I'm protected by powerful forces," he went on, trying a different tack. "Forces you can't even begin to imagine, little girl. If you harm me, you shall know the wrath of he that is darkness and terror. Stand down, she-witch. Your defeat is at hand."

Realizing that she could use his weirdness against him, she decided to run with the scary Willow iteration. Getting herself in character, she pushed him soundly against a brick wall. "Shut your mouth. I am a she-witch, a very powerful she-witch, or witch, as is more accurate. I'm not to be trifled with. I am Willow." *And I sound like the Wizard of Oz. But he's buying it.* "I am death. If you dare defy me, I will call down my fury, exact fresh vengeance, and make your worst dreams come true." She raised her brows. "Okay?"

He believed her, and she forced him to go to Buffy's house with her.

She marched him into the house, where his old enemies—Xander, Anya, plus the cute sister, Dawn, all regarded him with . . . scorn.

Anya stepped on his coat!

Then they tied him up police-interrogation style and threatened to hurt him if he didn't tell them why he was back in town.

"I haven't done anything wrong," he pleaded.

"Then you won't mind if we ask you a few questions," Xander said.

"Yeah, okay," Andrew murmured.

"What were you doing buying blood at the butcher shop?" Xander demanded, as Anya listened, too.

He gave them his pre-thought-up story: "I-fell-in-love-with-a-beautiful-vampire-girl-down-in-Mehico-and-now-we're-trying-to-make-a-go-of-it-on-the-straight-and-narrow-and-put-our-lives-back-together-here-in-Sunnydale."

Xander privately suspected he was getting his material from Tarantino's *From Dusk to Dawn*.

"You think this is a *game*, junior?!" Anya yelled at him, grabbing him, shaking him. "People are dying! Our friends are in danger!"

Andrew whimpered in fear; Xander looked genuinely surprised at Anya's behavior.

"And you want to waste our time with *deceptions*? Not on my watch!"

And she backhanded him a wicked one across the face. He screamed in pain.

Xander stopped her, asked to speak to her privately. They went into the bathroom, giddy over their performance.

"Did you see that?" Anya asked. "I actually made him cry!"

"You were perfect," Xander told her. "I was worried I overdid it with the whole easy way/hard way thing."

"No, that was great," Anya congratulated him.

She shook her hand like it was stinging. "I wasn't sure if I should slap him, but then he made me want to slap him so I thought, 'Slap him.'"

"He'll be singing in no time," Xander said happily.

"What do we do now?" she asked.

"Now we let him stew in his own juices for a bit, then we give him the hard brace," Xander told her.

Anya nodded. "Right."

Buffy came out of her room. Anya didn't miss a beat, nodded to her, all tough and *NYPD Blue*.

"What's the status with your guy?" she asked Buffy.

"He hasn't talking yet," Buffy admitted

Anya reported happily, "The weasel wants to sing. He just needs a tune."

"He's primed," Xander agreed. "I'll be pumping him in no time." Amending that, he tried again. "He'll give us information soon."

Buffy nodded and returned to Spike.

"It's all flashes here and there," the white-haired vampire admitted. "It's like I'm watching someone else . . . do it, kill people. I've been losing time for a while now, waking up in strange places. Things have been wonky since . . ."

He hesitated, and she filled in. "Since you got your soul." He lowered his head in assent. "How did you do it?"

He sighed at the memory. "I went to seek a legend out. Traveled to the other side of the world, made a deal with a demon."

"Just like that?" Buffy asked sharply.

"There was a price," he said, face stony. "There were trials, torture, pain, and suffering . . . of sorts." He looked at her. "I have come to redefine the words 'pain' and 'suffering' since I fell in love with you."

Xander got into character and went back into the room, where a very frightened Andrew flinched at the sight of him. He offered Andrew some water. After he drank, he muttered, "That chick's psycho."

Xander let out his breath and looked sad. "You don't know the half of it. She's a vengeance demon, you know." He sat down. "She's bad news."

"This one time I saw her having sex with Spike," he told Xander.

Xander winced but said nothing. Then he continued. "She's killed a lot of men. She tortures them. Anyone who incurs her wrath. There was this one guy . . . she took stopped his heart, then she replaced it with darkness . . ." Seeing that his own personal pain was not impressing Andrew, he added, "then she tore out his intestines and rubbed his face in it."

That worked.

Then the door flew opened and Anya charged into the room, all hellfire and fury, and shouted, "You're gonna tell us what we need to know, and you're gonna tell us right now!"

She went for Andrew's throat, knocking his chair

backward in her wrath. As Xander pretended to try to stop her, she slapped him, gave him a visual apology cue, and got back to her interrogation.

"Get her off me!" Andrew shouted. "I'll tell you what you need to know."

Hearing the ruckus, Buffy left the room to see what was going on . . .

. . . leaving Spike with his double, who leaned against the wall, smirking at him.

He walked toward Spike, who was still tied in the chair, and said, "Well, we've got ourselves a problem."

Anya and Xander looked to be beating the truth out of Andrew, which was fine with Buffy; She started to go back into her own when she overheard Spike from behind the closed door. It sounded as if he was talking to someone.

And . . . singing?

She opened the door and entered the room, warily looking around.

She eyed Spike, who seemed to have calmed down quite a bit.

"Who were you talking to?" she asked him.

"Nobody. I was just keeping myself company," he said steadily.

He was so different from the unhappy mess she'd left less than a minute before . . . composed, at ease.

"Are you okay?" she asked him.

"Fine," he rejoined, as if the answer should be obvious. "Feeling a bit peckish, I suppose." He looked over at the bags of pig blood on the night table by the bed. "Do you mind?"

Buffy kept her eye on him, her spider-sense tingling. The abrupt change in his mood was startling. Something was up with him.

She turned her head for just a second when she went to get the pig's blood . . . and that was when he vamped out again.

He roared with vampiric fury, breaking the chair arms in his struggle to free himself. He stood; Buffy dashed at him, ready to fight, but he pushed her down and turned on his heel, racing in the other direction.

Where, in Dawn's room, Andrew was against the wall, spilling his guts.

"We needed more blood to activate the seal of Danthaza—"

A hand broke through the wall behind Andrew, just like in *Night of the Living Dead*. Another hand grabbed his chest. Screaming, Andrew was yanked through the wall, breaking the plaster, and into the next room.

He was in Spike's clutches; the raging vampire pushed his head to one side, and chomped into him.

Buffy threw Spike off Andrew and threw him against the wall. Spike gazed up at her, mouth dripped, his face a contortion of confusion and misery . . .

. . . as he gazed at his double, standing behind the Slayer, looking very disappointed in him.

Buffy kicked Spike in the face, knocking him unconscious.

* * *

While he was out, Buffy and Xander dragged him into the basement and chained him to the wall. Then Buffy met with the others in the living room, trying to understand why he had changed so much.

"Spike and I were having a conversation, and he was fine. I mean, you know, fine as Spike can be. And then I went to check on you guys, and when I got back it was like he was a completely different person."

"Different like 'William the Bloody' type different?"

"He was talking to someone," Buffy remembered. "And then he started singing. He mentioned something about a song in the cellar. And he changed there, too. I mean, instantly became another person."

Xander got it.

"Trigger," he announced. "It's a brainwashing term. It's how the military makes sleeper agents. They brainwash operatives and condition them with a specific trigger, like a song, that makes 'em drastically change at a moment's notice."

"Is this left over from your days in the army?" Willow asked him.

Xander favored her with one of his patented self-deprecating looks. "No, this is left over from every Army movie I've ever seen. But it makes sense. We've had ghosts or something haunting us, right? Well, what if Spike's ghosts have figured out a way to control him?"

"Spike said he's been seeing things since I found him in the basement," Buffy put in.

"So he gets his soul back, he starts seeing spooky things, and he goes extra-extra crazy."

It was making sense to the Slayer. "This trigger. How do we make it stop?"

Xander was not as much help there. "Well, usually the operative completes his task and either blows his head off or steals a submarine."

"All right," Buffy said to the group. "If Spike's a bomb, then I need to know how to diffuse him." To Dawn and Willow, she added, "I want to know what did this to him. Spirits, ghosts, demons—check the lot of them. Look for anything that could haunt or possibly control like this. I need to know exactly what we're dealing with."

Principal Wood was finished with his day job. He had threatened two boys with a visit from the police if they didn't repair their vandalism; he had attended innumerable meetings; he had filed out piles of paperwork.

It was time to go . . . to the basement.

There was a dead boy sprawled over an elaborate disc.

Robin Wood stared at him impassively.

Then he got a shovel, loaded the body in his car, and drove it to a quarry.

Within a few minutes, he had put the boy's body into a hole and began to shovel gravel over it.

It was a shallow grave for a useless victim, dug by a man who seemed not at all surprised to be doing so.

Powerless. In pain.

Spike lay inert on the basement floor, his hands and feet chained to the wall. The shadows shifted as

Buffy walked across the floor with a bowl of water and a towel in her hands, giving Spike the illusion of movement.

She knelt and tenderly dabbed the blood off his face, and he opened his eyes. Weakly, fearfully, he asked, "Did I hurt anybody?"

"You took a good bite out of Andrew," she told him. "Tucker's brother. He'll be okay."

"I don't remember," Spike said. He sounded weary and defeated.

"It's okay." She knew she sounded the same, as she rose and walked to the sink.

"Buffy, I don't know why."

"We think we do. Something's playing you. Some ghost or demon has figured out how to control you. Got the gang researching it now. Xander has this theory that you're being triggered."

Spike pulled himself to a sitting position and said, "Kill me."

She faced him. "You don't understand. When I left the room earlier, I heard you talking to someone."

He ignored her. "Do you have any idea what I'm capable of?"

"I was in the cellar with you," she reminded him. "I saw what you did."

"I'm not talking about the cellar," Spike insisted. "The people in the cellar got off easy. I'm talking about me. Buffy, you have never met the real me."

She crossed her arms and raised her chin. "Believe me, I'm well aware of what you're capable of."

"No. You got off easy, too." He rose, and his face

hardened with purpose, with self-loathing. "Do you know how much blood you can drink from a girl before she'll die? I do." He swallowed, determined to go on. "You see, the trick is to drink enough so that they'll still cry when you . . ." He began to lose his composure, but he held on. "'Cause it's not worth it if they don't cry."

Buffy refused to rise to his bait, refused to react. But inside, she was thinking of another vampire who had hoped to make her hate him by revealing his atrocities—Angel, who had boasted about eating his entire family "with a song in my heart." Angel, whose life had centered around penance, and need . . . and the realization that he could never, ever pay enough for the awful things he'd done.

"It's not your fault. You're not the one doing this," she said, but her voice was strained.

"I already did it," he reminded her. "It's already done." He paced, an animal in misery, then stepped toward her. "You want to know what I've done to girls Dawn's age?" He saw her glance tick away, saw that he'd gotten to her.

"This is me, Buffy. You've got to kill me before I get out."

She knit her forehead at that, frightened. "We can keep you locked up. We'll figure out—"

"Have you ever really asked yourself why you can't do it?" he asked.

She raised her chin. "You fought by my side. You've saved lives. You've helped—"

He rolled his eyes and cut her off. "Don't rationalize this into some noble act "

He paced back and forth, light to shadow, and then the darkness swallowed him as he said, "You like people like me who hurt you."

"No." Her eyes were wide to prove the truth of her assertion.

"You need the pain we cause you. You need the hate. You need it to do your job. To be the Slayer."

"No," she said firmly, her voice rising. "You think you have insight now because your soul's drenched in blood? You don't know me. You don't even know you. Was that you who killed those people in the cellar? Was that you who waited for those girls?"

"There's no one else . . ." Spike began.

"That's not true," she said firmly. She took a moment, and then she said, "Listen to me. You're not alive because of pain. Or hate. You're alive because I saw you change. I saw your penance."

He lunged violently at her, but the chains held him back. "Window dressing," he scoffed.

"It would be easier, wouldn't it? If it were an act? But it's not." She came up to him, her face filled with emotion.

"You faced the monster inside of you and you fought back. You risked everything to be a better man."

"Buffy," he moaned.

She got close, in her heart, in her spirit, as she said, "And you can be. You are. You may not see it, but I do. I believe in you, Spike."

His face radiated hope and amazement.

Then at that moment, the lights flickered and went out. The glass in the basement door exploded inward, and a black-hooded figure burst into the room.

He was carrying a staff and he smacked her across the face with it, sending her flying across the room.

"Buffy!" Spike shouted, and over his voice, she heard the sounds of more attacks coming from upstairs.

They came through windows.

They broke down the doors.

Hooded figures burst upon Willow and Dawn in the living room. From the kitchen more swarmed in; one of them hit Anya in the back of the head with his staff. She dropped to the floor.

Xander moved to take him on when he was hit from behind by two more of them. Their hoods fell back, their faces were revealed. Symbols carved in black covered their eyeless faces.

Chaos continued to unfold: one of them rushed Willow, whacking her across the neck with his staff. She flew back, hit the wall, and dropped to the ground.

Another one charged Dawn, who dropped to the ground and flipped him with his own momentum, sending him crashing into the wall.

Then Buffy flew through the door to the basement, shattering it to pieces. She joined the fray, aware that some of the attackers had broken off and were headed upstairs.

She shook off the others and followed after them into her room, where one of the robed figures burst into the room, dropped his staff, and took out two crescent-shaped daggers. He made for the bed, where Andrew lay bound. Andrew's eyes widened as he rolled off the bed and the figure stabbed the mattress with his vicious blades.

Buffy grabbed the attacker; another one dashed into the room. And another. As Andrew managed to stand, she grabbed him and used him as a battering ram à la Jackie Chan, holding him by the shoulders and driving him into the chest of one of the figures. He fell back, and she repeated the maneuver with the other one.

Then she heaved Andrew out of her way, grabbed Two-Knives' weapons, and stabbed him as he rushed her, directly in the stomach.

The other figure rushed her, and she stabbed him in the stomach with the other knife, so that her arms were crossed mummy-style over her chest. Then she drew out both razor-sharp knives, uncrossed her arms, and slashed each of them again with the opposite knife.

They fell to the floor, dead.

"Buffy!" Xander shouted, running into the room. He was carrying one of staffs, all action man and yecch face as he saw the bodies.

"Dawn?" Buffy demanded.

"She's okay." He looked around. "I thought there were more of them . . ."

She got it at once: there had been more of them. And they had gone elsewhere.

"Spike," she said.

They raced out of the room and into the basement.

Spike's shackles were empty . . . and he was gone.

* * *

Aftermath.

In the living room, the wounded tended to each other and to themselves. Willow brought The first aid kit and was just sitting down when Buffy and Xander came into the room together. There were dead guys lying around, too.

"They were so fast," Xander observed. "And organized."

"They were after Spike all along," Buffy replied.

"And we were just in the way," Xander added.

Then Buffy knelt to inspect one of the robed people lying face-up on the floor.

"I know these guys," she said, as it all came together. "I fought them before. This isn't some demon." She had figured it out. "It's all the same thing. Spike's ghosts, the people you guys saw, from beneath us, it's all the same thing.

"I know what we're up against." She paused, frightened. "The First."

London, Watchers Council Headquarters

The members of the Council were in an uproar as they tried to contain the damage that had been inflicted upon them.

The building had been ransacked—maps torn off walls, files cabinets emptied and overturned. The atmosphere was frantic, though some of the Watchers cleaned up and spoke on phones with characteristically grim Englishness.

Through this all, walked Quentin Travers, surveying the damage, a grave look on his face.

Phillip briefed him.

"They took our files, wiped out our records. We've lost contact with operations in Munich, Switzerland, and Rome. We've got casualty confirmations coming in from as far away as Melbourne."

Lydia, the young blonde, blurted, "Sir, we are crippled."

Quentin gazed at her, and soothed, "It's all right." Then he quoted Winston Churchill, who had been Prime Minister of Britain during World War II, when London was being blitzed on a regular basis by Adolph Hitler's Nazis: "'We are still the masters of our fate, we are still the captains of our souls.'"

The words worked their magic on the young woman. Then Quentin said to the group at large, "Our fears have been confirmed. The First Evil has declared all-out war against this institution. Their first volleys have proved to be most effective." He paused for dramatic effect. "I for one, think it's time we struck back."

All gazes were riveted on him. He could practically hear the others saying, "Hear, hear."

"Get me confirmations on all remaining operatives. Begin preparations for mobilization. Once we're accounted for, I want to be ready to move. We'll be paying a visit to the Hellmouth."

He continued, "My friends, these are the times that define us. Proverbs 24:6: 'For by wise counsel, you shall make your war.'"

And in the next moment, the Council Building

exploded into a huge conflagration of bombs and flames. . . .

Spike's double grinned evilly at Spike as the shirtless vampire was strapped to a sort of Catherine wheel above a large disc carved with a pentagram and other arcane symbols. It was scene directly out of *The Black Cat*, starring Bela Lugosi and Boris Karloff, only it was real life.

"You'll have to excuse the spectacle, but I've always been a bit of a sucker for the ol' classics," Spike's double said, as if it could read his mind.

Metal scalpels flashed in the light as the robed figures lay them out, passing them to one another. There were other sharp objects, torture instruments—Spike was familiar with them all. He'd used them all himself, at some point in his long, horrible life. He'd had Marcus, the skilled vampiric torturer, use them on Angel to make him tell them where the Ring of Amarra had got to.

They began to use them. Spike was shocked at how much The First slice hurt, then stunned even more by the second. Unbelievable pain, unimaginable . . .

He screamed and screamed.

"Hey, don't look at me," his reflection ordered him. "I wanted to do this more subtlelike. My Harbingers have a tendency to call attention to themselves."

More pain.

Spike screamed again.

His double leaned forward and said, "*You're* the one who couldn't hold his end of the bargain. *You're* the one who couldn't take care of what's-his-name.

You're the one who had to make breakthroughs and learn something about himself."

Still more pain . . . oh, God . . .

"So now, fittingly, you're the one who gets to do the honors," his double continued. And then . . . it changed into Buffy, her smile evil and lustful, who drawled, "I have to admit, I'm glad it worked out this way. I was going to bleed Andrew, but you look a lot better with your shirt off."

At her signal, one of her minions . . . her Harbingers . . . cranked a wheel that hoisted Spike's Catherine wheel into the hair. He hung horizontally from the disc, ritual cuts carved into his chest, and they were bleeding steadily on the disc below him.

"To be honest, I'm getting a little tired of subtle," "Buffy" drawled as she watched him dangling. "I think it's about time we brought some authority to our presence. Now, Spike, do you want to see what a real vampire looks like?"

Spike's blood was pooling on the grooves of the seal, running around the circumference. The Celtic knots between the points of the pentagram began to glow.

One by one, the points of the five-pointed star lifted, then folded into themselves, forming a pyramid. Once formed, it sank into the center of the disc, and then the entire disc itself began to submerge into the abyss in portions, like a great medieval death machine.

Light streamed out of it, blue and sickly, a portent of what was to come.

And then a single hand shot out, followed by

another. The flesh was gray, desiccated; the nails long and gnarled.

Dressed in black leather like the Master, the creature climbed forth. Its bald head stamped with exaggerated vampire features—forehead, teeth. Its cheeks were sunken and its eyes . . . its eyes were filled with demonic, unbridled power.

The it raised its hands and roared with fury.

And Spike could do nothing but watch.

And bleed.

Chapter Ten: "Bring on the Night"

In Buffy's living room, Xander swept up the broken glass from any and all windows in the entire Summers' home, for heaven's sake. Buffy and Willow were at the table doing computer research, while Anya and Dawn sat on the couch with very old and musty-smelling books.

"It's a loop," Xander said, exasperated. "Like the mummy hand. I'm doomed to replace these windows for all eternity. You know, maybe we should board these up until things are less Hellmouthy."

Anya, who had on her reading glasses to alleviate her eyestrain, was equally frustrated. She held up a notebook she'd been reading and announced, "Nothing. And nothing." She held up two books. "Cliff Notes to nothing. Nothing abridged . . ."

Willow glanced up from the laptop. "Yeah, my search isn't turning up anything, either." She asked Buffy, "Are you sure this thing called itself 'The First.'"

Buffy gave a thoughtful shrug. "Pretty sure. It claimed to be the original evil, the one that came before anything else."

Anya peered over glasses and rolled her eyes. "*Please.* How many times have I heard that line in my demon days? 'I'm so rotten, they don't even have a word for it. I'm bad. Baddy bad bad bad does it make you horny?'" Off everyone's startled glances, she added quickly, "Or terrified. Whatever."

"It wasn't a line," Buffy argued. "When I came up against this thing, I felt it. It was ancient and enormous. It nearly got Angel to kill himself. And if we don't rescue Spike soon, God only knows what The First'll get him to do."

She felt helpless at the thought, and tried to push her fears away, concentrate on the situation at hand.

Xander shot a look at Andrew, who was back in his chair and unconscious again. "I wish Sleeping Ugly would come to," he grumbled. "He's been out all night."

Anya added, "He was just starting to squeal when the spooky SWAT arrived. Said The First was held up at the Seal of Danzar something?"

Dawn walked over to Andrew, regarding him suspiciously. "Maybe he's just faking so he doesn't have to answer any more questions." She slapped him and stood back to gauge the effect. "Or maybe he's in a fugue state." She pulled back her hand in preparation to slapping him again, but Buffy interrupted her.

"He'll come to when he comes to. If we're going to rescue Spike, we need how to figure out how to fight this thing."

Dawn pouted as she headed back to the couch. "Anya gets to hit him."

"Hey," Willow called excitedly. "Here! The First!" She kept reading, grimaced, and added, "Bank of Delaware. Sorry."

Sighing, Buffy said, "Hand me the Watcher's Codex again."

And then, as she took it . . .

"Can I get you something else, baby? How about some tea?"

Joyce Summers stood beside Buffy, her face sweet and kind and solicitous. She was so beautiful, so vibrant and alive. But she wasn't really there. Buffy knew that, and yet, she couldn't staunch her reaction.

She closed her eyes and said, "You're not real. You're The First."

"Oh, baby, you're so tired, you're not making sense," Joyce said kindly. "Maybe you should get some sleep."

"No," Buffy murmured, though the idea of sleep was unbelievably tempting.

Joyce's gaze filled with concern. "You can't win against this thing. Not if you don't rest."

Visibly shaken, Buffy said, "Stop. Stop being like this. It's a lie."

"I don't want to scare you," Joyce continued, "but

I want you to take care." She bent and said slowly, "You need to wake up."

"What?" Buffy asked, frowning in confusion.

Then Xander said, "You're dreaming. Buffy, wake up."

She roused, sitting upright as she realized she had been asleep. She looked around and said, "Did you see it?"

"There's nothing to see," Xander reassured her. "You were just doing a little dream talking. That's all."

"Oh," she said pensively.

He eyed her. "You okay? What did you see?"

She shook her head. "Nothing. It was nothing."

To the dirgelike chant of The First's Harbingers, Spike was dragged face up along the floor of an underground cave. Torchlight flickered on his ruined face and the symbols on his chest. He managed to focus long enough to make out the image of the . . . what should he call it? The Ubervamp? It was the monster that was dragging him along. He flashed to another time he had been dragged powerlessly along—by the Initiative soldiers—and wondered what would happen to him this time.

Keepin' me alive for something . . .

Then The First appeared to him as his double, sneering at Spike's condition, and said to the Ubervamp, "Go on, Give it a kick, then. You always liked that, didn't you?"

As he spoke he morphed into Drusilla, and Spike

had to remind himself that this wasn't really Dru.

"Kick a dolly when he's down," she said in her Cockney accent. "That was always your style."

She watched, pleased, as the Ubervamp kicked him so hard he rolled. She said evilly, "Has buckets of energy, poor dear. He's been laying in wait for his moment since before the bug walked."

She said to the monster, "There, there, pet. Soon as the moon comes, you'll have your carnage. Little girls tear so easily . . . like pink paper." The Ubervamp kicked Spike again.

And again.

And again.

Buffy walked in just as Dawn splashed Andrew with cold water, which worked, but Dawn and Anya didn't want to get in trouble with Buffy so Anya blurted, "Silly Andrew. You drooled all over yourself."

Andrew gazed at Buffy hero-worship style and said, 'I was about to be dead. You saved me."

"For the time being." She crossed her arms just like Wonder Woman and said, "But if you don't tell us what we need to know, then I'm going to offer you to The First on a platter and let him chop you into tiny pieces."

Andrew swallowed, composing himself. He was about to talk when he stopped, confused, and asked, "The First what?"

"It's the name of the evil thing that pretended to be Warren to get you to kill Jonathan."

He was disappointed. "Not very ominous sounding. An evil name should be like Lex or Voldemort or—"

"Hey, I was intimidating here," Buffy groused.

"Oh, sorry," Andrew said contritely. "Go ahead."

She sighed. "Forget it. Where's the Seal?"

And then they were in the basement, staring down at the disc, and Xander said, "Whoa. Check out the goat-heady badness."

"What does it do?" Buffy asked.

"I don't know. It didn't work 'cause there wasn't enough blood."

Dawn was examining a strange wheel-cross thing as she said, "There's blood on this. Lots. Looks like The First made a sacrifice. Or a music video."

Buffy was worried. "The Seal could've been activated. I bet that's what The First needed Spike for."

Andrew began to panic. "That's wasn't there before," he insisted, indicated the crossworks. "I had nothing to do with that."

"Thanks for clearing that up," Xander drawled, "'cause otherwise we might've thought you were up to no good here at the satanic manhole cover." In exasperation, he added, "You killed your best friend!"

Andrew murmured, "He's in a place of joy and peace. He told me."

Buffy rolled her eyes as Xander said impatiently, "No, nobody told you. You got tricked by a fake ghost."

"Can we save the encounter session?" Buffy demanded. "We need to cover this thing up."

She grabbed one of the shovels that Andrew and Jonathan used to uncover the Seal and tossed it toward Xander and Andrew.

Xander got one too, and everyone began digging.

When they were finished, they walked out of the room and into the hallway. Andrew muttered, "Man, this place gives me the creeps. It's like in Wonder Woman, issue 297-299."

"Catacombs," Xander said reflexively. "With the skeletons."

Simultaneously they both said, "That was cool."

Okay, I did not just massively geek out, Xander thought.

"So what next?" Dawn asked . . . and then she and Buffy both clammed up as Principal Wood emerged from another corridor, carrying a shovel of his own.

"Buffy . . ." he began.

"Hey," she replied.

They eyed each other. And the shovels. It was . . . odd.

"Apparently somebody left this in the courtyard, and I was just returning it," he told her.

She raised her brows. "That's some full-service principaling."

The principal in turn looked at Buffy's shoulder.

"Oh." She said earnestly, "And I was just down here helping Dawnie with her project."

"For science," Dawn volunteered.

"We buried a . . . time capsule," Buffy informed him.

Dawn said, way too brightly, "Hello, people of the future! Kids now like Red Bull and *Jackass*!"

They moved off awkwardly, but not before Principal Wood asked her if she could come back to work.

"Things are backing up," he told her.

"I'll be back tomorrow," she promised him. "One hundred percent ooze free."

After they got home, Willow and Anya made preparations for a locator spell, to see if they could find The First.

Xander tried to get Buffy to get some rest, but she demurred. They watched on as Willow finished her oblation, pouring magical powder on the table from a bowl.

Then the area on the table exploded, sending Anya flying. Wind whipped through the room, scattering objects in a maelstrom. The bowl superheated as Dawn shrieked and jumped away. Crimson light from the bowl twisted into twin funnels that shot into her nose. Willow threw back her head and screamed as her eyes and hair went black. Then The First, as Buffy had first glimpsed it years ago, erupted from Willow's mouth.

It was enormous, a glowing red apparition derived from every nightmare of hell, its eyes two flaming pits, its talons at the ready as it lunged at Buffy. Then it was immediately sucked back inside the Wicca.

"Will!" Buffy cried.

Willow stood, her body shaking as red lightning bolts shot from her mouth. The bolts knocked Buffy down and shot her across the room.

A demonic voice erupted from Willow, bellowing, "You only make me stronger!"

Xander, who had snatched the bowl that held the spell ingredients, smashed it against the dining room wall. Just as suddenly as everything had started, it all went back to normal. Willow's eyes and hair—everything.

Willow's knees buckled and she fell to the floor. She was sobbing and shaking, and as Buffy knelt at her side, Willow cried, "It's still in me. I feel it!"

"No, it's not. It's gone. You're okay," Buffy soothed.

Willow could not calm down. "I don't want to hurt anybody. Please, Buffy, don't let it make me. Oh, God!"

"We won't. I promise. We won't use magic to fight this thing until we know what we're doing."

Shortly thereafter, Buffy put on her coat and gathered up a few weapons, preparing to go after The First herself.

"At least let me go with you," Xander insisted. And when she refused, he pointed out, "You said so yourself you don't know how to fight The First. Or even where it is."

Buffy reached for the door. "It's out there. It's hurting my friends. I'll find it."

She pulled the door open.

Giles stood on the front porch, a nimbus of light around his head.

"Buffy," he said.

"Giles." She couldn't believe the relief that flooded through her at the sight of him. She went to hug him, but at that moment, three young girls she'd never seen before walked right into her house.

The First one looked all *Ghost World*—lunchbox for a purse, and as she came in, she said, "Nice place. Bit of a mess."

The second one, more polished, smiled at Buffy and drifted in, saying nothing.

The third one—very beautiful—gave Buffy a once-over and said, "This is the Slayer? Huh." She sounded unimpressed.

"Sorry to barge in," Giles said, a tad wry. "I'm afraid we have a slight apocalypse."

In the living room, Dawn inspected the three new girls as she said, "They're all Slayers?"

"Potential Slayers," Giles explained. "Waiting for one to be called. There were many more like them all over the world, but now there's just a handful, and they're all on their way to Sunnydale."

Buffy got it, realized what she had been seeing in her dreams—Potential Slayers being murdered.

"We always feared this day would come," Giles said. "When there'd be an attack, against not just an individual Slayer, but against the whole line."

Buffy got it. She said, "The First. That's what it wants."

"Yes," Giles said. "To erase all the Slayers in training and their Watchers, along with their methods."

"And then Faith, and then me," Buffy said shortly.

"And with all the Potentials gone and no way of making another, it's the end. No more Slayer. Ever."

Willow was confused. "But we haven't found any information on The First. No documentation."

Giles crossed his arms as he explained. "That's because it predates any written history, and it rarely shows its true face. The only record we know was in the Council Library." He looked uncomfortable.

"What about the Council? What do they say about this?"

"Gone," Giles replied. "Obliterated. They were in session, and there was an explosion."

"That means all the Council's records are—are destroyed?" Willow asked anxiously.

"Annabelle," Giles prompted, and the young Potential stepped forward with a backpack. She pulled out a pitiful number of files and books.

"That's what's left," he told them. "The mystic secrets of the Watchers, and whatever I could find on The First."

"But what do these records say about The First?" Buffy asked.

"Uh, very little," Giles admitted. "It can change form. It only appears in the guise of someone who's passed away. Also, it's not corporeal. It can't touch or fight on its own. It only works through those it manipulates. And its followers, the Bringers."

"Yeah, with the hoodies and the crazy alphabet eyes," said the Potential named Molly.

"Molly," said Annabelle, Mr. Giles doesn't need us prattling on."

Giles at on the arm of the couch. "The First is unlike anything "we've faced before. I mean, there's evil and there's the thing that created evil, the source.

He continued. "It has eternities to act, endless resources. How to defeat it . . . honestly, I don't know. But we have to find a way. If the Slayer line is eliminated, then the Hellmouth has no guardian. the balance is destroyed."

He walked up to Buffy. "I'm afraid it falls to you, Buffy. You're the only one who has the strength to protect the girls—and the world—against what's coming."

"But no pressure," Xander said angrily.

The pretty Potential walked to the center of the room and said in disbelief, "That's it? That's the plan? I don't see how one person, even a Slayer, could protect us. And if this thing is the root of all evil, isn't the Hellmouth going to be its number one vacation spot? I mean, don't you think we should be hiding our asses on the other side of the globe?"

"Kennedy!" Annabelle cried.

"No, she's not wrong," Buffy said. "We need more muscle. That's why we need to find Spike."

Anya looked dubious. "Yeah, he'll help. If he's not crazy. Or killing people. Or dead. Or you, know, all of the above."

In the underground cavern that had become Spike's torture chamber, Spike prayed for the true death to free him of his torment.

The First was still wearing Drusilla's skin and it matched her inventiveness—and her viciousness—in causing pain. At her command, the Ubervamp was forcing Spike's head beneath the surface of a filthy pool of water, waiting for him to expire, then yanking him out to revive.

Then Spike would sputter to life, coughing up water, gasping in agony.

"That's why our kind make such good dollies," The First said. "Hard to kill." She glared at him. "Tried to enlighten Little Buffy, didn't you? Spilled our secrets like seed." She reached down with her long, thin arms and raised her dress, undulating slowly.

"But you forgot. I say what you tell and what you know. I saw when this is over." She let go of her skirt and put her hands behind her head. "And I'm not done with you yet. Not nearly."

She clicked her tongue at the Ubervamp, and it shoved Spike back in the water . . . to be drowned all over again.

Sunnydale's Main Street was decorated for Christmas. Buffy and Giles walked together, as she and Angel once had done.

"This place, where you last saw The First, you say it was in a Christmas tree lot?"

"Under it," Buffy corrected him. "There was a hidden cavern, just happened to be under a tree lot. The Bringers were doing some kind of ritual." She took a breath as she gazed at her old friend. "Giles, this is bad, isn't it? A new kind of bad."

"Just in time for Christmas," Giles said dryly.

Sighing, Buffy took in their surroundings. "You know, I didn't even realize it was December. Maybe when we get home, we should decorate the rubble." She gazed at him fondly. "Think you'll ever just show up for a real visit? The kind where the world isn't about to end?"

"If we survive this, I promise," he said with a wistful smile.

"Good. 'Cause I miss you."

"I miss you, too," he told her.

There was a lot going on in Buffy's house. Young Potentials were getting ready for bed. Xander was boarding up the windows.

I wish Jonathan could see this. I'm actually hanging out in Buffy's house with her gang! Andrew thought.

Still in tied-up hostage mode, Andrew asked Xander, "So, how long have you followed Buffy?"

Xander looked annoyed. "I don't follow her. She's my best friend."

"Huh. She seems like a good leader. Her hair is shiny. Does she make you stab things?"

Meanwhile, Willow was trying to organize the sleeping arrangements, which Kennedy kept vetoing. Apparently, yakking all night and snoring was a common affliction among Potential Slayers. She finally gave up, handing the sheets to the pretty young Potential named Kennedy, and said, "You want to do the sleeping arrangements?"

Kennedy grinned at her like a sly little cat and said, "You better not hog the covers."

Willow blinked. "She's new!" she blurted to Dawn.

After that, it was a time to worry about food. Blackened mac and cheese, pizza, plain or veggie, and . . .

"Brill! Biscuits!" Mollie crowed.

So everyone ate cookies.

Buffy and Giles got to the place where the Christmas tree lot had once stood. As Buffy stepped on some wooden boards, they broke beneath her weight and she tumbled into the entrance to the cave.

"Found it," she announced, picking herself up.

Giles put on his glasses and peered down at her. "Good Lord," he said, "are you all right?"

"Peachy," she said, dusting herself off. "Except my knees bend backward now. Okay, Giles, stay up there. I'm going to check it out."

She walked among the outcroppings and cave formations; she thought she saw a flicker of movement, but when she turned around, there was nothing.

She walked on, turned around again.

This time something was there, in her face. He was hideous, gray and deformed, a grotesque of vampiric aspect, an unbelievably hideous monster.

He made an uppercut that sent her slamming around the cavern. He came at her again, and her blocks were ineffective.

She retreated; he followed. She managed a few blows, but she barely managed to stay upright. Yet her opponent was barely winded.

Inside of a minute she was bleeding, spent . . . and very frightened.

He swung, connected, swung again; but this time she dropped and rolled . . . and sprang to her feet with stake in hand. Before the creature could react, she drove the stake deep into His heart.

Hah! she thought triumphantly.

But he did not dust.

He grinned, and pulled the stake out. Then he came at her with it. She managed to avoid his stabbing motions, and the stake splintered inches from her face.

The monster was after her, punching her in the stomach, throwing her against the wall. Blow after blow rained down on her. She tried to hit him. He grabbed her fist and broke bones, then drew her forward so that her head rammed into a stalactite, which she broke off and slammed over his head, and he finally loosened his grip on her and fell to the ground.

Buffy ran.

She leaped to the rock wall where she had fallen in and started scrambling up, as fast as she could, hand-and footholds crumbling . . .

She was halfway up when she felt his taloned hand gripping her ankle. . . .

Buffy struggled mightily to pull herself out of the cave hole, almost freeing herself, but he managed to yank her back in. She dug into the soft earth, her fingers leaving treads. . . .

And there was Giles, haloed with a nimbus of light once more, this one of rosy dawn . . .

The sun was rising.

As Buffy finally got all the way out of the hole, the monster behind retreated in snarling fear.

When they got back to Buffy's house, the Potentials were eating breakfast, having made themselves at home.

"Sorry about the British invasion," Kennedy said. Then she looked at Buffy as the Slayer walked into the kitchen and said, "You all right? You look . . ." She trailed off.

Buffy shut the door and said, "Yeah, I just got into a fight, is all." She said to Giles, "You want to tell me with what?"

Giles hesitated. "Buffy, don't you think we should discuss this privately?"

"You mean, not in front of the next generation? No time to coddle them." She said to the Potentials, "Welcome to the war room, guys."

A thrill rippled through the girls. Annabelle grabbed a pen and a pad of paper.

"What you fought was a vampire, but it was something more than that," Giles explained. "It was a Turok-han. As Neanderthals are to human beings, the Turok-han are to vampires. Primordial, ferociously powerful killing machines, as singleminded as animals. They are the vampires vampires fear. An ancient and entirely different race. Until this morning, I thought they were myth."

Buffy took that in. "So The First shows up—and now this. Think it's a coincidence?"

"More likely, the Turok-han is here as an agent of The First," Giles replied.

The girls processed that. Then Annabelle nervously raised her hand.

"Did you slay it?"

"No," Buffy replied. "It's still out there. Somewhere."

"What's it want?" Molly asked.

"All of us dead," Buffy said frankly. "But for now it looks like sunlight is keeping this Ubervamp away."

"So, until sunset, I suggest you get some rest," Giles urged Buffy. "A few hours sleep will do a world of difference."

"Somehow, I don't think taking on prehistoric evil comes with nap time. I'm going to go to work, see what I can find out. I'll be back before sunset."

Giles looked skeptical. "How do you plan to research something as ill-defined as The First?"

"I have the best plan ever," Buffy informed him.

Okay, maybe not the best plan, Buffy conceded, as she sat in her cubicle at Sunnydale High. Typing the single word "evil" into her Web browser had yielded 900,517 results.

Unbeknownst to Buffy, Principal Wood had come up behind her. He read off her screen, "Manifestations of Evil?"

Buffy jumped, but calmly typed, "In The Movies."

"You're searching for evil movies?" the principal queried.

"I know it's not the all-time most kosher use of office hours, but, ah, I'm facing a little downtime here and what can I say?" Buffy asked disingenuously. "I

just love those evil, evil movies. Like *The Exorcist* or
Blair Witch."

"As opposed to, say, Rob Schneider's *oeuvre*," he
put in.

"Different evil," she said.

"You okay?" He studied her. "You've looked better.

She frowned, a little hurt.

He added, "I'm not that big a fan of scary movies,
even the hokey ones. Sometimes they go to a place I
think kids could stand to avoid."

She demurred. "Well, this isn't for the kids . . ."

"Once you see true evil, it can have some serious
afterburn. You can't unsee what you saw. Ever."

They stared at each other, and she wondered if he
was giving her some kind of message beside the message that See No Evil was his, um, message.

Then he shrugged. "Just one opinion," he offered,
and he was friendly about it.

A bit shaken, she watched as he turned back to his
office. She said,

He paused. "Mysteries," he replied. "I love finding
out what's underneath it all at the end."

And there it was again, the sense that he was saying more than he was saying.

He walked away.

Still dressed in Drusilla's face, The First continued to
torture Spike, who was beaten and hurt so badly he
could hardly move.

"Think of it as a game," she suggested. "A fun,

funny game. Without all the rules, or any of the bother-
some winning part. But still, there are sides. You have
to choose a side, Spike. Then we can fly, be free and
visit all our friends as they come squirming from out
the earth."

She began to dance, slow and dirty. "I know you
like a good wriggle and a giggle and a squiggle."

"You're not Drusilla," he told her. "She was crazier
than you."

She made a show of covering her ears with her
hands. "Ooh, daddy. No kicking. It's almost Christmas
Day and you've gone spoiling it. I've been so very
good all year." She smiled and growled at him.

"But I could be bad if you like."

He looked away from her, but the Ubervamp
punched him in the head.

"Bad daddy. Needs a caning. Never learned his
headmaster's lesson while all the school bells
ring . . . and ring . . . and ring." She pantomimed ringing a bell.

"Choose a side," she whispered in his ear. "Choose
our side. You know that it's delicious." She mimed
licking his face. "What do you say?"

"Dru . . . love . . ." He set his jaw, knowing what
was to come. "Get bent."

"Stupid stubborn daddy," she pouted.

Then she folded her hands over her heart and
danced . . . as the Ubervamp mercilessly beat Spike.

In the bathroom in her house, Buffy examined her
injuries. They were bad. No wonder Principal Wood had

asked her how she was. She looked terrible. Then a hand was touching her arm . . . her mother's hand . . . and Joyce Summers was all concern and affection.

"I tried to warn you," she began, then looked abashed and said, "The last thing you need now is one of my helpful Mom's guilt trips. I'll get you some ice."

She turned to go. Buffy stopped her. "No, Mom, I can't," she said.

"Buffy, you have to heal," Joyce said.

Buffy replied, "I don't have time."

"Are you worried about the sun going down?" Joyce asked sweetly. "Because there's some things you can't control. The sun always goes down. The sun always comes up."

"Everyone's counting on me," Buffy asserted.

Joyce's brow wrinkled. "Well, they do that, and I'm sorry, Buffy, but these friends of yours put too much pressure on you. They always have."

"Something evil is coming," Buffy said.

Joyce gazed upon her with infinite patience. "Buffy, evil isn't coming. It's already here. Evil is always here."

Buffy lifted her chin. "I have to stop it."

"How are you going to do that?" Joyce queried.

"I don't know yet, but—"

"Buffy, no matter what your friends expect of you, evil is a part of us. All of us. It's natural. And no one can stop that. No one can stop nature, not even . . ."

And then the school bell rang, and Buffy woke up at her desk. A young male student was sitting across from her, looking hurt and pissed off.

"Oh, um, I'm sorry," she said. "What were we talking about?"

"Only my life," he said with supreme irritation. "You're just like all the others."

He gathered his things and rose to go.

"No! I'm different!" she proclaimed. "I'm hip and relate to the young people. Don't go . . . uh . . ."

"Roger," he said angrily.

"Roger. See, I knew that."

Enough was enough. He was out of there.

In the living room at Buffy's house, preparations for siege were underway. Xander was in the loop, finishing boarding up the living room window. Giles was pacing. Dawn and Willow were selecting weapons from the chest.

The Potentials sat together, looking useless and scared.

"This day's almost over," Giles said, looking at his watch. "And the sun will go down in seventeen minutes."

"Hey, junior Slayers, don't look so worried," Xander piped, smiling at the three young girls. "I mean, sure, we don't know where Spike is, or how to fight The First, or when the super-style vamp is going to attack us all. However, the house"—He tapped his hammer on the wooden panels he had installed— "boarded up. Now all we gotta do is trap this Ubervamp in the pantry, and it's game over."

Willow raised a brow at him. "Xander? Newbies. Let's ease them into the whole 'jokes in the face of death' thing."

"Who's joking?" Xander shot back in mock innocence. "Are you saying M. Night Shamalayan lied to us?"

Buffy said to the Potentials, "You'll be okay."

Coming up to Buffy, mace in hand, Willow said encouragingly, "Okay, or even better. It's like our guarantee." To Buffy, she added, "Um, Buffy, I just, I want you to know that I'm really sorry for letting you down. You know, here before with the magic going all 'aah' and me going all 'eee' and everything getting all 'rrrr.' I wish I could help out."

Buffy was touched. She said, "No one expects you to make everything right."

However, Willow's guilt was not assuaged. "So, I can't do everything, but I should at least be able to do something. I have so much power, but when I try to use it . . ."

"Don't, okay?" Buffy told her.

"Okay." Willow was still earnest face. "But you need help, Buffy. I know you and I'll know you'll never admit it, but you need help."

Buffy shrugged. "I'll be okay. Okay, or better. It's like my guarantee."

A moment. Between friends.

Then Kennedy approached, bordering on agitated, as she said, "Hey, are we getting weapons? Trained fighters, badness coming? I've heard worse ideas."

Annabelle said primly, "We'll be armed when the Slayer feels we're ready."

"I feel ready," Molly volunteered.

"You're frightened," Annabelle insisted. "You must learn to control your fear."

Kennedy said huffily, "Hey, you know what would help with that?" She looked at Buffy. "Weapons. We're sitting ducks without them."

Annabelle countered, "We're with the Slayer. Safe as houses."

"Do you see the house we're in?" Kennedy scoffed.

And Annabelle's balloon of courage pfffted . . . revealing a very young girl, filled with very pure dread.

Buffy saw it and said, "We should load them up, Giles."

Xander walked into the dining room, where Andrew was still tied in the chair. The blond bad boy said, "Listen to me, man. I've got a bad feeling about this. My spider-sense is tingling. This is going to get hairy. I'm talking weird with a beard. Better untie me."

Buffy joined them. "And that'll help us how?"

Andrew sighed mournfully. "Okay, I know what you're thinking. Andrew. Bad guy. You think I'm a super villain, like Dr. Doom, or Apokalypse, or . . . or the Riddler."

The last reference was lost on Xander, but he merely shrugged.

"I admit I went over to the Dark Side," Andrew went on, earnestly. "But only to pick up a couple of things and now I'm back. I've learned. I'm good again."

As she and Xander walked out of the room, Buffy muttered, "And when were you good before?"

"Okay, technically . . . never. Touché." He called after her, trying to get free. "But I'm like Vader in the last five minutes of *Jedi*, with redemptive powers minus a redemptive struggle of epic redemption which chronicles . . ." Realizing the futility of both his diatribe and his struggle , he sighed and added, "These ropes itch."

Buffy joined Giles at the window. Sunset was imminent. Their time was at hand.

"You have all my faith," Giles told her. "And they're depending on you."

She gave him a wry look. "Giles, that's not exactly what I needed to hear right now."

Then Molly came into the room. "Guys? Annabelle split!"

Escape.

Darkness had fallen, over the city of Sunnydale and across Annabelle's reflexive prime directive: survival. Her mind had gone into primitive overdrive; it was fight or flight, and something deep inside her had chosen the latter.

She was frantic, racing for her life, putting distance between the Slayer's house and her safety and—a hideous monster jumped from behind a dumpster and grabbed her by the throat. With a roar it hoisted her off the ground, her eyes bulging, her legs kicking . . .

Escape . . .

* * *

It didn't take Buffy long to find Annabelle's body. She was sorry, so very sorry; here was one she had not saved, could not save.

Then thoughts of mourning fled as the Ubervamp rushed up behind her and slammed her to the ground. Buffy crawled around the Dumpster, crouching, and then she launched her attack.

It took her only seconds to realize that she was doomed to repeat the battle in the underground cave: she kicked, and he ducked. He blocked her fists. Then he launched his counterattack, giving her far worse than she gave. She would up on the ground, face first; he yanked her up and started to choke her, and the only thing that saved her was when she spit blood at him, startling him into dropping her.

In the instant she had while he savored the taste of Slayer's blood, she limped away into the bowels of the building where their battle had led them, all pipes and machines and pieces of gigantic tubing.

Like the Terminator, the Ubervamp came after her, and Buffy was given no chance to rest. As before, she went on the offensive, hitting him over the head with a large piece of pipe, but it did no damage at all. He wrested it from her and they fought bare-fisted . . . and as before, he had the upper hand.

Punching, kicking, maiming. She was in pure defensive mode. She backed up, he came forward. She weakened, he gained his stride.

Her ribs were broken. Her head rang as he back-handed her, sending her at least thirty feet across the vast interior of the room.

As she lay gasping, he ran toward her. Then she saw a block and tackle holding up a pallet of metal rods. Three tons, she estimated. She followed the line to a rusted lever and pulled it.

The Ubervamp looked up just as the crate of metal rods came rushing down upon him. The impact was thunderous. He was buried beneath dozens of rods, beneath thick wood.

Silence.

She sagged with relief, her pain flooding into her consciousness now that she was safe. Slowly, painfully, she rose. She had to get home, share the good news . . .

Then she heard the horrible sound of twisting metal crashing.

She turned.

Impossible.

The Ubervamp was rising from the wreckage.

She couldn't believe it. Nothing could have survived . . . and yet here it came, loping after her in long strides.

She ran, but it was no use. She was far too wounded. He blocked her way as she nearly made it out, grabbing her, assaulting her with killing blows.

He threw her into a concrete wall, then crawled up the wall to gain force as he kicked her. She went down, hard. He kicked her in the head and grabbed her arm. Then he threw her through the wall.

Down it all came, chunks of rubble and bricks and concrete, slamming down on the Slayer, on the doomed, unconscious Slayer.

* * *

In the underground cavern, Spike's torment did not end. The First, still wearing Drusilla's image, seemed to have tired of their games.

She asked him, "Do you know why you're alive?"

He was so injured he could barely speak, but he managed it. "Never figured you for existential thought. I mean, you hated Paris."

She hissed, "You're alive for one reason, and one reason only. Because I wish it. Do you know why I wish it?" She held her hand to her heart. "Because I'm not done with you."

He had the brass to snicker at her. "Give it up. Whatever you are, whatever you get away with, I'm out. You can't pull this puppet's strings anymore."

She snapped around to face him. "And what makes you think you have a choice? What makes you think you will ever be any good at all in this world?"

"She does," he managed. "Because she believes in me."

Xander, Giles, and Willow found Buffy and brought her home. Her face was battered, both eyes blackened. She sat in a chair in a fetal position, beaten and injured, and listened to their conversation in the next room.

"We could make plans as we always do," Giles said, "but the truth is, Buffy was our plan. There is no backup."

"Giles," Willow ventured, "she looks bad."

"She does," Giles replied, sorrow in his voice. "I'm afraid there may be internal bleeding."

"What do we do if she can't fight?" Willow asked.

"We're back at square one," Giles stated flatly.

"Which square would that be, exactly?" Xander's voice had taken on the caustic tone he had when his back was up against the wall.

"I'm not sure," Giles admitted. "The First predates everything we've ever known, or can know. It's everywhere. It's pure. I don't know if we can fight it."

Then the Slayer unfolded herself, rose, and moved slowly into the room, and everyone turned, gazing at her in surprise, as if they hadn't even expected her to be able to walk.

"You're right," she said, her voice hoarse from the injuries to her voice. Through her ruined face, her eyes blazed. She held herself upright as proudly as she could.

"We don't know how to fight it. We don't know when it'll come. We can't run, can't hide, can't pretend it's not the end, 'cause it is." She took a breath. "Something's always been there to try and destroy the world. We've beaten them back, but we're not dealing with them anymore. We're dealing with reason they exit. Evil. The strongest. The First."

Her eyes shone. There was something about her, an aura of command, of power. This was no defeated girl; this was a Slayer.

"Buffy, I know you're tired," Giles said.

She looked at him. At all of them. "I'm beyond tired. I'm beyond scared. I'm standing on the mouth of hell, and it is going to swallow me whole."

A beat.

"And it'll choke on me."

A fierce resolve crept into her voice, and the others unconsciously responded. She took a step forward.

"We're not ready?" she asked. "They're not ready. They think we're going to wait for the end to come like we always do.

"I'm doing waiting. They want an apocalypse? Oh, we'll give 'em one." She almost smiled.

"Anyone else who wants to run, do it now. 'Cause we just became an army," she announced. Her passionate calm was almost unearthly; it was the interior serenity of a warrior, a champion, whose business is death and who had enacted many transactions in the coin of the realm.

"We just declared war."

Her voice gained momentum. "From now on, we won't just face our worst fears, we will seek them out. We will find them, and cut out their hearts one by one, until The First shows itself for what it really is. And I'll kill it myself."

The others were locked up in her passionate calm. Everyone was moved: Giles. Willow. Xander. And Andrew, in tears.

"There is only one thing on this more powerful than evil. And that's us."

She looked around at them all.

"Any questions?"

Chapter Eleven: "Showtime"

Rona was the last one off the bus. As she slowly went down the metal steps, she looked around at the deserted area, anxious that no one was there to meet her.

She crossed to the payphone, picked up the director dangling from a cable, and flipped through the pages. The one she needed had been torn out. No Summers listing for Rona.

Then, as she looked up, one of the black-robed, eyeless men she'd encountered before ran full tilt at her. He was armed with a wicked-sharp knife, and his grotesque face was grim with purpose. In terror, she turned to run. There were two more, their curved knives flashing as they arced over their heads.

Panicking, she backed up against the wall, her breath shallow and dizzy as she sank to the ground.

Oh, God, they're gonna kill me . . .

The two suddenly sprang into the air and went flying off into opposite directions.

And Buffy the Vampire Slayer stood where they had been.

The third attacker retreated while The First two rushed Buffy. As one swiped at her, Buffy grabbed his hand and stabbed the other one with his buddy's knife. He doubled over, and Buffy kicked him, hard. After a tussle, she broke the neck of the other one.

Then she called to the one who was retreating, "Hey! Try picking on someone my own size!" She hurled the knife at him, and it sliced into his back.

He fell.

Then Buffy crossed to Rona and said, "Rona, right? I just got word you were arriving."

Rona accepted Buffy's help as she got to her wobbly feet. "You're her," she said, in a daze.

"Here is me," Buffy concurred.

Rona took that in . . . and took in, too, that she had only been in Sunnydale mere seconds before she'd been attacked.

"I thought, uh, they told me I'd be safe here."

"Right," Buffy nodded. Then she backtracked slightly, adding, "Well, you are. I mean, you will be . . . safer . . . with me around."

"That's good," Rona allowed.

Buffy started to walk away, and Rona followed her. "Next time you're attacked—"

"Whoa, whoa," Rona protested. "'Next time'? You saying I'm gonna get attacked again?"

"Welcome to the Hellmouth," Buffy said frankly.

* * *

Kennedy watched Willow shifting uncomfortably on the floor in her sleeping bag and said, "You don't have to do this." She patted Willow's bed invitingly, "Nice big comfy bed right here. I mean, you ought to know. Your bed."

"No," Willow assured her, stiff on her back, "I'm just, uh, uneasy 'cause Buffy's out."

Kennedy nodded. "Right. How many girls arriving this time?"

"Just one," Willow told her. "But since Giles has the coven searching for other Slayers-in-waiting to send 'em our way, I'll bet we'll be seeing a lot more soon enough."

Kennedy propped her head on her hand. "With this many girls, well, if we don't get another bathroom in this house soon, things are going to get ugly."

Willow smiled. "Sounds like somebody had to share mirror time with a bunch of siblings."

"Somebody, but not me," Kennedy insisted. "I only have a half-sister and her bedroom was in another wing of the house."

Willow stared, impressed. "Wing? Your house had wings?"

"Yeah." Kennedy looked abashed. "Just a couple. A few. Our summer home in the Hamptons didn't have any at all. Well, one, actually."

"Huh." Willow took that in.

"But never mind my deal," Kennedy went on. She regarded the redhead with interest. "What's your story, Willow? I mean, witchcraft? That sounds new-agey."

Willow shifted. "No. It's safe to say that what I practice is definitely old-agey."

Absorbing that, nodding, Kennedy urged, "So, show my a trick."

"A trick?" Willow echoed with mild dismay.

"You know, pull a rabbit out of something, or make something float."

Willow shifted uncomfortably once more. "Um, yeah, listen, Kennedy, it's almost morning. We really need to get some sleep."

Kennedy scoffed. 'Hey, if I wanted to sleep, I'd be downstairs catching Zs with the other girls."

But no Zs were to be caught belowdecks, as several of the Potentials listened to Molly's recounting of everything that had happened before they had shown up. She spoke in a singsong voice as if she were telling a ghost story at a campfire, and the girls' eyes were huge, avidly taking in everything she was telling them.

"Annabelle was all, 'Control your fear, control your fear.' Meanwhile, she's the one that goes scampering off, right into that Turok-han vampire. Poor Annie."

One of the Potentials interrupted her. "Great, so the Slayer's who's supposed to protect us let her go get killed?"

"She didn't 'let' her," Molly corrected. "Annabelle was foolish. Buffy can't be faulted by arriving too late."

But then a brunette Potential sat up, arguing, "It's

not like she could've stopped it. I mean, the super vampire messed her up pretty good."

Then a redhead took the floor. "No lie. She still looked like a big bruise when I got here, and that was already like the day after."

The blonde added, "And why isn't she back yet? She left to get the new girl over an hour ago. You don't think she was too late again?"

Molly swallowed. "Maybe—"

"Maybe we can save the maybes for a more dayish part of the day, girls," Xander announced from the couch as he turned on the lamp. "Potential Slayers can function without sleep. Me, I'm no good without my usual ninety minutes."

Andrew, still tied up, but facing away from the rest of the group, said, "I'm with him. Keep the chatter down. Or speak up so I can hear you." He added plaintively, "I'm bored. *Episode One* bored."

Then Buffy walked in the front door with the Potential in tow. She looked around and said, "You guys are still up?"

Xander sat up with a fake smile plastered on his face. "Ah. Who needs sleep?" he said ironically.

"Everybody, this is Rona," Buffy announced.

The others greeted her. Then Rona gestured to Andrew and said, "Why is that guy tied to a chair?"

Xander smiled tightly. "The question you'll soon be asking is, 'Why isn't he gagged?'"

Anya walked into the room with a sleeping bag in her arms and Giles came after, suggesting to Molly that she show Rona where the kitchen was.

"Fair enough. I'm a bit peckish meself," Molly said.

Rona echoed warily, "'Peckish?'"

"That's English for 'hungry,'" Anya told her as she unrolled the sleeping back and spread it over the floor.

Rona muttered, "Oh. Here I thought 'hungry' was English for 'hungry.'"

Buffy told Anya, Xander, and Giles about the welcoming committee. No one was thrilled. Obviously The First knew that Potentials were arriving in Sunnydale.

"The First's always going to be one step ahead of, Giles," Buffy pointed out. "I need to know how to stop it. No, not stop it, hurt it." Her features hardened as she looked at her former Watcher. "Tell me how."

"I don't know, Buffy." Taking off his glasses, he squatted on his haunches, eye level with the rest of the room. "I've exhausted all the sources I have left with little result. The Watchers' records are still all we really have to go on."

Anya looked similarly frustrated. "I made the rounds myself. Tried to dig up anything useful from the demon community. The ones that didn't attack me, didn't know anything or didn't talk. Either way, we've got squat."

"Well, squat's not gonna cut it," Buffy said shortly. "What about the Turok-han?"

"The vampire time forgot?" Xander riffed.

"Time may have forgotten him, but I sure won't," Buffy replied. "We know stakes don't kill it, but anything in those ancient books about what does? Sunlight? Fire? Germs?"

From the other room, Andrew called, "So, Giles, with that thing guarding the entrance to The First's crib, how will Buffy get to Spike?"

Giles had no answer to that. Then the blonde Potential asked, "Well, do we any kind of plan to keep us from dying?"

Standing, Buffy sighed. "We're working on it."

Giles joined Buffy. He said reluctantly, "There is one avenue that we haven't tried yet . . ."

"Giles!" Anya protested.

"Beljoxa's Eye," Giles continued. "It's an oracle type creature that exists in a dark dimension. Only demons can open the gateway to it."

"Excuse me," Anya said hotly, "Ex-demon here."

"You've still friends in the fold," Giles argued. "Murderous acquaintants, anyway."

Anya appealed to Buffy. "Look there's no reason to think this Beljoxa's eye will have any of the answers we're looking for."

"Anya, please," Buffy said. "We're running out of time. Spike's running out of time."

They were getting ready to do another ritual down in the cave, them chanting and preparing to slice open his belly. But this time Spike was ready for them. He swept up his legs to break the neck of the Bringer stupid enough to come to close; then he took out the other bloke with the torch and raced for the exit.

And there she was, waiting for him like a goddess. *Buffy* . . .

. . . except that Spike was still shackled to the wall,

and none of it had really happened.

"Dreaming of me again, aren't you?" The First taunted. Now she wore the guise of Buffy, and she was heartbreakingly beautiful.

"Poor Spike," she continued, pacing before him. "He still thinks I believe in him. Be realistic. I don't even believe in myself." She stopped pacing and moved toward him, her smile filled with amusement. "At least not enough to risk my skin to save your ass. Not enough face . . . that."

Behind her, the Turok-han postured and growled.

But Spike had blocked her out; his eyes were closed and he was muttering to himself it was like a chant, something to keep him from irretrievably shattering. . . .

"She will come for me. She will come for me. She will come for me."

"No," The First said in her Buffy guise. "I won't."

Anya was making the rounds of the demons she had made the rounds with, and no one wanted to help her and Giles contact the Beljoxa's Eye. The demon named Torg was no exception.

"You broke my heart, Anyanka," he reminded her as he threw out the trash can behind his restaurant in the strip mall. He would have wrinkled his brows except that petals of flesh fanning the bridge of his nose prevented such a humanlike expression of love's bitter aftertaste

"Don't be so dramatic, Torg," she said. "You don't even have a heart. Six spleens, two stomachs, half a brain, maybe, but no heart."

She went on. "It was one date. And it wasn't even a date. We just happened to be invited to the same massacre."

"I remember," he said, then softening, added, "You wore pink."

"Those were entrails," she informed him. Then she played her key card. "Open this tiny little gateway to the Beljoxa's Eye for me and I'll . . . you and I . . ." She sighed and made the ultimate sacrifice. "I'll have sex with you again."

That grossed him out. "Please, you're human. The way you look, now, I wouldn't touch you for all the kittens in Korea."

She was stunned. "What I am, a leper in this town? I can't even give it away!"

Torg looked unmoved. "Come back when you are a leper," he told her.

Giles tried another tack. "Perhaps this might change your mind. You help us, and the Slayer won't kill your clientele and burn your establishment to the ground."

That did the trick.

Torg pulled claws like levers, growled in his particular form of Demonese, and flung blood or some other fluids from his wounded hand toward the back of the alley. A glowing white portal shot into existence.

"Don't let it hit you on the way out," he snapped at Anya.

She frowned and said to Giles, "It's the hair, right? Not attractive?"

Then they went into the black and windy demon

vortex dimension and found the Beljoxa's eyes, which was more like a conglomeration of eyes all fused together into a meta-eyeball shape, resting in a metal cage dangling from chains. The many eyes comprising blinked at the two supplicants.

"Oh, hi!" Anya said, with forced casualness, giving the oracle a jaunty wave.

At Buffy's house, while Willow took a call from the coven back in Britain, Xander finished untying Andrew.

"Ow, watch it," Andrew whined. "That's my joystick hand."

"Not touchin' that one," Xander said under his breath.

Buffy went back over the reasons Andrew was being let go.

"We don't have time to baby-sit a hostage."

"Especially a hostage that's gotten a little ripe," Xander put in.

Suddenly aware of that, Buffy made a face and took a step back.

"So . . . did you ever see the movie *Misery*?"

"Six times," he answered eagerly. "But the book was scarier than the movie 'cause instead of crushing his foot with a sledge hammer, Kathy Bates chops it off with . . ." And then he got it. He said in a little voice, "I'll be good."

Willow came in from the kitchen, saying, "Buffy, word from the underground. Another Potential arrived in town yesterday. She's a the Sun Spot Motel, near the highway. Harbringers killed her Watcher before he could tell anyone he'd sent her. If it wasn't for a particularly powerful seer in the coven, we wouldn't even know about it now."

Buffy glanced out the window. There were at least a couple of hours of daylight left.

"I'll go with you," Xander said.

Andrew stood. "All right, retrieving a Potential! Let's do it!" he cried. Then, sensing that he was not welcome—perhaps because of the way Buffy and Xander were glaring at him, he said meekly, "Or I could just go wash up."

As Xander and Buffy left, Dawn asked Willow where they were going, and Willow mused, "The more, the better, I figure. We need all the help we can get."

Dawn was hesitant. "Not sure more scared Slayer wannabes translates as help."

The other Slayer wannabes—the Potentials—were training in the basement . . . and one, at least was very scared.

Her name was Eve, and she was pissing Kennedy off with her morale-busting whining in her sweet Southern-belle accent.

"Why are we all bothering?" Eve was saying. "It's not like we can make a difference."

"We have to be ready," Kennedy pointed out. "If something comes down—"

"Something's already come down," said a Potential named Chloe.

"And what are we supposed to do about it?" Eve asked. "I mean, I've never seen a real vampire in my whole life, much less slayed one."

"I've seen one," the Potential named Vi volunteered. As the others turned to look at her, she added, "Well, my Watcher showed me a photograph of one." She hesitated. "A blurry photograph."

"See, that's what I'm saying," Eve argued. "Not one of us is remotely prepared to be activated as a new Chosen One."

Kennedy shrugged and retorted, "I feel pretty prepared."

Rona shifted. "Excuse the newness of me, but, huh, just so I understand. If the Slayer dies—"

"*When* the Slayer dies," Eve corrected. "I mean nobody lives forever, right?"

Rona started to grasp the harsh realities of what Eve was saying. "Then one of us . . ."

"Gets activated," Eve finished.

Molly said, "I prefer 'called.'"

The redheaded Potential said, "I heard there's more than one Slayer. There's another one, somewhere."

"That doesn't make any sense," Molly argued.

"Like any of this does," Eve pressed. "No matter how many there are, one of us is going to be the next Slayer, with the weight of the world on her shoulders."

She looked at each one in turn. "It could be anyone. Especially since there are so few of us left. They'll just run through each one of us, one after the other. Kinda creepy, huh?" She made a face. "All we do is wait around for each other to die."

She sighed and added, "Just my personal opinion, but I don't think the Slayer can protect us from The First."

At the Sunspot Motel, Buffy and Xander briefly cased the joint, because the joint was so deserted.

"Tourism must be down," Buffy observed.

"Right in the middle of apocalypse season," Xander mused.

Buffy knocked. "Hello?" Knocked again. "It's okay. We're friendly and we have eyes."

Xander peered through the window. Then he said, "Buffy, kick down the door."

She did. They raced to the body on the floor. It was a girl, facedown in a pool of her own blood.

"She's cold," Buffy told Xander. "She's been dead for days."

"Poor kid," Xander said. "Made it all the way to Sunnydale just to get herself killed."

Then Buffy rolled the girl over and saw her face. It was Eve.

"Eve, who's in our house?" Xander asked.

They left.

In her living room, Dawn was really wishing Andrew was elsewhere . . . at least tied up and gagged. He was driving her insane, and she was trying to discover more stuff about The First, maybe something that everyone else had missed.

"Okay, here's another interesting thing: How come the Slayer is always a girl?"

"I don't know. 'Cause girls are cooler?"

"I think a guy Slayer would be badass," Andrew said enthusiastically. "Like, like, if there was this ninja, a guy Slayer would be like, 'You may be silent, but this'll shut you up!'" He did a karate move.

"Buffy could stomp ninja ass," Dawn murmured, barely listening.

"The silent warrior? Ha, ha, I think not. She can't even slay that special vampire." Dawn glared at him. He shrugged. "Everyone's saying."

Dawn looked at him coolly. "Well, everyone should shut up. And you should stop pretending anybody here is your friend."

He was hurt, which only compelled him to keep yammering. "And also, why's she so about saving Spike? He's a way worse killer than me by . . . a way lot."

"Spike was being controlled by The First," she explained. "And he has a soul now. Besides, we need his help."

"What about me?" he demanded, squaring his shoulders. "Did it ever occur to anyone that I could be a lot more useful around here? I used to be an evil genius. Hello?"

Dawn got in his face. "And what was your genius thing?"

"Well, um, raising demons mostly." At her smirk, he shrugged and said, "Okay, so, not now, but also there was planning. There were . . . blueprints." Now she glared at him again. "I can be in this, kicking it righteous. Yeah!"

She said evenly, "Buffy said if you talked enough, I'm allowed to kill you."

"Not even," Andrew said timidly.

"Even."

He swallowed, then returned to geek yammer mode. "License to kill, huh?" At Dawn's nod, he said, "Pretty cool. You know, Timothy Dalton never got his props 'cause he came in at the end of an old regime. But he had it goin' on. He went rogue with the Broccolis. They were just treading water stylistically."

Dawn stared in revolted fascination. "Is there a language that you're speaking?"

He lost his groove, then, and went to sit on the couch to sulk. "I'm so alone," he mourned.

"They maybe you shouldn't have killed your only friend."

She walked away as he shot back, "The Slayer's not getting it done. I have got my ear to the ground, and that's the word!" With no response, he added hopefully, as he lay on the couch, "You wanna play 'Kevin Bacon'?"

Then the Slayer burst in—*oops, feet on the furniture!*—and rolled her eyes as she went past him and down the stairs to the basement, Xander following her.

Andrew trailed after as she shouted at one of the Potentials—Eve?—and said, "Get away from them!"

Eve grinned at Buffy. "What's the problem, officer?" she drawled.

Dawn, who had also followed, said, "Buffy, what did Eve do?"

"That's not Eve," Xander announced.

"Eve's dead," Buffy told the group.

They were stunned, backing away from Eve, as Rona said, "I don't . . . I don't understand . . ."

Wow. She's The First! Andrew realized. Then he freaked. *And if she thinks twice about, um, killing me . . . I'll be dead.*

"Whoops, one more down," Eve said cheerily. "Oh, well. Can't save 'em all, can you, Buffy?" She grinned at the Potentials. "Thanks for the slumber party, girls. It's been real fun the last couple of nights. I learned a whole lot . . ."

"Shut up and get out!" the Slayer yelled, enraged.

Eve faced Buffy. "Or you'll do what?"

Buffy went all silent ninja on that one.

"I'll be sending a guest over to visit y'all later on tonight," The First announced. "After the sun goes down, of course." She smiled like the Southern belle she most certainly was not. "Try and make him feel welcome before he rips y'all to pieces. Bye!"

Then she became a long thread of light that winked out in the middle like an old-style picture-tube TV going off.

Andrew was about to wet his pants. So he cleverly covered it up by saying loudly, "I need to go wash up again."

The information the Beljoxa's Eye was imparting to Giles and Anya was doing nothing for Anya's morale.

"It cannot be fought, it cannot be killed," it told her and Giles. "Since before the universe was born, long after there is nothing else, it will go on."

"I refuse to believe that," Giles asserted. "There must be some way to destroy it."

"What, am I talking to myself here? There's no way," the Eye insisted.

Giles pressed. "If The First has been around for all this time, then why hasn't it attempted something like this before? Why now?"

"The opportunity has only recently presented itself," the Eye replied. "The mystical forces surrounding the Chosen line have become irrevocably altered, become unstable, vulnerable." It continued, "The First Evil did not cause the disruption, only seized upon it to extinguish the lives of the Chosen forever."

"Then what has caused the disruption?" Giles asked. "What is responsible for letting this happen?"

"The Slayer," replied the Eye.

Buffy, Willow, Dawn, Xander, and, unfortunately, Andrew, were holding a pow-wow with the Potentials were gathered around the dining room table. The girls were in not loving the lack of a countermove against their invasion by The First.

"We should run," Vi insisted.

"And go where, Vi?" Kennedy asked pointedly.

"Annabelle ran," Dawn observed. "Look what it got her."

"It's safer in than out," Buffy insisted.

"How can you say that?" Molly demanded, staring

at the Slayer. "It was here, Buffy. *In the house.* Living with us for days."

"And you didn't even know it," Chloe added accusingly.

"None of us knew it," Xander argued, which, perhaps not the right thing to say . . .

"It could still be here," Vi said. "It could be any one of us."

Willow spoke up. "No. The First can only take the form of dead people."

"Yeah, well, there'll be plenty more of those soon enough. We're dropping like flies here."

The girls started talking at once, arguing with each other, until Buffy called out, "Hey!"

They stopped, looked at her.

"Look, I know you're all scared. You know what? I am, too, but Giles and Anya will be back soon, and hopefully the will have the information that we need to stop The First. In the meantime, we have to stick together, okay? We're stronger that way. We can't afford to fall apart now."

Andrew stepped up to the table. "She's right," he proclaimed. "Where would the Justice League have been if they hadn't put their differences aside to stop the Imperium and his shapeshifting alien horde?" He crossed his arms as if to say, *Well?*

Buffy gritted, "Don't help me."

Xander hesitated, then said, "Buffy, the sun goes down, and Ubervamp's on its way. A plan would be good about now."

Buffy turned to Willow with an uncertain expression and said, "Will, I'm sorry to ask but . . ."

Willow was tense, but she'd been expecting this for some time. "I know. We need a barrier."

"A major one," Buffy agreed. "Something tells me this vampire doesn't need an invitation to get in the house." She studied the Wicca carefully. "Can you do it?"

Willow said, "I'll try."

"Try?" Rona echoed.

"You heard her," Kennedy shot back.

Xander didn't want to speak in front of the girls, but he said, "You sure about Willow doing the hocus pocus again, Buffy? I mean, last time—"

"We don't have a lot of choices, Xander," Buffy reminded him.

"And what if it doesn't work?" Chloe asked shrilly. "What if that monster gets through?"

There was a pause, and then Buffy said, "Then we'll deal with it."

The girls looked at each other in shock.

"Deal?" Rona asked. "Fight, you mean. How are we supposed to do that?"

Vi chimed in, "And with what?"

"With whatever it takes," Kennedy insisted. She looked at Buffy. "Right?"

Molly was not convinced. "Buffy, you fought the Turok-han. And it almost killed you."

"And you're the real Slayer," Chloe added.

"What chance do *we* have?" Rona asked.

They went on, sinking into defeat, drowning in it . . . and Buffy formulated Plan B. . . .

* * *

Night.

Finally.

Dressed in the guise of the dead Potential named Eve, The First looked over at the Turok-han, who had been eagerly awaiting the word.

"The time has come," Eve said, as above them, darkness fell, "For all good children to say, 'good night.' Take them all," she urged it. "Except for her. Have fun."

Snarling, the Turok-han raced off to enjoy a blood-bath . . .

While Eve turned to Spike and said lustily, "Well. Alone again. I just love having you all to myself."

Night.

Too soon. Way too soon.

The Harbingers of The First continued to congregate on the grounds of the Summers' home. They seemed to be waiting for something, and their presence was terrifying the girls, who were receiving weapons from the Slayer.

"Why aren't they doing anything?" Molly asked. "Attacking?"

"They don't want in," Buffy told her. "They're here to make sure we don't get out."

Swords, spears, a crossbow for Kennedy, who knew how to use it . . .

"Can I have something?" Andrew pleaded. "C'mon. The Turok-han's coming for me, too, you know. I have a right to defend myself." Buffy raised her brows and he added weakly, "If you say so."

She handed him a bottle of holy water, who clutched his only defense possessively to his chest.

Kennedy watched Willow working herself up to do the magics as she murmured to herself, "Facing my fear, I'm facing my fear. . . . Hear that, Fear? I'm facing you. . . ."

She had been holding a votive candle in her palm. Now it levitated, hovering in the air.

"Wow," Kennedy ventured, "you really can float stuff."

The votive plummeted; Willow caught it in her hand.

"Just testing," Willow said shortly.

"Oh, right." Kennedy cocked her head. "Heard this voodoo once turned you into the big scary. Big, scary Willow . . . that's something I'd almost like to see . . ."

Willow turned her head sharply and snapped at her, "No. You wouldn't."

Kennedy pulled back. "I said 'almost.'"

"I needed to make sure," Willow told her. "Last time I tried using magic . . . The First turned it around on me. Got inside. I felt it surging through me." Anxiety coursed through her as she remembered. "In every fiber of my being. Pure, undiluted evil. I could taste it."

After a moment, Kennedy asked, "How's evil taste?"

"A little chalky," Willow told her.

A moment, and then as they walked back into the living room, Dawn called, "Guys? Something's happening."

On the lawn, the Harbingers were parting to make way for the Turok-han, who strode toward the door.

"Here it comes," Buffy said.

It began to beat on the door, growling

It was Willow's cue. She closed her eyes in deep concentration, reaching down to find the power, to wield it . . .

"Caerimonia Minerva, saepio saepire saepsi . . ."

With equal concentration, Andrew murmured, "Um, deflector shields . . . deflector shields up!"

"Willow," Buffy urged.

The door broke, and the Turok-han stood on the threshold.

"Saepio impedimentum!" Willow cried, as her eyes went black.

The Turok-han slammed up against an invisible force field. Enraged, it began to pound violently on the barrier, the impact causing the shield to ripple. With each strike, Willow grunted, her eyes flashing black.

"It's working!" Chloe cried.

"For the moment," Vi said.

Buffy checked in. "Will?"

"It's . . . it's strong," Willow grunted.

"It's hurting her," Kennedy said, as everyone moved back farther into the house.

"Hang on, Will," Buffy said.

The Turok-han pounded at the barrier more feverishly. Willow was beginning to convulse.

Dawn cried, "She can't hold it!"

"What do we do?" Rona shouted, panicking. "What do we do?"

Buffy looked at her, coming to a decision. "Run. Everybody run!"

Xander led the way outside, leading the Potentials, who were carrying their weapons. As Buffy herded everyone along, Kennedy launched into action with her crossbow. Armed with a battle axe, Xander fought hand-to-hand, but he was overpowered. Just as his opponent was about to take him out, Buffy stabbed the Bringer.

The roar of the Turok-han carried over them as the barrier fell.

"Come on!" Buffy said to Xander, and everyone raced away as fast as they could move.

Anya and Giles stepped from the vortex where the Eye lived, windblown and, in Anya's case, limping. They were all right, but Anya was confused.

"I don't understand how Buffy's death mucked up the whole Slayer mojo," she said. "You know, it's not like she hasn't died before."

Giles shook his head. "It's not because she died. It's because she lives. Again." After a pause, he added, "Buffy's not responsible for that."

"Oh." Anya frowned, dismayed. "*Oh*. Willow and me and Xander and Tara. We're the ones who brought Buffy back. We're . . . we're the reason The First is here, the reason those girls were murdered." She took the news like a hit to her solar plexus. "It's our fault. The world would've been better off it Buffy had stayed dead."

* * *

Buffy and everyone else were racing away from Revello Drive, trying to put as much distance between
themselves and the Turok-han.

Xander looked over his shoulder and said, "Okay,
no Harbringers following. I guess they'll save us for
old snaggletooth."

"Willow, take everyone and find a safe location,"
Buffy ordered, as she yanked Andrew's bottle of holy
water from his grasp.

"I know a place," Xander said.

"What are you going to do?" Dawn anxiously
asked her sister.

"Gonna try to slow the Turok down," Buffy told her.
"Lead him away from you guys. Get him to chase me."

Then they were gone, all of them, and she faced
the Turok-han along. It growled as it stood at the end
of the street like a nightmarish gunslinger waiting to
draw.

Then Buffy launched herself at the Ubervamp,
kicking it in the chest. It didn't phase it, but the effort
made her fall to the ground. She got out the holy water,
smashing the bottle against its face. As its flesh burned,
it yelled, and Buffy seized the moment to run.

It began to come after her, and then it stopped.

And then it went in the same direction the others
had fled.

Xander had taken everyone to a construction site. A
huge pit had been excavated. Scaffolding had been
erected everywhere, and Xander exhorted everyone to
climb down for their lives.

Andrew whined, "Climbing's not my thing. I got an inner ear condition."

"Is falling your thing? 'Cause if you don't pick up the pace, I'm gonna come up there and drop your ass."

"Way to keep up morale in a crisis," Andrew sniped. He jumped down. "No wonder Buffy's the leader."

"Some leader," Rona muttered.

Everyone followed Xander around the site to a big open area.

"Future site of the new public library, opening up May 2003. If I ever get back to work, that is."

Rona was incredulous. "You call this a safe location?"

Willow said, "This'll do. Okay, everyone. Spread out, take positions. And don't make a sound."

Rona's voice was shrill. "That's the plan? Spread out? That thing is going to kill Buffy and then it's going to come after all of us. For all we know, it's killing her right now."

Kennedy stared in horror past Rona and said, "Or it could just skip that part and come here."

The Turok-han strode toward them, death in its eyes, its fingers flexing and eager to rip apart little girls who tear like pink paper . . .

Kennedy loaded her crossbow. Molly began to panic.

Suddenly the flood lights surrounded the excavations pit illuminated the pit with an intense glare. And as they all looked up, Buffy stood beside the light, arms crossed, on a ledge.

The girls reacted, asking questions, while Kennedy aimed her crossbow at the Turok-han.

Willow gestured for her to cease and desist.

"It's showtime," the Wicca announced.

She led the group from the pit, and they all climbed the scaffolding. They hung onto the crossbars; Andrew looked as if he were in a state of ecstatic bliss.

Buffy said to the Turok-han. "Looks good, doesn't it? They're trapped in here. Terrified. Meat for the beast, and there's nothing they can do but wait."

She executed a perfect forward somersault into the open area. "That's all they've been doing for days."

She strode toward her enemy. "Having nightmares about monsters that can't be killed. But I don't believe in that. I always find a way. I'm the thing that monsters have nightmares about. And right now I'm going to show 'em why. It's time. Welcome," she said distinctly, "to Thunderdome."

"Two men enter," Andrew murmured reverently. "One man leaves."

And they clashed, the Slayer and the great evil that The First had unleashed upon them. It was brutal, and punishing, the Ubervamp gaining the upper hand almost at once. It rammed her into the ground. She got back up.

He threw her across the pit.

She grabbed Kennedy's crossbow and shot him.

The bolt to his heart gave him only a moment's pause, and then he came for her again.

And again.

A pipe from the scaffolding became a staff for the

Slayer, then a pole to vault away from him.

He followed.

She swung a pickaxe at him, but he ducked . . . and then he pushed her into the construction trailer wall.

And as she battled, Dawn realized that her sister had set this up, concocted a plan with Willow and Xander to bring all the Potentials here so they could watch her take out the Turok-han . . . or die trying. Because Slayers fought; they did not cower. They did not wait to be massacred. They did not spend their days and nights in terror of the end.

They ran out to meet the end, and to survive it.

As her sister fought like the true champion she was, Dawn choked back tears and thought, *If only I could be like that. Be a Slayer like Buffy . . .*

Then eventually, on one of Buffy's assaults, the Turok-han grabbed her by the throat and lifted her off her feet, crushing the air out of her. Buffy's struggles were to no avail.

"It's killing her," Rona said, her Slayer's heart kicking in.

"We . . . we have to do something!" Molly cried.

"Wait," Willow told them.

Then Buffy reached down to the arrow protruding from the vampire's heart, and twisted it. That hurt him; she snapped the bolt in half and plunged the broken shaft into his eyes.

He roared with pain and dropped her. Summoning every last ounce of her Slayer strength, she began to pummel the wounded Ubervamp, dealing it a severe, bone-crushing volley of punches and kicks.

Staggering, the Turok-han tried to fend off the blows, but his wound was distracting him. Buffy pressed her advantage, merciless, driving the super-vampire back where she could bang his head into the metal scaffolding.

Then she grabbed some barbed wire and wrapped it around the Turok-han's neck and pulled with all her strength, garroting him.

Its head was severed from his body, and he exploded into dust.

The Potentials watched in silent awe as Buffy wiped her hands together.

"See? Dust. Just like the rest of them," she said in clear, ringing tones.

They continued to stare.

"I don't know what's coming next," she told them. "But I do know it's gonna be just like this. Hard. Painful. But in the end it's going to be us. If we all do our parts, believe it: We'll be the ones left standing."

She regarded them all.

"Here endeth the lesson."

The Slayer walked away. And The First, as Eve, stood on the scaffolding and glared at her with hatred.

She will come for me, she will come, she will come.

It was the mantra that kept Spike from going completely insane.

And then she was there again with one of those bloody curved knives, and he didn't know what else she could to him, how else The First could torment him . . .

"You can't hurt me. You're just a bloody figment," he murmured.

She moved in and stared to cut his bindings. In her eyes . . . pain, empathy.

It really was Buffy.

It really was.

He began to weep.

Then slowly, she let him lean on her, and they walked away together, out of the cave, out of the nest of vipers . . .

Out of hell.

She had come.

Chapter Twelve: "Potential"

It's about Potential, Buffy thought, as she put the Slayers-in-training through their paces. *And they've all got it. They've got to learn that, know it deep in their bones. Because if I die . . .*

. . . oh, God, don't let me die . . . because they're not ready for that yet.

She watched as Vi and Ron walked through the graveyard, stakes awkward in their hands. A shadowy figure rustled through the bushes, pumping up the volume; the vampire swooped in and pushed Rona to the ground, grabbed Vi, came in the for the kill with his fangs brushing her neck . . . and stopped.

Spike allowed his vamp face to fade away

"Okay," he said loudly, "these two are dead. Why?"

As she wiped the dirt off her overalls, Rona muttered,

"'Cause the black chick always gets it first?"

"What's that, Rona?" Buffy pushed, as Spike gave Vi a little pressure on her arm, making her cry out, "Ow, ow!"

Rona frowned. "I'm dead because . . . he's a vampire. I don't have Slayer strength, Slayer speed. It wasn't a fair fight."

Still with his hold on Vi, Spike asked the redheaded Potential, "Vi, do you think I care about a fair fight?"

"Um, no. No, sir. You don't play by the rules. And I have learned a valuable lesson of some sort. Ow!"

"Okay, Spike," Buffy said. He let go of Vi, who hurried over to Molly, who was taking notes, and Kennedy. "You don't have Slayer strength. But that doesn't mean you're not strong. You have inherent abilities that others do not have."

Molly wrote something on her notepad and said, "Not like you do."

Buffy addressed them all. "No, not yet. But it's there. You have the Potential. You have strength, speed, instinct. You just have to learn to trust yourself." She turned her attention. "Rona, what did you instincts tell you to do just then?"

As if she were reciting from a book, Rona replied, "Block his attack, keep him off balance, gain the advantage . . ." She trailed off.

"No, they didn't." Buffy looked at her, waiting for the truth.

"They told me to run," Rona confessed.

"Don't fight on his terms. Your gut's telling you to

run, run. Okay? Regain the higher ground. Make the fight your own. Spike, what did your instincts tell you to do just then?"

"Hunt," he said without hesitation. "Kill."

Buffy took center stage and said to Spike, "Come at me full speed." To the girls, she said, "He needs to kill to live. That's all you need to know."

Spike vamped, growled, and charged at Buffy. Feinting, she stepped away as if she were going to run, then dropped to the earth. Spike sailed over her, head-first into a tombstone. Buffy straddled him and raised the stake directly over his heart.

"Instinct," she told the Potentials. "Understand him, but trust yours. You were Chosen for a reason."

Spike groaned, and Buffy murmured, "Are you okay?"

He gave her a pained smile. "I'm . . . fine. Couple of ribs ain't quite set right since . . ."

Since he had been tortured by The First. She began to lift his shirt to inspect his ribs. He took her hand, holding it to stop her.

"I'm gonna be okay," he told her.

It was a moment, one of tenderness and sweetness and something acknowledged that wasn't going to go away.

Vi called to her, "Careful, Buffy. Just when you think it's part of the lesson, he'll hurt your arm."

Buffy stood, offering her hand to Spike who rose. "Molly, Kennedy, let's go."

She faced the girls. "Next lesson."

* * *

The Potentials were doing a half-assed job of training, taking some time, and Dawn sat on the basement steps and watched them wistfully. Not too long ago, she was the only girl Buffy was training. Now she didn't merit any training at all.

Buffy had had it with the goofing off—Dawn knew that look in her eye—and Buffy hurled her battle axe at a bull's-eye target on the wall. It landed perfectly in the center, of course.

Startled, the Potentials stopped talking and looked at her.

"You're all gonna die," she announced. "But you knew that already. 'Cause that's the cool reward for being human. Big dessert at the end of the meal. Don't kid yourselves, you guys. This whole thing is all about death."

She stopped walking. "You think you're different 'cause you might be the next Slayer? Death is what a Slayer breathes, what a Slayer dreams about when she sleeps. Death is what a Slayer lives. My death could make you the next Slayer."

She walked to the target to get her axe. "Oh, good. Rapt attention. I love that so much." She yanked the axe free, set it down, and came back to the front of the group.

"If we go with what Anya's resources are telling us, The First is in remission for a while. As best we can tell, he—or precisely, 'it'—was putting a lot of stock in the Ubervamp thing, the Chaka Khan."

"Turok-han," Dawn corrected her.

Buffy went on, ignoring her, pacing as she spoke.

She reminded Dawn of a prowling lioness. "So when I kicked its ass, the whole Firsty circus decided to back off for a while. Good news? Means we probably don't have to worry about it pulling Spike's strings for a while."

She faced the girls. "Here's the half-empty. Time away means time to regroup. And part of that regrouping is coming stronger than ever.

"The odds are against us. Time is against us. And some of us will die in this battle. Decide now that it's not going to be you."

She walked toward them, and, as if to take the sting from her brutally honest words, her voice shifted and became warmer. "I know you're all tired, far away from home, anxious. But you're all special. Most people in this world have no idea why they're here or what they want to do. You do. You have a mission, a reason for being here. You're not here by chance. You're here because you are the Chosen Ones."

She turned from them and came upstairs, tossing off to her little sister, "Dawn, you better hurry up and eat something so you're not late for school."

School. Another world, and yet . . . not so much.

Buffy was on the phone with Xander, who had called to complain about the girls spying on him while he took a shower; she asked about Giles, who was picking up a Potential named Chao-Ahn from Shanghai. And then . . . there was Amanda, the girl who liked to beat on the insecure boys who picked on her.

Amanda was back for more advice. "One of the

boys who picks on me, I kind of . . . see, if a guy picks on you, is it weird to think he's cute? My mom says when a guy teases you, it means he likes you. Is it weird? We're mean to each other, and we like each other?"

"Well, it depends," Buffy ventured. "Sometimes that's how people relate. Being mean to each other. Even mortal enemies . . ." She nodded, getting with the program. "Then with the . . . and that leads to no good, absolutely no good. And with much confusion. A-And then it's over, absolutely seriously definitely over. And that's confusing, too. The over part. Which it is. Over."

Whoops.

Amanda was staring at her in utter bewilderment.

"So, maybe," Buffy said firmly.

The house was a disaster, furniture was now firewood, and there was much dysfunction in the air as Xander, Vi and Rona were shouting and Andrew was practically weeping about the shouting; it was very family, depressingly so.

Buffy was not in a mood to deal with it . . . and she didn't have to, because Willow had news.

"Althenea said the seers located another Potential Slayer here in Sunnydale. Someone that already lives here."

Grouped around the dining room table, the others of the . . . dining room—Xander, Anya, Willow, Dawn, and purely by default, Andrew—cabinet reacted.

Anya groused, "All these girls flocking to town, and this one's already here and under our noses?"

"Wait," Xander put in, "the seers couldn't find out her name or, like, her address or anything? Am I getting the definition of *seer* wrong?"

Buffy was torn. "I was going to take the girls out tonight, a little show and tell, but maybe now I shouldn't."

"They were so excited," Andrew murmured. "You're going to break their little hearts."

"This town is lousy with Bringers," Buffy went on. "I don't want to risk that they find this new girl first."

"No, you should go," Willow assured her. "I can do a spell to find her tonight. I just have to get together a few ingredients. But you . . . you shouldn't skip your training. It's too important."

Buffy looked cautiously at Willow. "Do you think you can handle it?"

"No problemo," Xander assured her.

From the doorway, Dawn reminded her sister, "You guys have more important things to do."

Buffy didn't even acknowledge her as she said, "Okay, I'll take 'em."

The Potentials were all excited about their field trip, choosing weapons, stylin' for the deathdealing, while Dawn put away the leftovers and tried to be a good sport about having to stay home with Andrew.

Kennedy sauntered in and said, "Hey, we gearing up already?"

Dawn was scraping the casserole into the garbage. "Oh, right," she said. "Your little group patrol."

"More than that," Vi said, puffing up like an important puffer fish. "It's an outing."

Kennedy looked excited. "I'm thinking tonight? We might actually get to kill things."

Dawn said shyly, "I've killed stuff sometimes . . ."

But any discussion about that was lost as the Slayer entered in patrol clothing, with Andrew on her heels.

"I am *not* begging," Andrew begged.

Buffy was irritated. "You're like a small dog dancing for Snausages."

He pouted. "You don't want me coming along 'cause you think I'm evil."

"He doesn't seem evil. Exactly," Vi pointed out.

"He's not evil," Buffy said, crossing her arms. "But when he gets close to it, he picks up its flavor like a mushroom or something."

"But I'm reformed," Andrew insisted. "I'm like Vegeta on *Dragonball Z.* I used to be a pure Sayan, and now I fight for the side of Goku." When she shook her head, he whined. "It's not fair. Spike killed people, and he gets to go."

"Spike didn't have free will, and you did."

He sighed. "I hate my free will."

Then Spike strode in, all strength and purpose, and said, "This is where you're all hiding. You ready to go, or what?"

And they trooped out, reminding Dawn of gladiators. Amazons . . .

"You wanna play *Dragonball Z?*" Andrew asked her.

* * *

Later, in the living room, Willow, Dawn, Xander, and Andrew got ready to do Willow's spell to find the Potential.

"Okay, I got my tumbleweed, my eggs, got my chrysalises . . . chrysali? My butterfly transformer pods."

Andrew picked up her snakeskin, making it wriggle as he said, "At you sssservice, Miss Rosenberg, ssssir."

Dawn wondered aloud if she knew the Potential. "Could be the glamazon in gym class. Or my lab partner, Margot, the freak. Boy, I hope not, because she totally fainted right in the middle of our fetal pig dissection."

"Killing pigs is just so wrong," Andrew said feelingly. "And also hard," he added.

"Well, we'll know soon enough who the next Potential is. Somebody's life is about to change," Willow said. "The spell will conjure up this brilliant light, and the light will find the Potential and it'll illuminate her with a glowing aura. I've enchanted this map so we can track her basic location. We'll have to hotfoot it, but I'm betting we find her tonight."

Anya and Xander joined them for the actual ritual. Willow starting throwing the ingredients into the fireplace, reciting her incantation:

> *"To light the aura of the new,*
> *skin of snake and chrysalis too.*
> *To indicate the fresh reborn,*

> *tumbleweed and rosebush thorn.*
> *An egg that means the life to come.*
> *Take this, oh spirit, and my spell is done."*

Immediately the room bloomed with unbelievably stinky glowy orange smell. Everyone started coughing.

"Oh, good God, what is that smell?" Xander cried.

Covering her mouth and nose, Willow said, "The smell will lead us to the Potential."

"Or some poor soul who ate too many chimichangas."

The orange smoke had concentrated into a blob about six feet in diameter that hung and quivered in the middle of the living room. And it hung there. And hung there.

It wasn't working.

"I suck," Willow said, dismayed. "I'm sorry, you guys. Maybe we can figure out something on the computer."

"Good call," Dawn said. "I'll open the door and let this place air out."

Dawn headed toward the front door, unaware that the blob had contracted into a glow and was shooting toward her and *vshoosh!* it hit her hard in the gut like a medicine ball, pinning her to the door. The orange smoke surrounded her, radiating around her like an aura.

"I think it worked," Willow said, stunned.

Oh, my God, Dawn realized. *I am the Potential.*

It took everyone a moment to process the revelation.

Anya said, "One second you're just a klutzy teenager with fake memories and history of kleptomania and now suddenly you're a hero." She realized what that also meant. "A hero with a much abbreviated life span!"

"It makes sense," Willow argued. "I guess. Remember that thing about they share the same blood or whatever?"

"She has to die," Dawn realized, sinking into a chair. "I mean, if I was ever the Slayer, it would mean she died."

Anya said brightly, "Well, it's a lot like being the Pope in that way, except you don't have to be some old Catholic."

Willow said, "I've got to call Buffy. She's going to be so excited."

"No, we can't," Xander reminded her. "She didn't bring a cell phone."

Dawn nodded. "Well, sure, 'cause all the important people are with her."

Xander shook his head and pointed at her. "You are important now."

Dawn was freaking out. "Wh-What happens now? I need to know what happens to my life."

"Well, I guess Buffy trains you," Willow told her.

"Right. I train with the Potentials . . . the other Potentials."

"We also have to protect you from the eyeless guys, the ones with the sharp, sharp knives," Anya put in helpfully.

"Bringers," Dawn said anxiously. "What if they saw the spell?"

"Saw the spell?" Xander echoed. "Dawn, they can't see flashcards. *Big* ones."

"We did a big orange powerful spell. What if they sensed it? What if they're on their way?"

Andrew strolled in, saying, "Are we gonna replace the microwave? 'Cause I was thinking some Orville Redenbacher with fresh butter flavor . . ." He saw the agitation and said, "What's going on?"

"Dawn's going to be a Slayer," Anya announced.

"Holy crap!" Andrew cried. Then he grimaced as Xander yelled at her and said, "Excuse me." He went back into rapture mode. "Pluck from an ordinary life, handed a destiny . . ."

Xander looked sternly at Andrew and pointed an equally stern finger at him. "Say Skywalker, and I smack ya."

"Well, we'll tell Buffy as soon as she gets back," Willow decided.

"Let's not . . . just not right away," Dawn pleaded. "Guys, when Mom appeared to me, she said . . . something about Buffy and I'm just not sure Buffy will be happy for me."

"Of course she will," Willow asserted, like a proud aunt.

"Will she? I mean, I'm not even sure I'm happy for me. Everything is different for me now."

"That's because you're part of something larger," Anya counseled her. "Like being swallowed. By something larger."

Shaky, Dawn rose. "This is too much for my head." She ran upstairs. "I . . . can't. I need to be . . ."

After Dawn fled to her room, Xander said to Anya, "Nice job with the 'getting swallowed' analogy."

Anya said emphatically, "Well, it is a mixed bag, you know. If she gets to be the Slayer, than her life is short and brutal. And if she doesn't, then it smells of unfulfilled Potential."

"It's not like that," Willow argued. "She's part of this huge power. I know what that feels like. It feels wonderful."

Andrew raised his chin, bringing it all home. "It's like, well, it's almost like this metaphor for womanhood, isn't it? The sort of flowering that happens when a girl realizes that she's a part of a fertile heritage stretching back to Eve, and—"

Xander covered his face with his hands, then lowered them and pleaded disgustedly with Andrew, "I'll *pay* you to talk about *Star Wars* again."

Anya stayed on target. "This isn't about womany power. This about the fact that Dawn just might have bought herself an early death."

Willow argued, "We don't know that."

"Right," Xander asserted. "All we know is that everything just changed."

In her room, Dawn stared in her mirror and said, "I'm Chosen."

Why hadn't she felt it before? It was obvious. She could see it in her clear eyes, the way she carried herself . . . the way she climbed out of the window, so freaked out she couldn't think straight.

* * *

The First stop on the Potentials' field trip was a demon bar.

They were astonished. Vi cried, "Like a gay bar only with demons!"

One of the clientele sauntered over to Spike and said, "Spike, long time. Nice of you to bring snacks."

"Touch 'em and lose your privates," Spike warned him.

"Do they card?" Vi asked.

"Nope. Go ahead," Buffy said grandly. "Down all the yak urine shots and pig's blood spritzers you want."

"Gross," Vi managed.

"Got that right," Spike big off. "Prices they charge, you should get human blood straight from the body." He gave the frightened Vi a look and said, "Vampire?"

To the girls, Buffy said, "Look, if I come in here, it's 'cause I have to wring some information out of something large, scary drunk, and with a roomful of friends who don't care much for the Slayer. Remember that. Not a being in here wouldn't be glad to rip your throat out."

Then saggy-baggy Clem rushed up and cried happily, "Buffy! Girl! How ya been?"

They hugged. "You look great!" she enthused. "So toned!"

Kennedy muttered under her breath, "He's ripping out her throat right now."

They yakked about the History Channel; the girls wondered if Buffy had also dated Clem, and then he came up to the girls and said, "So you girls are gonna deal with demons, huh?"

Then he went all Beetlejuice on them, all his wingly dangly ooky flangies sproining from his face. Got the right point across, as Vi gasped, "I could use a shot of that yak urine about now."

Oh, my God, I'm Chosen, Dawn thought as she walked down the street. *Deep inside me, I've got the power. Me, Dawn Summers.*

Then farther up ahead, she saw that weird Amanda chick from school, the one who was in Buffy's office now and then for beating up guys. She had a gash on her forehead, and when Dawn asked her about it, Amanda got nervous about it and said, "Um, I don't think you'd exactly believe me."

Dawn was concerned. Also excited. Here was someone who needed help.

And I can *help. I've got the power.*

"Try me," Dawn urged her.

"I was at school late because of, you know, Swing Choir, and I tore my sweater, you know, the striped ones we wear, and I went by Home Science to sew it up."

"Uh-huh," Dawn urged.

"And by the time I was done, the place was empty. It was sort of all echoy and lonely, and there was this guy . . . or *thing*. And it . . . it scratched me, and I kinda of dodged it, and it kind of hit is head."

Dawn was even more concerned. And more excited. "What kind of thing?"

Amanda anxiously shook her head. "I don't know. It was . . . messed up. In the face. 'Round here abouts."

"She ran her fingers up and down her nose and between her eyebrows.

"And when it scratched you, did it . . ." She took a breath. "Was it scratching with its teeth?"

Amanda gaped at her. "Is it really? Was it really a vampire?" She let out a nervous, slightly loony giggle. "I bet you think I'm crazy."

"I believe you," Dawn said.

"Yeah, well . . . cool." She went on. "The thing is, after it hits its head, I kind of freaked out. I trapped it in a room, and it's still there, and now I don't know what to do."

I do. I am a Potential.

"It's okay," Dawn said aloud. "This is totally dealable. Don't worry."

Amanda hesitated. "Well, I was thinking of getting your sister. I've heard people talking. A lot of 'em think she's some kind of high-functioning schizophrenic."

That made Dawn grin.

"But I also heard that maybe she could help with this kind of thing. Do you think we should go get her?"

"She's out," Dawn informed her. Then, "I'll take this one."

They climbed into school through a window. Dawn pulled a muscle but Amanda was okay.

"Come on," Amanda said. "The vampire's upstairs. Are you spooked out?"

"No," Dawn said. "I—I can do this. It's mostly instinct. I think."

They kept walking. "So, I was thinking, we don't have to kill the vampire, do we? Just suppose he got out and maybe like encouraged toward the gym while the marching band was playing because they look down on the Swing Choir. It might be, you know, funny."

Dawn stared in disbelief, and Amanda chuckled, "I'm just saying."

They finally walked up to the classroom door where Amanda had trapped the vamp.

"Had" being the operate word.

The door swung open, and there was no vamp to be seen.

"Where'd it go?" Amanda asked.

"I don't know," Dawn replied, but we have to get out of here."

Just like a big exclamation point at the end of her sentence, the vampire fell from the ceiling, where he had been hiding, and loomed up a them, fangs at the ready.

Dawn and Amanda ran off screaming; trying a different route. But he was there, in front of them, heading them off. Then Dawn spotted a fire extinguisher, broke the glass . . . and couldn't remember how to make it to a . . .

She threw it at the vamp; knocking him down, but he was up again and so she hit him again, and threw the extinguisher at him.

Then she and Amanda headed back upstairs, Dawn pretty much in a panic.

* * *

Next stop on the Potentials' field trip, one of Sunnydale's twelve fine cemeteries.

"Who can tell us where we are?" Buffy prodded her students.

"It's a nice cemetery," Rona replied.

"How can you tell?" Buffy queried, handing the flashlight to Spike.

Kennedy made a face. "Only a vamp could live like this."

Spike was mildly offended. "Some, yeah. As a group, we're not known for our tasteful décor, but in all fairness to the race . . ." He looked around. ". . . this place is seriously lacking in style."

"He has a point," Buffy said. "Vampires can live anywhere. Anyway they want."

Molly asked Spike, "Where'd you live?"

"What, you mean . . . before?" Off her nod, he said. "A crypt, actually, but nicer. A bit more . . . I don't know if posh is the right word, but it was more like—"

"Comfy," Buffy supplied.

Then she sent them to look around, see what they could find—clues that vamps had been there. After a few moments, they found . . .

"It's a body," Molly said, gaping at the corpse.

Buffy took a look, let go of it. "It's not a body. It's leftovers," she told them.

The body—correction, the vampire—jerked, growled, and glared at Buffy.

Stake in hand, she allowed it to get into battle posture while the Potentials grouped behind her, watching.

"No one's safe. Not here, not ever," she said. "See this guy?"

Kennedy faltered, "B-But he was dead a minute ago."

"That was a minute ago," Buffy said reasonably. "Now . . ." She slammed her fist into his face.

"Hey!" the vampire protested.

"He's the enemy," she continued. He got up and came after her like a shot.

"You can't think too much," Buffy told them. "Reacting's better. Could be the difference between staying alive and that other thing."

She punched the vampire; her stake clattered to the floor and Buffy took him on hand-to-hand. Kennedy moved to help her, but Spike held the Potential back.

"The question's never, 'What do you think?' It's always 'What do you know?' You have to know it. If you don't, if you make one mistake . . ." She trailed off as she hit the vampire hard, and he whammed onto his back on top of the lid of the sarcophagus. When he tried to kick her, she grabbed his foot and slammed her fist into his face. Then, using his leg against him, she flipped him over and threw him off the lid.

The Potentials watched, agape.

"It takes just one vampire to kill you. So you've got to know you can take him. Know your environment. Know what's around you, and how to use it. In the hands of a Slayer, everything is a Potential weapon, if you know how to see it. When you're fighting, you have to know yourself, your brain, your body. Know how to stay calm, centered. Every move is important. Every blow's got to be part of your plan, 'cause you make that one mistake, and it's over. You're not the Slayer. You're not a Potential. You're dead.

"What do you know?" she asked again. "Right now, the only thing you know for sure is you've got me."

She picked up her stake; the vampire leaped at her, kicking her in the face. She ducked, then gave him as good as she got—no, better. Finally grabbing him by his shoulders and throwing him across the crypt.

The she deliberately dropped the stake again and strolled through the crypt doors. Spike closed the doors after her . . . shutting the Potentials inside.

Let the lesson begin.

The vampire lurched toward them.

Dawn and Amada flew down another hallway, found an empty classroom, and raced inside.

"Help! We need to barricade this!" she cried, shutting the door. Amanda grabbed a chair, but Dawn said, "Too small."

Dawn tried to drag a filing cabinet toward the door, and Amanda went to help push.

"Too big," Amanda grunted, but together they succeeded in getting the cabinet pushed up to the door; then, drained, they sank to the floor.

"Stay down," Dawn cautioned.

"Think we're safe?" Amanda asked her.

As if taking that as his cue, the vampire growled

on the other side of the door, pushing the door against the filing cabinet. Dawn and Amanda pushed with their feet, straining to keep him out.

"Amanda?" Dawn said. "We're going to get out of this. Both of us. Alive!" She screamed as the vampire kept trying to force open the door. "Alive! You believe me?"

"I believe you," Amanda managed.

"Good." Dawn's heart raced. Her mind raced. She forced herself to stay calm and think. "'Cause I got a plan." She took a breath. "I'm not guaranteeing it'll work."

"Better than mine about him eating the Marching Band," Amanda said drolly. "Besides, your plan'll work."

"In case you haven't noticed," Dawn confessed, "I don't' know what I'm doing here."

"You're getting it done," Amanda said loyally.

The adults finished processing the changes in Dawn's new life and decided it was time to help Dawn do the same.

But as they knocked on her door, they're was no answer.

"Want me to kick down the door?" Anya offered. "It'd be funny. Besides, she's been sulking in there forever."

Xander turned the knob, discovering that the door was not locked, and pushed it open.

Then they saw the open window and Anya said, "Crap. Double crap."

"Gone," Xander said. "We've got to find her before the Bringers do."

Willow mentally raced ahead, saying, "I can do a locator spell, but we've got to hurry. And find Buffy."

Too late for the plan, too late for anything. The vampire shattered the glass on the classroom door. Through the shower of sparks, Dawn and Amanda got up and bounded away as the vampire knocked over the file cabinet and plunged into the room.

He spotted Dawn, came for her between the lab desks. She backed up, trying to put obstacles between herself and the vamp: lab desk, a chair; she threw empty flasks at him. Nothing slowed him down. Then a beaker with something in it, and as it made contact with his chest, chemical sizzled; smoke rose.

As he winced and looked down, she ran to a classroom flagpole with a California state flag suspended from it. She tried to snap the length of wood across her knee, but it didn't break, just hurt like hell.

She rapped it down on the edge of a lab desk, losing the flag end as she held up her nice, jabbed piece of wood. She slashed blindly at her opponent, then lost her balance at fell on the floor.

Amanda was cowering, terrified, as the vampire pounced on Dawn. Dawn struggled, giving it everything she had, screaming, "Help! Amanda! Help me!"

But the other girl was frozen with terror. "I can't!"

"Amanda!" Dawn shrieked, the vampire's fangs brushing her neck.

Then the windows shattered. Something was coming and Dawn thought excitedly, *Buffy!* Taking advantage of the vampire's distraction, Dawn pushed him away from her with her feet.

Bringers! Now I'm really dead!

The evil-eyed figures brushed past her and went straight for Amanda, who pushed herself against the wall as if to shrink inside it, wild to get away.

"No! You don't want her!" Dawn cried courageously, trying to draw their attention to their true quarry—Dawn, the Potential.

One of the Bringers pulled his curved dagger from his waist as the others came for Amanda, throwing desks out of their way. They were singleminded in their purpose, completely ignoring Dawn. They hoisted Amanda up by the arms.

"You want . . . me," she said in a deflated voice; because it hit her: She was not the quarry.

Amanda was.

Because Amanda was the Potential.

And I have to save her, Dawn thought.

As the Bringers prepared to slice Amanda open, Dawn lit a gas jet on one of the chem tables. A brief explosion knocked the Bringers off their feet, and she picked up her broken flagpole, calling, "Amanda!"

They raced down the hallway, Dawn carrying the jagged spear. Up the stairs they fled, and at the top, Amanda gasped, "What were those?"

Speaking rapidly but clearly, Dawn said, "Amanda, listen to me." She gazed at her. "You know how you said I was special? Well, I'm not."

Amanda wasn't with her. She was still focused on the danger and the terror and her own white fear.

"You're . . ." Amanda finally managed.

"But the thing is, you are," Dawn finished. As Amanda stared at her, Dawn continued, "This is your battle, Amanda."

Amanda shook her head. "No. No! I can't . . ."

"You can," Dawn ordered her. "You've got to."

And then the Bringers were on their way again, seconds away from them.

"I got your back," Dawn said, "but this is something you can do. It's something you were born to do."

From halfway up the stairs, Xander, who was arriving with the rest of cavalry, watched Dawn present a tall girl with brown hair a jagged wooden dowel, and he got in an instant what had gone done. No time for that now. He shouted, "Buffy!"

Buffy and Spike followed him up, but the Bringers were already on Amanda.

And after a couple of uncertain swipes, the power rose up in her veins, the Potential brimming inside her guided her moves, spoke to her of strength. And she began to knock the hell out of her assailants.

Buffy and Spike began stabbing bad guys; then a vampire showed up and went after the Potential. Without thinking, acting on pure instinct, the girl wheeled, pinned the vamp, and stabbed the vampire straight through the heart as if . . .

. . . as if she'd been born to do it.

Buffy dispatched the last Bringer, breaking his

neck, as Amanda turned to Buffy and said in a rush, "One minute I'm in Swing choir, and the next . . . what the hell's going on? You tell me to come to you with problems. Turns out, a vampire attacked me. Problem. So I go to your house, and when I get there, this orange cloud hits me."

Xander was standing next to Dawn; he could see the disappointment etched on her features as she said to him, "She was at the doorway."

"And I don't know if you're into the drugs," Amanda continued, "but that's not my deal, all right? That cloud hit me, and I got a little dizzy and discombobulated."

"It was Willow's spell," Dawn continued. "She's the Potential Slayer."

And the new Potential was welcomed into the charmed circle at the Summers home, sharing her story with the other girls, who were chattering about their big night out with Spike and the Slayer.

Rona was grinning as she said, "I'm sure the vampire thought we were, like, what four helpless girls. And then Vi—Vi actually yells, 'We're just four helpless girls!'"

"That was part of my plan," Vi giggled.

Kennedy rolled her eyes, and Rona went on, more soberly, "When it all started going down, it was like we knew what we were doing. For real."

Molly grew more serious as well, as she turned to Rona and said, "Yeah, like when you dodged that first attack, and then cracked him across the jaw."

"Aw, no, no, no," Rona said modestly. "See, I wouldn't have been able to do that if you hadn't have pulled his legs out."

"I hurt his arm," Vi announced. She nodded, pleased with herself. "Yep. And an arm can be as lethal as a mouth."

Molly said to Kennedy, "When you staked him, seriously, the rush was like . . ."

Kennedy deflected the praise by saying to Amanda, "So, you took one out solo?"

Molly looked at Amanda. "Yeah, what was that like?"

Shyly, Amanda moved her shoulders. "I don't know. I mean, I saw the vampire . . . vamp," she corrected, self-consciously.

"'Vampire' is good, too," Kennedy assured her. The others nodded.

"Cool," Amanda murmured. "Yeah, when that vampire attacked me, I found this kind of charge, you know?"

Kennedy did know. "Like, you realize in one instant that your whole life is different."

"Exactly," Amanda agreed. "It's that rush you're talking about."

"Hey," Buffy said behind Dawn. Dawn brightened and turned to her sister. Xander was there, too. "You okay?"

"Yeah." She nodded. "I . . . was thinking of hitting the books. Do some research on The First. It's in retreat mode right now, but you're still gonna need to know how to fight it," she offered.

Buffy nodded back. "Great. Sounds good." She looked past her sister to the Potentials. "Hey, you guys wanna head downstairs? Get our newest arrival up to speed?"

The Potentials rose and followed their leader. Each passed Dawn and no one looked her way. Except Amanda, all shyness and eager smile, and then she went after the others.

Forlorn, Dawn sat down, opened a book, and began to read. After a moment, she realized someone was watching her. It was Xander.

"What's up?" she asked.

"Aw, I'm just thinking about the girls," he said as he walked into the room. "It's a harsh gig, being a Potential. Just being picked out of a crowd, danger, destiny." He grinned. "Plus, if you act now, death."

"They can handle it," Dawn said, feeling loyal to the girls.

"Yeah." He sat in a chair in front of her desk. "They're special. No doubt. The thing is, not one of them will ever know," he said. "Not even Buffy."

She raised a brow. "Know what?"

His voice dropped its sass as he said, "How much harder it is for the rest of us."

"No way," she protested. "They've got—"

"Seven years, Dawn," he cut in, deadly serious. "Working with the Slayer. Seeing my friends get more and more powerful. A witch. A demon. Hell, I could fit Oz in my shaving kit, but come a full moon, he had a wolfy mojo not to be messed with. Powerful. All of them." He sighed. "And I'm the guy who fixes the windows."

She looked to cheer him up by saying, "Well, you had that sexy army training for a while, and . . . and the windows really did need fixing."

He didn't lose his vibe. He said, "I saw what you did last night."

"Yeah, I . . ." She shook her head, feeling stupid. "I guess I kind of lost my head when I thought I was the Slayer."

"You thought you were all special," Xander countered. "Miss Sunnydale 2003. And the minute you found out you weren't, you handed the crown to Amanda without a moment's pause. You gave her your power."

There's that word again. "The power wasn't mine," Dawn protested.

"They'll never know how tough it is, Dawnie, to be the one who *isn't* Chosen. To live so near to the spotlight and never step in it. But I know." And he did; she could see that. "I see more than anybody realizes because nobody's watching me. I saw you last night. I see you working here today. You're not special." He paused, and his face glowed with pride in her.

"You're extraordinary."

Then he rose and tenderly kissed her on the forehead, and stood to head out toward the front.

"Maybe that's your power," she called after him.

He paused and half-turned to her. "What?"

"Seeing," she said. "Knowing."

"Maybe it is." Then quietly joking, he murmured, "Maybe I should get a cape."

"Cape is good," she replied steadily.

They regarded each other, the not-quites, those who didn't have the power. Their smiles were as sad as they were strong.

Then Xander left the room, and Dawn, tearless, went back to the books on the desk.

Chapter Thirteen:
"The Killer in Me"

It was much with the preparations in the Summers household as Giles prepared to take the Potentials into the desert on a vision quest. He was not pleased about leaving Buffy and Dawn behind, and not shy about saying so.

"Now, you're sure you'll be all right here?"

"You'll only be gone for two days," Dawn pointed out.

"I think we've managed without you for a bit longer than that," Buffy reminded him.

"Right." He gazed coolly at her. "Well, thank goodness I needn't worry myself with the idea of bad things happening in my absence. You getting shot, for example. Or throwing everyone in the basement and trying to kill them. Or Willow turning evil."

"Oooh, don't forget," Dawn piped up. "Anya turned evil, too."

Buffy turned, stared at Dawn, not amused. She turned back to Giles.

"Okay, just leave."

Giles glanced over and saw Vi's notebook, said, "Dawn, Vi left her notebook next to the TV. Would you mind taking it out to her in the car?"

"Sure." Dawn picked it up and headed for the front door.

"And maybe whack her in the head with it as a reminder not to leave it lying all about?" Giles added.

"On it," Dawn sang.

She left, and Giles turned to Buffy.

"I'm just a bit twitchy about leaving you alone again with things in such a state of flux."

"I know," she said, but you should go. It's important for the girls to understand the source of their power, and to know how to use it."

"Do you think they understand the gravity of what we're undertaking?" Giles asked Buffy. "It's frightening, and it's difficult. And apparently, someone told them that the vision quest consists of me driving them to the desert, doing the hokey poky until a spooky Rasta-mama Slayer arrives and speaks to them in riddles." He gave Buffy his patented Giles Look.

Buffy went for wide innocent eyes as she prevaricated, "That's not exactly how I put it." Then, as Willow came into the room, "Hey, how's Kennedy?"

"Still flue-y," Willow told her. "Bummed about missing the field trip," she added. Then, to Giles, she said, "She says you she wants you to meditate extra hard for her and to bring her back some s'mores."

Giles looked martyred as he sighed, "Ah, yes, s'mores." He looked at Buffy. "I'm going to end up singing campfire songs, aren't I?"

Then Xander came in with a weather report from the car—the girls arguing over who got to drive first, since Giles had let his California license lapse: Molly jumped into the trunk; the car horn blaring. It was like the old days when Buffy was fifteen and Giles was already world-weary of parenting an impetuous young Slayer . . .

Buffy went down to the basement after Giles left, to visit with Spike. The vampire had insisted upon being chained up in his spot as before, and he sat on his cot, now, smiling as they talked about the glories of being free of the kids.

"Gives us all a chance for a breather, eh?" he observed. "From the constant pitterpatter of clomping teenage girly feet?"

Buffy shrugged and said, "No, I enjoy my responsibility as mentor, role model, life guide . . . oh my God, I cannot believe I have my bathroom all to myself for two whole days," she finished, flopping down beside him. "Have you seen the kitchen since they've been here?"

"I'm just trying to stay out of their way."

She regarded the chains. One hung across his back; he was manacled. It was not without some . . . allure. "I've noticed."

"This is better," he said. "Believe me, it's safer."

She shrugged. "Okay, but you've been fine."

He looked at her hard. "With you by my side, yeah. And that's the way it's gonna be until we're sure The First is done making me its bitch. Either we're together, or I'm on the leash."

"We just need to make sure the trigger's deactivated then. We've got a couple of days, lack of pitter-patter and all."

Spike leaned forward and gazed earnestly at her. "Buffy," he said. "Ow."

"Ow?" she echoed, puzzled.

His face contorted, twitching. "Ow, ow, ow!" He leaned back, thrashing against the wall.

"What's wrong?" she cried, as Buffy pressed his hands to his head, clearly in pain. "Spike, what is going on?"

"The chip," he groaned. "God. Why would . . ." And then he screamed and writhed in agony.

Upstairs, Willow was making tea for Kennedy, and she looked at Buffy as the Slayer came upstairs. Buffy was ragged.

"Hey," Willow said by way of greeting. "How is he?"

Buffy sat wearily. "Oh, in the 'goes' part of 'comes and goes.'"

"Well, there seems to be a definite lack of screaming," Willow ventured. "That's good."

"You'd think." She indicated the tea that Willow was brewing. "That for the other patient?

"Yeah." Willow's features softened. "Thought I'd bring her some tea, help her feel better." At Buffy's teasing smile, Willow murmured, "It's just tea."

Buffy chuckled. Then she said, "Will, how much do you know about Spike's chip?"

"Spike's chip?" Willow thought. "Well, I remember trying to dig up stuff back then but you know, turns out when a secret government agency studies vampires and puts chips in their brains that keeps them from hurting people, they don't really build Web sites. Why?"

Buffy was concerned. "Even with the chip, Spike was able to hurt all those people when he was brainwashed."

"Yeah, but he was under the control of The First," Willow argued.

"Maybe something's wrong with it," Buffy said.

"The chip is misfiring all on its own, then," Willow said slowly. "Well, this'll be fun."

Buffy looked at her wryly. "Remember when things used to be nice and boring?"

"No," Willow deadpanned. Then she walked out of the kitchen with the cup in her hand.

"Have fun," Buffy called after her. "Delivering tea."

"Okay, not when you make it sound all dirty like that," Willow mumbled as she went upstairs. "It's just tea."

But the not-so-English patient was not lying in bed retching with flu. She was getting dressed.

"Hey," Willow began, "I figured the best thing for a cold is a nice hot cup of . . . boots?"

"Hey," Kennedy said, not so embarrassed at being busted.

"For someone who's sick," Willow observed, "you look surprisingly dressy." She was shocked. "You were never sick!"

"No," Kennedy said, still without the contrition. "I was never sick."

"Oh, you are so busted," Willow said. "Xander's going to have to drive you to the desert, and—"

"Willow, chill." Boots laced, she stood. "There's a reason I didn't go. I have a thing. A separate thing." She put on her coat. "Something's coming down. I have my own mission. And I need your help."

So Willow helped her . . . to the Bronze.

Band playing, boozy drinks with the little umbrellas and cherry garnishes . . . it was almost like a date.

Which Willow finally got, and, sighing, got ready to go. She was not equipped for playing hooky during an apocalypse . . .

"Come on, come on," Kennedy urged her. "Just hang out with me a little."

Willow weakened, just a little.

"You're sexy when you pout," Kennedy told her.

"Why do you do that?" Willow asked, a little sharply.

With a sexy pout of her own, Kennedy said, "To get you to stay."

Willow caved. "All right. I'll stay for one drink. Then I'm going home."

Brightening, Kennedy agreed to the terms of

surrender. "Okay. One drink. I can work with that." She settled in. "Let's start with the easy stuff. How long have you known that you're gay?"

Willow sputtered. "Wait, that's easy? And you just assume that I'm—presume much?"

Kennedy smiled, amused. "Okay. How long have you enjoyed having sex with women?"

Willow was astonished. "Hey! Do you think you have some special lesbidar or something?"

"Okay, you know there's a better word for that, right? You really haven't been getting out there much, have you?" Kennedy asked her.

A bit ruffled, Willow said, "Well . . . can you always tell, just by looking at someone?"

"That wouldn't be any fun," Kennedy said coyly. "The fun part is the process of getting to know a girl. It's like . . . flirting in code. It's using body language and laughing at the right jokes and looking into her eyes and knowing she's still whispering to you, even when she's not saying a word. And that sense that if you can touch her just once, everything will be okay for both of you. That's how you can tell. Or if she's really hot . . . you just get her drunk."

Willow flushed, pleased. "Three years ago," she said. "That's when I knew. And it wasn't women. It was woman. Just one."

"Lucky woman," Kennedy said simply.

Buffy went back to check on Spike, who was lying on his cot with his head on a pillow. His nose was bleeding and his eyes were bloodshot. He looked awful.

"Popped another blood vessel, I think."

She grabbed a towel and wiped blood from his nose, watching him soberly, as she said, "There's got to be a reason why the chip is going all wonky. Maybe it's related to the trigger or maybe it ahs something to do with the new soul . . .

"Or maybe it wasn't meant to last this long." He gazed at her. "One more thing you and I have in common, eh, pet?"

She gave him the small reaction he wanted, then said, "Well, we'll fix it. We'll hit serious research mode . . ."

"Good. Try 'Behavioral Modification Software Throughout the Ages,'" he quipped.

She sighed. "Okay, you're right. Not a book thing. It's a phone thing."

"Who you gonna call?" Spike asked her, then, "God, that phrase is never gonna be useable again, is it?"

"Doubt it," she said.

They went upstairs and Spike sat on the stairs, listening as she dialed a number and started talking to some bloke about him.

"Tell him we're having a problem with Spike's chip. No, his chip. Spike."

Spike shook his head. "Listen, pet . . ."

"No, no," she said into the phone. "Finn is his last name. Yeah. Well, did he used to work there and then he got transferred? Is this actually a flower shop, or is this one of those things where I'm supposed to play along and show that I know it's really secret ops? Oh, maybe I shouldn't have said that."

Unbeknownst to her, the chip misfired again, sending Spike into paroxysm of pain.

"Okay well, I guess if some guy named Finn shows up to buy flowers . . . right. Thanks."

She hung up. "Wrong number. Or a giant government conspiracy . . ."

She turned and saw the aftermath of another powerful spasm splashed across Spike's face.

This one seemed easier than the others," he told her. "See? Probably just gonna fade . . ." He screamed, holding his head.

Kennedy asked Willow, "Do your parents know?"

"Yeah. My mom was all proud like I was making some political statement. Then the statement mojo wore off and I was just gay. She hardly even met Tara. We're private." She paled. "Were."

Kennedy reminisced. "It was *Gone with the Wind*. I saw that, and I knew I wanted to sweep Scarlet off her feet."

"You were five," Willow said, busting her.

Kennedy grinned. "Well, I'm not saying the sweeping would have been easy." She smiled and popped her maraschino cherry into her mouth. "What?"

"I just . . . I still don't get it." She moved her shoulders. "Why you like me. I mean, you don't even know me."

Kennedy was incredulous. "Have you seen you? Willow's cheeks reddened.

"And we like the same things," Kennedy continued. "Italian, skate punk, Robert Parker mysteries, fighting evil . . ."

"I don't like any of that stuff," Willow countered. "Except the fighting evil part. And even then, I'd prefer a nice foot massage."

"Okay." Kennedy got real. "I dig the way you always turn off the *Moulin Rouge* DVD so it has a happy ending. I like the way you speak. It's interesting. And your freckles. Lickable. I'm not so into the magic stuff. It seems like fairy talk crap to me, but if it matters to you . . . you care about it, so it's cool."

Willow looked down, enjoying it all.

Enjoying it very much.

Okay, a couple more umbrellas, and then they were back in the homestead, roommates but not like that, and Willow was a little tipsy. As she turned into her room, she slurred a little, "Well, this is my stop." She turned on the light and added, "So. Glad we talked."

Kennedy boldly came in with her. "Yes. Kinda cleared the air."

Willow nodded sagely. "Yeah. Totally. Air cleared. Check."

Then Kennedy moved in slowly, gently . . . for a kiss. Her lips touched Willow's slowly, passionately . . . and Willow was taken aback by Kennedy's reaction to their kiss. "Are you okay?" She laughed anxiously. "I'm not used to literally knocking girls off their feet with just the power of my own lips."

"What are you?" Kennedy demanded.

Perplexed, Willow crossed to her mirror . . . and saw Warren, the guy she'd flayed alive, staring back at her.

She rushed downstairs with Kennedy and raced into the living room, where Xander, Anya, and Dawn were seated. They jumped to their feet and Xander shouted, "Get Buffy! Tell her The First is back!"

"No, I'm not The First! I'm Willow!"

Then Andrew walked in, dropping his bowl of food. And as Willow protested that she was not Warren, he said firmly, "No more listening. I know who you are now. I know what you made me do. Your promises of happy fields and dancing schnauzers and being demigods won't work on me any more."

"Buffy!" Anya yelled. And when the Slayer came into the room, she punched Willow in the nose.

"Ow!" Willow cried.

"Wait," Anya ordered. And everyone did . . . because Buffy should not have been able to hit The First. It could not assume solid form.

"You're back!" Andrew said, smiling, and hugged Warren from behind, his hands touching Warren's chest . . . which was, for Willow . . .

"Bad touching!" she cried. Then she said, "Everyone please stop it. I'm Willow."

"Are you sure?" Xander asked suspiciously.

She walked slowly, head held up. "There are other stories from kindergarten. Non-yellow-crayon stories in which you don't come out in such a good light. An incident involving Aquaman Underoos, for example. You want me to start talking?"

"Hey, *Willow*!" Xander said, smiling as he rushed up to her.

As everyone gathered around, Anya asked, "What happened?"

"I don't know," Willow replied, "but I probably brought it on myself. I have a history with my witchy subconscious making things go kerfloopey."

Everybody started touching her, which made her twitchy. Buffy said, "Okay, say you're right, and you did do this to yourself. Why would your subconscious turn you into Warren?"

Willow raised her brows. "Obviously because I feel bad about killing him."

Then Spike had another misfire, and as Buffy was distracted by his agony, Willow said, "I'll handle it. I'll fix it. I'll be back before you even know I'm gone."

She walked out the front door. As the others gathered around Spike, Kennedy slipped out after her.

Then she caught up with Willow and said, "Okay, safe to say no one will ever accuse you of being too butch."

"Kennedy, go home," Willow said firmly.

"If you take a step back, serious, there's a certain element of humor here." As Willow froze, turned, and stared at her, Kennedy said quickly. "Well, a really big step."

"I killed him. It's hard to see the chuckles," Willow said.

"So, you got a plan?" she asked.

"Yeah, get some help reversing it," Willow told

her. "I'm going to see some old friends of mine. It's been awhile, but maybe they can help."

Old ghosts, Buffy thought, as she and Spike moved through the woods. *This place is filled with them.*

"Are you sure you want to go back in this place with me?" Spike asked her.

"Eh, nothing good on TV tonight," Buffy ventured. She found the place they were seeking beneath the bushes and the dirt. "You think the stuff's still good?"

He dug through the dirt with her. "Worked pretty good when the Initiative held me captive here. Every time I'd get a little . . . rambunctious, the chip would kick in. I'd feel like my head was going to explode. They'd dope me up, and everything would be all daffodils and teddy bears. For a couple of hours, anyway."

"Maybe we should search for files and stuff," Buffy said. "Find out everything we can about the chip. Shelf life."

"I'll take whatever I can get," Spike said flatly, grabbing the chain to the grate.

They pulled together, hoisting up a metal grate. Then they both jumped down into the exposed shaft.

They had just reentered the Initiative complex, years after the government guys had said they had poured concrete into it and sealed it up.

It reeked of death . . . they had left the dead behind, both human and demon. Buffy gritted, "I'm thinking brief stay."

Then they found the door to the med lab, and Buffy walked in first. The room was bathed in a dull red light. As they walked through slowly, they heard something shuffling around.

But when they aimed their flashlights to investigate, there was nothing there.

Back at Buffy's house, the phone rang and Andrew leaped to get it.

"I'm supposed to get a call when the new *League of Extraordinary Gentlemen* comes in," he said excitedly.

"Ooh can you see if you can get two?" Xander enthused; then, realizing that he had once again crossed the line into nerdonia, gritted at Andrew, "Loser."

But Andrew was not getting news about the L.E.G.; he was speaking to a W.A.T.C.H.E.R.

Named Robson.

Xander took the phone from him, listened, and then debriefed the others. Giles had been to see Robson, and as he was trying to help him, a Bringer attacked . . .

"Robson blacked out," Xander went on. "But the last thing he remembers is Giles's head about to get really familiar with a Bringer's very sharp axe."

They stared at each other. They had been dealing with The First, who could take on the visage of any dead person it wished to . . .

"Because if you want to infiltrate the inner circle of the Slayer," Xander began.

". . . become the one person she trusts more than anybody else," Anya finished.

"But there's no way we can know," Dawn piped up.

"Actually, that's not true," Andrew reminded them. "The First can't take corporeal form, so it can't touch anything."

"Oh, it's not like Giles hasn't touched anything, right?" Anya did a mental review and looked a bit uncertainly at everyone else. "Has anyone seen Giles touch anything since he got back? Hold anything? Has anyone hugged him?"

She was very serious, very scared. "Think very hard!"

They each ran through all their observations and interactions with Giles. Exchanged a look; faces paled; no one could remember a thing.

He asked me to take Vi's notebook to the car, Dawn remembered. *Was it because he couldn't?*

Pale and worried, Xander stood and walked toward the door. Anya and Dawn followed, and Andrew trailed after.

"Wait!" he cried. "Where're you . . . ?"

"The desert," Xander said grimly. "We're going to find Giles."

"Oh, good," Andrew enthuses. "Let me just get some tapes for the car. I've been working on this mix—"

"You're not coming," Xander said.

"What? Why?" Andrew demanded. "'Cause I used to be evil?"

"No, actually, 'cause you're annoying, but that's a good reason, too," Xander shot back as he turned toward the door.

"Wait! Don't leave me here. I keep getting attacked in this house."

"Actually, Xand," Dawn said in a maybe-he-has-a-point voice.

"If you leave me here alone, I'll do something evil, like burning something or gluing things together."

"For crying out loud, Harris, let's just take him," Anya said. "At least we can keep an eye on him."

So Andrew got to go.

Deep within the Initiative complex, Spike and Buffy heard the rustling sound again, followed by a scraping sound. They stopped and moved into defensive posture, scanning for it.

"Think something survived?" Buffy asked Spike.

"Sounds like," Spike replied.

Something moved behind them. They turned to look, but saw nothing there. Walked on.

Then something attacked Buffy. She dropped her flashlight as she fought with it. It was a demon, and Spike joined in . . . and then the chip misfired again.

"Not now!" He grabbed his head and fell to the floor.

The demon dropped the Slayer and went for the vampire, grabbing him by his heel and dragging him out of the room.

As soon as she could pull herself together, Buffy followed after with her flashlight in hand.

Then it pounced on her. She grabbed a shovel and swung hard. In retaliation, it threw her across the room. She kicked it away with her feet. Then she slammed the shovel into its chest and the monster collapsed to the floor.

"Spike, are you still with us?" she asked.

"Yeah," he managed.

"That, guys, was . . . just the beginning," she said, as the lights blazed on the room . . . and half a dozen army guys trained their rifles on them.

"Miss Summers," said one of the soldiers. "Agent Finn reported that you tried to contact him today."

"I knew it!" she cried. Then she whispered to Spike, "Government conspiracy."

The soldier made a soldierly gesture and the other army guys lowered their weapons. "We're to provide you anything you need to help assface here," he continued. "Those were his exact words, ma'am."

They took him to an examination room. Buffy paced, waiting to find out what was wrong, when the solider finally came up to her with the diagnosis.

"Med team tells me they took a look at the chip. You were right," he told her. "It's degraded. Leave it as it is much longer, it'll be fatal to him."

No. No, not what I wanted to hear.

"Agent Finn said it was your call, ma'am," the soldier continued. "All decisions regarding Hostile 17 are to be left in your hands. The chip—we either repair it, or remove it."

Not what I even thought of hearing.

What should I do?

With Kennedy in tow, Willow did another locator spell and found the campus Wicca group. They were sitting in a circle, candles lit before them, glowing crystal pendants dangling around their necks.

The High Priestess was praying, but Willow blurted out, "Okay, wow, this is new."

The women looked at her. Willow shuffled and said, "Oh, hey, I'm sorry. Willow. We actually met when I was a freshman." She made a face. "And also not a boy." She gestured to Kennedy and said, "This is Kennedy."

"You're Willow?" the High Priestess said in disbelief.

"Yeah. Wow, look at you guys. Campus Wiccans. Guess you got past the whole bake sale phase."

"Um, no, we still do that, too. Second Tuesday of every month. I'm . . . I'm kind of having a hard time with the whole guy event thing."

Then a member of the circle spoke up. "It's actually her. I can tell. I know her."

Willow was stunned. It was Amy. Formerly Amy the daughter of a witch whom Giles, had sent into a cheerleader trophy; later Amy, who accidentally had been turned into a rat. And later still, Amy, Willow's enabler when she got hard into the black magics . . . and whom she had asked to stay away, forever, if possible.

Amy began to make amends in a rush. "I wanted to come find you and tell you that I was here working on things with these guys. And that they're good. And that I'm sorry. But you're here, looking like, wow, how did this happen?"

"I got hit with, like, this glamour thing, and I can't seem to shake it myself. I was hoping someone here might be able to help."

Amy said, "We'll try."

They made a circle, and as Willow held a crystal, Amy led with a spell: *"Give back the form the soul requires. See that the balance is put right."*

The crystal glowed and heated, and Willow dropped it as she screamed.

Startled, Amy got to her feet, blurting out, "It didn't work?"

"No, it didn't, you dumb bitch!" Willow yelled. Then she hauled off and slapped Amy across the face.

"Willow!" Kennedy cried.

"You slapped me!" Amy said, gasping.

"No. I didn't. It wasn't me." She felt sick, terrified. "It was Warren."

She raced out of the room, terrified, Kennedy on her heels.

"It's not a trick," Willow despaired. "It's not a glamour. I'm becoming him. A murderous, misogynist *man*. Do you understand what he did? What *I* could do? I killed him for a reason."

"Getting angry isn't helping," Kennedy pointed out. "We can still try to—"

"You understand nothing about magic," Willow flung at her. "In case you hadn't noticed, our little date? It's over."

She stalked off, creating a magical barrier to keep Kennedy from following.

There is friction in the space between us. . . .

Much tension in Xander's car as they barreled through the night. Andrew wanted to play Ghost, and everyone else wanted to kill him.

"If this is The First, and I'm not saying it is," Anya began, "what're we expecting to find?"

"He didn't bring them out here to meditate," Xander said tersely.

Andrew said to Dawn, "Kinda makes you grateful you weren't a Potential after all, doesn't it? Safer."

"Not so fast with the big 'phew,'" Anya said.

Xander was hunched behind the wheel. "He might know we're coming."

Anya took that in. "Which means we're already too late, and we're heading out to the middle of nowhere . . ."

"With no Slayer," Dawn said anxiously, "no powerful witch . . ."

"Just a teenager, a powerful former demon, and two big geeks," Anya finished.

As Willow struggled to keep herself intact she wept, sinking down on the ground and then . . . there was no friction in the space, and Warren stood up, disgusted, saying, "Look at me. Crying like a little girl."

He strode down the street.

He had a gun to buy . . .

As Giles had dreaded, there were, indeed, s'mores and campfire songs. And now his charges were asleep, but he had decided to stay up and stand guard . . .

And then he was attacked—tackled and thrown to the ground.

"Touch him! Touch him!" one of his assailants shouted. It was Xander, of all people.

And then Dawn, grabbing him by the shoulder and saying, "Oh, I feel him, I feel him."

"I feel him, too," Xander said, feeling his chest.

"Me, too. Good Lord, that was Andrew, touching his leg!

Giles said, "We all feel each other. Including some of us who don't know each other well enough to take such liberties, thank you." He gave Andrew a look. "And I assume there's a perfectly reasonable and not at all insane explanation here."

Anya said helpfully, "We thought you might be non-corporeal evil."

"We got a call," Dawn added in. "We couldn't remember you touching anything."

"We had to make sure you were okay. We were worried," Xander concluded.

"Oh. That's very sweet." He pondered a moment, then added, "Now wait a minute. You think I'm evil if I bring a group of girls on a camping trip and I *don't* touch them?"

Kennedy went back to the Wicca room. Everyone had cleared out except Amy.

"It was too creepy, even for us," Amy explained. "You're really worried about her. She's going to be fine, really. She's good at this. She's strong. She's dealt with a lot worse." She smiled at Kennedy. "Long before she ever went out and found herself a big old Potential Slayer bodyguard, okay? Just have a little faith in her."

Kennedy stared at the witch. Then she said slowly, "I never said I was a Potential Slayer."

Amy was all innocence as she replied, "Oh, no, I think you did. When you first got here . . . you told us."

"No, I didn't." Kennedy advanced on Amy. "How did you know who I was?"

Amy smirked at her and said, "Oops."

Kennedy was furious. "Tell me why you did this to her," she demanded, getting into Amy's face. But the witch performed a magic charm and sent Kennedy flying away.

"Just your standard penance malediction." Putting it more simply, she said, "I put a hex on her."

"But why Warren?" Kennedy pushed. "And why did it happen after we kissed?"

Amy smiled broadly. "You? Oh, that's rich. Must have been some kiss. You must be good."

"Answer me!"

"The hex I cast lets the victim's subconscious pick the form of their punishment. It's always better than anything I come up with."

"Undo it. Let her out," Kennedy ordered her.

"Okay," Amy said breezily. "Oh, wait, I forgot. No."

"Why would you do this to her?" Kennedy demanded. "You really hate her that much?"

Amy drew herself up. "This isn't about hate. It's about power."

Kennedy blinked, and Amy continued.

"Willow's always had all the power. Even before she knew what to do with it. It came so easy for her. The rest of us, we had to work twice as hard to be half as good. But no one cares how hard you work."

She shook her head. "They just care about cute, sweet Willow. They don't know how weak she is—she gave into evil, stuff worse than I could even imagine. She almost destroyed the world! But everyone just keeps on loving her.

"So what's wrong with having a little fun? Take her down a peg or two."

"Fun?"

"Hey, I'm not the bad guy here," Amy protested. "I wonder where he'd be right about now?"

She waved her hand . . . and Kennedy was in the back yard of the Summers residence, just as the sun began to rise . . .

And Willow stood before her, very shaky, and holding a gun.

"You think you can just do that to me?" she shouted. "That I'd let you get away with it?"

Her gaze on the gun, Kennedy said calmly, "Okay, let's not get excited."

"It's too late!" Willow cried. "This is what I am. I made it happen, and I'll make it stop!"

"Willow," Kennedy pressed, ever so gently, "what did you make happen?"

Willow waved the gun, losing control. "You were there, bitch! You saw it! I killed her!"

She means Warren, Kennedy realized. "You mean 'him,'" she corrected.

"Him! Her! You know what I mean!"

"But you said 'her.'"

"No," Willow said, for a moment herself, though

still on the verge of completely breaking down. "That was Warren . . ."

"No. No, it wasn't," Kennedy insisted. "You said I was there. Who did you kill, Willow?"

"It was your fault. Slut! You tricked me! Got me to forget!"

Kennedy understood. "Tara . . ."

"Shut up!" Willow raged. "Shut! Up! You do not get to say her name! Offering it up to whoever's there. Tricking me into kissing you . . ."

She stopped, confused. "I . . . I can't hold on . . . He's winning."

Willow lowered the gun, scared. "I'm being punished. I kissed you, just for a second, but it was just enough.

"I let her go," she grieved, tears rolling down her cheeks. "I didn't mean it."

Kennedy shook her head. "Kissing me didn't mean . . ."

"No, she was never gone, she was with me. We should have been together forever . . . and I . . . I let her be dead. She's really dead. And I killed her."

Shattered, she sank to her knees, sobbing, "Oh, baby, I'm so sorry, don't leave me again; come back. I'm sorry. Come back . . ."

Kennedy came to her, terrified.

"Willow," Kennedy said. "I don't think you did anything wrong. This is just magic. And I think I'm figuring the whole magic thing out."

She closed the space between them, saying, "It's just like fairy tales."

"What are you doing?" Willow asked.

Kennedy's gaze was filled with sympathy, empathy, and all the love in the world . . .

"Bringing you back to life," she said.

And her kiss was for Willow, for all her pain and her grief and her loveliness and her splendor; and it was for Tara, who was not gone and never would be. In that kiss, she was restored forever, to her Willow, her dear, darling Willow . . .

Kennedy broke the kiss, and gazed at Willow.

"Hmm, I *am* good," she murmured.

Warren's face was gone. Willow was Willow again.

"It's me? I'm back?" Willow asked hopefully.

Kennedy nodded, and Willow swayed with relief.

"Oh, God."

"You all right?" Kennedy asked.

Willow glanced up at the bedroom window . . . at the smile there, at her girl . . .

"I have no idea," Willow confessed.

She laid her head on Kennedy's strong shoulder. Together they walked back to the house.

"I'm so tired," Willow murmured.

And Kennedy replied, "I'll make you some tea."

Chapter Fourteen: "First Date"

Giles had brought the Potentials back from the desert, including the newest one Chao-Ahn, and as they patrolled through one of Sunnydale's cemeteries he was explaining to them all how he had managed to survive the Bringers' attack back in London—the same attack that had felled his colleague, Robson.

"It was extraordinary good luck, of course," he said with typical British modesty. "And training. Years of training." To the new girl, he said, "Chao-Ahn, keep up. You're new here, Chao-Ahn, so take note. Remember about the training. But I honestly feel the largest part of it was instinct. Instinct and reflexes. There's a sort of watchfulness I've developed over the years. It's like another sense—"

And from out of nowhere, completely catching the watchful Watcher by surprise, Spike tackled him and threw him to the ground.

"Spike!" Buffy cried, as both Watcher and vampire shouted, "Hey!"

"You're not in pain," Giles said with astonishment.

"You're not The First," Spike said in like fashion.

"What?" Giles demanded.

"Anya said you were The First," Spike told him. "Said you were evil. You're supposed to be all go-through-able." He stood and walked over to Buffy.

Giles stood as well, regaining his composure as he said, "Then what the hell did you tackle me for, you berk? What's that supposed to do?"

Spike was abashed. "I, uh, didn't think of that."

"More importantly," Giles continued, "you just hit me. Why didn't your chip go off."

"Yeah, well . . ." Spike looked down.

Buffy stepped up to the plate. "Well, uh, when we were the Initiative . . ." She glanced at Spike, who looked back at her.

"There was a choice . . ." he ventured.

Buffy turned her attention back to Giles. "Right." She bobbed her head. "Either repair the chip, or to remove it."

Giles was astounded. "You . . . had it removed . . . *you removed the chip*?"

"Yeah." Buffy went for innocent voice, innocent tone.

"Had to make a choice," Spike chimed in.

"It really is okay," Buffy assured Giles.

"What's a chip?" Amanda piped up.

"They removed the chip?" Kennedy put in.

In Chinese, the new Potential, Chao-Ahn, said, "I don't understand a word any of you are saying."

Buffy was accessorizing for school—V-necked red sweater, big good hoop earrings. *Lookin' okay.*

"You know this is very dangerous," Giles said, stopping in the doorway, watching her.

"Ah, you just heard the horror stories," she said as she put the post on the back of the second hoop. "Wear hoops, they'll catch on something, rip your lobe off. Lobes flying everywhere." She cocked her head. "You mean Spike not having a chip. Free range Spike?"

He did. "I have to ask. Why on earth did you make that decision?"

She shrugged. "I guess it was instinct, like you were talking about."

"I made that up!" He walked into the room. "I knew the Bringer was there because his shoes squeaked." He perched on the edge of her dressing table and gazed at her with real concern. "Buffy, it's crucial that we keep these girls safe. I can't count the dangers. The First, the Bringers, random demons, and now Spike."

"And the Principal," she added helpfully.

"*What?*" he demanded.

"He was in the school basement, holding a shovel, acting evasive. Plus he's got that whole 'too charming to be real' thing going on. I'm looking into it."

He rose and said dryly, "Oh, well, that sounds very responsible of you. Balances out the vampire-on-the-loose issue."

She rose as well and walked across the room, started folding laundry. "Nothing's changed, Giles. Spike had a chip before, remember? When The First had him kill all those people?"

"We have no idea if his chip was working then," he said, then took off his glasses, a sign that he was quite stressed, weary, and flummoxed. "A new chip might restrain him should The First attempt to activate him again."

"Spike has a soul now," Buffy arguing, facing him. "That's what's gonna stop him from hurting people."

"Buffy . . ." Giles began.

"He can be a good man, Giles. I feel it. But he's never going to get there if we don't give him the chance."

She walked to her closet to put away the clothes. He came up behind her and said, very seriously, "Buffy, I want more for you. Your feelings for him are coloring your judgment. I can hear it in your voice."

Buffy sighed, and he pressed on. "That way lies a future filled with pain. I don't want that for you."

"We haven't . . ." she began, and then how could she go on? How could she talk about that with Giles? "Things have been different since he came back."

He did not skirt the issue. "It doesn't matter if you're not physical with each other any more. There's a connection. You rely on him, he relies on you. That's what's affecting your judgment."

"You think I'm losing sight of the big picture, but I'm not," Buffy assured him. "When Spike had that chip, it was like having him in a muzzle. It was wrong.

You can't beat evil by doing evil. I know that."

He walked out of the room, and Giles called after her calmly, "Well, I hope you're right. You're gambling with a lot of lives."

Big tool, Xander thought admiringly, as he watched a massive saw cut through a metal pipe. He was in the El Niño lumberyard, where men where men were men and . . . *wow*.

A very beautiful young woman was examining lengths of rope.

Oooh, accent on length, he thought hopefully, and said, "Can I help? You seem kind of confused."

She eyed him. "You're not wearing a green apron."

He gave her props for that. "Confused, but sort of randomly observant."

"Sorry." She smiled at him. "I just mean . . . you don't work here, right?"

"Oh, right. Just helpful. I'm Xander."

"Lissa." They shook hands. "And I guess I could use some advice. I can't even figure out if I've got the right kind of rope."

"That depends on what you need it for," Xander said pleasantly. "Something like functional around the house, or you, know, recreational." That got a grin, so he continued in the same pleasant vein, "By which I mean, for example, boating or mountain climbing—not tying someone up for sexy, funky fun."

She laughed and he played off his embarrassment.

"In conclusion, rope can be useful in various ways."

"I have a kayak," she said, with a bit of sparkage.

"Again with the random. I like it."

"Sorry. I need it to store my kayak. So I was thinking maybe I could sort of suspend it from the ceiling in the garage with ropes and a pulley or a winch thing."

"Not a bad plan," he told her. "You'll need stronger rope than that. Wanna have coffee with me later?"

She was startled. "What?"

"Oh, you're the only one that gets to be random?" he asked.

Oh, bingo . . .

Much with the creeping, as Buffy snuck into Principal Wood's office and pretended not to realize that she was looking through the files on his desk.

"Now, if I were a sign of being evil," she murmured, "where would I be?"

She had just tiptoed over to a big wall cabinet when Principal Wood called her name from the doorway.

"Principal Wood," she said with the big innocence. "It's you."

"You looking for something?" he asked.

Uhhh . . . "File folders," she decided. "And mechanical pencils. Well, I want to write on a file folder with a mechanical pencil."

"The supply cabinet in the outer office has those things," he said, not without warmth.

"Oh. This isn't a supply cabinet?" she asked, trawling on more well-intentioned oopsiness. "My bad. Okay. Thanks!"

She started to leave, when he stepped in her way and said, "Hey, Buffy, what're you doing tonight?"

As if this were a test that she could easily pass she said, "Preparing for tomorrow's counseling sessions?"

He smiled faintly. "No, really."

"Watching a reality show about a millionaire," she confessed.

"Well, then . . . I'd like to take you out to dinner, if that's all right with you. I mean, you don't have to. I'm certainly not saying come to dinner if you enjoy having a job." He chuckled, then realized what he'd just said. "You know, I may have to make up a document saying I didn't just say that and have you sign it."

Buffy smiled at him. "Sure. I'd be happy to have dinner with you."

"Great." He smiled back. "I'll draw up the paperwork."

Once she was gone, Robin shut his office door and pulled the bloody handkerchief out of his pocket. He unfolded it, revealing the ornate bloody stiletto inside, and calmly and cautiously cleaned the blood off it. Then he opened up the cabinet Buffy Summers had been just about to open and pushed up the Dry-Erase board inside.

His knives and swords were beautifully displayed and very shiny. A good fighter cherishes his weaponry, or so his mother's Watcher had always said. And she should know . . .

He slid the stiletto into its appointed place on the field of velvet, then closed up the cabinet . . . and went back to his day-job life.

* * *

In the living room, it was Willow's turn to fold the laundry in their vast commune of Potentials and their socks and underwear —*next field trip should be to Urban Outfitters, not a graveyard*, Buffy thought—as Willow asked cheerily, "So, he asked you out to dinner?"

"Yeah," Buffy said. "Isn't that weird? I mean, he's a principal. He's a young, hot principal with earrings, but he's a principal. Why do you think he asked me out. I mean, he could be interested, right?" she asked, flushing a little.

"Yeah, sure," Willow said, rolling socks. "You're a frisky vixen."

"Or it could be work-related," Buffy mused. "Maybe I'm getting promoted for doing such a good job."

Willow burst out in a flurry of giggles, then caught herself and said, "Oh, right. That makes sense, too."

"Or, maybe he knows that I suspect he's up to something and he's taking me out to kill me."

Willow considered. "Well, then, you'll have to dress for the ambiguity."

"You know," Buffy went on in that vein, "it's not even that he's acting suspicious. It's just . . . there he is. On the Hellmouth. All day, every day." She knit her brows. "That's got to be like being showered with evil. Only from underneath."

"Not really a shower," Willow agreed.

"A bidet," Buffy said, eyes wide. "A bidet of evil."

"Buff, if he's really interested . . . are you interested back?"

She blushed again. "I don't know. he's good-looking and he's . . . he's solid, he's smart, he's normal. So not the wicked energy, which is nice 'cause I don't want to only be attracted to wicked energy." Then she frowned and added in a rush, "Or what if he is wicked, in which case that's why I'm attracted to him."

Willow smiled at her and drawled, "I'm gonna wait for that sentence to come around again before I jump on."

Buffy's grin got bigger. "I mean, I think I like him. And he'd be good for me."

"Right," Willow said sagely. "Help you move on."

Buffy frowned and said in a defensive tone, "Why does everybody in this house think I'm still in love with Spike?"

"No," Willow cut in, "I mean move from this imposed super-self-reliance. Let somebody else get close."

"Oh." The front door opened and she was delighted for the distraction to get her out of the conversation. "Hey, someone's here."

That someone was Xander, who entered much with the joy and said, "Guys, guess what happened."

"Buffy got a date!" Willow answered brightly.

"No. I did!" Then he gave Buffy a friendly grrr look and said, "Fine. Way to steal my thunder."

"Sorry," she said. "It if makes you feel better, it's Principal Wood, and I think he's aligned with The First."

Xander's protective eyebrows shot up. "Also, like ten years older than you, right?"

Loyally, Willow came to the rescue. "Which is like one hundred years younger than your type!"

"Yay," Buffy drawled. "Someone who doesn't remember the Industrial Revolution."

"I think they're going to end up making out," Willow said confidentially. 'Oh, Principal Wood,' she'll gasp, 'I love your lack of wicked energy.'"

Buffy threw socks at her. "Watch it, or I'm going to make you take about your new girlfriend who you hold hands with under the dinner table and think we don't notice."

Willow reddened, changed the subject.

"How about yours, Xander. Is she evil?"

"Well, she's interested in me, so there's a good chance, but I'm hoping for the best," he announced. "We're going for coffee. She has a kayak."

Then Giles and the new Potential, Chao-Ahn, burst through the door. Both were carrying large and colorful shopping bags.

"Dear Lord," Giles said. "I hate that mall. The shop assistant are rude. And everything in the food court is sticky."

"That's gotta be rough," Xander said. "Getting pulled out of your home, being told you're a Potential Slayer, not being able to bring anything."

"Yes," Giles concurred, as Chao-Ahn looked on blankly. "And the language barrier is formidable. I was concerned that my Mandarin is a little thin, but as it turns out, she speaks Cantonese, which is . . . thinner. But we muddled through." He beamed proudly. "And, as I suspected, ice cream is a universal language."

In Chinese, Chao-Ahn told them, "Like many from Asia, I am lactose intolerant. I'm very uncomfortable."

"She's grateful to be in the land of plenty," Giles translated. To the new girl, he said in a loud, slow voice, "Let go and put away your new clothes."

"Hey, Will, do you think you can do a computer check on Principal Wood?" Buffy asked. "See if you can find anything out?"

"Yeah. Sure." Willow looked at Xander. "Want me to check your girl out while I'm at it, Xand?"

"Nope. I'm going in blind," he told them both. "I'm going to be an optimist about this. Why go looking for trouble? If it's gonna find you, it's gonna find you."

This was one microwave that wasn't gonna have the clock part flashing on and off.

Andrew was standing in the kitchen of Slayer Central with the instruction manual, hard at processing, when a voice from his murderous past said, "You don't need a manual. It's intuitive."

It was Jonathan. Or rather, The First masquerading as Jonathan. Andrew was terrified, and stared in horror.

"There's a button marked 'Clock Set,' for pity's sake," Jonathan continued. "What kind of a nerd are you? No wonder you crashed your jet pack."

"No," Andrew said breathlessly. "Get thee behind me!" He whipped a cross out of his jeans pocket. "I rebuke thee. Take that, The First!"

Jonathan rolled his eyes. "Look, you monkey." He walked up to Andrew, extended his arm, and passed his hand through the cross. "Ooh, ahh, it burns as it inef-fectually passes through me." He lowered his arm. "I'm non-corporeal, remember? Also, not a vampire, so . . . a cross?"

Abashed, Andrew put the cross down. "What do you want from me, Jonathan-slash-The First?"

"I have an assignment for you," Jonathan/The First announced.

Andrew did not love that information. "I follow Buffy's orders now. I'm redeeming myself for killing you, I mean, for killing Jonathan."

"Really? Why?" Jonathan laughed. "So you can earn a spot on her little pep squad? You think she'll ever let you in? You're a murderer."

"Confidentially, a lot of her people are murderers," Andrew told him/it. "Anya and Willow and Spike."

"And yet you're the only one she makes seek redemption. Does that seem fair to you?"

Andrew shrugged anxiously. "I guess not."

"You know we're headed toward a fight, don't you? What do you think the world's going to be like after that? Newsflash: There's not going to be a Slayer gang any more. And as long as there is Evil, I live. And as long as I live, you can dwell by my side."

"That sounds nice," Andrew said tentatively.

Jonathan pressed his advantage. "Your assignment won't be hard. They're just little girls."

Shocked, Andrew blurted, "You want me to hurt the girls?"

"Just the Potential Slayers. The girls must die. It'll be easy. Willow brought something to this house, something good, something you can use."

Andrew thought hard, then said proudly, "The new microwave!"

"The *gun*," Jonathan corrected him.

In the bathroom, Anya tried to scrub out the pizza or blood or whatever it was on Buffy's blouse while they talked about her upcoming . . . event.

"I don't think it's really a date," Anya said, much with the scrubbing.

"That's why I chose a top that says, you know, I'm comfortable in an a stodgy office or a swinging casual setting, or killing you if you're a demon."

"I was talking about this sham date of Xander's," Anya said heatedly. "I think it's part of a plan to make me jealous."

"We'll, it's not working," Buffy said, in a bid to support her.

"Are you nuts? Of course it's working. Observe my bitter ranting. Hear the shrill edge of hysteria in my voice . . . and go, leave me here to stew in my impotent rage. I have to pee."

Buffy walked out of the bathroom in her camisole, her ruined top in her hand . . . and Spike approached. Much fumbling with awkwardness. He had heard about her date, and then he said calmly, "I'm all right. Think I still dream of a crypt for two with a white picket fence? My eyes are clear."

"Thank you," she said gratefully.

"Never much cared for picket fences anyway. Bloody dangerous."

* * *

And speaking of dangerous . . . Xander was in the coffee shop with the big fancy French cup, and no girl, because it was 8:30 exactly, the time of their date, and—

There she was!

Did you think I was going to stand you up?" she asked, when he seemed so thrilled that she was there right on time.

"Well, it would be kind of karmic," he admitted. "Forget it. I'm just glad you're here. You're going to love the coffee. Got myself a redeye; it's black coffee with a shot of espresso. It's kinda rough if you're not used to that sort of—"

She took it from him, tasted it. "It's hot cocoa," she said.

Busted. "Well, sometimes I don't sleep too good." He made a face. "I just lost macho points, didn't I."

She shrugged. "Hey, who wants macho? I like that you like hot cocoa." Then she said to the water, "Redeye please." To Xander, "Sounded good."

Okay, much with the weirdness on Principal Wood, as Willow searched for data on him, Kennedy, Dawn, and Amanda looking on.

"I've Googled till I just can't Google no more," she asserted.

Then Anya and Giles stomped into the room, Anya with a stack of papers. Anya handed them to Willow and said, "Giles made these for Chao-Ahn, and now she's locked herself in the bathroom."

"Those are flashcards," Giles said. "I—I made them to facilitate her training. Chao-Ahn never had a Watcher."

Crude black-and-white stick figures were swathed in blood as they were menaced by various knife-wielding evildoers labeled VAMPIRE and BRINGER. TUROK-HAN was especially hideous, looming over a girl who had been ripped in two. They reminded Willow of the pictures Giles had drawn when the Gentlemen had glided into town and stolen everyone's voices.

"Perhaps I'll rethink the approach," Giles conceded.

Then Willow invited him to get researchy, and that was The First Giles heard about Buffy's . . . event.

"Buffy has a date?" he asked, blinking.

Anya grimaced. "Didn't you hear? Everybody has a date. Buffy has a date. Willow's been completely making out with this girl—" She pointed to Kennedy, who said, "Hey!"

"Xander's out with some hardware-store-whore," she continued. "It's Date Fest 2003."

With that, she sat down.

"Buffy's actually investigating Principal Wood," Willow allowed. "It's not a date."

"Really?" Giles asked, somewhat mollified.

"It might be a date," Willow said guiltily.

"For God's sake!" Giles cried. "How can anyone think about their social life? We're about to fight the original, primal evil. These girls are in mortal danger. Didn't you see the flashcards? This isn't right!"

Neither is what I'm doing, Andrew thought, as he spied on them.

"This isn't right," Buffy said, hesitating as Principal Wood—*let's call him Robin*—led her down a small dark alley.

"I know it doesn't look promising," he said, "but I swear this place is great. The best-kept secret in town. It's just down this way."

They headed into the alley, and then . . . vamps attacked!

They came at them from the shadows, surrounding them, and Buffy got into melee mode. She vaulted over one to land on the back of another, staking him through the back, and landing on the ground while he dusted under her. Then she kicked out with her feet from that position to work on the other two; she was dusting another one and then doing a flip and shouting at her date, "You set me up!"

And then she had the chance to observe him in action and he dusted two vamps in quick succession, *pffft pffft,—yeeeea*! just like that.

He held out a hand to help her up.

"The restaurant's right there," he said.

And so it was.

Lissa was not only hot, but she was a great listener, too, so Xander poured his heart out about Anya. After all, they had just had their not-anniversary, so, ouch. But she said, "It turned out good for me, and that's what really matters, right?"

He laughed and nodded, and said, "I should have taken you on a nicer date than this."

Her answering smile was sexy. "Well, I can think of something fun to do. . . ."

The restaurant was intimate and romantic, just the place for good food and true confessions, as Robin opened up to Buffy about the battle they'd just won.

"I've had a little practice," he allowed. "Never took on two at once before, but I've taken out a vamp here or there. And some demons."

"So, you're . . . freelance?" she asked.

"Freelance." He considered that. "Yes, I guess that would be a good way to put it."

"And you know who I am?" she asked him.

"You're the Slayer."

"Right." She took that in. "So . . . I'm guessing that you don't work in an office about fifteen feet over a Hellmouth because you love educational administration."

He grinned at her. "I actually do enjoy the work, but you're right, I maneuvered myself into that school, that office, just like I maneuvered you there. The Hellmouth draws the bad things in close, and now we're headed for something big, Buffy. Really big." His demeanor lost all traces of amusement. "Really big, and I need to be here where it happens. I want to help."

"So, you didn't want me for my counseling skills?" she asked obliquely.

He burst into a flurry of laughter much like Willow's, the caught himself and assured her, quite seriously, "They're valuable, too."

"Why didn't you tell me about you?" she asked, cocking her head.

"I wasn't sure about things yet. Not sure I was ready yet. Now the fight is starting and I don't have time to worry anymore. I have to do something."

"So, you knew who I was before you even came here," she said. "How do you know about Slayers?"

He nodded, as if they were getting down to brass tacks. "See, when I was a little boy, my mother was one. The one, actually. The Slayer."

"Your moth . . ." She caught her breath, shaken. "Wow. I didn't know that any Slayers had children."

"Well, I don't know of any others," he conceded. "She was killed when I was four. I still remember her, but it's a little . . ." He searched for a word. "Fuzzy? You know?"

She had to ask, although she didn't really want to: "Um, something got her . . . a demon?"

"A vampire." He got a faraway look in his eyes. "I went through this whole 'avenging son' phase in my twenties, but I never found him. So now I just dust as many of them as I can find. I figure eventually I'll get him. That's probably why we got jumped outside. I'm not very popular with the bumpy-forehead crowd. I bet you aren't, either."

She shook her head. "No. Not most of them. Um, so, do you have any Slayer powers?" She laugh self-consciously. "I'm sorry, I—I'm just so floored. I—I have no idea what to ask."

"No, I don't have powers," he told her. "No super-strength or mythic responsibilities. I'm just a guy with a few skills 'cause her Watcher took me in and raised me."

"So you decided to tell me . . . in a darkened, little romantic French restaurant?"

He gazed at her, and it was a man-to-woman kind of gaze. "Yeah. I'm not really sure how that happened, but yeah."

Still mired in the wrongness, Andrew parlayed with Jonathan/The First in the living room. Andrew had a paper bag and Jonathan had a question:

"Did you find the gun?"

"Yes. It was in Buffy's underwear drawer. She has nice things," Andrew reported.

"Show me," Jonathan ordered.

"Well, I didn't take 'em," Andrew allowed, "but there were thongs and regular underpants . . ."

Irritated, Jonathan said, "Show me the gun."

"Oh." Andrew opened the paper bag to show him the gun. "Willow tried shooting Kennedy with that."

"Great." Jonathan got down to business. "There's going to be panic and fleeing when you start firing, so you're going to have to get them trapped someplace like the basement."

Andrew said, "Uh-huh. And we're killing them because . . . ?"

"Because they're the future of the Slayer line. When they're gone, the line is gone."

"Mmhmm, uh-huh. So why not have Spike do it?" Andrew asked. "He's the one with the trigger."

"It's not time for him yet. You can wait for the next

time they're training in the basement, but don't rely on a locked door."

"Okay." Then Andrew asked, with as much casualness as he could muster, "Say, um, do you have any weaknesses I should know about if I'm gonna work for you, like, uh, kryptonite or allergies? Ah, are you made out of the evil impulses of humans, so if everyone was unconscious at the same time, you would fade away?"

Jonathan looked at him suspiciously. "You're asking a lot of questions."

"Yes, well, I . . . because I'm evil." Andrew was nervously playing with desk accessories. "And I want to do the best I can at that, so I want to . . . know stuff . . . like when—when do we kill Buffy?"

"Are you wearing a wire?"

Uh-oh. 'Cause he was.

"Do you think you can trick The First?" Jonathan demanded. "I told you, Andrew. I made you do this . . ."

He pressed his hands against his sweater. They came back wet with blood.

"Jonathan suffered," The First murmured. "He was your friend, and he trusted you, and now he spends eternity in pain because of what you did."

"No," Andrew gasped. "What's happening to you?"

Like a time-delay special effects in an old horror movie, Jonathan's face began to decay, all white and green and shiny with decomposition.

"This is what you did to him. You started down a road with that action. You have to keep going."

"Stop looking like Jonathan," Andrew protested in a tight, frightened voice. "You're not him. You're The First, and you're trying to get me to shoot innocent girls, but I won't do it. I'm good now. When the fight is over, I'm going to pay for killing Jonathan."

The First shook his head. "You're going to pay for more than that. Do you know why? Because the biggest, baddest First Evil in the world is angry with you."

And Willow, listening in on Andrew's wire at the dining room table, finally thought she heard something.

"You think you can trick me, women?" Jonathan's voice boomed.

Beside her, Kennedy bolted out of her chair and took off Willow's headphones.

"You hear only what I want you to hear," The First proclaimed. "You see only what I want you to see."

Then Jonathan appeared behind Amanda, who screamed and backed away with the others.

He was gross, purple-black; one eye milky. His flesh was opening, putrefying, and it was terrifying to see those dead lips open and say, "So many dead girls. There'll be so many."

"See, I knew it," Xander said, resigned.

He and Lissa were in the Sunnydale High School basement. His date had tied him on the wheel Spike had been bounded to in order to be tortured, also for bleeding all over the Seal of Danthalzar, once more uncovered.

Lissa had changed into something more comfortable, a slinky High Priestess outfit all black and shiny like her hair—not unlike another wacky evil love interest of hers, the Inca mummy princess, Ampata.

"Thanks for your help selecting the ropes," she said. "The one I picked wasn't strong enough."

"Yeah, that would've been bad," he said. "Listen, is this because I'm a friends with Buffy?"

"Who's Buffy?"

"The Slayer," he answered miserably.

"You know the Slayer?" She was impressed.

She started winching up the rope, and the crossworks wheel started rising into the air. "This can't just happen," Xander groaned. "It just can't keep happening that demon women find me attractive. There's gotta be a reason."

"You just seem like a nice guy. That's all," Lissa replied. "And I wanted to get to know you."

"And kill me?" Xander asked shrilly.

Sure," she said pleasantly. "Do the ropes hurt?"

"Yes," Xander told her.

She smiled. "Good."

In the living room, Willow and her contingent of eavesdroppers briefed Anya, Spike, and Giles on what had just happened with The First. Dawn was trying to peel the tape off Andrew's chest that held the wire in place.

"So, we're thinking," Willow said in summation, "it didn't go too well."

As Dawn worked on the tape, she said to Andrew, "You should let me do this fast."

"No. No, no. I hate that. Ow!"

Spike couldn't believe what he was hearing. "You tried to record the ultimate evil? Why? In a complex effort to royally piss it off?"

Kennedy leaned over Willow's shoulder. "Guess we succeeded pretty good, huh?"

"God, I never should have gone in wired." He made his whiny Andrew moan. "Redemption is hard."

Giles frowned. "Getting back to Spike's question, why *did* you try to record it?"

"To study it," Willow told him, over more of Andrew's mewling. "To see if we could figure something out from what it was saying. Because, guys, we have to face it. We know nothing about The First."

"Well, we know not to record it," Anya ventured. "That's something."

"Why did it appear to this one, then?" Spike persisted, waving a hand at Andrew. "I thought it was supposed to be pulling *my* strings."

"It said it wasn't time for you yet," Andrew said. Spike reacted to that with a very concerned frown.

Then Andrew said, "Ow," as Dawn pulled off the last piece of tape. "Ow. I'm frightened. And my chest hurts where the tape was." Petulantly he said down.

"It's okay, Andrew. You did good. You stood up to it. That's really amazing."

Andrew smiled at her. "Thank you. You're a peach."

Anya said, "Yeah. What did it want you to do, anyway?"

"Shoot all the girls," Andrew told her.

"Shoot girls?" Dawn asked nervously.

"Not you," Andrew assured her. "Just the Potentials."

Dawn was relieved. "Oh, well, that's something anyway," she said. Then, catching herself, she said soberly, "Something tragic."

"This proves my point," Giles said. "This is a crucial time. We need to circle our wagons and stop doing things like going out on dates when gunplay is imminent. Willow, call Buffy. Get her back here. We need to dispose of the gun and figure out our next move."

"I'll go get her," Spike said.

Willow's cell phone chirped and Amanda said, "Bet that's her. Sometimes you're thinking about calling someone—"

Willow checked the phone. "No, it's a text message. From Xander. It's one of our signals. The system we set up awhile back. Like codes." She frowned thoughtfully. "Uh, this one's either 'I just got lucky, don't call me for a while' or 'my date's a demon who's trying to kill me.'"

"You don't remember which?" Kennedy asked incredulously.

Willow shrugged, made a face. "It was a long time ago."

Dawn ventured, "Well, if we play the percentages . . ."

"Something's eating Xander's head," Giles finished.

"Buffy will know what to do," Andrew piped up.

"I'll go get her," Spike offered. "I can probably

still track her scent. She'll be worried about the boy."

He was out like a shot.

And he made it to the French restaurant just in time to hear Buffy say to her *date . . . very much a date, thank you very much . . .* "Oh, my God, that might be the best thing I've ever had in my mouth."

And then he was feeding her, for God's sake . . . and then both looked up and saw Spike glowering there, and he said, "It's Xander."

I saw this movie, Xander thought as he hung kayak-style over the Seal of Dental Floss. *Lair of the White Worm*, Ken Russell director, starring that chick from *L.A. Law . . .*

"The end is coming," Lissa said, channeling the same movie. "The final fight, and everyone is hearing the drumbeat. It's telling us to pick our partners, align ourselves with the good or the evil."

She'd gone all lizard eyes, and she reached forward with a long, thin knife and stabbed him in the stomach.

His blood dripped down onto the seal as he screamed in agony, and the Seal began to glow. Appreciatively, the demon woman said, "Couldn't have done it without you, Xander. Thanks for the great date."

Buffy was not loving the cavalry car ride to save Xander. She was in the front next to Robin and Spike glowered some more in the back seat.

"You're sure he's in the high school?" she asked Spike.

"Willow did a locator spell. Usual stuff," he bit off.

Robin was equally uncomfortable as he asked, "So, how do you two know each other?"

"He works with me," Buffy blurted. "In the struggle against evil."

"Cool," Robin said.

But it was not cool. Ever so not cool.

Because as they burst into the school basement and the fight began, Buffy's coworker turned into a vampire.

But time for that then, as Buffy and Spike fought Lissa and Robin moved to free Xander. As he eased him down, one of the triangles on the Seal cracked open and the taloned hand of some hideous creature shot through. It grabbed Robin's leg.

Robin managed to throw Xander away from the Seal, cutting off the steady supply of blood. The triangle slammed shut, severing the arm.

From beneath the Seal, there was a scream.

Meanwhile, Spike launched himself at Lissa, hitting her high and knocking her back. Buffy was ready. When the demon flipped to her feet, Buffy swung with a sword she'd wrenched away from her and whacked off her head.

The headless body morphed into a pinkish humanoid shape with hairy shoulders, shark teeth, and black stitches.

Robin checked on the young man . . . Xander, while Buffy crossed to the vampire. Silently, they regarded each other and she checking him for injuries.

They were . . . intimate. That was the only word Robin could find for what he was seeing.

Then Buffy came to Xander's side. Tersely he said to Buffy, "I think your friend's gonna be okay."

Xander grimaced and said to Robin, "So, how's your date going?"

Robin could only stare at the vampire . . . with hatred in his gaze.

At the Summers residence, those who were dateless awaited the arrival of those who were not.

"Where are they?" Anya said angrily. "I can't believe Buffy hasn't brought him home yet. His slut ate him up."

"His slut didn't eat him up," Willow cut in. "And besides, I thought you were all angry at him."

"My feelings are changeable but intense," Anya replied.

"I understand your fear, Anya," Andrew commiserated. "I know fear myself, because, you know, I, um, enraged that primal force."

Then Giles walked in with a glass of milk, looked around, and said, "They're not back yet?"

Chao-Ahn came down the stairs and said in Cantonese, "Why is everyone up? Are the flashcard monsters attacking?"

"She says she can't sleep," Giles told the others. "I made myself some warm milk," he told her in a nice, loud, slow voice. "You can have it."

"You're trying to kill me!" she cried in Chinese.

"She's shy," Giles interpreted.

Then the daters arrived. Xander was bandaged up but he seemed physically all right.

"What happened? Willow asked.

"What do you think happened?" Xander asked, walking toward her. "Another demon woman was attracted to me." As Anya looked disgusted, Xander said, "I'm going gay. I've decided I'm turning gay." He gestured to the Wicca. "Willow, gay me up. Come on. Let's gay."

"What?" Willow asked, startled.

"You heard me. Just tell me what to do. I'm mentally undressing Scott Bakula right now. That's a start, isn't it?"

Andrew closed his eyes and said dreamily, "Captain Archer." He nodded.

"Come on, let's get this gay show on the gay road. Help me out here," Xander told Willow.

Amused, Buffy said, "What if you just start attracting male demons?"

Dawn giggled. "Clem always liked you."

"Children, enough," Giles ordered.

"I'd need some stylish new clothes," Xander continued.

"Enough!" Giles bellowed. "Have you learned nothing from tonight's assorted chaos? There's no time for fun and games and . . . and quipping about orientation."

He picked up his flashcards. "These aren't a joke. This . . . happens. Girls are going to die. We may die. It's time to get serious."

With that, he stalked out of the room.

* * *

Once all the assorted chaos had gone to bed, Spike joined Buffy in the living room. She was quiet, and he was subdued.

"Anyone tell you about what happened 'round here tonight?" he began. "The First talked to the little boy. Said it's not time for me yet." He paused, and then he said it, "I should move out. Leave town. Before it *is* time for me."

Buffy looked up at him. "No," she said. "You have to stay."

He shrugged. "You've got another demon fighter now."

"That's not why I need you here," she said.

"Is that right? Why's that then?"

Gazing at him steadily, Buffy answered, "'Cause I'm not ready for you to not be here."

Robin was brushing his teeth, washing his face, wishing that Buffy Summers did not have some kind of thing going on with a vampire, when a voice behind him said, "You look good."

He stayed calm and very still as the ghost of his mother regarded him with a big smile on her face.

"You're not my mother," he said icily.

She raised her brows. "I give you a compliment and you don't say thank you? Did I raise you that way?"

"You didn't raise me at all," he shot back.

"Well, I was dead."

He walked right through her, and she reappeared, facing him again.

"So, you're The First," he said. "Why are you here? Why now?"

"'Cause you've been coming up in the world, taking the demons out." She gave her head a toss. "It makes a mother proud."

"Yeah?" He took an aggressive step toward her. "Well, think how pleased she'll be when I help take you out. Until it's time for that, I've got no use for you."

He turned to walk away.

"Would you like to know who killed me?" his mother asked. "I know you went looking for him. You can check it out after I tell you. Check the timing, rereading what the witnesses said, and the people in the subway station."

His heart was pounding. "Who is it?"

"You met him," she said, savoring the revelation. "You know him. You fight at his side."

And then he knew. Deep in his soul, he had already known. He was nonplused by the revelation..

"Spike," he said.

She smiled. "Now . . . what do you say?" she chided him.

He looked down and softly said, "Thank you."

Chapter Fifteen: "Get It Done"

Patrol. In her own house.

Buffy kept watch over the Potentials. There were so many now, and from all over the world. In an effort to communicate, Giles had purchased stacks of foreign language books. In the living room, Buffy picked up one that was entitled "Greek" and placed it with the others.

She went upstairs, doing a sweep. Kennedy was in bed with Willow; other girls lay in sleeping bags wedged everywhere.

Then she heard crying and followed its path; a young girl was huddled on the floor at the end of the hall, her face hidden.

"Chloe? It is Chloe, right?" she asked.

Wearing an expression of utter despair, Chloe looked up at her. But before she could speak, a flash of motion smashed violently into Buffy. She and her assailant crashed down the stairs with a bone-rattling slam onto the foyer floor.

Buffy was pinned, strong hands holding her shoulders tight.

In her war makeup and her Rasta braids, the Primitive sat atop her chest like a nightmare and rasped at Buffy, "It's not enough."

Then Buffy bolted away.

Dream, she wondered, *or vision?*

Nightmare, Anya thought. As Buffy and Anya walked down an alley, she grumbled, "I'm a bright girl, good education, quick on the uptake. So tell me, why in the name of almighty Grothnar would I let myself become human?"

Spike favored her with a faint smile and said, "You're really talking to the wrong fella."

"I mean, sure, the vengeance demon gig has some downsides . . ."

"All jobs do," he pointed out.

"But being human? You're always icky on the inside, disgusting on the outside."

Spike gave her an appreciative once-over. "Your outside's not so bad."

She was pleased. "You know, the only thing worse than being human is being trapped inside a house full of humans."

"Preaching to the choir, love."

"I mean, it's like we live in Slayer central. I swear, if Buffy rooms or boards one more of the Potential girls, I'm gonna call a health inspector."

"I like my plan better," Spike mused. "Get up, get out, get drunk. Repeat as needed. It's just more elegant."

Then she nattered on, talking about drinking and sex . . . and more sex, until Spike looked heavenward for patience and said, "Would you let it go? You're like a dog with a bone!"

"So what?" she asked heatedly.

"It's my bone. Just drop it."

"Okay, okay. I wasn't proposing," she said. "Time goes by, girl gets hungry. You should know."

"Oh, thank God," he said, looking past her.

"What?"

"Demon," he told her.

And suddenly, a D'Korr demon rushed Anya, throwing her to the ground as he announced, "D'Hoffryn says you die!"

"Of course, he does," Spike said calmly, and kicked him in the . . . bone.

He doubled over, and Spike seized the moment to seize Anya and drag her the hell out of there.

There was fighting in the school as well, more violence, more vandalism, as the bad vibes escalated.

"It's started, hasn't it?" Robin asked Buffy, as they conferred in her office.

She nodded. "The Hellmouth has begun its semi-annual percolation," she informed him. "Usually, it blows around May. We're a little ahead of schedule."

He took that in. "I can't say I'm too surprised. I knew I signed on for something, but Buffy, I'm just a guy. Granted, a cool and sexy vampire-fighting guy, but still . . ."

She smiled at him. "Don't forget 'snappy dresser.'"

"Mmm." He liked that. "Thank you. But this is going to get bigger than me." He closed the blinds. "That's why I decided to give you this."

He reached down under her desk and placed a worn old leather satchel on her desk.

"It's an emergency kit," he told her. "This bag belonged to my mother."

"Wow." Buffy stared at it. "A Slayer keepsake. I couldn't."

"You have to," he insisted. "Technically, it should have been handed down through the years, directly to you, but after my mother died, I guess I just couldn't part with it. "I don't know what's inside, exactly, but I now it has something to do with her power. Well, your power now."

"I—I don't know what to say," she murmured, staring at the bag.

He grinned. "Try saying, 'Thank you, Principal Wood.'"

"Thank you, Principal Wood," she coyly mimicked him.

"Ah, call me Robin," he said. "Now, I'd like to see where you work."

"Uh, here, actually." She touched her desk. "Uh, this is my desk, and uh, these are my pencils . . ." She held up her pencil holder.

"No. Where you do your other work," he told her.

* * *

So she took him home, debriefing him about the Potentials on the way.

"We thought the Council could protect them," she told him as they went inside the house. "But unfortunately, no one was protecting the Council, and all their Watchers were killed. Word got out, and they've all been coming here since."

"Well, there's nothing like the end of the world to bring people together," he drawled.

Then Andrew stomped into the room, his baker man ensemble complete with a white apron and red-and-white checked oven mitts.

"Where the hell have you been?" he demanded, crossing his arms over his chest. "This funnel cake is kicking my ass."

"Robin Wood, this is . . . Andrew. Andrew is . . . actually, he's our hostage," Buffy finished.

Andrew said, "I like to think of myself more as a"—air quotes—"guestage."

"Well, he was evil, people got killed, and now he bakes," Buffy said. "It's a thing."

"Oh," Robin said.

Andrew narrowed his eyes at Buffy. "Could we try to just keep our secret headquarters a little bit more secret? Keep bringing people in, they're gonna see everything. They'll see the big board."

"Andrew," Buffy said patiently, "we don't have a big board."

Oh, yes they did.

Andrew fetched it, saying, "I made it myself."

"Oh, I wouldn't have guessed," Robin said, as he gazed at the dry-erase board labeled SUNNYDALE BIG BOARD with a Sharpie-drawn map and lots of pretty colors.

"This is us," Andrew said, pointing. "And this represents The First in various incarnations. There's no pattern to the naked eye yet, but the instant one emerges, yours truly is on it."

Buffy and Robin drifted away. Andrew called after Buffy, "Where do we put our receipts?"

They walked outside, where Kennedy was putting them through their martial arts paces.

"Punch block combo!" she bellowed.

"Huh!" the Potentials shouted, snapping to.

"Cross block kick!"

"Huh!"

They were doing well, all but one . . . Chloe, from Buffy's dream. She was not keeping up.

Kennedy noticed, too. She marched up to the girl like a drill sergeant and shouted at her, "What the hell do you call that, Potential? Try that in the field, you are dead. Drop and give me twenty!"

Chloe was confused. "Twenty what?"

"Pushups, maggot!"

Then as Kennedy turned, she spotted Buffy and Robin, and grinned.

"I love this job!" she crowed. "Did you see that? I called that girl 'maggot'!"

Buffy introduced Robin as an ally, and Kennedy said, "So, what do you think? My girls ready to kick some ass, or what?"

"Well, I'm just not sure The First has an ass that you can actually, you know, kick."

"Principal Wood, hi!" Amanda called, waving at him. "It's so weird seeing you outside of school."

Kennedy shouted at her, "What are you waving at, Potential? Attention!"

"Huh!" they all chorused.

Buffy and Robin turned away, and Buffy said glumly, "You're right. It's not enough."

"That's not what I said, Buffy," he argued. "It's an impressive group of recruits."

"They're not recruits," she said. "Recruits are recruited. These girls were Chosen."

"You're doing the best you can with what you've got."

She would not be mollified. "They're not all going to make it. Some will die, and nothing I can do will stop that."

Then Willow popped out the back door with her arms brimming with weaponry. She froze, deer in headlights, Willow-style.

"Oh, hi, hey. Well . . . Buffy . . . I see that our preparations for the school pep-dance-cheer-drill contest are coming along." She gave her head a little shake. "Bring it on!"

"Its okay," Buffy told her. "I filled him in on everything."

Willow heaved a sigh of relief. "Oh, thank God. If I had to explain all these weapons, I had nothing."

As she put the heavy weaponry down, Robin said, "You're Willow."

"You're Wood," she returned.

"Buffy tells me you've been, how shall I put it? Experimenting."

Willow shot Buffy a look.

"With the magics," he filled in.

"Oh. Yes," she said awkwardly. "Nothing too heavy, though. Just the lighter, safer stuff. Uh, if Kennedy asks, her pointy stuff's right there. See you inside." She added as she wheeled around, "So much cooler than Snyder."

Then she went inside. "She really almost destroyed the world?" he asked, intrigued.

"Yep."

"Remind me not to make her crabbing," he said flatly.

"It might be better if you did."

He was confused. "How's that work?"

She sighed. "It's just . . . The First is coming, and look at us. The army. We've got fighters with nothing to hit, a Wicca who won't use magic, and the brains of our operation wears oven mitts."

"Hmm." He was thoughtful. "Well, you're redefining the job, Buffy. That takes guts." A beat, and then, "This isn't your full arsenal, anyway." Off her look, he added, "Show me the vampire."

Spike and Anya were arguing in the basement about their encounter with D'Hoffryn's assassin the night before. Anya was pissed.

You fought like such a wimp-ire, with the lifting and the running," she said. "Why not just kill him?"

"Anya, think," Spike insisted. "I fight. Demon Boy gets lucky, knocked out, you get killed. True? We both know the safest and sanest way of saving your life was to keep you with me, away from danger."

Defeated but no less pissed off, Anya walked off.

"No need to thank me," Spike called after her. "I'm just the one who beat him off." He gave Buffy a droll looked. "Repelled him would perhaps be the better phrase."

He checked out Robin and said, "And just what brings our good principal to this neck of the gloom?"

"I'm showing him our operation," Buffy told him. "Us."

"Fine by me," Spike replied, nodding. "Big fight against evil coming up. The more good guys we got, the longer we'll all live."

Robin did not look at him. "Is that what you are? A good guy?"

"I haven't heard any complaints. Well, I have heard a few complaints over the years, but then I just killed whoever spoke up, and that was pretty much that."

Robin turned around and looked at him.

"He's joking," Buffy cut in quickly.

"No. He's not," Robin said.

"No, I'm not," Spike concurred. "But . . . that's the old me I'm talking about."

"Oh, now that you have a soul," Robin said. "And how's that working out for you?"

"In progress," Spike said, lifting his chin.

"Well, you've had some time. You've been in Sunnydale, what . . . ?"

"Years," Spike said.

"How many?"

"A few," Spike replied tersely.

"Before that?"

"Around." Spike was not loving the third degree.

Buffy felt the tension. She said to Robin, "We'd better get back upstairs."

Robin left, and Buffy and Dawn fell to sleeping bag duty in Dawn's room. It took a long time; there were a lot of Potentials sleeping at their house.

"So, I took a look in inside that emergency bag of Principal Wood's," Dawn told Buffy. "Smelled weird. Kind of like Grandma's closet, but worse."

Buffy made a face. "I didn't know that was possible. Anything we could use?"

Dawn shrugged. "Trinkets, weapons, one very large textbook." She held it up for display and began to flip through it. "Translation's going to be a bitch. Do you know that ancient Sumerians do not speak English?"

"They're worse than the French," Buffy quipped. "Anything else?"

"Yes," Dawn told her. "A big, fat unopenable box. I'm betting whatever the big deal about this emergency bag is, you'll find it in the box."

"Good. Keep on it." Buffy walked out of the room. "Don't you have any real homework?"

"Well, I've got a system," Dawn said, trailing after her. "It's called flunking out. No, just kidding! I'm paying someone to do my work." She giggled. "I'm kidding! I love to see your eyeballs change color when you think I'm gonna flunk out of—"

They sailed into another bedroom, and she gasped.

Chloe dangled from the ceiling. She had used a sheet to form a noose, and she had done it right. Her face was blue and slight puffy. She was dead.

Kennedy, Rona, and Amanda came out of the bedroom across the hall and joined Buffy and Dawn.

"What happened?" Kennedy asked. "We heard . . ." She gasped and covered her mouth.

"Dawn," Buffy said, staring at the corpse, "get a knife."

"Good thinking," said Chloe . . . standing beside her dead body. Buffy stiffened, knowing that they were gazing at The First. "Good thinking," she said. "But, on the other hand, why rush? Up or down, I'll still be dead."

"You're not Chloe," Buffy said coldly.

"Yeah, well, neither is she, anymore," The First said, as if she really didn't care. "Now she's just . . . Chloe's body."

"What did you do to her?" Kennedy demanded.

"Nothing! We just talked all night." She made a little face. "Well, I did most of the talking but Chloe is . . . I'm sorry, *was* . . . a good listener. Till she hung herself." To Kennedy, she added, "Like when you called her a maggot. She really heard that."

"Don't listen to it, any of you," Buffy ordered. "It's The First."

"Oh, let 'em," The First drawled. "The only reason why Chloe offered herself is 'cause she knew what you're not getting. I'm coming, you're going.

All this . . ." she gestured ". . . is almost over."

"We'll be here," Buffy said grimly.

"All of you?" The First asked, with a raise of her brow. "But wait. I thought . . ." Her voice altered, becoming that of Buffy. "'They're not all going to make it. Some will die, and there's nothing I can do that will stop it.'" She shifted back to Chloe's voice. "Hey, I didn't say it. But I'll be seeing all of you, one by one." She added cheerily, "TTFN!" Then she disappeared, like a flash of light on the horizon.

"What's TTFN?" Buffy asked stolidly.

Rona swallowed hard. "It's 'ta ta for now.' It's what Tigger says when he leaves."

Amanda added anxiously, "Chloe loved Winnie the Pooh."

Buffy's voice was choked with anger and sorrow. "Dawn," she managed, "where's that knife?"

Buffy dug the grave alone, placing Chloe next to Annabelle. Next to the Slayer's failures.

She went back into the house, where everyone had gathered; some were sitting in traumatic silence, others were sobbing quietly. Everyone was grieving.

"Anyone want to say a few words about Chloe?" she asked, gazing around the group. No one spoke. "Let me."

She paced, and then she said harshly, "Chloe was an idiot. Chloe was stupid. She was weak. And anyone in a rush to be the next dead body I bury, it's easy. Just think of Chloe, and do what she did. I'll find room for you next to her and Annabelle."

As they stared at her, she continued, "I'm the Slayer. The one with the power. And The First has me using that power to dig our graves." She punctuated her point by throwing down her shovel. Willow flinched. Kennedy noticed.

"I've been carrying you —all of you—too far, too long. Ride's over."

Kennedy jumped to her feet and cried, "You're out of line!"

"No," Willow said clearly, "she's not."

Kennedy looked at Willow. "You're going to let her talk to you like that? Willow, she's not even the most powerful one in this room. With you here, she's not even close."

Buffy turned her attention to the young Potential. Close. Calm. "You're new here," she said, "and you're wrong. Because I use the power that I have. The rest of you are just waiting for me."

Xander ventured forth. "Well, yeah, but only because you kind of told us to. You're our leader, Buffy, as in 'follow the.'"

"Well, from now on, I'm your leader as is 'do what I say,'" she shot back.

"*Ja wohl*," Xander said, with an edge. "But let's not try to forget, we're also your friends."

"I'm not," Anya piped up.

Buffy whirled on her and said, "Then why are you here? Aside from getting rescued, what is it that you do?"

Anya was caught off balance. "I . . . provide much-needed sarcasm," she said.

Xander raised a hand. "Um, that would kind of be my job, actually."

"You're here because you're scared," Buffy said to Anya.

"Same goes for everyone in this room," Xander argued.

"Fine," Buffy bit off. "Anya, all of you: Be as scared as you like. Just be useful while you're at it."

"Come on, Buffy," Willow said. "You know everyone's here already doing everything they can."

"The First isn't impressed. It already knows us. It knows what we can do, and it's laughing. You want to surprise the enemy? Surprise yourselves," Buffy said to the group. "Force yourself to do what can't be done, or else we are not an army—we're just a bunch of girls waiting to be picked off and buried."

Spike rose and walked toward the door.

"Where are you going?" Buffy asked.

"Out. Since I'm neither a girl, nor waiting, all of this speechifying doesn't really apply to me, does it?"

"Fine," she called after him. "Take a cell phone. That way, if I need someone to get weepy or wailed on, I can call you."

Spike froze. Cold with fury, he turned and said, "If you've got something to say . . ."

"Just said it. Keep holding back, Spike, and you might as well walk out that door."

He blinked. "Holding back? You're blind. I've been here, right in it, fighting, scrapping . . ."

"Since you got your soul back?" she asked, leading him.

"Well, as a matter of fact, I haven't quite been relishing the kill the way I used to."

"You were a better fighter then," Buffy observed.

He was thrown. "I did this for you. The soul, the changes; it's what you wanted."

"What I want is the Spike that's dangerous," she told him frankly. "The Spike that tried to kill me when we met."

He retorted angrily, "Oh, you don't know how close you are to bringing him out."

"I'm nowhere near him," Buffy said. Without taking her gaze off Spike, she said to Dawn, "Get the Potentials upstairs. I'm declaring an emergency."

Buffy invited Robin for the opening of his mother's Slayer's bag. He showed, a bit bleary-eyed but ready for action. Buffy had cleared the room of Potentials—the core group was there—Robin, Buffy, Willow, Dawn, Xander, and Kennedy. Everyone except Spike.

They had taken everything out of the satchel and laid it out on the table in the living room. Dawn said, "This emergency bag's got some neat stuff in it—weapons, charms, advanced reading assignments."

She held up the big fancy book she had shown to Buffy.

Xander examined a goblet and said, "Cool stuff, but we've seen it all before."

Anya pointed to an arcane-looking wooden box with a metal lock on it. "Not this, we haven't. What's inside it?" Anya asked Robin.

"I don't know," he admitted. "It hasn't been opened since . . ." Buffy broke the lock off with her bare hands. ". . . well, since now."

Xander reached in and pulled out some metal figures. He held them for a moment, and then he said, "Puppets. That's it! The First hates puppets. Now, if we can just airlift Kermit, Fozzi, and Miss Piggy into town, The First'll be a-runnin'."

"Those are Muppets," Willow corrected him.

Dawn took the puppets from Xander. "And these things are shadow-casters," Dawn said. "You put them in motion, and they tell you a story." She looked down at the book. "It says you can't just watch. You have to see."

"What the hell does that mean?" Anya said.

"It's cryptic." Xander made a face. "Every time instructions get cryptic, someone gets hurt. Usually me."

"That's where all my fancy translating skills break down," Dawn said, "but I think it's an origin myth." She looked freaked. "The story of the very First Slayer."

Buffy was shaken. "I saw her. The other night. In my dream." She looked at the group. "That's got to mean something, right?"

They were about to find out, as they figured out how to put the device together—it was like a zoetrope, or a magic lantern from Victorian times. They took the paintings off the walls, leaving them blank. Then Xander stuck a match and lit the wick at the center of a five-sided turntable of what might have been copper. Light glowed, giving Dawn the means by which to read her book.

"According to this," she told the group, "you put on those puppet guys one by one. They cast shadows and the shadows tell the story. First there is the Earth."

Xander placed The First metal figure into one of the sides. As the light threw the shadow of hills and the crescent moon against the wall, ghostly drumbeats echoed softly.

"What's the sound?" Kennedy asked anxiously.

"Okay, so far, so creepy." Xander drawled.

"Then there came the Demons," Dawn read.

Xander inserted the next figure, and the image of hills was chased by the crude image of a monster. A roar rose above the drumbeats.

"After Demons, there came Men."

The third shadowy tableau was of three men with staffs, appearing behind the demon and the hills.

"The Men found a Girl," Dawn read.

Her sound was a scream, and a ripple of unease floated around the room. As if in response, the turntable started to spin faster.

"The Men took the Girl. To fight the Demon. Um, all Demons. They . . ." She hesitated. "They chained her to the Earth."

Xander added the last image—of Chains—connecting the Girl image to the Earth. The rattling sound added to the growing cacophony.

"And then . . . I can't read this. Something about darkness," Dawn said.

The magic lantern spun, making the shadows on the wall dance and move, taking on a life of their own. They moved, and acted out the story.

"It says you cannot be shown," Dawn said over the noise. "You cannot just watch, but you must see. See for yourself, but only if you're willing to make the . . . exchange."

Xander called, "When did you get so good at Sumerian?"

But the words on the pages of the book were glowing and melting away into nothing, leaving each page completely blank.

On the wall, Demon attacked Girl, who shrieked in her chains. The device whirled faster, out of control, then a bright blue light flashed into the center of the turntable, shooting in all directions until it was the size and shape of a regular door. The glare was intense, blinding . . . terrifying.

"But what's it mean?" Xander cried.

"It means I have to go in there," Buffy said.

"No, it doesn't!" Willow protested. "It doesn't say that? Where does it say that?"

"Buffy, you don't even know what you're exchanging," Robin put in. "You don't know if you're ready yet."

"That's the point," she remarked, walking toward it.

"No, Buffy," Willow pleaded. "We don't know where you're going or how we'll get you back!"

"Find a way," Buffy told her.

Then she jumped through the doorway. The second she disappeared into it, the device snapped shut.

The others were stunned into silence. Then Anya said, "What was that about an exchange?"

As soon as the words were out of her, there was an

afterflash of light and a blast of energy—and an enormous demon appeared where the portal had stood.

"Ah. This must be the exchange student," Xander quipped.

As if in reply, the demon grabbed him by the collar and threw him across the room.

They moved into fight stance as Kennedy said, "Willow, use your magic! Send it back!"

Willow said, "I'm trying . . . *Redi!*" *Return!*

The demon responded by backhanding the Wicca. Then Robin dipped into his mother's weapons bag and attacked the demon with throwing stars, moving in for fearless hand-to-hand. The demon dropped him to the floor.

"Weapons!" Kennedy cried. Dawn handed her a sword and kept one for herself. The two charged the demon, but it was too strong and too fast for them. Dawn was thrown left; Kennedy, right.

Then Spike rushed in, assessed the situation, and leaped onto the demon's back.

"Get out of here, all of you!" he shouted. "Unless you want to end up all dead and useless!"

"What are you going to do?" Kennedy asked from the couch.

"What I do best," Spike replied.

He grabbed the demon by the head and bashed it against the wall, and for a moment there was hope that he had actually slowed the monster down. Then it heaved Spike toward the ceiling. The vampire shot through so hard that he broke through it and landed on the floor upstairs.

Triumphant, the demon broke through the French doors and left the house.

"We need Buffy," Willow said.

Xander nodded. "You've got to get her back," Xander told her. "Looks like it's spell o'clock."

"Which spell?" Anya asked. "I mean, didn't you see that thing? And you expect to reopen the portal without sending Willow off the deep end."

Frowning, Willow ducked her head. "Thanks for your support."

"Well, it's true," Anya said. "We're going to have to find another way."

Willow shook her head. "There isn't, and Buffy knew it. I've got to get her back."

"We don't even know where she went," Kennedy said.

Guess that worked, Buffy thought.

She was in the desert where she had once before gone with Giles, and met The First Slayer. She walked, orienting herself, aware that this was no ordinary desert; magic swirled everywhere.

Magic, and death.

Then she came upon three men in tribal robes and turbans, each holding a tall staff

"Hello?" she said. "I'm Buffy. I'm the Slayer."

Though they spoke in another tongue, she understood what they were saying:

We know who you are.
And we know why you're here.

We've been waiting.

The three began circling her.

> *We have been here since the beginning.*
> *Now, we are almost at the end.*

"The end of what?" she asked.

> *You are the Hellmouth's last guardian.*

"Latest. You mean latest guardian," she said.

> *No.*

Ignoring that, she said, "Okay, I have The First to fight. So just tell me what I need to know. I came to learn."

> *We cannot give you knowledge. Only power.*

"You know what I think?" Buffy asked sharply. "I'm not really here at all. None of this is actually happening. This is a like a play . . . like some shadow-play," she added, thinking of the magic lantern. "Some nonreality reenactment hologramy—"

One of the men clubbed her with his staff, and she collapsed to the ground.

As soon as Buffy disappeared, Dawn's book went all Sumerian. Willow tried to work the magics. She was lost, panicked. She went into the kitchen to get the first-aid kit for Kennedy, with everyone following her, giving her advice.

"Why not try all thirty-two flavors?" Kennedy suggested. "Worst thing that happens is you go brunette."

"That's not the worst thing than can happen," Willow said shortly.

"We have a choice," Anya pointed out. "We can risk Willow's life and the rest of our lives to get Buffy back or we can leave her out there."

Robin spoke up. "If we play it safe back here, Buffy could stay lost."

Anya looked at him. "You missed her 'everyone sucks but me' speech. If she's so superior, let her find her own way back."

"Anya," Xander said, "The First is up and running. Every second that Buffy's not here, is an opportunity for it to show up and rip us to pieces."

Then Dawn helped Willow focus by asking her how another witch would bring Buffy back, and that got Willow talking to Anya about the laws of conservation of magical energies, and . . . again, the need for an exchange.

The demon that had run off would do just fine.

"Get cracking on that portal," Spike said. "Don't be stingy with the mojo. The demon's mine." He walked toward the door.

"Where are you going?" Robin asked.

"Thing I need," Spike replied.

Ultimately, Willow went with creating a barrier of protective sand on the floor of the living room.

"The sand forms a circle," Dawn said, understanding. "The circle acts as a barrier. And the barrier contains the portal."

"Now what?" Kennedy asked. "We hold hands and chant kumbaya or something?"

Willow handed her the bag of sand. "Maybe, till we get the magics up and running. I'm kind of working on my best guess here."

"Will, maybe we should wait," Xander suggested. "See if Spike can bring back that demon."

The Wicca so wished they could. "Opening a portal this size could take days," she told Xander.

"Better get started," Kennedy said.

She began, breathing deeply, then taking her place on the floor in the middle of the circle. She concentrated her energy, found her power, and began to chant.

"Via temporis, iam clamo ad te, via spatii, te jubeo aperire!"

Nothing.

Willow gathered her authority. *"Aperi."*

Still nothing. Willow turned to Dawn.

"Dawnie," she said, "you better put on some coffee. This could take all . . ."

Energy coursed through the room, exploding in a flash of light. Everyone was blown away from the circle, in which the Wicca sat, her eyes black and her voice raised in a roaring, demonic shriek.

Buffy came to. She was in a cave; the three men were looking at her . . . and she was chained to the walls, one manacle on either wrist, connected to . . .

. . . the Earth.

"What is this?" she demanded.

The Men answered:

> *We are at the beginning.*
> *The source of your strength. The well of the*
> *Slayer's power.*
> *This is why we have brought you here.*

"I thought *I* brought me here," Buffy said.

The Men . . . the Shadow Men . . . made no answer, only pounded the Earth in a strange, hypnotic rhythm with their staffs.

"Listen, you guys," she said, "I'm already the Slayer, bursting with power. Really don't need any more."

Then one of them said to her, *The First Slayer did not talk so much.*

Then, as she yanked on her chains again, the men continued to pound the Earth. The one who had spoken brought a box to the center of the circle. Cautiously he opened it, and the three Men stood away, standing like sentinels with their staffs in their hands.

> *Herein lies your truest strength.*
> *The energy of the demon. Its spirit.*
> *Its heart.*

Comprehension dawned. "This is how you?"

> *Created the Slayer? Yes.*

Slowly, a black ether undulated out of the box, tendrils curling and extending, reaching and growing; it danced to the rhythm, it sought . . . home.

The Men were impassive, alert.

It must become one with you.

"No!" Buffy struggled harder against her chains.

This will make you ready for the fight.

"By making me less human?" Buffy demanded.

This is how it was then. How it must be now. This is all there is.

And she struggled as the mist rose, growing fuller, taking shape, entering her through her nose and ears. She screamed, fighting against it, and it must have been her screaming that blocked its entry, for it rose to the ceiling of the cave and came back down to her, encircling her hips. Still, she resisted.

"Make this stop!" she gritted, her jaw clenched.

This is what you came for.

"No! This isn't the way!"

Do not fight this.

* * *

You can tell by the way I wear my coat . . . Spike thought to himself, as he went through the boxes he'd left in the school basement, where his soul had nearly driven him insane. He found his old duster, shook it out, put it on. His armor.

Robin had come back to the school to see if he could find something more to help with the magics. Hearing Spike's footsteps, he leaned out of his office.

Where you going?" he asked Spike coldly.

"Got a job," Spike returned.

Then Robin saw . . . oh, my God, my mother had a coat like that. She was wearing a coat like that last time she said good-bye to me . . .

"Nice coat," he managed neutrally. "Where'd you get it?"

"New York."

Spike walked on.

Black-eyed Willow sat in the middle of the living room, her hair whipping, the eye in the storm. The others gave her wide berth, wary and watching.

"*Via, concursus, tempus, spatium, audi me ut imperio . . .*" Unable to deal with the strain, she shouted, "Screw it! Mighty forces, I suck at Latin, okay? But that's not the issue! I'm the one in charge, and I'm tell you, open up the portal, *now*!"

"It's not happening, Will," Xander said after a moment.

"Give her time," Kennedy protested. "She's getting it."

"Or something's getting her," Xander shot back.

"Will, thinking you better back up a little—"

"*No!*"

Feral, half-crazed, Willow extended her arms toward Anya and Kennedy and hoisted them into the air. Power drained from them in waves, surging into Willow. They writhed; she gave them no quarter. Her hair went black; she opened her mouth and from her, and energy vortexed out.

The portal shimmered before her.

Xander broke the protective barrier, grabbed her up in his arms, and carried her out of the circle.

Her hair immediately turned red . . . and Kennedy wobbled brokenly in shock over what she had done.

Gonna get this job done in record time, Spike thought as he engaged the enemy, which he had found raging about in one of Sunnydale's darker and more loathsome alleys. Spike was tricked out in duster and vampface. *Demon not hard to find, gonna be a piece of cake to kill.*

"Oh, come on now, Nancy, call yourself a demon? I thought you were up for a proper fight!"

They traded blows, big 'uns; head-butting and kicking and all the rest, Spike was up for it the way he used to be before he got all nice and soul-filled. He was a monster, same as the other one—two demons, and if his pockets had been jingling he'd have bet it all on himself. Hell six crowns and tuppence, even more . . .

"Yeah!" he shouted, laughing maniacally.

* * *

In the desert cave, Buffy glared at the Men, who continued to watch, but did not see . . .

As the mist probed for its prey again, Buffy was half-mad with anger. "You think I came all this way to get knocked up by some demon dust?" she demanded. "I can't fight this. I know that now. But you guys? You're just men." She ripped her chains free. "Just the men who did this . . . to her. Whoever that girl was before she was The First Slayer."

You don't understand.

"No, you don't understand!" she shouted. "You violated that girl, made her kill for you because you're weak, you're pathetic, and you obviously have nothing to show me."

She let loose with the chains, which were connected to her manacles, swinging them at the legs of one Man, at the staff of the other. She knocked them down. They rose, and with their staffs, began to fight her. The black mist rose and undulated, presiding over the violence.

Then two of the Men were down, and the third stood with his staff, steady as she approached. She grabbed his staff and broke it.

The black mist vanished.

"I knew it," she crowed. "It's always the staff."

We offered you power, the Man said, looking very sad, and not at all wise.

"Tell me something I don't know."

As you wish.

And with great sorrow, and reverence, he placed his hand against Buffy's head. . . .

* * *

The demon and Spike kept on with the fighting. The demon pinned him against the wall, but Spike did what he did best: grabbed the bastard's head and gave it a right yank. Its neck snapped, the demon died, and Spike contemptuously tossed its carcass to the ground.

Fully vamped, loving it all, he took out a cigarette and put it in his mouth. "I don't know your feelings, big guy," he said, "but to me, a tussle like that . . ." He struck a match on the demon's ear and lit his cig; let his face go back to human again. ". . . is good for the soul."

He hoisted the wreckage over his back, carried it back to Buffy's place, and tossed it into the portal.

As fast as it flashed through . . .

. . . Buffy reappeared.

No one greeted her aloud; no one ran to hug her. No one moved. No one could manage to do anything but . . .

What I saw . . .

What I saw her do, what I felt, Kennedy thought, as Willow approached her. *My God, I thought it was about fairy tales. I was so naïve . . .*

"Hey, you okay?" Willow asked anxiously. "You've been kind of quiet since . . ."

"You sucked the life out of me?" Kennedy accused her.

Willow took it straight on the chin. "Yeah. Since that." She regarded her young lover and said, not pulling any punches herself, "It's important you know.

What I am. What I'm like when . . . I'm like that."

Kennedy faltered. "I thought it would be . . . I don't know, cool somehow." A beat, and then, "It just hurt."

"I'm really sorry," Willow said. "It's just, you were the most powerful person nearby and . . . well, that's how it works." She added with rigorous honest, "That's how I work."

"I got that," Kennedy said. "You told me." She took a breath. "I'll . . . see you in the morning."

Kennedy went into her room . . . and shut the door.

Willow walked on, pausing on the threshold of Buffy's room. Buffy was awake, staring straight ahead, seeing things Willow could only imagine. Or not.

"Thanks for bringing me back. Again," Buffy said.

Willow walked over. "Well, that's what I do." She perched on the edge of the bed.

"I was hard on you guys today," Buffy began.

"Aw, it's all right. You needed to be." She wrinkled up her nose and gently added, "Although, Twinkies and kisses? Also peachy motivational tools."

That failed to make Buffy smile. Somberly, she said, "I think I made a mistake." She turned to Willow. "Those men that I met? You know, the Shadow Men? They offered me more power . . . but I didn't like the loop hole."

Willow raised her brows. "So you turned it down? It's okay, Buffy. We'll get by." She added, "We always do."

"I don't know." Buffy gave her head a little shake.

"They showed me . . ." She trailed off.

"Showed you what?" Willow asked her.

"That The First Slayer was right," Buffy replied, ticking her glance toward her old friend. "It isn't enough."

"Why, Buffy?" Willow asked. "What did you see? What did they show you?"

A cave. beneath. And in it, a Turok-han roared with battle fury, wild, frenzied, its blood fever raging.

And behind it, and around it, and beneath it . . .

Thousands more.

Thousands upon thousands more, a sea. An army, massing.

Apocalypse.

Hundreds of thousands, preparing to march.

To devour.

Chapter Sixteen: "Storyteller"

INT. MY ELEGANT STUDY—NIGHT

My camera pans across my elegant study—there they are, my Time-Life collections of Nietzsche, Joseph Campbell, and Tolkien—the masters! Then my Science Fiction Book Club leather-bound editions of the seminal works of Wager's Kane and Edgar Rice Burroughs; then my backed and bagged Spiderman's, my Batman's, and the complete Gor saga . . .

Then my first close-up, my elegant smoking jacket and my pipe. Diana Rigg, where are you now? I don't notice the camera at first, and then I do.

I close the book on my lap.

ME

Oh! Hello there, gentle viewers!

(closing my book)

You caught me catching up on an old

"The world is **seriously** doomed"

The Potentials

Clem

"Grr, argh!"

"Why didn't I die?"

Harbringer

"That's my girl, always doing the stupid thing."

"Anything you say is just going to sound like good-bye."

favorite. It's wonderful to get lost in a
story, isn't it? Adventure and heroics and
discovery, don't they just take you away?
(puffing on my pipe except that if I cough, just
set it down on my beautiful crystal ashtray)
Come with me now, if you will, gentle
viewers. Join me on a new voyage of
the mind, a little tale I like to call, "Buffy,
A Slayer of the Vampeers."

ME SOME MORE
It was cold last night, and the wind was crew-ell,
but the Slayer had a job to do. . . .

Buffy was on patrol in a hot outfit, and the vamp that
was after her was eager to turn her into his vampiric
spawn, perhaps even his bride of blood. But ah ha! She
tricked him, flipped over him to vault to a very tall
tombstone, and pause in a handstand there, a total 10 if
she were in the Slayer Olympics. And then she shot
him with her custom crossbow.

Little did she realize, however, that another vamp-
peer lunged from the shadows, ready to spawnize her
as well.

AND YET MORE ME
Ouch! My goodness! Things look bad
for the Slayer, don't they?

And then someone was pounding on the door. Andrew,
sitting (fully clothed) on the toilet set as he taped him-

self, jumped as Anya burst into the bathroom.

"For God's sake, Andrew!" she cried. "You've been in here thirty minutes. What are you doing?"

Flustered, the young auteur of the cinema replied, "Entertaining and educating."

"Man," she barked. "Why can't you just masturbate like the rest of us."

Oh, hot, Andrew thought, using his USC Film School–quality imagination.

EXT. CEMETERY—NIGHT

Buffy was being attacked by Vampire #2, then *yeaah! dust!* and Andrew thrilled. He ran up to her, and enthusing, "That was great! I completely got you dusting that guy on film. Hey, why do vampires show up on video?"

Buffy scowled. "I told you I didn't want you doing that! It's distracting!"

And off she stomped, totally breaking his fourth wall, as he caught up beside her and said, "Okay, I'll cut the footage together and do the intro tomorrow. 'She was a woman in danger . . . or was she?'" He added, "It's a valuable record. An important document for the ages: a Slayer in action."

She glared at him. "A nerd in pain. Would they like that? "Cause we could do that.'"

AND WE JUMP CUT TO . . .

Anya dragging Andrew out of the bathroom. There was quite a line of Potentials waiting to use the bathroom, with their little toiletry bags and fuzzy slippers, so young, so sweet, too young to die!

"The world is going to want to know about Buffy," Andrew told Anya as she dragged him along the hall. "It's a story of ultimate triumph tainted with the bitterness for what's been lost in the struggle. It's a legacy for future generations!"

Anya was unmoved. "If there are any. Buffy seems to think that this apocalypse is going to actually be, you know, apocalyptic. Your story seems pretty pointless."

"Oh, and I was going to interview you later today," he said offhandedly, but with the guile of Anthony Perkins in *Psycho* (why did Van Sant even bother? Heresy! Except that Viggo was in it, pre-Aragorn, and that was cool) "You know, 'cause you have that unique perspective on the whole thing. Give it editorial balance and . . . glamour . . ." He trailed wistfully off.

And . . . *bingo*!

"Balance is important," she said. "People don't always take that into account. I could bring you that, absolutely."

THE EXPOSITORY NARRATIVE

. . . provided by me, standing in front of the Big Board, and shot in the basement . . . and on the board, the school with the Hellmouth beneath with a big bunch of black Dry-Erase (I'll make a demon shoot out of it for emphasis); then some Bringers—say, five, with their eyes Xed out and pumpkin mouths; then big, red scary THE FIRST in the upper right . . . cool . . . I can probably storyboard for Lucas someday . . . he needs me, I can help him write more interesting stories than that hideous Episode Numero Uno, that's for sure . . .

"Let's explore the world of our story, shall we? Buffy lives in Sunnydale, California. There's a Hellmouth underneath the high school. And now there's that thing in the basement of the high school called the Seal of Danzal-Danzalthar. Um, due to some circumstances it got opened up . . . a little bit . . . recently . . . and this nasty, nasty vampire thing came out of it. It was just awful. Awful!

"This whole thing is being orchestrated by something called The First. It's made up of all the evil in the whole world. Oh, there's also these guys." *I point to the Bringers.* "They work for The First. We don't know much about them except that they're very ugly, and they're very mobile from blind people." *I smile.* "Is that clear?"

MIDDLE SHOT

Andrew brought his camcorder into the kitchen as the Potentials prepared them hearty repasts of kids cereal and cried loudly and lustily for the low-fat milk. Xander the man who was the heart of the Slayer machine, was fortifying himself right out of the box, and tension was rampant over some new development.

"Oh, um, we're out of Raisin Bran," the young sister of the Slayer informed Anya, the twice-reformed former vengeance demon and now glamorous spokeswoman for balance.

Then there she was, in a total Ridley Scott commercial, pouring herself a bowl of cereal . . . Buffy, her hair windswept and free. With a lion's heart and the face of an angel.

"She's never afraid because she knows her side will always win," Andrew breathed.

Then Spike appeared in the viewfinder, shirtless, and brushed his hand against his Slayer-woman. They moved to embrace, the tamed alpha male and the woman who had conquered him . . . their clinch every inch a Fabio moment . . .

"You can feel the heat between them," Andrew murmured, "although technically, as a vampire, he's room temperature."

Anya appeared next, sucking grapes off the stem . . . popping one into her delectable mouth . . .

"Anya, a feisty waif with a fiery temper and a vulnerable heart that she hides even from herself . . ."

IN FRONT OF THE CAMERA

"Oh, for God's sake," Buffy said to Xander, "Is he doing that again? Can't we make him stop?"

Rona looked thoughtful. "I don't know. If we save the world, it will be kind of nice to have a record of it."

"If we don't save the world," Amanda added, "then nothing matters."

Her spoon halfway to her mouth, Kennedy stared at Amanda. "That's catchy, Amanda. Let's make that our slogan."

Xander said, "It is kind of a shame you keep saving the world and there's not any proof."

"And it helps the girls with their training," Willow offered. "You know, reviewing the tapes."

"Come on," Buffy said. "No one else thinks this is idiotic?"

Spike—wearing a shirt in real life—shrugged. "Long as he's not pointing that thing at me, seems like a fine way to keep the boy busy."

"This is not about keeping busy!" Buffy said, frustrated. "This is about war." She paused, then added, "I'm sorry to jump all over you guys, but . . . I have to tell you what's going on. There's something new."

Oh, my God, this is like the Osbournes, Andrew thought.

"You have to get ready. No one here is ready. We can all survive what's coming . . ." Buffy was saying.

Oh, God, rewind, Andrew thought.

He wandered into the dining room and trained the camera on a far more interesting subject:

ME AGAIN
    Honestly, gentle viewers, these
    motivational speeches of hers get a
    little long. I'll take you back in
    there a little later. In the in-between-
    time, I thought you might
    want to know a little about me, your
    humble host. I'm a man with a
    burden, a man with a dark past. You
    see I was once a . . . Supervillain.

INT. SCIENCE LAB—DAY
    In his fashionable suit and stylish sunglasses, Andrew completed the latest in a series of diabolical inventions intended to thwart the Slayer as his adoring

sidekicks, Warren and Jonathan, raptly attended to his every word:

"Thus , the validity of the Bronsted-Debye-Huckel equation at low ionic strength has been amply tested and the charges on the reactant ions are well known, if their reagents are properly characters," he concluded.

"What'll it do to Buffy?" Warren was dying to know.

Andrew could barely stand how amazingly neat he was. "Make her . . . *super-magnetic.*"

"Wow," Jonathan gasped. "She won't be able to get out of her car."

"And knives and other sharp things will fly at her," Warren said, clearly stunned by Andrew's super-genius.

"We could walk right by her and she wouldn't be able to stop us," Andrew elaborated.

"Unless we were wearing, like, metal belt buckles," Warren pointed out, concerned. "'Cause then we'd stick to her."

Andrew raised his chin. "In my plan, we are beltless."

Jonathan and Warren took off their goggles and goggle-free, were goggle-eyed at their incredible leader.

"Wow," Jonathan said, "you're the best, Andrew."

"Yep," the hero-worshipping Jonathan added. "Good-looking, and smart, too."

BACK TO BUFFY . . . OR NOT?

". . . more than just a battle," the Slayer was saying. "It's going to be a battle like we've never seen before."

Andrew murmured, "She's not done. Even Willow

looks bored, and she's usually can take a lot of that stuff."

Through the viewfinder, Kennedy gave Willow a shy caress on her beautifully proportioned lesbian arm.

"Oooh, do you see that? That's important. Willow and Kennedy have been in a kind of a bad place lately, but things are looking up.

"You see, Kennedy pursued the reluctant Willow and won her heart, only to find herself frightened when she glimpsed the darkness that still lies within the witch's mind. Side note: I once had my own personal encounter with Dark Willow." [PRODUCTION NOTE: SEE IF MAGIC BOX SECURITY CAMERA CAUGHT ANY OF THIS. IT WAS WHEN SHE CAME AFTER US LAST YEAR.]

FLASHBACK TO MAGIC BOX—LAST YEAR

"Jonathan, Andrew," Dark Willow said scarily. At least, her uncanny voice worked its desired effect upon Jonathan, who was weaker of will. Andrew stayed proud, and true . . .

"You boys like magics, don't you?" Dark Willow intoned. Then she put out the lights and taunted them, saying, "Abracadabra." Her soul-searing Death Spell rent the very fabric of time itself as it blasted toward them like a very cool CGI force created by noted Santa Monica–based wizard Loni Peristere. Terrorized, Jonathan ducked.

"Haltem," Andrew said calmly, barely raising a finger.

The spell evaporated.

"Okay, I didn't see that coming," Dark Willow conceded.

"That's because we have power you can't imagine," Andrew explained kindly.

"We do?" Ah, that was from Jonathan, Andrew's guileless protégé.

"You, Dark Willow, wield a force of mighty evil it is true, but you are new to the game, little one."

She tried again. and he deflected her again with an idle wave of his hand..

"Damn," Dark Willow blurted, not able to conceal her admiration. "That is one effective counter-spell."

"Thank you, little one," Andrew said, as Jonathan gazed worshipfully on.

BACK TO BUFFY . . . OR THE KITCHEN?

"I think she's done talking," Andrew announced. "That usually means she had to go to work. Let's see what those little locusts left for breakfast, shall we?"

School was a madhouse, a madhouse. Kids fighting; shy girl starting to go invisible; girl rushing out of the girls' room sobbing that the mirror said she was fat. "It said it!" she wept, running away.

Then a stressed-out boy was ranting about his trig exam, which covered three extra chapters, and his English paper and—

"I feel like I'm gonna explode!"

Uh-oh.

Buffy walked up to the boy and said, "You just need to relax, you know?" To his friends, she said,

"You know, um, maybe one of you guys could give him a foot rub?"

Then she went in to see Robin, who was holding an ice pack to his head. He told her, "Someone threw a rock at me as I got out of my car. Didn't get really get a good chance to see who."

She took a Band-Aid from the open first-aid kit open on the office counter and prepared to stick it on his head. "Yeah, well, it could have been any of them," she said. "Students, teachers . . . something is going on today."

Robin grimaced as she taped on the bandage. "Yes, well, that occurred to me as I ducked the other two rocks."

She nodded. "There's a thing that happens here. In this school. Over the Hellmouth. Where the way a thing feels, it kind of starts being that way . . . for real. I've seen all these things before, just not all at once."

He processed that. "So, what? It's like hell's a bustin' out all over?"

ME HERE IN FRONT OF BIG BOARD, NODDING. THIS WILL BE A LOT LIKE PROFESSOR DR. EVERETT VON SCOTT IN *ROCKY HORROR PICTURE SHOW*.

"Exactly," Buffy said. "Being in a high school can feel like being at war, so now it's true. The students feel like the teachers are out to get them. The Chess Club resents the French Club for taking the activities room, and well, everybody hates the cheerleaders. If we don't do something about this, we're going to have a riot on our hands. And a lot of other nasty stuff too."

Ka-BLAM.

Brain matter splatted against the window.

Buffy said sadly, "He really should have had the foot rub."

INT. SUMMERS' HOUSE—DINING ROOM / FOYER / LIVING ROOM—DAY

MOI
Dawn is a typical American teenager.
Bubbly and sweet with a hunger for
fun and a smile that lights up the room.

DAWN
Hello.

MOI SOME MORE
Dawn used to be a key.

INSERT CLOSE-UP OF THE KEY ET TU, MOI
I have no idea what that means.

INT. LIVING ROOM AT BUFFY'S HOUSE—DAY

AND YET . . . MOI!
Hey, here's something I think you're going
to be interested in.

Pan pass Kennedy and Willow making out passionately on the couch to show a . . . CLOSE-UP on the window behind the sofa.

YOU GUESSED IT: ME

Look at the fine work Xander did on replacing that window sash. You can't even tell it's new, it blends in so well. He's extraordinary.

Buffy and Robin had spread blueprints all over his desk, working on the school blowups one by one.

"You've dealt with this before? I mean, you've seen stuff like this in the high school?"

She got a little nostalgic. "Well, sure. You know, swim team monsters or killer prom dogs. Again, not all at once. My guess? It's that Seal thing in the basement. It's like all the Hellmouth's energy is trying to escape in that one little spot, and it's getting all . . ."

"Focusy," he finished.

"Careful," she told him. "You're starting to speak like me now."

INT. LIVING ROOM AT BUFFY'S HOUSE—DAY [THIS IS XANDER AND ANYA INTERVIEW #1 FOR "BUFFY, THE SLAYER OF THE VAMPEERS" OR ELSE: "BUFFY, THE SLAYER WHO KNEW NO FEAR."]

ME

I understand that exactly one year ago today you left Anya at the altar. Any comment on that?

XANDER

Whoa, what the hell?

ANYA

What *do* you have to say for yourself one year later?

XANDER

I've apologized enough. That's what I have to say.

ME

But you think it was something that called for an apology.

XANDER

Well, yes.

ME

So, then you don't think it was the right then to do.

ANYA

Of course he doesn't think it was the right thing to do!

XANDER

It was the right thing to do.

ANYA

What?!

ME

Interesting. I feel like we're getting to something here.

XANDER

Look, Anya, if I'd married you, it would have always been against what I thought was best. It wouldn't have worked.

ANYA

But-but we still spark! I get jealous of you, you get jealous of me! You still love me!

ME

Ooh, is that true, Xander? Do you still love her? *(Oh, my God, I am better than Larry King!)*

Buffy and Robin had moved down the basement . . . where, sure enough, the Seal of Danzalthar lay fully exposed in the dirt floor.

"I swear we just covered this thing up," Buffy said.

"It doesn't want to stay hidden any more," Robin countered. "It wants to turn these kids into monsters and victims and who knows what."

Buffy took a breath, let it out. "It's more than that. I had a vision the other day."

He was intrigued. "You have visions?"

She nodded. "Sometimes."

Intrigued further. "How do you know they're not just dreams?"

She smiled. "You're running to catch the bus naked? That's a dream. An army of vicious vampire creatures? That's a vision. Also, I was awake."

"A bus to where?" he teased. "I mean, an army of how many?

"Hundreds. Maybe hundreds of hundreds. All I know is that the last Ubervamp I faced crawled out of that very hole."

He knelt on the Seal, and she came along for the ride, saying, "Willow did a search on the symbolic database, but it turns out everybody loves a good goat's tongue. Rock groups, covens, and Greek cookbooks. She said she couldn't narrow it down."

He gave her a penetrating look. "And you trust her?"

She blinked. "Yes. Why wouldn't I trust her?"

"I don't know why any of you should trust one another," he said. "You've all been evil at some point, right?"

Buffy shook her head. "No. Willow had a bad patch, but I've never been."

His voice was growly in an evil way as he turned to her and said, "Evil is as evil does, and I know what you're doing." He stood, and his eyes glowed milky white. "You're with that vampire, screwing that vampire, you filthy whore!"

He charged at her and she dodged him and he ran into he wall. Panting, he said, "Whoa. What happened?"

"I think it was controlling you," she managed.

He was abashed . . . and worried.

"Buffy, we've got to get rid of this Seal. We've got to shut it down before it starts affecting everyone."

"I think I have a pretty good idea who we should talk to," Buffy ventured. "The guy that fed it its first drop of blood."

As if on cue, a very cute little pink piglet chittered

past them, scampering off into the shadows.

"God, I hope that's not a student," Wood murmured.

SPIKE, TAKE #1

Spike glared at the camera and realized he was being taped. He flicked his cigarette butt toward the lens and lunged toward it in a move that would make Randy Rude of the WWE PROUD!

"Thought I told you to piss off with that bloody camera. And here you are again with that thing in my face!" he thundered. "Sod off 'fore I rip your throat out and—"

CUT! BAD LIGHTING!

SPIKE, TAKE #2

Spike glared at the camera and realized he was being taped. He flicked his . . .

[Oh, my God, the tale of Xander and Anya must be told . . . over and over and over and over and over again!]

As they sat on the sofa, Xander said, "I mean, you were the one who didn't want to keep seeing each other."

Anya frowned. "And here's where we hop on the merry-go-round of rotating knives. I blame you and you blame me and we both end up all cut to shreds. Please, just tell . . . do you still love me?" Her voice broke.

Xander nodded. "Yes. I still love you. I always will. I just don't know if that means anything for us anymore."

Anya said, "Well, I love you, too. I don't know if that means anything, either."

"Well, that's nice to hear," Xander said tenderly. "I'm not going to find anyone out there like you, am I?"

"Doesn't seem likely," Anya replied.

"I guess I'm more replaceable, obviously."

He's talking about when she had sex with Spike!

"No. There's no one like you, Xander. You were willing to stand up to danger, even when your hands had no weapons. You were ready to protect me with your life."

Xander gazed at her. "I guess we fit together pretty good."

"We fit together great." She smiled back at him.

"You know," Xander confessed, "sometimes I want you back in my life."

She gazed at him tenderly. "I hope you know you never left my heart."

And over and over and over AGAIN!

And then, gentle viewer, I was intruded upon!

Buffy and her handsome young principal friend-slash-sidekick burst into the basement. They talked so fast and urgent that someone who was trying to write down every word they sent would have a heck of a time of it unless they had gone to school to become a court reporter, or something.

"Heads up, Andrew. We've got to talk," Buffy said to Andrew.

Robin said, "We just spent the day keeping a lid on a war."

Andrew stood, excited, and said, "Oooh, that would be very exciting on tape!"

Buffy looked irritated as she crossed her arms and continued, all Miss Practical, "The school is out of control with energy from the Hellmouth. It's time for you to help, Andrew."

And here he was, Mr. Art. "Well, right now, I'm really more about the recording of the . . ."

"No," she insisted, as firmly as a producer, *whose job, let's face it, is to say no. Look at Gareth Davies.* "The Seal thing is your baby, and you have to get in there before it tears everything apart."

Once in the basement of Sunnydale High School, lived a mama Bezoar who hatched some eggs that took over everybody's minds and made them attack each other.

Variation on the theme, but with the volume pumped way up: the Seal of Danthalzar began to summon the students of the new school, and they answered, stumbling down the stairs and walking through the passages, to come upon the seal, kneel, and chant above it in Latin.

And it began to glow.

[PRODUCTION NOTE TO ME: WE COULD SHOOT THIS SCENE ON THE UNIVERSAL BACKLOT. THEY HAVE A VERY CUTE MEXICAN VILLAGE THERE. THE TRAM RIDE GOES THROUGH IT, DURING WHICH THERE IS A MOCK FLOOD TO SHOW HOW SPECIAL EFFECTS WORK. BUT WE COULD ASK THEM VERY NICELY TO GIVE US A FEW MINUTES TO SHOOT THIS NEXT SCENE,

MAYBE WHEN EVERYONE IS HAVING LUNCH OR SOMETHING. WE'LL GET DAWN TO ASK. NO ONE COULD SAY NO TO HER. OR ELSE WE WILL ASK BUFFY TO THREATEN THEM.

BUT FIRST, THE SCARY MONTAGE/DREAM SEQUENCE]

It was Mexico, the dingy hideout of Andrew and Jonathan. They slept fitfully, tormented by horrible images: the Seal of Danthalzar; a Turok-han; a Bringer stabbing the Istanbulian Potential; the Cheese Man; the Turok-han reprise; cheese slices; the Frankfurtian Potential dying; the Turok-han again, even scarier; the Seal opening, more more more more. . . .

And a voice, vaguely reminiscent of the one in the Pirates of the Caribbean ride in Disneyland, booming "*DEZ-day ah-BAH-ho tay DEV-or-ah.*"

They woke up simultaneously . . . and not for the first time.

Jonathan was panting "Omigod," and Andrew breathed, "Hay-sus."

Tears formed in the tormented eyes of Jonathan as he said, "*Desme abajo tay devorah.* What does it mean? What does it mean?"

For a while, they had guessed that it had been part of the lost footage of Klaatu's speech in *The Day the Earth Stood Still*, which had been excised because the censors thought it was blasphemous and was certain to upset the American audience. But they'd checked into that, and though the words have been close, they weren't close enough.

Now Jonathan said, "Let's try looking it up again in the morning in the *dictionario*. Holy cats, that was terrifying."

Andrew nodded. "We're fugitives, haunted by our past, tormented by a message we don't understand."

"We're hunted men," Jonathan concurred, "driven mad by forces beyond our understanding."

"We're men of hidden power," Andrew continued, "tortured from within by . . . by a voice from out of nowhere." (That sounds like the Disneyland guy's voice. In fact, he is also the voice of Amtrak. This is especially evident when the train pulls into the Anaheim station . . .

Oh, Anaheim! How I miss you!)

"I don't deserve this," Jonathan blurted. "I wasn't even that evil."

"I thought you were evil," Andrew assured him. As Jonathan glanced questioningly at him and they both sat up, Andrew said, "I respected your ideas for evil projects and I thought you had good follow-through."

"Oh." Jonathan got a little lift from that. "It's nice that you noticed."

CUT.

"Okay," Willow said, "I think we're getting a little off track here."

In Buffy's living room, Willow, Kennedy, the young and handsome Principal Wood, Spike, and La Buffeleta Sumprema were all staring at Andrew, who was supposed to be staring at a glowing memory crystal in order to evoke his memories about the Seal.

"I'm all tense," Andrew murmured. "Can't I have a

cool, refreshing Zima?"

"No Zima," Buffy snapped. "You were The First one to uncover the Seal and feed it blood. How did you know it was there? How did you know what to do?"

"I—I don't know. Stuff happened." He shrugged. "I forget. I'm not a part of this. I document, I don't participate. I'm a detached journalist, recording with a neutral eye—"

"Andrew, stop it, or I'm going to smash this camera over your head," Buffy said, hefting his sacred camcorder in her powerful grip. Clearly she had no idea it was as precious to him as a Panavision once had been to Spielberg, who was The First director ever to use one in a commercial film—*Sugarland Express*, starring Goldie Hawn.

"Actually, I'm gonna do that anyway, so you might as well talk," she added, and all was despair, despair . . .

"Stop going off topic," Willow ordered him.

"I wasn't going off topic," Andrew told her. "It's going to get relevant in a second, because Jonathan's going to go to the bathroom."

And so, we return to México, where . . .

"I'm going to go to the bathroom," Jonathan announced.

Off he went, and Andrew idled away the time by singing "La Cucaracha" to himself . . .

Then there he was, dead Warren, only looking great, and he said, "You get the knife?"

Andrew gasped and got to his feet. "Oh, gosh! I'm glad to see you!"

"Me, too," Warren said fondly. "You're looking

good."

"Am I?" Andrew was sure he was being polite. He rubbed his face. "I probably have pillow creases . . ."

"No, no, it's good," Warren assured him. "You're a man on the run. You've got kind of a wild, desperate thing going." He came nearer and said again, "Did you get the knife?"

"Yeah, it wasn't easy. I had to meet this demon guy who sells all kinds of weird weapons and stuff."

"Yeah?" Warren asked. "Show me."

Andrew got a little anxious. "Well, I didn't buy them, but there were poison arrows and this sort of collapsible sword . . ."

"Show me the knife!" Warren said impatiently. "Quick, before the shortcake comes back."

"Oh, it'll be awhile. He's got a shy bladder." He called over to the bathroom. "Jonathan, you okay in there?"

"Don't talk to me," Jonathan snapped. "I'm fine."

Andrew got the knife from under the bed and showed it to Warren. It was not of the Ginzu variety. "Pretty knife," he said. "Except the, uh, stabbing. I don't . . . I don't think I can do it. Jonathan has been a good friend to me here in Mexico." He smiled faintly. "He said he'll buy me a burro."

Warren didn't take the knife, which Andrew was almost hoping he would do, just so he wouldn't have to keep track of it anymore; but then Andrew remembered that Warren couldn't take corporeal form just now.

"Oh, you can stab him," Warren encouraged him. "It's all part of the plan. That boy's blood is a powerful tribute.

It's a gift to something very big, very important . . . and ultimately, won't even hurt him! We get a reward," he reminded Andrew. "You and me and him, too."

"We live as gods," Andrew murmured.

He saw them in his mind's eye in the Elysian Fields, as presented in *Young Hercules*, or rather, *Fern Gully*—the three of them in blazing white togas and wearing crowns of laurel leaves, frolicking with harps among daisies and poppies. Butterflies flitted; bars of gold gleamed; a unicorn flitted past and it was all very Loreena McKennitt, or maybe the cover of the Kenny Loggins CD. At any rate, much airbrushed joy as they strummed and sang, "We are as gods! We are as gods!"

"There's power in the knife," Warren reminded him. "Drive the words deep into him. It's the only way for us to get our reward."

"Got it. If I kill him with this knife," Andrew said, "We live as gods."

CUT TO THE RELENTLESS INTERROGATION OF THE MISUNDERSTOOD HERO IN BUFFY'S STYLISH LIVING ROOM

"We need to see that knife," Willow mused. "There's something there."

Buffy turned to Willow's young and hot lesbian girlfriend and said, "Kennedy, search his stuff. There's something there."

"It's not in my stuff," Andrew told her. "It's in the kitchen. In the cutlery drawer." He said to Buffy, "You didn't have any steak knives."

Willow stared at him in revolted fascination. "You

put your old murder weapon in with our utensils?"

He shrugged, not quite getting the problem. "I washed it."

Willow continued, "The First said something about words. 'Drive the words deep into him.'"

Andrew thought a moment. "There was some carving on the blade. I just thought it was a pattern."

"Found it," Kennedy called out.

She handed the knife to Willow, who showed it to Andrew.

"Okay, you're Mr. Demon-summoner. How are you with demon languages?"

He stared down at the hilt, and realized that he had been staring at the runes upside down *all this time*!

"Whoa, you were right," he said. "It's in Tawarick. It's, uh, like proto-Tawarick. It's really, really old." He studied it a moment. "It says, 'The Blood which I spill, I consecrate to the oldest evil.'"

Wow.

In the way of popular and powerful individuals who have worked hard and played hard together, everyone else except Andrew, who was left out, went into the dining room to make a plan. Andrew doubted it had much to do with him . . . until Buffy came back to him and said, "Guess what, Andy. You just won yourself a free vacation to the beautiful downtown Hellmouth."

"So he can do what?" Spike demanded. "Yell at it in its own language?"

"Maybe," Will said.

"What?" Robin was puzzled. "I'm not following."

"Look, we have to deal with the Seal right away. We already might have to just shut the school down, and I'm not losing any more territory to The First. Besides, it's the only thing we've got."

Willow explained, "The Seal responds to this language somehow, or The First wouldn't have needed this knife. Andrew knows the language, so he can talk to it, maybe give it commands."

Oh, God. This can't be happening.

The Supervillain swayed with terror.

(And so here I am, filing the war zone that has become Sunnydale High School . . . it's like in *Pitch Black,* when Vin Diesel as Rick Riddick stands all alone on the planet of New Mecca and darkness shades the planet. He must face the overwhelming hordes monsters bursting from every corner of everywhere . . .)

DIE CHEERLEADERS was spray-painted on the wall, and MARCHING BAND RULES. There were fifty-five gallon drums spewing flames and smoke, and chaos, and noise.

"Nice way to run a school," Spike drawled. "There's got to be kids injured in here."

Principal Wood glared at him and said, "Yeah, easy pickings for the likes of you, eh?"

"Hey, to help, you know," Spike shot back, giving him a look.

"Check out Spike and the principal," Andrew said into the camera. "There something going on there.

Sexual tension you could cut with a knife."

The belly of the beast was filled with books, trash, and rubble. Some students ran past, amok. Then one jumped out from behind a corner and hit Principal Wood with a fire extinguisher! Another ran off with Buffy!

And yet another hit Spike with part of a locker.

As Andrew wisely retreated, he murmured, "Oh, God, struck down before I achieve redemption."

Not burdened with cameras, the others fought back; Buffy freed herself and *el prinicpale* grabbed the locker door. Spike started beating up one of the boys.

"Then Buffy said, "Spike, Wood!" I need you to stay here, holding the line of retreat."

Then she grabbed Andrew and dragged him down, down, down the rabbit hole of doom—*the basement.*

"We make our way down the stairs carefully, alert for any danger," Andrew whispered.

Buffy took his camera away. "No more." She clamped the viewfinder shut with her powerful yet beautifully manicured fingers.

"But I want the world to see what you do," he protested.

"What I do is too important to show the world," she replied.

"Ooh, I like that," he said appreciatively.

"Be quiet!" she snapped at him. "I don't want a biographer, especially a murderer."

Ouch-iewawa.

"Yeah, well, see, about that . . . we just keep tossing that word around," Andrew said nervously, but that's not really what happened."

"*What*? You stabbed Jonathan to death. What were you trying to do? Scratch his back from the front?"

"It was confusing," Andrew protested. "Jonathan and I were digging, but Warren was there, and only I could see him. . . ."

CUT TO THE TRUE VERSION OF WHAT REALLY HAPPENED

Andrew and Jonathan were in the basement uncovering the Seal of Danzalthar while Warren was observing.

"Not one of them cares about you," Andrew was saying to Jonathan.

"But I care about them. That's why I'm here," Jonathan replied.

"Do it. Stab him," Warren urged him.

"No! I can't do it!"

Jonathan stopped digging. "What?"

"Do it now," Warren insisted.

"This isn't right," Andrew said firmly.

"Stab him. Spill the blood."

Jonathan frowned. "Who are you talking to? What isn't right?"

And then Andrew pulled out the knife, saying to Warren, "Did you actually think I could use this?"

"A knife?" Jonathan asked, wide-eyed. "You tricked me, damn you! I'll kill you!"

"Stab him! You have to!" Warren shouted. "If you fail, you'll die a lost soul and I'll hate you forever!"

"I'll kill you! I'll kill you!" Jonathan screamed.

They wrestled with the knife; Andrew tried with all his might to stop their mortal combat, but then

Jonathan fell against the knife, *fell, I tell you!*

And Jonathan fell to the ground.

(Then there was a dramatic pull-back as I raised my hands to the unforgiving heavens and cried:

"Nooooooooooooooooooooooooooooooooooooooo!")

"See, I'm a man trapped by circumstances into paying for a crime I didn't even . . ."

"I thought you would say that," Buffy said. "I saw the Seal possess Wood like that earlier today."

CUT TO THE TRUE VERSION OF WHAT REALLY HAPPENED, FROM A DIFFERENT BUT EQUALLY VALID PERSPECTIVE

Jonathan said, "That's why I'm here."

Then the hideous Seal of Danzalthar, cunning, baffling, yet powerful, possessed Andrew spirit, body, and soul. His eyes went white in the throes of his possession as he shouted, "Die! Die! Die!" stabbing his friend from many angles.

Then he saw Warren, watching him, and regained the color of his irises as he shouted, "What have I done? Get out of my brain!"

(There was a dramatic pull-back as I fell to my knees and cupped my hands to my temples, screaming like Charlton Heston in *Planet of the Apes*:

"Aaaaaaaaaaaaaaaaaaaaaaaaaaaaaaaaaaaaaaaaaaah!")

Buffy glared at him. "You just completely changed your entire story."

"Did not," he said,

"You did too," she insisted.

But as they reached the outer portal of the evil, beating chamber of the black heart of Sunnydale, strange chanting filled Andrew's ears.

"There's someone in there. We're going in. Just be prepared, okay? The Seal could have done anything to them."

They entered the chamber.

Five students had carved the damned sigils of The First into the faces, thus mutilating themselves . . . and then they had mystically changed into Bringers, servants of The First.

"Nope, they're okay," Buffy drawled.

A ROMANTIC INTERLUDE

Xander and Anya lay together on a cot in the basement, speaking in tones vaguely reminiscent of the poignant scene in Stephen King's *The Shining* as Wendy recalls her lovemaking with Jack.

"Wow," Xander said. "That was nice."

"Certainly was, you carpenter, you," Anya murmured, pleased.

Xander glanced at the wall. "It's too bad Buffy took Spike's chains down, huh?"

"You said it," she agreed.

[LONG BEAT.]

"Mmm, I feel good," Xander said.

"Well, yeah. I'm a spitfire in the bedroom," she said proudly.

[LONG BEAT.]

"Yeah, I always knew we'd do that again."

"Yeah, one more time, anyway."

Xander asked gently, "Is that what it was?" He looked at her. "One more time?"

They looked at each other with tenderness.

"I think maybe we're really over," she said. "Which is . . . it's good, right? I mean, now we can move on."

The Seal was glowing as Buffy fought the student-Bringers. One of them threw her to the ground as she kicked his knees, sending him to the ground on top of her. Buffy launched the dead weight of the injured student up at the next attacker.

"She's like a woman fighting for more than life," Andrew said into the microphone of his camera, which he had retrieved. "She fights like fighting *is* life. It is the air she breathes, and she knows she will win because there is no alternative."

Then she knocked out the last Bringer and whirled on him. "It's your turn, Andrew," she announced.

She pulled out the knife and walked toward Andrew.

He backed away. "So, you figure, what? I, uh . . ." He put down the camcorder. "I stand on the seal, and hold the knife and command it to stop glowing in, uh, Tawarick?"

They faced each other on opposite radii of the goat-faced disc. Walking around the circumference, Buffy tried to approach Andrew as he tried to maintain his distance.

"Doesn't really make sense?" Buffy said menacingly. "Bringing you here to talk to it. This thing doesn't understand words. It understands blood."

(Oh, my God. It's like a Warren thing. She tricked me into coming here!)

"Blood opens it," Andrew pointed out. "You don't want to open it. Opening it would be bad."

"Well," Buffy said, still walking around the circle. "Willow did a little research. Looked into that. Seems the blood the man that awoke it . . . *you* . . . that's a different kind of deal. Reverses the whole thing."

Oh . . . my . . . God . . .

"How much blood are you going to . . . ?" he asked, his heartbeat picking up.

"I don't know," she said simply. "Maybe not enough to kill you."

He faced her, but he couldn't make himself stand still, He kept backing away from her. "So, this is my redemption at last. I buy back my bruised soul with the blood of my heart. Not enough to kill . . ."

She stood directly before him now, knife out, her facial beauty a synergistic combination of good lighting and righteous anger.

"Stop that!" she shouted at him. "Stop telling stories! Life . . . isn't . . . a . . . story!"

"Sorry. Sorry," he managed, terrified.

"Shut up!" She was nearly in tears, so she was furious. "You always do this! You make everything into a story so no one's responsible for anything because they're just following a script!"

"Please don't kill me," he begged. "Warren said Jonathan would be okay. I trusted him, and I lost my friend."

"You didn't lose him!" Buffy thundered at him. *"You murdered him!"*

"I know," he managed, "but you don't need to kill

me. You said we'd all get through this."

"I made it up," she bit off. "I'm making it all up. What kind of hero does that make me?"

He shook his head. "No, you're doing great. Really. Kudos."

"Yeah?" Her eyes flashed. "Well, I don't like having to give a bunch of speeches about how we're all going to live, because we won't. This isn't some story where good triumphs because good triumphs. Good people are going to die! Girls. Maybe me. Probably you. Probably . . . right now."

He shook his head, terrified, pleading with her as she dragged him toward the Seal. He leaned over it. She was holding the back of his collar so that he didn't fall. She pointed the knife at him. The Seal of Danzalthar glowed brightly.

"Don't, please, *don't*!"

"When your blood pours out, it might save the world. What do you think about that? Does it buy it all back? Are you redeemed?"

And something in him broke. It just . . . broke, and he began to cry.

"No! Because I killed him." He sobbed, tears streaming down his face. "Because I killed him! I listened to Warren, and I pretended I thought it was him, but I knew . . . I knew it wasn't. And I killed Jonathan!"

He sobbed harder.

"And now you're going to kill me. And I'm scared, and I'm going to die. And this . . . this is what Jonathan felt."

His tears dripped onto the Seal, and as he wept . . . the Seal stopped glowing.

Buffy released him. He fell to the ground, and the knife with him.

"It . . . stopped," he said slowly.

She gazed at him. "Didn't want blood. It wanted tears."

He was mystified. Yet as he got back up, he said, "Thanks."

She was kind to him now, gentler than she ever had been. "Sorry I had to . . ."

He swallowed hard. "You . . . you weren't really going to stab me, were you?"

"I wasn't going to stab you," she told him.

"What if . . . the tears didn't work?"

Buffy the Vampire Slayer smiled at him enigmatically—Buffy, the Slayer, and he grabbed his camcorder and trailed after her.

Spike and Robin had been battling together. They were both bruised and battered but not beaten; and Spike could have been staked with any number of things with weapons from the woodshop.

Then the students simply stopped—bell had rung, time for the next period—and wandered off.

"She got it done," Robins observed.

"Always has," Spike said, a tinge of pride in his voice.

"So far," Robin replied.

(I am not sitting in my fancy library. I'm sitting on a toilet. I am not suave and debonair. I am . . . just Andrew.)

"Here's the thing," he said into the camera. "I killed my best friend. There's a big fight coming, and I don't know what's going to happen. I don't even think I'm going to live through it."

He looked down, centering himself in the real world, the one beyond the story, the world in which he lived.

"That's uh, probably the way it should be. I guess I'm . . ."

He turned off the camera.

Chapter Seventeen: "Lies My Parents Told Me"

New York City, 1977

It was raining hard, and Robin's mama was fighting for her life.

Her coat whipped like bat's wings as she faced down the vampire, and they were kicking and hitting each other like comic book heroes. Robin was very, very scared as he hid behind the park bench.

He had seen a fight like this before. She got so badly beaten; monsters tried to bite her and kill her. She always beat them.

But even at four, Robin knew his mama might die one night . . .

His mother was Nikki the Vampire Slayer, and right now she was double-kicking the white-haired vampire in the chest. He went down, then rolled back up and bouncing on his heels like a boxer on TV.

"Well, all right!" he said. "Got the moves, don't you? Gonna ride you hard before I put you away, love."

"Sure about that?" she challenged him. "You seem a little wet and limp to me. And I'm not your 'love.'"

She charged him, launching another attack. They collided, fighting and smacking each other. The vampire dodged her punch and twisted her arm behind her back. Then he wrapped his other arm around her throat and pulled her close to him.

Robin jerked in his panic, knocking into the trash bin next to him.

The vampire was distracted by the noise, and Robin's mama seized the chance to butt him with the back of her head and break free.

As he staggered back, Nikki somersaulted to her feet, reached into her long black leather coat, pulled out a stake, and threw it at him.

The white-haired vampire caught it in midair.

"Tsk, tsk, tsk," he said to her. "Taken me a long time to track you down. Don't really want to end the dance so soon. Do you, Nikki? Music's just getting started, 'in'it?"

As he turned to go, he tossed the stake aside.

It clattered to the ground, very close to Robin.

The vampire turned back again; Robin froze.

"Oh, and . . . *love* the coat," he said, striding off into the darkness.

The Slayer watched him go for a moment until Robin said anxiously, "Mama?"

She turned her attention toward her boy, who emerged from behind the bench. She went to him and crouched next to him as she straightened the hood on his rain slicker.

"Did real good, baby boy," she told him warmly. "Stayed down just like Mama told you."

His teeth were chattering. He was hungry.

"Can we go home now?"

She shook her head. "Nuh-uh, not safe there anymore." She smiled at him. "Hey, how about I leave you with Crowley? He's got those spooky doodads you like playing—"

"No," he said quickly. "I want to stay with you."

She took that in. Then she looked in the direction where the vampire had headed off, paused, and said, "Yeah, I know you do, baby. But . . . remember, Robin, honey . . . what we talked about. Always gotta work the mission."

He looked away.

"Look at me," she said firmly. "You know I love you. But I got a job to do. The mission's what matters, right?"

He nodded.

"That's my baby. C'mon."

She stood, taking his hand, and they walked off a bit before Robin pulled free of her grasp, turned, and ran back to retrieve the stake that was lying on the ground. He picked it up.

"Robin!" she called.

Lighting flashed . . . and the four-year-old became Principal Wood, fighting in an alley with Buffy and the very same vampire, now wearing his mother's duster. Buffy was squaring off with a large vampire while Spike, sent his adversary crashing into a Dumpster, then decapitated him with a shovel.

But Robin with a jagged piece of wooden crate in his grip, was going down.

He had gotten in a few licks, but the tide had turned. The vampire swept his legs out from under him and he was down.

Now the demon was loomed over him, ready to strike.

Then the vampire exploded in a cloud of dust . . . revealing Spike gripping the splintered end of the shovel's handle.

"Little tip, mate," he said. "The stake's your friend. Don't be afraid to use it.

He has on her coat, Robin thought, livid. *The vampire who killed my mother just saved my life.*

Sensing some unfinished business, Spike wheeled around and said, "What?"

Robin shook his head slightly, as if to say, *Nothing.* Spike was still not convinced that they were finished, but he moved off toward Buffy.

"Just waiting for my moment," Robin said stonily.

He was squeezing the stake in his hand so tightly that blood dripped from his fist.

At the Summers' home, the phone rang. Dawn got it, and to her surprise it was Angel.

"Dawnie, hi, it's me," he said on the line. "Is Buffy home?"

"Yeah, hold on a sec," she replied brightly.

But the line had gone dead.

Weird, she thought, and made a note to mention it to Buffy.

But she forgot.

Sunnydale High School was thrashed and trashed. The wreckage of the riot caused by the Seal was everywhere. Painters rolled paint over the graffiti; Buffy doubted that the custodian realized that what he was scraping off the window was the residue of the stressed-out student's exploding head.

"Situation still normal," Buffy commented to Robin Wood as they watched through the blinds over his window. "Or as normal as this school ever sees."

"So it appears," Wood drawled.

"Well, no fires," she said, looking on the bright side. "And the Swing Choir and the Marching Band have gone back to their normal, healthy, seething resentment."

"Been pretty quite around here since you shut down that Seal. You just may have stopped this thing, Buffy," Robin said, gazing at her.

She demurred. "I saw an army of Ubervamps in my vision. To think I stopped The First . . . No. It can't be that easy."

He raised a brow and smiled faintly. "Call that easy?"

"Hey, any apocalypse I avert without dying, those are the easy ones."

Smiling warmly, he moved toward her and said,

"Y'know, you're something else, Miss Summers. I've been watching you when we're out patrolling. You remind me of my . . ." He trailed off.

She gazed at him with real sympathy. "Your mother," she finished for him.

"What I remember of her, anyway," he said faintly.

Her answering smile was wry. "Gotta tell ya, not a line every girl likes to hear. But in this case . . . compliment taken."

It was a moment that became another moment. She felt herself relax a little, liking this nice man, this guy, this vampire-slaying ally . . .

"Maybe you're right," she said. "Maybe everything's fine."

"Everything's terrible!" Giles cried, sailing into Robin's office. "A full catastrophe!"

"Giles, what's wrong?" She hadn't even realized that he was back in town. He was wearing a sheepherder's jacket and he actually looked kind of good.

"Have you seen the new library?" he demanded, in high dudgeon. "There's nothing but computers! There's not a book to be seen. I don't know where to begin. Buffy, who do we speak to?"

"That'd be me," Robin said, extending his head.

Giles moved into charming mode and said, "Yes, I'm sorry. Rupert Giles. Buffy's told me you're something of a freelance demon fighter."

"Oh, yes?" Robin asked as he shut the door.

"I'm relieved," Giles continued, aware that he had lacked discretion. "We're running dangerously low on allies."

Buffy heard what he was saying between the lines. "So. I didn't stop it, then."

"No," Giles informed her. "The seers in the coven are certain The First is continuing to gather its forces." He added gravely, "I'm afraid war is inevitable." A beat, and then: "So we should go to the school board."

"What?" Robin asked, as if he assumed he was missing Giles's point.

"Well, I can have my backup library sent from home in the meantime. It's not much, but—"

"Giles," Buffy cut in.

"Knowledge comes from crated bindings and pages, Buffy, not ones and zeroes."

Buffy thought of the conversations about computers versus books that Giles used to have with his lost love, Jenny Calendar.

My God, we've been at this a long time.

"So," she said, returning to the topic, "did you bring back any Potentials?"

"Ah, no. Actually my trip was about something else," he told her. "Regarding Spike. I told you my concerns when you recklessly chose to remove the chip from his head."

Robin stirred. "Wait. Sorry. Chip?"

"Long story," Giles said.

Buffy turned to him. "The military put a chip in Spike's brain so he couldn't hurt anyone."

"And that would be the abridged version," Giles said with asperity.

"But he wouldn't hurt any one, Giles," Buffy insisted. "He has a soul now."

"Unless The First triggers him again," Giles argued.

"Triggers the chip?" Robin asked, trying to keep up.

Buffy shook her head. "The trigger's a post-hypnotic thing The First put in his head. Made him . . ." She took a breath; it was difficult for her to say. "He was killing again."

"So he has a trigger, a soul, and a chip," Robin summarized.

"Not anymore," Giles said, making it obvious that he was saying it for Buffy's benefit.

Buffy frowned at him. "It was killing him, Giles."

"The trigger?" Robin asked hopefully.

"The chip. The trigger's not working any more."

Robin tried again. "Because the military gave him a soul." Buffy just looked at him and he said, "Sorry."

"We don't know that the trigger's inactive," Giles argued. "But what I've brought may help us to disarm it. And ascertain what it is, exactly, that causes Spike's behavior."

"It was that song, Giles," Buffy said. "I'm telling you, it was the song he was singing."

"Yes, but he has no memory of it," Giles pointed out. "Is there any part of it that you can remember?"

"It wasn't like it had a catchy hook or anything, like, 'I'm Comin' Up So you Better Get This Party Started.' It was boring, old and English. Just like yo . . ." She caught herself as he glowered at her. "Ul," she said quickly. "Yul Brynner." A beat. "A British . . . Yul Brynner."

Robin was intrigued. "This thing you brought. To keep Spike from killing again. How does it work?"

"That will require a bit of magic," Giles said enigmatically.

A bit of magic, and some chains . . .

Muttering to himself, Xander shackled Spike to the basement wall.

"Could have put the chains back up a week ago," he muttered, "Oh, no, we have to work on Spike now, of all times . . ."

"What?" Spike demanded.

"Nothing," Xander replied.

Spike spotted Robin Wood standing a bit away from the others and asked him testily, "What you doin' here? You came to see the show?"

"I thought you might need the support," Robin drawled.

"Uh-huh," Spike said, completely unconvinced. He turned to Giles and said, "Right. Let's get this over with. What're you going to do? Some hypnobeam or disarming spell?"

"Not exactly," Giles said. "The First has brainwashed you. There's something in your subconscious that it's using to provoke a violent reaction."

He held up a small strange object. "So we have to put this in your brain."

Spike stared in horror at what appeared to be a pebble between Giles's fingers. "Bugger that."

"The Prokaryote stone will move within your mind to reveal the root of the trigger's power," Giles explained. "It can unleash ideas, images, memories. Hopefully, once you understand what's setting you off, you can break its hold on you."

"'Hopefully,'" Dawn echoed. "So it might not work."

"The stone's only a catalyst for the process," Giles explained, replacing the stone into a box. "The rest is up to Spike."

"And how d'you expect to get that hunk of rubble into my cranium?" Spike demanded waspishly.

Giles turned to Willow who, as was her wont, was holding a large, ancient text. She took a step forward and said, "Okay. Just hope my pronunciation's in the ballpark."

She began:

"Kun'ati belek sp'sion. Bok'vata im kele'beshus. Ek'vota. Mor'osh boot'ke."

The stone began to slither and stretch into an unappetizingly leechlike creature.

Spike was distressed, to say the least.

"Oh, you have got to be joking," he said loudly. "What now?"

Calmly, Giles explained, "It has to enter your cerebral cortex through the optic nerve."

"Oh, bollocks." Spike stared at the creature. "All the rubbish people keep sticking in my head . . . it's a wonder there's any room for my brain."

"I don't think it takes up that much space, do you?" Giles asked.

Giles lifted the box to Spike's cheek. The creature undulating out of the box and crawled onto his cheek, then flattened like a worm and eased its way into his eye.

Then he cried out in pain and yanked on his chains.

Contact.

Buffy hurried to him, sitting beside him as she took his hand, trying to still him as he thrashed in pain.

"Listen to me, Spike. You all right?"

He was breathing hard; he nodded, obviously not all right. Then he gritted, "How am I supposed to know if this bug ugly's doing its—"

And it was London again, 1880. He was alive again, and with his dear mother in their parlor. She had a handkerchief in her hand, which she held tightly as he read her some of his poetry, another ode to the loveliness that was Cecily.

"*'Her eyes, balls of honey . . . angel's harps, her laugh . . . oh, lark, grant a sign/if crook'd be cupid's shaft . . .*

"*'Hark, the lark . . . her name it hath spake . . . "Cecily" it discharges from 'twixt its wee beak."'*"

His mother beamed at him. "Oh, William," she began.

"It's just scribbling," he said, suddenly shy.

"Nonsense. It's magnificent." She smiled at him. "This 'Cecily' of whom you write so often . . . would that be the Underwoods' eldest girl?"

"Oh, no," he said quickly, "I don't presume . . ."

"She's lovely," his mother cut in. "And you

shouldn't be alone. You need a woman in your life."

He gazed at her. "I have a woman in my life."

She was surprised . . . and pleased. "But you've never . . ."

Then she realized that it was she to whom he referred, and she smiled at her son.

He smiled back. "Well, do not mistake me," he told her. "I have hopes that one day there will be an addition to this household. But I will always look after you, Mother," he said firmly. "This I promise."

She gazed at him with love, and then she began to cough. It overtook her, racked her body. She brought her handkerchief to her lips and when she lifted it away to drink from the glass of water he offered her, he saw the bloodstain on it.

He was alarmed. "Should I send a coach for Dr. Gull?"

"I'll be all right. Ah." She smiled again. "It's passed. Just sit with me awhile, will you?"

"Of course." He sat at her feet, covering his alarm, savoring this fine moment that they were together, and her illness was not so advanced that she could not enjoy the simple pleasures of womanly life, such as her needle-point. Then, to complete the moment, she began to sing the ditty he loved best, one from his nursery days.

"Early one morning, just as the sun was rising, I hear a maid sing in the valley below."

The song echoed . . . reverberated . . . seethed . . .

Before anyone could stop him, Spike lunged from the basement cot in a frenzy, full-on vamp mode. He hit

Buffy, slamming her across the room, lunging, fighting. He picked up his cot and flung it across the room, hitting Dawn. She fell to the ground.

"Dawn!" Willow cried.

She hurried to help Dawn, then Anya took her upstairs. Buffy prepared to take on Spike when he froze. Then the Prokaryote slithered out of his eye and clattered to the floor, once more a solid object.

Spike morphed back to human guise, and he stared in shock and shame at Dawn, whom he had wounded in his blackout. He caught sight of the principal as well, the man silently observing, and obviously intrigued.

"Get me out of these sodding things already!" Spike cried, humiliated. "I'm fine." He said to Giles. "Stone of yours is out, in'it? Did its job. So, I'm de-triggered, right?"

"Spike," Giles asked. "What do you remember? About the song?"

"Oh, yeah." Spike sighed. "The song. It's called 'Early One Morning.' Old folk ditty."

"What's it mean to you?" Robin queried.

"Mean? Nothin'. Just . . ." The next word did not come easily. "My mum. It was her favorite. She used to sing it to me." Self-consciously he added, "When I was a baby."

"And . . . ?" Giles prodded him.

"No 'and.' That's it," Spike shot back. He looked at Buffy. "Shouldn't you check on Dawn? Clocked the niblet pretty fierce."

"She'll be okay," Buffy told him. "She's tough."

* * *

Willow and Anya were taking care of Dawn upstairs.
She had a bad gash on her head and as Willow minis-
tered to her, she said, "Ow!"

"Sorry," Willow said. "It doesn't look like anything's broken."

"Did you use a magick X-ray?" Dawn asked.

"No, it's just what people usually say," Willow told
her.

Looking on, Kennedy tried to process what was
going on. "So Spike's trigger's been active the entire
time?"

Rona was shocked. "How can Buffy take this for
granted? He lives in our house! We've trained with
him!"

Anya waved a hand. "Don't waste your time.
Spike's got some sort of 'get out of jail free' card that
doesn't apply to the rest of us. I mean, he could slaughter a hundred frat boys . . ." Then, seeing the looks on
Xander and Dawn's faces, she moved to pretend all
was well, by saying, "Forgiveness makes us human,
blah blah blah blah . . ."

The phone had rung, and Andrew had gone to get
it. He said, "Willow, a call for you from L.A. Somebody named Fred? Guy sounds kind of effeminate."

Down in the basement, Buffy unchained Spike, to
Giles's dismay. Buffy pulled her former Watcher
aside and whispered, "This is pointless, Giles. He
doesn't know anything. Your prophylactic stone
didn't work."

"Because he's not cooperating," Giles insisted. "This process takes time. He's blocking whatever's flooding his consciousness, and as long as he does so, he's endangering us all."

Robin joined the conversation. "So the trigger's still working?"

"As much as ever," Giles replied.

And he was back in his London townhouse, with her, so beautiful in her black lace, her black eyes, her black heart . . . Drusilla, his love, his passion, his sire . . .

"Oooh, such a pretty house you have, sweet Willy," she cooed. "Smells of daffodils and viscera."

"Don't get too attached now," he cautioned her, pleased, "Won't be here for long now, love."

"Well then . . ." She sat on the couch, patted it insistently. "Shall we give it a proper good-bye?"

"You are a saucy one, aren't you?" he asked. He grinned at her, plopped down next to her, and pulled her up and over his lap, burning her lips twixt his . . .

"Oh, Dru, we'll bring this world to its knees," he said hotly.

"It's ripe and ready, my darling," she rejoined. "Waiting for us to devour its fruit."

"We'll ravage this city together, my pet," he vowed. "Lay waste to all of Europe. The three of us will teach these snobs and elitists with the folderol just what—"

"Three?" she echoed cautiously.

"You, me, and Mother," he answered, missing the darkness in her tone. "We'll open up their veins and bathe in their blood as they scream our names across the . . ." He saw her expression. "What?"

"You . . . you want to bring your mum with us?" she asked.

"Well, yeah," he answered. "You'll like her."

"To eat, you mean?"

He grinned at her good joke. And then . . .

"William?"

His poor mum walked painfully into the parlor. She had gotten worse; she used a walking stick now.

"Mother!"

He was a bit abashed to have been caught on the couch with an unmarried woman, but before he could explain, she continued, "Where have you been? I've been beside myself for days . . ."

He puffed up a bit. He had such news about his activities!

"You needn't have worried, Mother," he assured her. "You'll never have to worry about anything again. Something . . . has happened. I've changed."

She looked at him with puzzlement; her gaze swept over to Drusilla.

"Who . . . who is the woman?"

Drusilla rose and glided toward her. "I'm the other that gave birth to your son."

"I beg your pardon?" His mother was astonished.

"It's true, Mother," William said excitedly. "Drusilla . . . she has made me what I am. I'm no longer bound to this mortal coil." He straightened his shoulders. "I have become a creature of the night. A vampire."

His mother was completely bewildered.

"Are you drunk?"

"Little bit," he admitted. He moved to her. "Think of it. No more sickness. No more dying. You'll never age another day. Let me do this for you."

He reached out to touch her, but she drew away from him.

"What are you talking about?" she asked him. "And why are you acting so strangely?"

"It's all right, Mother," he told her. "It's only me." He embraced her tenderly. "We'll be together forever."

Then he changed into a vampire, and as he held her, prepared to bring her into eternal health. "It only hurts for a moment," he promised her.

Spike jerked out of his memories, aware that Buffy had unchained him. She was watching him closely and would have said something, except that Willow trotted down the stairs, announcing, "Hey, I just got a call. I'm going to have to take off for a little while. Maybe a day or so . . ."

"Is something wrong?" Buffy asked her anxiously.

"Nothing you need worry about," Willow answered. "I'll give you the full scoop later. Hopefully I'll bring back some good news."

Buffy looked first at her, then at Spike.

"Could use a little of that." She shrugged. "Okay. Guess now's as good a time as we're likely to see for a while. Just hurry back."

As the Wicca went back upstairs, Giles said to Buffy, "Think about what you're doing."

She bit off, "I have unchained Spike."

"Buffy . . . ," he began.

She turned away from him. "Don't."

She and Spike headed upstairs as well. Giles was just about to follow when Robin Wood said, sotto voce, "Mr. Giles, do you have a moment?"

Watching Buffy and Spike go on up, Giles turned to the young man.

"What's on your mind?" he asked.

"Same thing that's on yours," Robin said. He looked toward the top of the stairs. "We've got ourselves a problem."

Giles understood.

"Spike," he said.

Robin nodded. "If that trigger's still working, The First must be waiting for the right time to use it against us. Awhile back it slipped up, told Andrew 'it wasn't time yet for Spike.' Whatever The First's ultimate plan is, Spike must be an integral part in that.

"Something needs to be done."

They stood looked at each other like two courtiers planning to depose the king—nervous, frightened, building up their resolve.

"Buffy would never allow it," Giles murmured.

"Buffy would listen to her Watcher, wouldn't she?" Robin asked.

Giles smiled wryly. "I don't think you know very much about the Watcher/Slayer dynamic."

Wood gave him a look. "As a matter of fact, I was raised by a Watcher."

Giles blurted, "You what?"

"Bernard Crowley," Robin filled in. "Took me in when I was a young boy. Trained me."

Giles processed that. "Crowley . . . I remember the name. New York–based Watcher. Resigned shortly after his Slayer was . . ."

Giles was stunned. "You're Nikki Wood's son."

"Yes," Robin told him.

And there it was: "Spike killed your mother." A beat, as the full ramifications hit home. "Does Buffy know this?"

"She knows my mother was a Slayer," Robin told him. "She doesn't know about Spike."

"And this has nothing to do with personal vengeance," Giles said with supreme understatement.

"Does it matter?" Robin pressed his advantage. "He's an instrument of evil. He's going to prove to be our undoing in this fight. Buffy's undoing. And she will never, never see it coming."

And then he brought home his case.

"Now, I'm talking about what needs to be done for the greater good. You know I'm right."

Giles took his time.

"What . . . exactly do you propose?"

"I just need you to keep Buffy away for a few hours."

Giles's silence was his consent.

. . . whereby we'll kill a king . . .

It was night, just the two of them, a Slayer grown up, and a Watcher toughened, seasoned . . . and determined. Giles could tell she was ignorant of the true purpose of the mission as they walked together through the graveyard.

"I dunno, Giles," she said. "Is this really a primo time for a training mission?"

"I'm still your teacher, Buffy," he asserted. "And no matter how adept a Slayer you are, there'll always be new things to learn. Now more than ever it's crucial to maintain the focus upon your calling."

She gave him a look as they walked along. "You're talking to me like I'm sixteen again."

"Sometimes the most effective way of moving forward is to start at the beginning," he observed. *Words to live by . . . we started together so long ago. Though I knew my calling was vital, I did not want to become a Watcher. Nor did she take on the burden of Slayer with any joy. Now we have young Potentials to protect . . . the only children she . . . and I as well, will have, of that I've no doubt. They are our investment.*

They are the power of the Slayer line, and we must do everything we can to protect them.

They came to a stop near a fresh grave. Buffy turned to him, saying, "In case you haven't noticed, our plates are kind of full right now. Plus, not sure how I feel about Robin looking after Spike at his place."

He said frostily, "For what it's worth, everyone in your house seemed quite relieved by the arrangement." Then, "Buffy I may not technically be your Watcher anymore, but the fact that your life is such chaos only underscores the importance of the lessons I can impart to you."

She shrugged. "Fine. Impart away."

So he began. "We are on the verge of war. It's time we looked at the big picture."

"Hello?" She sounded incredulous. "All I *do* is look at the big picture. The other day I gave an inspirational speech to the telephone repairman."

"It takes more than rousing speeches to lead, Buffy," he pressed on. "If you're going to be a general, you need to make the difficult decisions, regardless of the cost."

"Have you *seen* me with those girls? The way I've treated my friends and my family? And Andrew? Believe me, I know how to make hard decisions."

"Well, that's what we're here to find out, while we work on the basics."

Behind them, a hand shot from the fresh grave. They both glanced at it: new vampire, about to emerge.

Wood escorted Spike past the door to his apartment and toward the padlocked side door of his garage. Spike was a bit taken aback.

"Live in a garage?" he asked.

As Wood started unlocking the padlock, he said, "This is just my work room. Kind of my . . . sanctuary."

"Little place to unwind, huh," Spike ventured, while Wood opened the door and started inside.

"Hard day principal-ing got you down, you need a place to cut loose, let down your hair. So to speak."

They were inside and stood in darkness for a moment. Not a problem for Spike, who, as a vampire, could see in the dark . . . and then the lights went on and he registered the dozens and dozens of crosses, all shapes and sizes, blanketing the walls. It looked like something out of the bloody *Omega Man*

"What the bloody hell's this?" he demanded. He felt as if he had just swallowed ice.

Wood said affably, "I told you. My sanctuary. It's the Hellmouth, Spike. You can never be too careful."

On a tool bench sat a laptop, surrounded by bookcases filled with books. Wood gestured. "Stay away from the walls. You'll be all right."

Spike looked around the room. "Bit much, in'it?" He scrutinized the principal. "What's your story, Wood?"

He turned on the computer. A menu came up and he began to type. Spike's spider sense was tingling.

"No story, really," he said. "Trying to do what's right, make a difference." He looked over his shoulder at Spike. "How about you? What kind of man are you, Spike?"

"Sorry," Spike said tersely. "Not much for self-reflection."

"Yeah," Wood replied, equally tense. "Makes sense."

Whatever the principal had on the screen appeared to satisfy him. Then he pulled open a large drawer in the bench. Spike couldn't see what was inside, but it had caught the man's attention.

"See," the man said, "you strike me as the type of guy who careens through life completely oblivious to the damage he's doing to everyone around him."

Spike bristled. "That right?"

"I know more about you than you think, Spike,"

Wood continued. "I've been searching for you for a very . . . very long time." He glared at the vampire. "Ever since you killed my mother."

Spike's anxiety level decreased. *Oh, is this all that's about.*

"Killed a lot of people's mothers," he said.

Robin turned back around and said in a dangerous voice, "Oh, you'd remember mine."

Then, as Spike looked on, he fastened metal braces onto his arms, one extending down to end in a rack of brass knuckles, bit of gladiator-style studded spike at the base of the elbow. The other brace was smaller, fitting over his hand like a wrist protector.

"She was a Slayer," Wood added, with soft, deadly menace.

Ah. It all came together in one package wrapped in revenge. "So that's it, is it? Brought me here to kill me?"

Wood slowly turned around to face him. "No. I don't want to kill you, Spike. I want to kill the monster who took my mother from me."

Then he tapped a key on the laptop, and from the speakers spilled a Scots Joan Baez–like folk version of Spike's mother's favorite song:

"Early one morning, just as the sun was rising . . . "

Spike tensed, gaze darting with fear as his face morphed . . . *No, no . . .*

"Oh, there he is," Robin Wood said calmly, staring at the enraged vampire

Nikki the Vampire Slayer's son had called out his enemy.

* * *

It was night in their London townhouse. Spike had left with Dru to hunt, and now was back to check on his mother. He had no idea how long the transformation should take; he did hope that he had returned in time to see her blossom into eternal life.

He saw her nowhere—did see, however, the bloodstains on the settee, where he'd reclined her lifeless body. Her walked stick was propped up by the fireplace.

"Mother?" he called.

Then her heard her music box, the dulcet tones of their song tinkling over the stillness: "*Early one morning . . .*"

His mother walked into the light, radiant with health and smiling brightly at him; in her arms she carried her music box.

"Hello, William," she said.

He was overjoyed. "Look at you," he murmured delightedly.

"Mm, yes, all better." Her eyes were clear. She was truly well.

"You're glowing," he went on happily.

She focused on the music box almost dreamily. "Am I? I suppose I have you to thank for that, don't I?" She looked up at him. "How will I ever repay you?"

"Seeing you like this is payment enough," he assured her.

"Oh, William, you're so . . . tender," she said sweetly, smiling up at her boy.

"Well, this is as it should be, Mother. You and I,

together. All of London laid out before us."

"Aaah, yes. Us." Smiling to herself, she set down the music box and closed it.

"First we'll feast," he told her. "And then the night is yours. The theater perhaps. Dancing. Tell me. What's your pleasure?"

"Pleasure?" She never lost her enigmatic smile as she said, "To take my leave of you, of course."

At his confusion, a cruel smile replaced her sweetness. *"The lark hath spake from twixt its week beak,"* she mocked. "You honestly thought I could bear an eternity listening to that twaddle?"

CRACK!

The memories were forcibly beaten from Spike's brain as Wood hit him in the face. Feral, instinctual, the vampire snarl and struck back, hard.

"That's right, dog," Wood said, bleeding and filled with hatred. "Bite back."

Then the principal's studded elbow slammed into Spike's jaw.

CRACK!

William's vampiric mother smiled at him in a way mothers ought not smile at sons.

"I hate to be cruel . . ." She stopped, thought about that, and started again. "No. I don't," she corrected. "I used to hate to be cruel. In life. I find it quite . . . freeing." She gazed coldly at him and added, "Nothing less will pry your greedy little fingers off my apron strings, will it?"

He was horrified. "Stop, please."

"Ever since the day you first slithered from me, like a parasite. Had I known, I would spared myself a lifetime of tedium and dashed your brains out when I first saw you."

CRACK!

Robin slammed the demonic murderer across the face, ramming him—it—against the cross-laden wall with one arm across the throat, the other pummeling its abdomen. Smoke sizzled as the crosses burned the hellspawn, and it howled.

CRACK!

"God, how I prayed you'd find a woman to release me," William's mother flung at him, advancing on him. "But you scarcely showed an interest. Who could compare to your doddering, housebound mum? A captive audience for your witless prattle?"

CRACK!

The crosses on the wall seared the monster's face as Robin held it there; then, wild with pain and fury, the demon shoved Robin off him, sending him sailing . . . and shouting in English—almost like a person—"Nooooo!"

CRACK!

It was as if each word William's mother spoke was like a slap across his cheek. She said to him, "Whatever I was . . . that's not who I am any more."

"Darling, it's who you'll always be. A limp, sentimental fool."

Each word, the harshest of blows.

CRACK!

Nikki's boy kicked the creature in the face; it slammed back into the bookcases. Shelves broke; books tumbled like boulders. Robin loomed over him and rain blows all over its grotesque features, its distorted parody of a human face.

"Hurts, don't it?" Robin cried. "This is what it felt like, when you beat the life out of her?" He hit it, over and over. "When you toyed with her? Before you snapped her neck?"

CRACK!

In the graveyard Buffy fought with the vampire, who had finally emerged from fresh grave, flipping him onto his back, straddling him, and whipped out her stake. *Another night, another vampire.*

She was about to finish him off when Giles said, "Don't kill him yet."

Both she and the vamp looked over at Giles. "Why not?" she asked.

"Because I'm asking you not to," he informed her.

Buffy shrugged. No big. She elbowed the vampire and rolled away. The vamp got back up on its feet and they squared off again.

Giles said, "Would you let this vampire live if it meant saving the world?"

"Sure."

She glanced at the vamp. "Seems like a nice enough guy."

"Thanks," the vampire said uncertainly.

"No problem," she said pleasantly.

He added awkwardly, "My name's Richard."

"Hi, Rich."

They fought a little to stay in the game, and then Buffy turned to her former Watcher and said, "Giles, we've had this conversation before. When I told you I wouldn't sacrifice Dawn to stop Glory from destroying the world."

"But things are different now, aren't they? After what you've been through. Knowing what you're up against. Faced with the same choice now . . . you'd let her die."

She hesitated . . . and realized he was right.

"If I had to. To save the world, yes."

The vampire spun-kicked her in the head; she scowled and said, "Ouch! Can I kill this guy yet?"

"No," Giles ordered her.

Irritated, Buffy started wailing on Richard, giving him what for as Giles said, "So you really do understand the difficult decisions you'll have to make. That any one of us expendable in this war . . ."

She couldn't believe how he was droning on. "Have you *heard* my speeches?" she demanded.

"That we can't allow any threat that may jeopardize our chances of winning," he continued.

"Yes. I get it!"

She and the vampire fought, trading blows. She was getting very frustrated, wondering what the point was, and then Giles said, "And yet, there is Spike."

What?

She paused to look at him.

The vampire tackled her.

CRACK!

The vampire was nearly comatose, its eyes glassy as if it was on drugs. Blood streamed down its face; its face was pulpy from the beating.

"Animal like you," Robin flung at it, "never cared for anyone but yourself."

He striped his mother's coat off the monster's body and laid it gently on the table.

It felt as if her ghost moved in the room . . . and he knew that soon, she would be at peace.

"No one else mattered," Robin said to the creature. "Just all about the hunt."

He pulled a small wooden cross off the wall with a bit of effort.

CRACK!

"You want to run, don't you?" William's mother asked him as she backed him against the fireplace. "Scamper off and cry to your new little trollop. Do you think you'll be able to love her? Do you think you'll be able to touch her without feeling me?"

She picked up her walked stick as she regarded him with utter contempt. "All you ever wanted was to be back inside. And you finally got your wish, didn't you? Sank your teeth into me, an eternal kiss . . ."

"No," he insisted. "I only wanted to make you well."

She glided closer still. "You wanted your hands on me," she said with contempt. "Perhaps you'd like to finish what you started, hmmm?"

"Please. I loved you. I did. Just . . . not like this."

She watched him suffer, smiling cruelly, enjoying her power over him. Toying with him, and savoring its effect.

"Just like this," she said. "This is what you wanted, all along."

"Stop it!" he cried.

"Come on. Do it." She mocked him. "Who's my little dark prince?"

"No!" He shoved her away. She stumbled, and her smile vanished.

"*Get out!*" she shouted.

And then she grabbed her walking stick and swung at him. William blocked the block, catching the cane; she fought to get it back, snarling into vampface as she sneered at him, "There, there, precious. It will only hurt for a moment."

Then his vampire's heart broke. It was not true that the creatures of the night could not love or show mercy . . . "I'm sorry," he said softly.

"What?" Robin demanded, back in the garage.

And William plunged the shard of the walking stick into his mother's chest.

For one last instant, she was his mother again,

kind, gentle and loving. Her eyes, sick and tired, but filled with light . . . for him.

Then she dusted, and was gone.

Forever.

I'm free, Spike thought in wonder. He felt himself released from the trigger, felt the guilt and shame evaporate along with his memories. His face had changed to his man's features.

He grabbed the principal's arm and kicked him in the chest. The other man reeled backward.

"Sorry?" Wood demanded. "You think 'sorry' is going to make everything right?"

"I wasn't talking to you," Spike tossed off.

That enraged Wood, who launched a full attack, but Spike defended himself skillfully, deflecting each blow. Then he executed a round kick to Wood's head, dazing him.

"I don't give a piss about your mum," he informed Robin Wood. "She was a Slayer. I was a vampire."

Wood attacked; Spike gave it right back.

"That's the way the game is played."

"Game?!" Wood shouted, astonished.

"She knew what she was signing up for," Spike retorted, punishing Wood with a brace of hard blows.

"Well, *I* didn't sign up for it," Wood argued.

"Well, that's the rub, in'it?" Spike said. "You didn't sign up for it, and somehow that's my fault."

Wood threw punches; Spike dodged and deflected them.

"You took my childhood . . . when you took her

away from me. She was all I had! She was my world!"

Spike stayed with the fight. "And you weren't hers. Does it piss you off?"

Wood hesitated, then came at Spike again.

"Shut up!" he shouted. "You didn't know her!"

His swing was awkward; Spike avoided it, then pummeled him, beating him to his knees.

"I know Slayers. No matter how many people they got around them, they fight alone," he said coldly. Then he beat Wood to his knees. "Life of the Chosen One. The rest of us be damned. Your mum was no different."

Bloody and beaten, Wood stared blearily up at him with desperate defiance. "She . . . she loved me."

Spike delivered the final blow. "So she said, I expect. But not enough to quit though, was it? Not enough to walk away. For you."

Wood did not respond. He could not. Broken on the floor, he was . . . shattered.

Spike gave each of them a few moments, and then he said. "I'll tell you a story. 'Bout a mother and a son. See, like you, I loved my mother. So much so, I turned her into a vampire so we could be together forever." He paused, then added. "She said some nasty bits to me after I did that. Been weighing on me for quite some time."

He paced, running it through.

"But you helped me figure something out. You see, unlike you . . ." He didn't mind saying that. ". . . I had a mother who loved me back. When I sired her, I set loose a demon that tore into me."

"But that was the demon talking, not her. I realize that now."

He finally understood, was finally free.

"My mother loved me with all her heart. I was her world."

Confidently he crossed to the laptop and hit a key. The folksy rendition of "Early One Morning" began to play. He listened calmly.

"That's a nice little song you got there," he said to the ravaged man on the floor.

He listened a little longer, then stopped the music.

"Thanks, doctor. You cured me after all."

Menacingly, he advanced on the defenseless man. "I've got my own free will now. I'm not under The First, or anyone's influence now."

He stared up at Spike looming over him.

"I just wanted you to know that . . . before I kill you."

He morphed into vampface, yanked up his enemy, and bit him, hard . . .

CRACK!

Giles was still yammering on about Spike while Buffy kept socking the vampire, even though both she and ol' Rich had grown tired of the game.

"Spike is a liability, Buffy. He refuses to see that. And so do you. Angel left here because he realized how harmful your relationship with him was. Spike, on the other hand, lacks such self-awareness."

Buffy was pissed. "Spike's here because I want

him here. We need him. I'm in the fight of my life," Buffy insisted.

"Really?" the vampire asked shyly.

"Not you, Richard." She bashed him hard.

"You want Spike here even after what he's done to you in the past?" Giles pressed.

"It's different now. He has a soul."

"Yes, and The First is exploiting it to his advantage."

"Exactly," Buffy insisted. "The First's doing this. Spike's innocent."

Then she staked the vamp as she focused her attention on Giles.

And do I tell you now? Giles wondered. *That I murdered Ben, the boy who had been forced to share his mortal form with Glory the Hellgod? That though he had not only been oblivious of her barbarism and her cruelties, and had tried to help us kill her . . . I put my hand over his mouth as he lay defenseless. I smothered him, and saved the world.*

I did what you could not to.

Do I tell you this?

He did not, but she did read something else in his face . . .

She staked the vampire.

"Oh, god, you've been stalling me." Her eyes widened. "Keeping me away!"

He made an attempt to connect and bring her to the place she needed to be in her mind.

"Buffy, it's time to stop playing the role of general and start being one."

She stared at him in shock, then turned and ran.

"This is the way wars are won!" he shouted after her.

CRACK!

The side door of Robin's garage opened and Spike stepped out. He was pulling on his coat, and he had been savagely beaten.

"Spike!" Buffy cried.

She came to him, full of fear for him, and for what he might have done.

Wordlessly he pushed the door open.

Robin Wood lay sprawled on the floor, barely recognizable through the blood and bruises.

"I gave him a pass," Spike said. "I let him live. On account of the fact that I killed his mother."

Buffy began to put the pieces together . . .

". . . but that's all he gets," Spike told her. He began to walk away. "He even so much as looks at me funny again, I'll kill him."

Buffy watched him go . . . then turned toward the garage. She went inside, saw all the crosses.

Walked to Robin's side and knelt beside him.

"I lost my mom a couple years ago," she said. "I came home and found her dead on the couch."

He wiped the blood from his mouth as he said, "I'm sorry."

He said of his mother, "She got herself killed. Being murdered."

"And none of it matters," she told him. "We're preparing to fight a war, and you're looking for revenge on a man who doesn't exist anymore."

"Don't delude yourself. That man still exists," Robin said bitterly.

"Spike's the strongest warrior I have, and we need him if we're going to get through this alive," she informed him. "If you try anything again, he will kill you. But more importantly, I'll let him."

He looked down, unable to meet her gaze.

"I have a mission: to win this war. To save the world. I don't have time for vendettas."

She turned her back on him and walked away.

"The mission is what matters."

And she left him.

Alone.

Alone, Buffy came home. She checked on her sweet little sister, curled up with her stuffed animals. Her head was bandaged, but she looked good.

Then she walked toward her bedroom . . . alone.

"Buffy," Giles called.

He was standing at the other end of the hallway. He came toward her and said, "I understand your anger." He let that sink in, then added, "Please believe me when I tell you we did—"

"He's alive, Giles," she said flatly, not looking at him. "Spike's alive. Wood failed."

She couldn't fathom the expression on his face, but she didn't turn around to see it.

"That doesn't change anything," Giles insisted. "What I told you is still true. You need to learn."

"No."

Now she did turn, did face him, and she stared at him as if she had never seen him before.

"No," she said again. "I think you've taught me everything I need to know."

She turned, shut the door in his face.

And stood alone.

Part Three: Resurrection

Chapter Eighteen: "Dirty Girls"

The Potential was running for her life.

So close, she thought desperately, *I'm so close!*

On the outskirts of Sunnydale, the breath in her lungs pumping, she kept her mind focused on one simple thought: *Buffy. Get to the Slayer. Safety.*

She woved and dodged but the evil, eyeless men had caught up with her; they were surrounding her. She wove and dodged, but they kept lunging for her. She broke away and sprinted out into the middle of the road.

There was a pair of headlights coming; waving her arms, she planted her feet, screaming, "Help! Stop, please! Please!"

The vehicle swerved and screeched to a stop. It was a battered old truck, and a young man was driving it.

She raced over and yanked open the passenger's side door. As she threw herself inside, he said, "What's going on?"

"Please!" she begged. "Get me out of here!"

"Is someone hurt?" he asked anxiously.

The evil guys had reached the edge of the road and were heading toward them. Shannon yelled, "Drive!"

Which he did, flooring it even before she got the door shut, leaving the black-robed creatures behind.

She panted, catching her breath, as the truck roared down the road. The man—he was quite young and handsome, with dark eyes, dimples and reddish hair, and wearing a priest's collar—studied her, then glanced in the rearview mirror.

"Well, that was . . . are you all right?" he asked her.

She nodded. "Thank you. Thank God you were there."

"Well, let's not give Him credit for everything. No, I'm funnin' ya," he said. "I don't believe in coincidence." He looked back again. "I also don't believe young girls should be out in the woods late at night." He gave her a look. "Should be tucked in bed."

"Wish I was," Shannon murmured.

"I expect you do at that," he said. I don't mean to pry, but those boys looked kinda like, well . . ." He gave her another hard look. "You didn't happen to fall in with devil worshippers, did you?"

She looked out the window, her hard history washing over her face.

"I'm sorry," the man said. "It looks like you've been traveling awhile." He blinked. "And I didn't think . . . is there somewhere you want me to drop you? Are you headed somewhere?"

"Sunnydale," she told him.

He smiled a bit bemused. "Going there myself. Never been, but I expect we could find a police station . . ."

"I just need to get to Revello Drive," she said firmly, staying on track. "But thanks, uh . . ." She glanced at his clerical collar. "Father?"

"Call me Caleb," he said to her. "I never was nobody's daddy."

"I'm . . . Shannon." She was reluctant to reveal even that—she had been warned by her Watcher to stay as incognito as possible—but after all, he was a religious person.

"Well, Shannon, you feel like telling me why those freaky joes were after you?" he asked.

"I—I'm not sure," she lied.

"Did you ever give thought that maybe they were chasing you because you're a whore?" he asked out of the blue.

She was shocked. "What?"

"I know what you're thinking." He smiled at her. "'Crazy preacher man, spouting off about the Whore of Babylon' or some such. That ain't me. I'm not here to lecture you. What's the point? My words just curdle in your ears. You don't take in a thing. So much filth inside your head, ain't no room for the words of truth. You know what you are, Shannon?"

When she didn't answer, he said, "Dirty."

Oh, my God, he's crazy! Shannon murmured, "I'm not . . . I don't want . . ."

"There's no blame here," Caleb said soothingly. "You were born dirty. Born without a soul, born with that gaping maw wants to open up and suck out a man's marrow. Makes me puke to think too hard on it."

Shannon tried to open the door on her side, realizing with a sickening rush of fear that there was no handle on the door. As she searched for another means of escape, Caleb pushed the car lighter in.

"Yeah, that door there's problematical," he drawled. "Don't know as I can recommend stepping out at this speed, either. Like as not to tumble some. Then there's my boys back there. They hate to miss a mark."

And it keeps getting worse . . . oh, God, oh, my God . . .

"Your boys," she managed.

He smiled easily at her. "Well, they ain't exactly my *blue-eyed* boys, but they're hard workers. And they don't truck with Satan." He confessed, "That was me having fun." He looked her in the eye. "Satan is a little man."

She tried to grab the wheel, but he slammed her back with one arm.

"I don't like back seat drivers!"

Then the lighter popped. Driving with one knee, he placed it against the ring on his finger, heating up the metal.

Shannon whimpered, "Please . . . don't hurt me . . ."

"Is this the part where you offer to do anything?" he sneered at her. "'Cause I've tried to make it clear you have nothing I want to explore."

He pulled the lighter away from his ring; the symbol on his ring glowed white hot. Then, before she could think of a way to stop him, he drove his fist into the side of her neck, smoke sizzling from the impression of the ring as she screamed.

"That's right!" he shouted. "That's a cleansing fire! Hallelujah!"

His laugh was wild and joy-filled as he released her, hands on the wheel again. She cowered against the door sobbing in the midst of her nightmare.

He glanced again in the mirror. "If I'm not mistaken, there should be a car a little ways behind us. And I believe there's some folk in it heading to the same place you are. Now I got a message for you to deliver, but it's not for them. It's for the other one. The one and only, original, accept-no-substitutes Slayer. Can you tell her something for me?"

"Y-Yes," Shannon managed.

"Well, thank you, Shannon."

He reached into the other side of his seat, whipped out an enormous bowie knife, and plunged it into her belly. The agony wrenched her out her power of speech, her ability to say or do anything.

He whispered to her, and then he pulled out the knife like a period on the end of his sentence.

"Now, let's see if we can't do something about that door," he told her.

He swung a leg around and kicked her, the door swinging open from her momentum as she tumbled out. She spun head over heels several times before stopping to a rest in the middle of the road.

* * *

Following behind the truck, Willow was mentally reviewing the ensoulment of Angel, which she had successfully accomplished as per Fred's phone call. That had gone well. Having her passenger figure out what was going on with Slayers . . . and nobody alerting her . . . not so well.

But all musing stopped when the Wicca saw the body fly from the passenger's side of the truck.

She managed to swerve just in time, tires squealing, her car rocking as if a tired had blown.

Then she jumped out into the crisis and ran to the girl in the road.

Willow's passenger got out more slowly. Her veins had recently been loaded with Morpheus, and she was still a little thrashed.

"Goddess," Willow breathed. To the girl, she said, "Can you hear me? Can you talk?"

But the girl was beyond any of that. As she lay in a glaze of unconsciousness, Willow looked up to her companion and said, "She's bleeding badly." Then she pulled off her T-shirt and pressed it against the girl's gut wound, trying vainly to staunch the flow of blood.

Then Faith took in the sight, looked out at the horizon. Her face was shadowed with wariness, and she already felt unutterably tired.

"Guess I'm back in Sunnydale," she murmured.

There was a young Slayer who lived on Revello Drive; she had so many Potentials she didn't know what to do. So she fed them all supper and sent many of them to stay at Xander's apartment, darn the luck.

Now stunningly gorgeous Kelly sat on the side of his bed in a baby T and boxers, and man, did she need comforting.

"I haven't been able to sleep the last few nights," she said in a hushed voice, trying not to wake the others.

"Hey, listen, it's going to be okay," he soothed. "Buffy knows what she's doing. She's not going to send you into battle until she's sure you're ready for . . . action."

Like me. I'm ready!

"That's just it, though. How will *I* know when I'm ready?" she asked anxiously. "For action?"

"You have to . . . trust us," he told her sincerely.

"I'm so scared, Xander," she confided, "and I'm so young."

"Believe it or not," he told her, "I was younger than you when I started all this."

She looked somber, wistful . . . so very, very young. And inexperienced.

"There's just so much I haven't done. So much I need to do. It's, like, I've never had a real boyfriend, you know?"

"Yeah?" he croaked.

She traced the bed sheet with her finger. "I've never been with a man. I could die tomorrow, and . . . I've never been with a man." Her look was vulnerable and seductive.

Then the Potential named Colleen, who had been sleeping beside them, roused and came over to the bed. She was wearing a nightie, and she was equally beautiful.

"I've never been with a man before, either," she said.

"Colleen," Xander murmured, trying to calm them both down.

"And I've never been with her in front of a man before," she added, pointing at Kelly.

"And I've never been with her in front of a man before," Kelly said, pointing at Colleen.

Both girls turned and looked at him. Colleen crawled on the bed toward him.

"Xander," Kelly said in a breathy voice.

"We can't," Xander said anxiously.

"We're so scared," Colleen reminded him.

"The others will hear us," Xander argued as they both glided toward him, wanting him, desirous of his special brand of comfort.

"No, they won't. They're okay," the two girls said.

The door to Xander's bedroom opened all by itself . . .

. . . to reveal the other Potentials having a pillow fight. All gorgeous, all scantily clad, all . . . there and young and so, um, *buoyant* . . .

Feathers, girlish laughter, nighties and bras and panties, all his favorite "ies . . ."

Then the door jerked open and Xander jerked . . . awake, realizing he had been dreaming.

"Xander, goddamn it!" Rona barked.

"What-what?" he asked guiltily. "I'm sleeping."

Rona said, "Dominique has the stomach flu and the toilet's backed up."

Behind her, the Potentials were milling around,

displeased, in their full-body jammies and um, orthodontic headgear.

"It actually backed up while she was on the toilet," Rona continued. "And she has the stomach flu." She gave him a moment to . . . digest that. "You should probably visualize that before you go in there. It'll make it easier to deal with."

"Be right out," Xander told her. "Just have a . . . leg cramp."

She went out, and he went down.

Willow and Faith were no strangers to the E.R., and their little friend too . . . who was fighting for her life, and no guarantees, there.

"Are you sure she's one of us?" Faith asked, and for a harsh second she almost laughed, because she sounded to herself like Tony Soprano talking in code about being in the Mafia. "She don't look like much now. Not a Potential Slayer, I mean."

Willow shrugged. "I don't know. Seems to fit, though. We'll know more when she regains consciousness."

"*If* she regains consciousness," Faith said. "Girl's been gutted like a catfish." They both looked back at Shannon, and Faith added bitterly, "Something's killing girls all over the world, trying to end the Slayer line . . . thing like that, figure I might get a heads-up."

Willow looked stricken.

"Guess it doesn't really matter," Faith went on. "Long as you got the true Slayer intact."

Red looked upset. Poor Red.

"You were in prison," Willow reminded her. "We figured you were safe there."

"Yeah, prison," Faith scoffed. "Safe as a kitten."

"Sorry," Willow murmured. "I—I don't know a lot about 'the big house.'" A beat, and then she asked, "Was it . . . I mean, did something happen in there?"

Faith cocked her head. "Someone came at me with this wicked-looking knife. Didn't know why . . . not till now."

Willow was all frowny eyebrows and big, shiny eyes as she said, "Faith, we didn't think—"

"Forget it. 'S cool," Faith said. "I get by."

She nodded toward Shannon, changing the subject. "What do we do about her?"

"We should find Buffy, tell her what's going on. I tried calling home. Dawn says she's out patrolling."

"Let's go look for her," Faith suggested. "Cemetery's more fun anyway."

Willow demurred. "One of us should stay here. In case she wakes up."

"Fine. Sit tight. I'll be back." Faith started to talk off.

"Wait," Willow called. As Faith did so, the Wicca swallowed hard and said, "Maybe you meeting Buffy alone isn't the best idea . . ."

"You told her the sitch, right?" Faith asked sharply. She knows I'm coming. Prob'ly up all night hanging streamers . . ."

"Yeah, it's not exactly you guys are study buddies exactly," Willow murmured. "Maybe it'd be better if I . . . eased her into the whole thing."

Faith shook her head. "I can't stay here, Willow. Spent too much time in hospitals. We don't click. Don't worry . . ."

She turned to walk out the door.

". . . I'm sure we'll get along fine."

In one of Sunnydale's many fine graveyards, a girl was running for her life. There was a vampire closing in behind her; and though it made no sense, she stopped to assess her options—*which way do I run?*—when running just about anywhere was preferable to standing still.

Stupid bint.

The vampire flung himself at her and she went down; she was struggling wildly and the vampire backhanded her. She went flying into a tombstone; and lay on the grass, helpless and unconscious.

He moved in for the kill . . .

. . . and a hand grabbed him from behind and yanked, hard, sending him across the graveyard and into a tomb wall.

He looked up at his assailant. She was dark, beautiful, and had a swagger that would put Colin Farrell to shame. Had killed for, in fact.

She walked toward him and said, "What did you want to do to her, vamp? Something like this?"

She charged. With a growl, he lunged at her. She easily blocked his punch and then gave him a bleedin' fantastic right cross that sent him flying all over again, right on his arse.

He devamped, and looked up her as he got up

and backed away, sizing her up.

"Nice punch you got there," he said. "Let me guess. Leather pants, hard right cross, doe-eyes, holier-than-thou glower." He nodded. "You must be Faith."

"Oh, goody," she deadpanned. "I'm famous."

"Heard you were coming," he said, nodding. "Right. Bit of a misunderstanding here. I'm—"

"Spike," she finished for him. Her eyes sparkled with private amusement. "We met before."

He tried to remember her. Shook his head.

"We have? I don't think—"

Without warning, she kicked him in the face.

"Bloody hell!" he protested. "What are you doing? I'm on your side!"

"Yeah?" she flung at him. She hit him again. "Maybe you haven't heard. I'm reformed."

"So am I!" He blocked her next punch and hit her square in the face. "I reformed way before you did."

She hit him again; they went at it, trading blows, and he said, "Stop hitting me! We're on the same side!"

"*Please,*" he said. "Do you think I'm stupid? You were attacking that girl!"

Whack! She got in a good one and then *wham!*—a punch flew out of nowhere and dropped Faith to the ground.

It was Buffy, who said, "Oops, sorry, Faith. Didn't realize that was you."

Faith rose and said, "It's all right, B. Luckily you still punch like you used to."

Girl's hurt, not about to admit it, Spike realized. Then Buffy walked over and helped him to his feet.

"You okay?"

"Yeah. T'riffic," he added, not about to admit it.

Faith looked confused. "You protecting vampires? Are you the bad Slayer now?" She thought a moment. "Am I the good Slayer now?"

"He's with me," Buffy told her. "He's got a soul."

Faith blinked. "He's like Angel?"

"No," Spike said quickly.

"Sort of," Buffy put in.

"I'm nothing like Angel," Spike assured Faith.

"He fights on my side," Buffy volleyed. "Which is more than I can say for some of us."

"Yeah?" Faith drawled. "Well, if he's so good, why's he chasing down defenseless—"

Then the formerly helpless girl tackled Faith and flung her to the ground. Bird was in full vampface, and Spike and Buffy looked on, making no move to help.

"That's one of the bad guys," Buffy said helpfully.

As she struggled with the frenzied demon, Faith gritted, "You should make 'em wear signs."

She pushed the vamp off her and rolled to her feet, got in Buffy's face, and yanked a stake out of Buffy's belt.

"May I?" she asked. Buffy nodded. "Thanks."

She whipped around, leaped on top of the vamp, and dusted her.

"Angel's dull as a table lamp," Spike muttered. "And we have very different coloring."

It had been bothering him.

Annoyed, a bit winded, Faith got to her feet. "Okay, catching up. Anything else I gotta know?"

Buffy looked at Spike. Spike looked at Buffy.

Buffy said to Faith, with total, dripping insincerity, "Nice to have you back."

I can't believe this is happening, Buffy thought, as they walked through Buffy's front door.

Faith said, "Whoa, memory lane. Same old house."

"Every piece of it has been destroyed and replaced since you left, so, actually, new house," Buffy drawled.

"Buffy," Dawn began.

"We have another houseguest," Buffy announced.

Giles and Dawn both stood up, looks on their faces filled with hostility, if not surprise.

"Hey," Faith said brightly, "got a spare bed for a wanted fugitive?"

"Hello, Faith," Giles said coolly.

Faith raised her chin. "Huh. Guess 'wanted' wasn't so accurate."

"Does she have to stay here?" Dawn asked Buffy. "'Cause there's some nice hotels that welcome tried-to-kill-your-sister types."

Faith looked impressed. "Check it out, brat's all woman-sized."

"Guys, we need to go to the hospital," Buffy told Giles and Dawn. "A girl was attacked on her way into town. She may be a Poten—"

"We know," Dawn told her. "Willow's been calling."

"She's still there," Giles added, meaning Willow. "She'll call if the girl wakes up."

Buffy's answering look was icy. She wasn't sure

she would ever feel warmly toward Giles again.

"Fine," she said.

The awkwardness grew, and then Giles said to Faith, "Well, Faith. I guess we should try to find a place to squeeze you in tonight."

Giles and Dawn left. Then Spike said to Faith, "Not all that tension was about you. Giles was part of a plan to kill me for Buffy's own good."

Faith considered that. "Well that makes me feel better about me." A beat. "Worse about Giles." Another beat. "Kind of shaky about you."

Who was it said about being the vine? Oh, yeah.

The vineyard was the power center; the vineyard was "where it was at," as they used to say back before Caleb and the serpent formed an understanding: no touching.

Now, in the cellar, Caleb poured himself a small one from one of the dozens of barrels and huge casks settin' about. Bringers hovered—not literally—in the musty corners.

"'Drink of this, for it is my blood,'" he said, quoting from the greats. He tasted it and continued his conversation.

"You know, I loved the story of the Last Supper, the body, the blood of Christ become rich red wine. I recall as a boy, though . . . couldn't help thinking, what if you ordered the white? Nice oakey chardonnay, or a white zin?

"I never did bring it up, but well, I never could stay with the same parish for very long. Just looking for answers, looking for the Lord, in the wrong damn places. 'Till you showed me the light."

The First stepped out of the darkness and into the light. She was wearing the face of a beautiful young blond woman. Corrupt, but an interesting choice.

"Do you think I'm God?" The First asked him.

"I sure do not," Caleb assured her. "I'm beyond concepts like that."

"But you still wear the outfit," she mused, indicating his collar.

"Man can turn his back on what he came from," he replied. "Besides, black is slimming. Everybody knows that."

"How do you like what I'm wearing?" The First asked him.

He shrugged. "Just another dirty girl. And since you only dress up in dead folk, I'm guessing it's one who has been paid her wage."

"Look hard," The First urged, amused.

He did, up and down, not with any lust, but carefully. He came close and stared into her eyes.

"What do you see?" The First asked him.

"Strength," he replied slowly. "And the loneliness that comes with real strength."

She feigned disappointment. "Nothing about my pert and bouncy hairdo?"

"You're . . . her," he said slowly.

"The Slayer," she affirmed.

He was mesmerized. "At long last," he said, then put his hand out to touch her face. It slid through the image, and as he pulled it away, he said, "All the work

I done for you, blowing up the Council, organizing the Ray Charles Brigade, and stickin' all those splits . . . you never showed me."

"Well, you've earned it," she told him silkily. "And you'll be meeting her soon. Am I right?"

"Oh, yeah," he said, savoring the thought. "She'll get the message."

"And what makes you so sure she'll come?" she asked him.

"Curiosity," Caleb replied. "Woman's first sin. I offered her an apple. What can she do but take it?"

The First smiled, and Caleb raised his glass.

He said to her, "See you soon."

And he drained it down.

The Storyteller was back, and he was telling of the legend that was . . .

ANDREW (VOICE OVER)
Faith.
And there she is, so ravishing and dangerous, a cool, dangerous beauty like in James Bond.
Faith tough. Faith dangerous, Faith sooooo seductive.

ANDREW (CONT'D; V.O.)
Her name alone invokes awe. "Faith."
A set of principals or beliefs.
Faith dancing in the Bronze with her hands above her head, reveling in the power of her womanhood!

ANDREW (CONT'D; V.O.)
Upon which you're willing to devote
your life.
Faith fighting various demons, kicking much ass!

ANDREW (cont'd; V.O.)
The Dark Slayer. A lethal
combination of beauty, power, and
death. For years and years—or to
be more accurate, months—Faith
fought on the side of good."
And then, hidden tiger, crouching . . . Slayer!
She is taking out five ninjas in a deserted alley!
They are wearing those kung-fu-style pajamas and
she is every inch a Bai Ling or a Michelle Yeoh!

ANDREW (CONT'D; V.O.)
Terrorizing even the most silent and
deadly members of the evil community.
The deadly ninjas attack at once. Like a flying
dragonness, Faith leaps into the air!

Faith leaped into the air and took all five of them
out with a flashy and glamorous circle kick. She
landed in a crouch among her vanquished enemies.
The she rose—the no-longer-crouching Slayer!—and
arched her back.

Ooooh.

ANDREW (cont'd; V.O.)
But, like so many tragic heroes,
Faith was seduced by the lure of the

Dark Side.

Then see her being very bad—shooting a bow and arrow, burgling!, punching people, holding a knife to Willow's throat . . . and jumping up and down on the bed!

ANDREW (CONT'D; V.O.)
  She wrapped evil around her like a
  large, evil poncho. She became a
  cold-blooded killer.

SHOT OF FAITH STABBING THE MAYOR'S ASSISTANT, THEN BATTLING THE SLAYER OF THE LIGHT . . . BUFFY.

ANDREW (CONT'D; V.O.)
  Nobody was immune to her trail of
  destruction. Not friends,
  not family.

THEN WE SEE FAITH BATTLING A VULCAN (CLASSIC-TREK VERSION.)

ANDREW (CONT'D; V.O.)
  Not even the most pacifist and
  logical of races . . .
  Blow for blow, and then the Vulcan went for the Death Grip. She caught his arm, twisted it behind his back, and with her other hand held up her knife, about to strike down and stab him in the stomach.

* * *

As Andrew held Rona en tableau, in the exact same pose, and also in the kitchen, Amanda said, "What the hell are you talking about? I thought Faith killed a *vulcanologist.*"

Andrew shook his head patiently. "Silly, silly Amanda. Why would Faith kill a person who studies Vulcans?"

There were nearly a dozen Potentials listening to his story, including Chao-Ahn, who probably didn't understand a word—okay, for sure didn't understand a word—and who all looked a little bewildered.

"He studied volcanoes," Amanda barked at him. "He was a professor."

"Ah." Andrew felt . . . awkward. "Well, regardless."

Molly squinted at him. "I thought you weren't supposed to be doing this anymore. Making up these stories."

"I'm not," Andrew insisted. "This is true, except for that . . . possible word misunderstanding." He leaned forward. "And there are some things you need to know."

He turned and looked out the window, where Faith was working out. Getting sweaty.

"Faith has a history that is not to be taken lightly." He turned back to the group. "She's a killer. Never forget that. You must stay on guard around Faith at all times. Your very lives may depend on it."

Robin was at his desk, still banged up from his encounter with Spike. When Buffy knocked on the door and poked her head in, she looked as uneasy as he felt.

She said to him, "You look better."

"No, I don't."

She smiled weakly. "No, you don't."

"But I'll be okay," he added, "unless, of course you start beating on me now."

"I won't," she promised. "I thought about it some, drew a couple little doodles, but, look, as far as I'm concerned, we're on even ground." She gave him a nod. "I mean what I said before—I don't have time for your vendettas—but I need you in this fight. I want you on my side."

"Thank you," he said sincerely. "That means a lot."

"So we're good," she concluded.

"Absolutely," he agreed. Then he said, "You're fired."

She smiled. "That makes me feel so much . . . what?"

"Effective immediately." He looked straight at her.

"You're firing me?" She couldn't believe it. "I just refrained from kicking your ass!"

He gestured. "Buffy, there's nothing here for you. People are leaving town, half the kids don't even bother to show up anymore. . . . You've got things to deal with that are worse than anything here. Look at the big picture."

She blinked at him and said, "Right, the picture of the big war with all the dead little girls."

"Not dead," he argued. "Not if you get them ready."

She sat down slowly, absorbing the reality. He was right; it was ridiculous to be worrying about anything besides preparations for the apocalypse.

"I don't want to lead them into a war, Robin," she murmured. "War can't be the right thing."

"Most wars aren't. They aren't right and they aren't necessary, and humans kill one another," he told her. "This isn't that war."

"The only question about this one is, are you going to be ready for it?"

"I don't know," Buffy admitted honestly. She was afraid to even think about it, much less talk about it. "These girls . . . they haven't been tested in battle."

He regarded her. "Then I guess . . . maybe you should test them?"

Buffy thought about that.

"Couldn't I just come to work part-time?" she asked, pretending it was a real question. "I could make flyers for encounter groups and post them around the school. Kids could bring snacks—"

"And you're fired again," he said. "Remember Buffy . . ." His voice took on a note of bitterness . . . "It's the mission that matters."

He was right.

Faith had had enough togetherness. It reminded her of prison.

So she took the stairs down to the basement for some quiet time and a smoke.

She sat on the last step and light herself a cigarette.

From the dark, a voice said, "You craving a moment alone in the dank, or can I bum one?"

Faith turned to see Spike on his cot in a corner. He was just sitting up from having been asleep, had off his shirt, hair a little tousled. He was not chained up, but his restraints were dangling from the wall.

Faith got up and moved toward him, extending the pack.

"Guess you can smoke all you want," she said. "The 'big C' not really an issue."

"Teeth get yellow," Spike said, "over an eternity. You gotta watch that."

"Huh," Faith said.

Spike followed her line of sight as he took a cig. She was looking at the chains over his bed.

"Right," he said. "Not what it looks like."

"Hey, to each his own," she said, shrugging. "This one guy I ran with? He liked me to dress up like a school girl and take this friggin' bull whip and— "

"I got dangerous for a while," he cut in.

"This before the soul or after?" Faith asked.

"After." He shrugged nonchalantly. "But I'm over her." Slid her a glance and said, "In case you get feeling dust-happy again after your long incarceration."

"Not if you're all repent-y," she said. "Takes the fun out of it."

They smoked, but they had not become smoking buddies. Still, they contemplated each other.

Upstairs, the girls were shrieking and laughing.

"No more Starbucks for the wannabes, man." She

rolled her eyes. "They've been spazzing for, like, hours."

"Yeah." He nodded. "Gets a bit much up there."

"They're good girls. Green, is all."

He cocked his head. "So how come you're not up there imparting?"

"That's Buffy's thing," she replied. "Anyway, I just spent a good stretch of time locked away with a mess of female types. Kind of had my fill."

"But you waited until Angel needed you to break out of jail," he ventured.

She shrugged. "Three squares, night weight room, and a movie every Sunday., It could have been worse."

He was thoughtful. "What movie?"

"Last one was *Glitter*." She gave him a weary smile. "Guess it couldn't have been worse."

"You had the power to walk away anytime. Nothing to stop you," he said softly.

"I stopped me." A beat. She tried to keep the haunted feeling out of her eyes. "I got dangerous for a while.'

And then . . . a connection. Their eyes met.

"You over it?" he asked her.

"More or less," she replied. "I pull for the good guys now."

"What's the 'less'?" Spike asked.

"Usual stuff."

He prodded. "Such as?"

She indicated the chain, said, "I was thinking about looking up the guy with the bull whip." Shifted. "Long incarceration."

Spike smiled. "You could do better. School girl thing is old hat."

"It's all old hat, man. Every guy has some whack fantasy. Scratch the surface of even the most crunchy granola dude? Naughty nurses and horny cheerleaders. I figure, you can't beat 'em . . ."

"Join 'em," Spike finished for her.

"Just don't forget who's on top," she zinged right back.

"I suspect that would be you," he said dryly.

"Got that right." She preened a little.

Thing's getting warm now, so to speak . . . and then she sat down on the end of Spike's cot, looking at him.

"I met you before," she told him.

"Yeah, you made quite an impression on my chin." He grinned at her.

"Not in the graveyard. Before that," she said. Then, "I was kinda wearing a different body."

His grin was a bit lascivious as he gave her an appreciative once-over. "Pity."

"You seemed okay with it," she said, teasing him.

He got it. "The body swap. With Buffy."

"She fill you in on that whole deal?"

"Told me it went down," he told her. "Failed to mention who was driving her skin around."

"I may have said a few things," she said.

"Like you could ride me at a gallop until my legs buckled, squeeze me till I popped like warm champagne?" He raised a lazy brow. "Not the sort of thing a man forgets."

"You should have known it wasn't blondy behind

the wheel," she crowed. "She'd never throw down like that."

"You *have* been away," Spike said.

She was amazed. "Don't tell me miss tightly wound is getting her naughty on."

"Not of late," he replied.

She gave her head a little shake. "Wow, *everybody's* full of surprises."

The vibe was getting more intimate . . . until they heard a noise on the stair. And of course, it was Buffy, come to spoil the moment . . . and all one hundred thousand and twenty-eight moments to come after it.

"Hey, B," Faith said cozily.

"Nice to see you two getting on so well." Oooh, she was pissed.

"Yeah," Faith said. "You know all the cool vampires."

"Yeah," Buffy bit off.

Spike looked at Buffy. "Aren't you usually at work about now?"

"Right," she said awkwardly. "I kinda am. I decided to cut back my hours."

Then Dawn called down, "Buffy? Is that you?"

"I'm down here," she called to her sister. Then, to Spike, "Figure I'm better off focusing on what's going on around here."

Dawn appeared at the head of the stairs. Her face was filled with anxiety.

"Buffy, Willow just called form the hospital. The girl's awake."

*   *   *

The girl was named Shannon, and she was a Potential, as they had suspected. She was barely alive, hooked up and still bloody through her bandages. As she told Buffy and Willow her story, Buffy got more freaked out, listened harder.

"He was a minister or something," Shannon told her. "At least, he dressed like one. I thought he was trying to 'save' me. At first."

Buffy frowned. "He picked you up on the side of the road?"

She nodded and croaked, "The Bringers were chasing me." She thought a moment, then added, "He said they were 'his boys.' Right before he burned me."

As she pulled back the bandage on her neck, she revealed the burn mark the guy—Caleb—had left there. Buffy gestured to Willow's purse; Willow pulled out a small digital camera and took a shot of the injury.

"He wanted me to tell you something before . . . before he cut me,"

she said in a tiny voice. "He told me to give the Slayer a message."

Buffy was barely able to control her anger at the horror the girl had faced. "What is it?"

She looked at Buffy, cold and hollow.

"He said, 'I have something of yours.'"

Full house, oh, was it: There were an even dozen, counting Buffy, and they included Xander, Willow, Giles, Spike, Dawn, Kennedy, Rona, Amanda, Molly, Chao-Ahn, and Andrew.

"We've got a new player in town," Buffy announced. "Dresses like a preacher. Calls himself Caleb. Looks like he's working for The First."

Dawn thought about that. "So he's like . . . The Second?"

Buffy shaken, angry, and in mood for riposting.

"He's taunting us. Calling us out. Says he has something of mine. Could be another girl. Could be something else. Don't know. I don't care."

She paused, fighting for control.

"I'm tired of talking. I'm tired of training. He's got something of mine? Fine. I'm getting her back."

Her gaze was flinty, her spine, ramrod straight. She was totally on the edge . . . and she said, "And you guys are coming with me."

Caleb was walking in the vineyard, and she was there . . . he didn't know her name, didn't care what it was. Seventeen or so, she was a filthy whore in a sundress that just advertised her soulless lust, and she slithering around like the serpent in the garden, just itching to cause a man's downfall.

"You're searching for something, girl," he said, coming upon her. "What would that be now?"

"Oh." She was startled. Then excited. "You. I was looking for you."

"That right?" Caleb said kindly.

She nodded. "I heard you speaking tonight. Preaching. I felt your words going straight to me."

"The truth is like a sword, isn't it, girl?" He felt himself filling with the fire. "Cuts deep."

"Yeah." She moved closer, trying some seduction, a little clumsy . . . but ready. "I got warm. The words made me feel that way. I got warm. It was your words that made me feel that way. All that power you was talking about. The temple coming down, and the end of days." She went for it. "Your words are strong, Preacher."

"You liked 'em," Caleb said simply.

She nodded, less shy before, still deferential. Something about men with the fire . . . women wanted it. So they could burn awhile, then suffocate the source with their lack of breath.

"Words I use got a power to 'em," he told her. "Power, now. They're not just 'words.' They're truth."

"They called you. And so you followed. Know why?"

"Tell me, Preacher." She put her hands on her own belly, breathing deep, taking his fire into herself.

"Because you're human," Caleb told her . "You got your urges. A woman's got hers, a man's got his. Our whole race can be so damnably weak. It's why we seek the strength. That power."

She murmured eagerly, "It's not wrong to be drawn to the power? Is it, Preacher?"

Moving into the deepest shadows, she stepped up against a wall. He followed her in.

Then she fell out of the darkness and into the light, hallelujah; she was bleeding, gutted like that other little whore he had picked up in his trunk. The Slayer's little whore girl, Shannon.

"No child. Not wrong. Just human," he told the corpse.

Then the body morphed, becoming Buffy the Vampire Slayer, fresh and unhurt as a little apple blossom.

She looked up at Caleb and said, "Most people don't like visits from their dead, you know."

"It's okay with me. Might unsatisfying, is all," he told her. "I must confess I miss the bite of flesh on a knife. Freeing a soul from its body should have . . . a *tug* to it," he mused.

"You can't complain," The First argued. "You tricked that girl. She followed you."

He shrugged. "I only told her the truth," he shot back. "And as for the following . . ."

He tucked his knife back in his belt.

"There'll be others."

The core group was in Buffy's room, and they were holding a big power pow-wow. Buffy paced in front of Xander, Willow, Spike, Giles and Faith, and her mind was brimming with plans.

"Start arming the girls," she said. "I want to be ready to move when we find him."

Willow was confused. "We don't even know where we're going."

"That's why I figured we'd do a little recon first, see what we can find out," Buffy said. She asked Faith, "You up for it?"

Faith shrugged: compliance but no obedience. "Point me where you want me."

Giles was also confused. "But are you certain this is the best course of action? You don't even know what this man has of yours, if he in fact has anything."

Buffy replied, "It could be a girl. A Potential trying to get to us."

"It could be a stapler," Giles rejoined.

She set her jaw and raised her chin, saying, "I'm going in, anyway."

"With the girls?" Giles asked. "Most of them have yet to be in the field at all, let alone in a life-or-death situation."

"Then it's time we test 'em. We'll just take the ones who've been with us the longest. The rest can stay here."

Spike likewise looked less than enthusiastic. "Could be that's what he wants you to do. Ol' bait and switch."

Nodding, Willow said, "He lures us away, then kills all the girls we leave behind."

"I know," Buffy said to Willow. "That's why I want you to stay with them."

Willow was still not following.

Buffy explained, "You're my most powerful weapon, Will. You can keep these girls safe if something happens."

Xander shook his head, so not loving this plan. "Unknown man breezes into tow, says he has something of yours . . . Buffy, this thing's got 'trap' written all over it."

Buffy glossed over that. "He won't be expecting a full attack. Not this soon. That's why we have to move."

"We know nothing about this man!" Giles insisted. "We cannot go into battle without preparation. We need time."

"Giles," Buffy said, "we don't *have* time. And you're not going into battle. I need you to stay behind with the others." She paused, and could not help herself from adding, "Help the girls who still need a teacher."

Her barb hit home, and Giles shut his mouth.

Tightly.

Recon a go. Faith was nothing if not good.

Buffy was with her, and they were following a Bringer, who was darting through the darkness in a brisk and furtive way.

"No eyes," Faith mused, "but look at him go. He got sonar or something?"

"Or something, I guess," Buffy said. "They're pretty good when they attack.

"They say your other senses get better," Faith said, as they both watched the buy. "Maybe all blind people are smokin' in a knife fight." As Buffy gave her a look, Faith said, "Not saying it's likely." She gestured to their robed target. "They just roam free 'round town?"

Buffy watched the Bringer. "Well, normally they show up out of nowhere and either stab or get stabbed and then run off." She paused and added, not all that happily, "This guys seems like he wants to be found."

"Lends weight to that whole 'it's a trap' theory," Faith observed.

"I'm through waiting around for people to attack us," Buffy insisted.

"Hey, I'm with you," Faith told her. "Drop me in the hornet's next. What the hell."

Buffy nodded, focused on the Bringer.

Faith took a shot at connecting.

"You've got a rough sitch here, trying to turn a bunch of little girls into an army."

Buffy didn't like the description at all. She said angrily, "They're Potential Slayers. Just like we were."

"Right," Faith said. "Maybe they'll do as good as us."

Buffy shot a glance at Faith, unclear if she was being sarcastic. She said, "They're getting better."

"I'll work with 'em," Faith offered. "Some of them seem real eager. Fashion disasters, yeah, but ready to fight."

Buffy let that go by. She let a few more seconds go by. Then she asked the question she had wanted to ask Faith ever since she showed.

"Why'd you come back?"

"Willow said you needed me. Didn't give it a lot of thought. Do you . . ." She looked hard at the other Slayer. "Am I getting that you want me to be not here?"

Startled, Buffy blurted, "That's not what I meant. I'm . . . glad you're here. It's good." She sucked it up. "Thank you."

"No prob. You know me," Faith said lightly. "I'm all about the good deeds."

"Willow told me you helped out Angel," Buffy said.

"Yeah." She made less of a deal out it. "He says, 'Hey.'"

"Really?" Buffy asked warmly.

"Sure." Faith gave her a quick smile.

Buffy took yet another moment, then gathered up herself and asked, "How is he?"

"Better," Faith said. "Had to do this whole magical mind walk with him."

"You were . . . in Angel's mind." Buffy sounded annoyed, and Faith couldn't help it. She liked that.

"Yeah. Very weird. We got close," she spun. "Saw all sorts of heavy stuff from his past. Tripped me out."

"Uh-huh," Buffy said.

"That whole vampire-with-a-soul tip, interesting, isn't it? I mean, the darkness and the light. I can see it in Spike."

"So . . . how much did you and Spike . . . ?"

It was almost painful, how easy it was.

"Buffy," Faith began, then nodded toward the Bringer up ahead.

Old no-eyes was gliding into a clearing, heading toward an old building, stone and vine-covered. Dark wood abounded; there were shadows, and it was quiet.

Abandoned, but not empty.

The Bringer went straight for a heavy wooden door, opened it, and went inside. He started down some stairs . . . and then the Slayers' view was cut off as the door slammed shut.

"What is this place?" Faith asked.

"Look." Buffy gestured. "There's more of them."

Bringers from the north of them, Bringers from the west. they walked out of the woods, maybe four of them, all headed for Door #1.

"Looks like we found our hornet's nest," Faith murmured.

Buffy concurred. "Let's go get the cavalry," she said.

Battle preparations.

In the living room, Dawn and Xander were helping the Potentials check their weapons and put on protective gear as the girls were going through their moves. Andrew was . . . there also.

Xander wanted very badly for there to be a noble sort of *Spartacus* air to the proceedings, but truth was, it felt more like Helm's Deep.

But they won at Helm's Deep, he reminded himself. *The Elves and the Walking Trees helped out. I'm sure we've got some Walking Trees around here somewhere.*

"Now, remember," he instructed, using Molly as his demonstration aid, "we're looking for killing blows only, people, so chest and throat if there're vampires. Stomach, chest, and face if it's a Bringer."

Rona asked, "What if it's a something else?"

Xander nodded. "Could happen, something otherworldly, and here's a handy rule: Don't waste your time with flashy tentacles just 'cause they're waving about trying to get attention. Go for the center—brain, heart, eyes. Everything's got eyes."

"Except the Bringers," Dawn piped up.

"Except the Bringers," Xander conceded.

Molly looked unhappy. "I don't want there to be tentacles. I'm not good with squishy."

Kennedy squared her shoulders and declared, "I don't care if it's Godzilla, I want to get in this thing."

Andrew raised a hand. "Godzilla's mostly Tokyo based, so he's probably a no-show."

"Besides, Matthew Broderick can kill Godzilla, so how tough can he be?" Amanda went on.

With controlled fury, Andrew appealed for support to his secret brother in geekdom. Xander said, "Matthew Broderick never killed Godzilla. He killed a big dumb lizard that was *not* the real Godzilla."

"Right, right," Amanda jibed, "the big slow guy in the suit was cooler."

"I can't hear this," Andrew moaned, with all the passion of one who agreed with the poster on the Internet Movie Data Base who said, in effect, that the filmmakers' contempt for *Godzilla* fans was obvious.

"She's young, bro," Xander reminded him. "She doesn't understand."

Rona shook her head as she looked up from her weaponry and her outfitry. "You people are even crazier than *her*."

"Than who?" Xander asked.

"Buffy, man. Taking us right into the bad guy's lair."

"Well," Xander began, "that's, generally speaking, where you find the bad guy. And I don't think you came here to fight *plaque*."

"I came here for protection," Rona informed him.

Xander argued, "Well, you signed on to fight with—"

"I know," Rona said, "but this plan is trouble. Buffy doesn't care how many of us she—"

Xander cut her dead. "Let me tell you something about Buffy. In fact . . ." he gazed around the room ". . . everybody should listen to this.

"I've been through more battles with Buffy than you all can imagine. She's stopped anything that's ever come against her."

He was unaware that Buffy and Faith and come into the house, and were silently listening.

"She's laid down her life—literally—to protect the people around her. This girl *died*, two times, and she's still standing.

"You're scared, that's smart. You got questions, you should ask."

He looked at them all again, very serious, very clear.

"But you doubt her motives, you think Buffy is about the kill, then you take the little bus to battle. I've seen her heart . . . this time *not* literally . . . and I'll tell you right now: she cares more about your lives than you will ever know. You have to trust her.

"She's earned it."

The room was pin-drop silent. Andrew fought not to cry; Dawn beamed at Xander.

Buffy was moved nearly to tears herself, while Faith said jovially, "Damn! I had no idea you were that cool!"

Everyone was startled to see them.

"Well, you always were a little slow," Buffy pointed out.

"I get that now," Faith said contritely.

But Buffy's gaze was for Xander, her gratitude

boundless. Then she stepped into the room, and put her martial aspect back on.

"All right, people," she said. "Let's saddle up."

Buffy's army approached the target: the strange vine-covered building in the clearing, which was as silent as the grave.

Which, Buffy knew, were rarely truly silent . . .

She signaled for them to wait. Faith, Spike, Xander, Kennedy, Rona, Molly, Amanda and five others—*take time to learn their names*—froze—armed, focused, ready for anything.

Buffy turned to Xander and Faith.

"Set up a perimeter," she told them. "Guard the door. I don't want anything getting in behind us."

She nodded to Spike. "My group will go in first, and check the place out."

Then to Xander and Faith: "You guys are our safety net. If this thing is a trap, we give the signal and you come in, guns blazing after us."

"What's the signal?" Xander asked.

"I'm thinking lots and lots of yelling."

Xander and Faith nodded.

"Got it," Xander said.

Buffy gestured to Spike and her squadron of Potentials. "Shall we?"

The seven of them crept downstairs into the vast main cellar of the building. It was a vineyard, Buffy realized, or had been. The cavernous room was filled with wine barrels and large casks. It smelled of must and wine. It was cold.

They were sharp, ready. Moving in formation, they spread out, guarding each other's backs.

This is a group of soldiers, Buffy thought, moved. *Not scared little girls.*

"What is this place?" Molly asked.

"It's like an old vineyard or something," Buffy answered, as they all scanned the area for intruders.

"An evil vineyard, huh?" Kennedy said dryly.

Spike nodded. "Like Falcon Crest . . ."

"Stay alert," Buffy commanded them. "Bringers are here somewhere. We just need to find where they went . . ."

"Shouldn't be too hard," Spike said loudly.

A phalanx of Bringers stepped forward into the light from the dark archways around the room. They were armed—knives, staffs—and they had the group surrounded.

As they had been trained, the Potentials circled in the middle of the room as the Bringers pressed forward . . . closing in on them.

Buffy tried to steady them. "Cover each other's backs," she reminded them. "Let them come to us."

And they did.

The Bringers attacked, bringing chaos and destruction with them.

But these girls were warriors now, and their pledge was to bring chaos to its knees; as Buffy and Spike traded rapid-fire blows with their Bringers, Molly caught an attacking Bringer's wrists and headbutted him. Rona kicked another one in the face; Kennedy blasted one with an uppercut.

All the girls fought, but the Bringers were skilled, too. One swept Kennedy's legs, and she hit the ground hard. He leaped on her, knife raised for the kill, when Molly caught his hand, spun him around, and cracked elbows with him in the face, dropping him.

Buffy and Spike finished off their opponents with kicks and punches, working in concert; then moved to help with the others. Spike took on Rona's attacker and dropped her, hard.

Molly, Kennedy, and two more fought and kicked, spun, and slammed their fists and their elbows and their feet into the minions of The First. The coppery scent of blood filled the room; screams and grunts bounced off the walls and the casks, silent sentries to the mayhem swarming and swirling all around them. Headswimming frenzy, alarming strength and power and the will to destroy; to survive, to maim and end.

The precious Potentials, heiresses to Buffy's mantel, took on the Bringers as if their lives were part of their arsenals; their weapons were their courage and their skill. They charged with warriors' hearts, like Willow's beloved Amazons.

They began to knock the Bringers back.

Buffy stepped up onto one of the barrels and leaped off, jump kicking a Bringer in the face, sending him flying. He hit the ground, struggled to right himself . . . and started backing away.

His brothers joined him, slinking back into the shadows like so much vermin, eager to be gone, to be safe, to regroup.

Buffy and her army breathed hard, looking each other over as they regrouped and advanced forward.

From the darkness just ahead of her, Buffy heard the soft clicking of boots on concrete.

Young man in a clerical collar . . . had to be Caleb. He was smiling evilly, and Buffy was reminded slightly of the Mayor. A chill washed over her, but she maintained her concentration.

"Well now," he began easily, "you girls are just burning with righteousness, aren't you? Problem is, you think you're blazing like suns, when really you're matchsticks in the face of darkness."

He walked toward Buffy, as calm as he could be.

"You having fun? Hope my boys haven't worn you out too much. Need you fit for when I . . . purify you."

"Save the sermon, padre," Buffy snapped. "I heard you had something of mine."

He smiled brilliantly, holding his hands up, gesturing to the Potentials.

"Well, I do now," he said, obviously amused. "You liked my little message, did you?"

Buffy stood stone-faced.

"You know, I ruined a perfectly good knife all that girl. Got her soiled blood all over the place. I may need a new truck."

She felt a ripple of fear run through the girls. All she could do now was show them how to do this.

"So you're the Slayer," he said, approaching her stealthily, his entire demeanor screaming that he was not one bit afraid of her. That was not a good thing, not at all.

"The Slayer. The strongest and fastest and most aflame with that most precious invention of all mankind the notion of goodness. The Slayer must indeed be powerful."

Without warning, he rocketed his fist at her face and punched the holy living hell out of her, blasting her up into the air and sending her sailing over the wine barrels across the room. She slammed into the back wall and hit the ground like a body thrown off the Empire State Building.

She lay unconscious.

Caleb looked calmly at the shocked faces of Spike and the Potentials: *Our leader has been taken out with just one punch.*

"So," Caleb drawled, "what else you got?"

He began to laugh.

Spike morphed into vampface. With a roar he attacked, launching himself at Caleb. Caleb met his attack head-on, blocking Spike's attack with glee. His movements were effortless, as if he were playing fair with lesser creatures.

He headbutted Spike and knocked the vampire back. Spike was dazed. Then Caleb stepped forward and punched Spike in the midsection, launching him straight back across the room. Spike's body crashed through one of the wine barrels, sending a deluge of red wine gushing like a crimson flood of blood.

Spike lay motionless in the wash.

Caleb laughed as he surveyed the room, holding out his arms and saying, "Well, c'mon boys, what are you waiting for? Let's show these ladies a proper time!"

The Bringers charged back out of the darkness, attacking the Potentials with newfound vigor. The girls were rattled, overwhelmed by what they had just seen. They were no longer the fine-tuned machine.

Kennedy, Rona, Molly, and two of their sister warriors traded blows with the Bringers, but the bad guys delivered punishing blows. They were being beaten, mercilessly so; and as the punishment progressed, Caleb walked gracefully through the killing filed, calm as could be.

Without so much as glancing her way, he backhanded Kennedy, sending her smashing through a full wine rack. Broken glass and wine cascaded everywhere.

Kennedy's body was lost in the mess.

"Kennedy!" Rona shouted, rushing toward her.

Caleb caught her as she was running by.

"Miss," he said, "I do believe you have your own problems you should be worried about."

He took her arm and snapped it over his knee. Rona shrieked as the pain filled every inch of her, leaving room for nothing . . . except more pain.

Carelessly he dropped her to the ground. Then he walked over and fetched up a knife from the ground, which he tossed to one of his Bringers.

The minion caught it and leaped on Rona. Just as he was plunging the knife down—

—*FWACK!*

—An arrow sliced straight through the Bringer's wrist, jerking him backward.

The cavalry had arrived; Xander, armed with a bow-and-arrow, charged through the doorway. Amanda, Faith, and three more Potentials dashed in behind him.

"Oh, good," Caleb drawled. "There's more of you."

"Something tells me that's our guy!" Xander cried.

"Two steps ahead of you!" Faith shot back.

She charged at Caleb, knives in her fists; she sliced and diced at him, but he dodged her flurry.

Then Amanda and the other Potentials rushed into the fracas, flying to the aid of their overwhelmed comrades. Fresher than the others, oblivious of the strength of the opposition, they fought well, and bravely.

But there were so many, and they seemed to withstand so much . . .

Xander assessed the scene: Faith was fighting Caleb; the Potentials were battling the Bringers. Spike was down; Kennedy, down . . . where was . . .

"Buffy!" he shouted.

She was on the ground, out cold. Xander moved to her just as a Bringer came bearing down on them. He cracked him with his bow, and the two exchanged blows, Xander pressing forward, protecting Buffy.

Faith couldn't put a stop to Caleb; couldn't wipe that stupid-ass smirk off his face. He blocked her attacks and knocked the knives from her hands.

"You're the other one, aren't you," he said. "The Cain to her Abel. No offense meant to Cain, of course," he added pleasantly.

She dodged his attack, and cracked him in the face with a good punch.

"Never was much for the good book," Faith gritted.

"Oh, it has its moments," he rejoined. "Paul has some good bits to say, for instance."

He caught her punch, spun her around, and grabbed her by the hair.

"But overall it's a tad . . . complicated. I liked to keep things simple."

He slammed her face down into one of the wooden barrels, and the wood shattered and exploded in a torrent of red wine. Faith's body hit the ground amidst the wood splinters and liquid, and Caleb stood over her, palms up, smiling as he mocked an old hymn:

"Good folk, bad folk . . ."

Then a Potential named Dianne stepped up behind Caleb with a sword. She swung as hard as she could, going for his head. He ducked easily, never taking his eyes off Faith, and grabbed Dianne by the throat.

He pulled her close to him, singing, "Clean folk, dirty folk . . ."

. . . and snapped her neck.

Molly screamed, "Noooo!"

Caleb turned and smiled, coming for her next.

"Yes," he said.

And it was coming to an end: the Bringers were winning, and the Potentials were being brutalized; they were going down, hurt very badly. They were going to die.

*   *   *

Buffy came to slowly, shaking the cobwebs away. She tried to get to her feet, staggered by the chaos. Her girls, laid low; Spike, down; Faith, down; and Caleb, walking toward Molly like a coyote after a mouse.

Buffy spotted Xander taking out a Bringer with a hard elbow across the face. She called, "Xander!"

He saw her struggling to get to her feet and rushed to help her.

"Buffy—"

"Get them out of here," she told him. "We have to retreat." Off his questioning look, she ordered, "Do it."

He nodded and rushed back into the fray, grabbing a fallen girl and helping her to her feet.

Caleb was still stalking Molly; he had backed her into a corner and she was terrified. The dagger in her hand was all she had; that and her heart . . .

"I wish there were an easier way to do this," he said sadly. "To *cleanse* you. I do. But I don't make the rules."

Molly girded herself for her last stand, rushing toward him and swinging her knife. He caught her wrist easily, and caught her up by the neck, tightening his grip around her throat. He hoisted her into the air, her feet dangling.

"Okay, that's a bit of a lie," he conceded. "I make the rules."

And Buffy fought to save her. She staggered across the room, backhanding a Bringer as he came at her, sending him flying.

No. No . . .

"What can I say?" Caleb said to Molly, her eyes

bulging. He put his hand around her knife hand. "I work in mysterious ways."

Buffy slogged toward them.

No. Nearly there. Inches away . . .

Then he plunged her own knife deep into her chest. Molly's eyes went wide with shock.

Caleb dropped her to the ground.

Eyes wide.

Dead.

Buffy screamed and threw herself at Caleb. She hit him as hard as she possibly could across his face. He dropped to one knee and came back laughing.

"That's it," he encouraged her. "Show me your fire."

She attacked; they traded vicious blows.

Xander, ushering the girls up the stairs, called to Faith as she struggled to her feet.

"Faith! We gotta go!"

Amanda helped another girl up and herded her toward the stairs.

Caleb and Buffy were pounding each other; he swung for her and she ducked it, then sent him flying across the room with a powerful uppercut. She lunged after him; then Spike grabbed her by the arm, halting her trajectory, as she said, "We're leaving."

She looked at him, coming to her senses. She nodded; they swept the area, saw Rona on the ground, and helped her up.

Faith hurried past Xander with a girl over her shoulder; then Xander raced over to Kennedy, who was struggling to extricate herself from the mass of broken glass from the shattered wine rack.

He rushed over to her, grabbing her by the hand, and pulled her up.

"You okay?" he asked. Stupid question, but she nodded. "Let's go," he told her. "Come on."

He pushed her ahead of him. She ran toward the exit. Then he paused for a moment, checking for stragglers.

That was when Caleb got him.

He grabbed Xander by the neck, laughing.

"You're the one who sees everything, right?" he taunted, throwing Xander's words—the ones he had shared privately, with Dawn—back at Xander as he struggled in his grasp.

"Let's see what we can do about that," Caleb said.

He took his thumb and plunged it deep into Xander's eye socket.

Xander screamed and screamed and screamed and screamed.

Buffy and Spike, who were helping Rona to safety, turned toward his screams.

"XANDER!" Buffy shrieked.

She and Spike rushed toward Caleb and Xander. Caleb rushed his bloody hand, about to destroy Xander's other eye, when Spike slammed him to him, grabbing his arm, and knocking him back.

Buffy was there to catch Xander, holding him in her arms as he clutched his face in agony.

Spike drilled Caleb with a nasty punch to the face; Caleb fell back and tumbled to the floor.

Then he turned to Buffy. She was in shock and he helped carry Xander and drove her away to the exit.

Retreat.

Nightmare.

Wreckage, disaster; bodies, death and . . .

. . . Caleb, on his feet again, staring at Buffy.

Smiling.

Buffy turned, and rushed Xander up the stairs with Spike.

And Caleb moved into darkness, his old friend, still smiling.

Aftermath.

Agony.

Defeat.

In the hospital emergency room, the girls fought new battles: against life-threatening injuries, against pain, against trauma and disbelief. As Buffy walked past each bed . . . against her.

Despair.

Surrender.

Extinction.

Oh, my God, Xander.

Buffy reeled as she stood at Xander's bed, which was at the end of the row. His head and his . . . eye . . . were heavily bandaged.

If thine right eye offend me . . . I'll pluck it . . .

Willow sat vigil, her hand around Xander's.

For Buffy, Willow had no words of comfort.

At her house . . .

Buffy surveyed the disarray of defeat, felt the shame, the anger, the blame. Kennedy being tended to on the couch; the other two survivors wounded, dazed, quietly talking to Dawn and four Potentials who were spared from battle duty.

The girls would not look at her. She had betrayed them. She had killed their sisters in arms.

She couldn't meet their gazes.

Shellshocked, she walked out the front door and bled into the darkness.

In the cellar, darkness laughed and capered. Darkness exulted.

Darkness had won.

"Now, it's a simple story," Caleb said. "Stop me if you've heard it.

"I have found and truly believe there's nothing so bad it can't be made better with a story. And this one's got a happy ending," he said . . . happily.

"There once was a woman," he intoned, moving himself back to his thumpin' days, back to the sweet days of little girls in sundresses begging to be gutted like fish. "And she was foul, like all women. For Adam's rib was dirty, just like Adam himself, for what was he, but human? But this woman, she was filled— with darkness, despair, and why? Because she did not know. She could not see. She didn't hear the good news, the Glory that was coming.

"That'd be you."

He glanced up at The First, who was wearing Buffy's image, and who smiling at Caleb, well pleased with her beloved son.

"The Kingdom, the Power, and the Glory are yours," he said. "Now and forever. You show up, they'll get in line.

"Because they followed her," he continued. "And all they have to do is take one more step . . . and I'll kill them all. See?" he said to The First, savoring each syllable, each word, as if it were a cut of his knife, a *tug*—

"Told you it had a happy ending."

Chapter Nineteen: "Empty Places"

Sunnydale was falling: The Hellmouth's jittery pressure cooker had finally boiled up into panic. It was worse than any war zone Buffy had seen on TV as the inhabitants of Sunnydale fled for their lives. Chaos raced up the street screaming alongside women, children, shop owners shutting down for the last time; the town was the picture by Edvard Munch called "The Scream." It was Picasso's "Guernica." It was superheated terror, and it was all that was left.

Surrounded by throngs, the Slayer walked alone.

Then floppy-faced Clem leaned out of a brand new bright red VW Beetle and called out to her, "Hey, you!"

She brightened, seeing a familiar face, and walked over to him as he said, "Can you believe this *mishegas*?"

She shook her head. "It's like these people have never seen an apocalypse before." Then she gave him a knowing look and said, "And you're just out for a quick spin, right? Maybe out to the 7-11 . . . in Nebraska."

Busted, Clem said, "It's getting bad here. Really bad. Hellmouth acting up again, people feeling it, getting crazier. And you can't swing a cat without hitting some kind of demonic activity. Not that I . . . swing cats. Or eat. Nope." He added weakly, "Cutting way back. Cholesterol."

Before she might possibly smack him, he scampered back to the less-controversial topic of mayhem.

"We've seen bad stuff in this town before, but, you know, this time, it's like, it just seems . . . different. More powerful. I don't think anyone's gonna be able to stop it."

He looked further busted and said, "I mean, I'm sure you're going to do fine. Complete faith in you. If anyone can do it, you can, 'cause . . . you rock!"

He added brightly, "If you save the world, I'll come back, we'll have a drink . . . *when*!" He nodded at her eagerly, flop-flop with the entire face, which, to an outsider, might seem to be made entirely of flappy bunny ears.

Then he added weakly, "Maybe . . . maybe you should just get out of town this time."

"Yeah," she said. I probably should."

But she didn't move an inch.

"You take care of yourself, okay?" he said to her. Which, to an outsider, might have seemed like a stupid thing to say.

He left, and then, in the wild, frenzied crowd, she stood alone.

In the evacuation madness, Willow and Giles were stood just outside the police station, Obi-wanning a young cop:

"Thank you, officer," Giles said sincerely. "I appreciate your help.

"Thank *you*, Inspector," the cop replied. "We don't get a lot of contact with Interpol, so we're happy to help with anything you need. Is there anything else?"

"No. Thank you," Willow said. "We're fine."

The cop nodded. "Right, because you're . . . wait . . ." Confusion crept across his features. "Who are . . . ?"

Willow put the whammy on him, saying firmly, "I'm with the Inspector."

And he was back in the mojo. "You're with the Inspector," he said. "Right. We don't get a lot of contact with Interpol."

They were interrupted by two more cops struggling with a guy who had completely lost it, and was screaming, "A single step! A single step and it is upon us! It is nigh! From beneath you it—"

One of the officers cuffed him as the other pushed him into the station.

"Freakin' nutcase," growled the cop who had put on the cuffs.

"Ow," Willow murmured. She remembered the people who had lost their minds when Glory had come to town. How they were the only ones who had sensed what was happening, but no one listened to them because of their chaos. It was like that now.

"People're acting up," the cop announced. "Getting nuts. We do what we can, but our hands are kind of tied. I mean, man, let us know if you need help with your guy, because we're itching to hand out some justice."

"He wasn't much of a threat," Willow argued.

"And you're . . . wait . . ." the cop murmured.

"We really out to go catch that flight back to . . . Interpol," Giles said to Willow.

They walked away. "My control was fading," she confided in him. "What's up with them?"

"Same thing as everyone else," Giles observed. "Hellmouth is active again."

"C'mon," Willow said. "I want to get back to Xander."

He lay in his hospital bed, bandage over his eye. . . where his eye should have been, and Willow could hardly stand it. She couldn't bear to see him so wounded. It terrified her.

". . . and that you should expect to see some bruising when you remove the bandage," Buffy was saying to him as Willow tried to focus, try to stay present. "Bruising around the . . . area. The . . . musculature and bone structure took a heavy hit."

"Okay," Xander replied.

"Also, the meds may cause some stomach discomfort," Buffy ventured, "so we're going to have to be, you know, careful." She took a breath. "About your diet."

"Can't really taste anything anyway," Xander confided. "I keep waiting for all my other senses to improve by fifty percent. Should kick in any day now."

"And we're looking at a possible release as early as tonight," she soldiered on. "Once your labs are back. Doctor Kallet says they should be a couple hours."

Then he pretty much dismissed the Slayer, which Willow didn't get at first. Buffy stood, picking up Willow's file from the nightstand and said, "Okay, I think you're all caught up. Thanks for this, Willow. Great work."

"Oh, but I thought we were going to . . . there were going to be card games," Willow protested.

"It's okay," Xander said to Buffy. "Gotta be done. And maybe I'll see you tonight. Without any depth of field, of course, but still . . ."

Buffy smiled at Xander, turned, and left.

"So, you're stuck with me then, huh?" Willow asked, too brightly. "Let's get us some cherry-flavored off-brand gelatin, and then I think we're going to be ready for a rousing game of—

"I'm gonna need a parrot," Xander cut in. "To go with the eye patch. You know, complete the look. I think I still have that costume from Halloween . . ."

Though her heart was breaking, she did her best to go with it. "Yes, well, don't underestimate the impact of a peg leg. The hospital can probably hook you up with a nice one. Maybe they have a two-body-parts-for-one kind of deal."

"Oh, you know what the best part is?" he said, pumping up the hilarity. "No one will ever make me watch *Jaws 3-D* again!"

"Right!" she said cheerily. "Plus . . . you never . . ."

She grew quiet, smile frozen in place, tears welling. She could no longer speak.

"Willow," Xander murmured. "Please. Don't."

He himself was barely holding it together. She understood that she was would drag him over the edge if she sailed off there herself.

Pulling herself back from that abyss was hard. But for Xander . . . she did it.

Meanwhile, at Command Central, Anya and Andrew were holding a training session in the basement. Potentials were squeezed in everywhere—on the floor, sitting on the washer and dryer. They were pissed and scared and bewildered. Not over the vineyard attack in the slightest.

Andrew stood next to a large easel with a stack of large posterboard cards on it while Anya conducted a lecture. The demoralized Potentials grouped all around them. Morale was subterranean, like the foe they fought.

"So we know that a battle is coming," Anya summed up. "Ubervamps galore."

Andrew wrote "Ubervamp" on one of the cards and showed it to the home audience with the grace and style of Vanna White.

"And we know the Ubervamps are hard to kill," Anya continued.

Andrew murmured to himself, "Hard . . . to . . ."

"But I've been out talking to my old contacts," Anya cut I, and they've provided some surprising bits of news. Yay for them."

The only person who reacted favorably was Andrew, who continued to work on his posterboard cards, with a dash and dedication that would make Giles proud.

"Ubervamps *can*, for example, be staked," Anya announced. Right in the heart—*Zing! Poof!*—like regular vamps. We didn't know that.

"Of course," she added thoughtfully, "there's an incredibly strong sternum on these guys, so it's like driving a wooden stake through solid steel . . . but you're all super strong, right?"

"Um, no," Kennedy shot back.

"Oh. Right." Anya seemed to remember that the girls contained the Potential for superstrength. The power of the Slayer didn't belong to any of them, yet. "But the heart thing is still good to know since holy water runs off these guys like they're Scotch-guarded, but guess what, they're not coming out during the day."

Andrew fashioned a lovely sun on the board.

"Also, stay away from their teeth and the claws they use to shed flesh."

Rona shifted impatiently, interrupting her. "Okay, you know what? I used to be afraid of the Ubervamp guys. Then the scary preacher blew into town, and now I'm just mostly terrified of him."

Kennedy added, "We saw him do stuff . . ."

"Right, well, we're working on getting info on him," Anya told them, "But in the meantime . . ."

Quietly, her fear evident, Amanda murmured, "Why bother?"

Everyone stopped and looked at her.

"Nothing works. Nothing will."

That stumped Anya, who began shuffling through her note cards as if answers lay there, when they didn't. There were no answers for what had happened to all of them.

"Right, well," Anya murmured. She stopped and looked up. "I know you're upset."

Then she put down the note cards and said, "I, myself, would very much like to be sitting at the bedside of my one-eyed ex-fiancé right now rather than killing time with you people in this overcrowded and, might I add, increasingly ripe-smelling basement, and I would be if not for a certain awkward discussion he and I recently had right over there on that cot immediately following some exciting and unexpected break-up sex."

The three Potentials who had been sitting on the cot gingerly slid off it.

"I need to give him space," Anya said. "So I'm doing what I can do. Contributing what I can." She smiled. "And so are all of you. You still need to have all this information. We can't stop just because something *else* is trying to kill you, too."

She smiled sympathetically at the girls; Andrew looked quite moved.

"Now, I've got more information on the Ubervamps, so perk up those ears," she said, shifting to a cheerier tone of voice. "They're primal, not like your . . . evolved, intuitive, and attractive demons. These guys are all instinct, so don't bother with the logic or, you know, pleading for your life . . ."

My life, Faith thought, sitting on the kitchen counter, eating potato chips. *It's been so long since I've gotten to do something like this.*

Kennedy approached her, asked, "Got enough to share?"

"I'll trade you for a carton of cigarettes and some soap," she said drolly. "Sorry. Habit." As she handed the bag to Kennedy, she said, "Shouldn't you be down at Hogwarts?"

Kennedy took some chips and came around to face Faith. She handed her back the bag and said boldly, "Probably."

Faith grinned at her. "All right, playing hooky. Score one for the boarding school brat." Then she gave her a wry look. "Anya's technique is probably a little different than what you're used to."

"Do you think there are going to be questions about her sex life?" Amanda asked as she came into the kitchen. "'Cause I really hope I don't have to study all that."

"Yeah, whenever she starts talking about getting all sweaty with Xander like that, I just remind her I had him first. Shuts her right the hell up," Faith informed them. "Might work less well for you guys."

"Thing is," Kennedy said, "what's the point? Studying demon hot zones and pressure points doesn't do a helluva lot of good when Preacher Man is out there ready to finish the job he started."

Faith took that in. "No one's come up with any info yet 'bout Caleb?"

"No," Amanda told her. "Nothing is working, not research, not Anya's contacts . . ."

Kennedy anxiously looked to Faith. "We're lousy with dead ends around here. Everyone's feeling pretty . . . pointless. We don't even have a place to start."

Then Buffy called, "Hey, who's here?"

Faith and the two Potentials went to the front door

to find Buffy coming in, a thick manila folder with her. Dawn came down the stairs.

"Buffy!" Dawn cried. "How's Xander?"

"He's doing really well. He's ready to come home, I think," Buffy said, going for the good news.

Faith gestured to the manila folder. "Whatcha got?"

"Info Willow and Giles were able to get from the police database," Buffy replied, dropping the file on the dining room table. "We figure, you know, with Caleb's overt religiosity thing, if we want to learn more about him, we should try finding out maybe where he's been."

Faith flipped through the file. "Incidents of violence and vandalism connected to California and religious institutions in the last ten years." She added, for the benefit of Kennedy and Amanda, "Looks like this gives us a place to start."

"Exactly," Buffy concurred. "We start with California. If nothing turns up, we expand the search to other areas. But a guy like Caleb didn't just get in the game. He's been playing for a while. We thought we'd try to find out where."

"So we look at recent events, see if anything smacks of Caleb's MO," Dawn ventured.

"Right. And if that doesn't work, we'll try something else," Buffy said. "Whatever it takes." She looked at dawn. "You okay to help?"

Dawn raised her brows in mock innocence as she drawled, "Well I was going to do lots and lots of homework, but darn all the luck, that's when they cancelled school. So it turns out I have the time."

"Good," Buffy said, settling in a the table.

There was a moment, and then Dawn ventured, "Hey, now, what was Xander's mood like, you know, exactly? 'Cause yesterday he seemed more resigned than morose, so I was wondering if he's trending upward still."

Buffy concentrated on the papers very hard. . . .

"Oh, and you were going to talk to his doctor about the meds, right, because it seemed like . . ."

Buffy kept her eyes trained on the papers, and Dawn finally got it. She said, "Or, we could make talk about this later."

"Okay," Buffy answered tightly.

Faith cut in. "Hey, pipsqueak. Why don't you go get some of the stuff you've already gotten from Giles?"

"Fine," Dawn said. "We can cross-reference all of this to Giles' files, see what we get." She thought a moment and said, "Plus, I could say 'Giles' files' some more. I'll be right back.

She tripped upstairs, and Buffy said to the group at larger, "Okay, so we're looking for anything that looks like Caleb, his church, his ring . . ."

". . . his ability to render a Slayer useless in just one punch," Kennedy shot back.

Buffy took the hit.

Kennedy backtracked. "I didn't . . . that was stupid. I don't know why I said that."

"It's okay," Buffy told her, although it really wasn't. She took a breath. "You know, I gotta get to the school anyway, pick up the rest of my stuff."

She got up and moved toward the door.

Kennedy followed her. "I really didn't mean to . . ."

"It's fine. Don't worry about it," the Slayer said firmly. Then she thought for a moment. "Hey, isn't Anya doing a thing for you guys today?"

Kennedy nodded. "Yeah, we were there. We should probably head down there now."

"Okay," Buffy said, approving. "I'll be back soon." She said to Faith, "See if you can get everyone started on this stuff in the meantime."

The school was lonely, dark, and deep. This was the second high school the Hellmouth had defeated, although some might argue that Buffy herself had personally brought down The First . . . *and before that, I burned down the gym at Hemery. If I can graduate, anyone can.*

Her face prickling, emotions churning, she sat down at her desk and looked at her things. She didn't move. . . . and then she finally saw a picture of Xander, Willow, and her . . . all so young, so filled with excitement and life. She picked it up and stared at the faces, almost as if she were gazing at children she had once loved and lost.

Oh, God . . .

It was too much, just too much . . . and then a voice drawled, "Au, now, look. Things don't go exactly your way, so here come the waterworks."

Buffy knew that voice. Hated it with every fiber of her being . . .

"Ain't that just like a woman?" Caleb drawled.

She stood, livid, ready to kill . . . and terrified.

"Get out of here," she ordered him.

He laughed and shook a finger at her. "Now, now, little girl. Manners. Though I do imagine that firebrand tongue of yours has inflamed many a man. Weak as they are."

He moved toward her desk as if he had no worries and plenty of time. Glancing around, he ventured, "This here's a *public* school, ain't it? Kind of deserted." He shrugged. "That's only just, I suppose. Folks work so hard at keeping the Lord out, and look what happens in return. God abandons you."

He grinned. "Not that He could do much good now, anyway."

As Buffy slowly, stealthily reached for her desk drawer, he shook his head in a playful, warning gestured. "Ah-*ah*, I wouldn't were I you, sweet pea. Fighting back didn't do you much good last time, did it?"

He grinned and moved closer to her. "And how is poor, sweet Xander. Let him know he's in my prayers. And any time he's willing . . ." He wriggled his thumb, and they both knew that meant.

". . . I'm ready to finish the job."

Buffy said, "You get near Xander again, I will end you."

Then Caleb suddenly, violently shoved Buffy's desk, tipping it on its side and out of the way. There was nothing standing between them now.

Buffy kicked at his ankles, but he easily stepped aside; then he grabbed her and dragged her up until she dangled off the ground, eye-to-eye with him.

"I'm going to find such sweet pleasure in taming you," he said.

Without a moment's hesitation, he tossed her through the window. She slammed against the opposite wall in the hallway outside, her momentum putting a huge hold in it as she crumpled, unconscious, to the floor.

Giles and Dawn were working on the island in the center of the kitchen, file pages spread everywhere, reports, press clippings and photographs littering the place.

"Show me what you have," Giles told her.

"Not much," Dawn replied. "Most of these places were hit by run-of-the-mill vandalism. Basic B and E, money stolen, sometimes colorful language painted on the doors."

She looked up. "Did you notice how I just kind of threw 'B and E' in there? It's a law enforcement term."

"Yes," Giles placated her. "Yes, excellent work. Very proud."

She got back to business. "Here's the one that stood out. It's a mission up north in Gilroy."

She slid a photo to Giles as Andrew entered.

Then Andrew came into the kitchen, much with the pissed-off hangdog, as he put forth his complaint: "Um, Mr. Giles? Faith stole the last meatball-and-mozzarella-flavored Hot Pocket out of the freezer even though I had called dibs on it."

Ignoring Andrew, Giles said, "I don't see anything."

"Exactly," Dawn concurred. "No vandalism at all."

"Then why is it in the file?" Giles asked, puzzled.

"Place was abandoned," she reported. "Locals started realizing after a few days no one was going in or out. Six members of the order lived there. When the cops showed up, all gone. Unsolved."

Doggedly, Andrew opened the freezer. "Yup. See? The Post-it's still there: 'Andrew's, please do not eat,' but the box is empty now."

Studying the photo, Giles said, "Oh."

"Oh?" Dawn was excited. "Oh, good?"

"Not sure. Here . . ."

Giles carried the photo into the living room, where about seven or eight Potentials were sitting around the room, quiet and depressed.

Andrew followed, saying, "See, it's not the Hot Pocket itself that matters, even though it had the new-and-improved thicker tomato sauce. It's just the fundamental lack of respect."

Sitting, Giles opened the desk drawer, pulled out a magnifying glass, and closely examined the police photo. As Andrew concluding his rant, he glanced up at him, and said calmly, "Sssh. Pay attention."

Standing he handed the magnifying glass to Dawn. "Do you see that knothole in the back wall?"

Dawn bent in closer, examining the photo. "It's not a knothole," she realized.

It was Caleb's mark.

"Amanda, " Giles said, keeping his voice even, "would you go down to the basement and get Spike?"

Amanda slowly got up, nodding, and left the room. Giles and Dawn looked around.

"These poor girls," Giles murmured.

They were poor indeed, thoroughly demoralized, caught and sinking in a quagmire of depression. Staring out the window, speaking in hushed voices and sad whispers—it was pervasive, relentless hopelessness.

"Maybe this will help," Dawn said to Giles. "If this does get us closer to Caleb."

Faith entered, popping the last bit of a Hot Pocket into her mouth. Andrew seethed; he barely registered as she said to the others, "Sounded like there was news."

Then Spike came in with Amanda and said coolly, "What's up, Rupert?"

"I have a mission for you," Giles informed him.

"Really." Spike mock-considered that information. "Because, you know, sometimes our missions end up with you trying to kill me. I'm not fond of those."

"This is . . . serious," Giles replied. "With real . . ." His gaze took in the room. ". . . ramifications. Have a look."

He showed the photo to Spike, who scrutinized it for a moment before replying, "Ah. Looks like our boys was here." He looked up at Giles. "You want me to go check it out?"

Giles said neutrally, "I need someone who can handle himself in case Caleb left any . . . souvenirs."

"You want me to just go walking in there alone," Spike stated, squaring off a bit.

"You'll be fine," Giles shot back.

Andrew whined forward, "Are we going to get to the food-stealing issue soon?"

"Take Andrew," Giles concluded.

Simultaneously, Andrew and Spike cried, "What?!"

"You're always saying you want to get out of the house more," Dawn pointed out to Andrew.

"Yeah, but . . . ," Andrew said anxiously.

"There might be demons," Giles pointed out. "Lurking about You never know. He's a demon expert, he can help."

Spike was disgusted. He rolled his eyes and said, "Oh, *please* . . ."

"He can bring that pan-flute thing of his," Giles continued. "Excellent. Off you go."

Without looking, Giles gave Andrew a small shove as Spike glowered at Giles, storming off. Tentatively Andrew picked up the file papers and followed Spike out.

Dawn turned to Amanda and said eagerly, "So, see? That's something, right? We'll have some news soon."

Amanda did not return the joy. "Sure. Maybe that'll get us somewhere."

She slouched back with the others. Dawn, Giles, and Faith registered the fact that the new development had done absolutely nothing to improve morale.

"Meantime," Faith said, "the 'troops' here have to sit and stew, feeling crappier by the minute."

"We should keep them occupied," Dawn ventured.

"Yeah." Faith brightened. "Yeah. I think I know how to keep 'em occupied."

It was the Bronze. It was time to party down and get a little a buzz on and let it all just frickin' go. It was Faith's show and the music was . . . okay, the kind of music they play at the Bronze, although Aimee Mann, Faith was sorry she'd missed her, but anyway, hot young Potentials were finally strutting again. Playing pool, dancing . . . and Faith dancing like, well, she'd been locked away in prison for three years.

"So, what kind of band plays during an apocalypse?" Kennedy asked Dawn, grinning.

"I think this band might actually be one of the signs," Dawn shot back, but it was kinda funny, not all scary. A little good.

A little like . . . life was still happening.

Buffy had barely gotten away with her life.

She staggered into the house, calling, "Guys? How's it—"

And there was Giles at the dining room table, astonished at her appearance. He came to her saying, "My God! What . . ."

"Caleb." She brushed him off. "Came looking for seconds."

"Good Lord," Giles gasped. "Is he . . . ?"

"Still able to make me see little cartoon birdies all around my head?" she cut in. "You betcha." Painfully she sat down. "The short lack of consciousness was nice, though. I feel rested."

Giles sat again, facing her, and they shared an awkwardly silent moment. Buffy made the first move, trying to get past it.

"How'd the police files work out? Was there anything helpful in there?"

Giles brightened at their brief détente, ready to work.

"Oh, yes, very much so, I think," he told her. "Evidence that Caleb may have made inroads up north."

"Really?" Buffy asked, smiling excitedly. "That's

. . . that's great! That could help us a lot! Good job."

"I sent Spike to look into it," Giles added, and then . . . oops.

"Oh," Buffy said tersely. There was a moment, and then she said, "So, is this a mission from which you intend Spike to return alive?"

"Yes," he said firmly. "I sent Andrew with him."

Buffy took that in. Then she deadpanned, "And again, I ask the question . . ."

"Buffy," he said reasonably, "you weren't here. Some decisions must be made in your absence."

"Well, those are the ones that have been scaring me," she retorted.

He raised his chin, not backing down, and told her, "I did what I thought was right."

She narrowed her eyes, not happy, and gave it right back, "You sent away the guy who's been watching my back. Again. I think—"

"We are *all* watching your back," he countered.

"Yeah. Funny how I don't really feel that lately." She bit off every word as she stood and moved toward the stairs. She was tired, and hurt, angry and . . . hurt.

"Buffy," he began.

She paused. "Where's everyone else? Faith, the girls . . . where'd everyone go?"

"Faith thought the girls needed some time away from their studies," Giles told her. "A chance to relax for an hour or two. I thought, given everything learned from our time . . ."

He capitulated under her intense, questioning scrutiny. "She took them to the Bronze."

She stared at him as though she couldn't quite believe it. Then she nodded, turned to the front door, and left.

The vineyard. The wine cellar. Caleb . . . and his god.

They walked, they talked.

"Know what I figured out tonight?" Caleb asked. "Every high school from one end of this country to the other smells exactly alike. Now why do you suppose that is?

The First, dressed in Buffy's body, stepped from the shadows and moved toward him.

"And how was our best girl?" The First asked him.

He shook his head, grinning. "They always think they should put up a fight."

"Did you lay the proper groundwork?" The First pressed.

"That I did." He preened a little. "Reckon she got the message, even if she doesn't know it yet. So now the big, strong Slayer goes back to those girls. She's so ready to just walk them right into it, and all we're going to have to do . . ." He reached up to The First's chest . . .

". . . is give her that one . . . gentle . . . final . . . nudge."

His hand passed right through The First, and The First smiled.

"Excellent," she said.

"Gotta say," Caleb continued, "I know she's supposed to be some great and powerful mystical force, but . . . I don't see it. I just don't." He smiled broadly. "She was so . . . *easy*."

"Of course she was," The First responded. "And now it's just a question of knowing how to exploit it. And when."

Buffy The First smiled a very happy smile.

At the Bronze the girls danced and drank; Faith took a drink away from Amanda and was having a wicked good time until the cops showed up, looking grim.

"I was wondering what was taking you boys so long," Faith said as she kept dancing.

One of the officers said to her, "We're gonna have to ask you to come with us, miss. Outstanding warrant."

She smiled brightly, shrugged, and said, "Yeah, or let's try this one on instead. How about you boys buy me a drink and we see where the evening takes us?"

But the guy got behind her and grabbed her wrists, and they began to Mirandize her: "You are under arrest. You have the right to remain silent. . . ."

And the yadas . . . and then, as Faith began to protest, she saw something spooky. Both cops had put black tape over their badges, which she knew is what cops did when they were about to do things they didn't want traced back to them.

Amanda, Dawn, and Kennedy must have seen what was going down, because they came over.

"What's going on?" Kennedy demanded.

Dawn said, "They're trying to--"

"You girls don't want to get involved in this," the lead cop informed them.

Kennedy raised her chin. "Yeah? And maybe we do."

Acting as one, the cops pulled their guns. End of discussion. The Potentials stood back, stunned.

And then the leader tossed a large, non-regulation machine gun to one of his fellow anonymous badges. That guy turned and faced the crowd in the Bronze, as the leader and his lackeys dragged Faith away.

They hauled Faith outside, roughing her up as she insisted, "I'm telling you! I'm not going back to jail!"

As she got free and turned toward the door, one of the cops slammed the door shut, trapping her outside with the them.

The leader said, "Who said anything about jail?"

Faith turned back around, and all the cops lifted their guns, aiming right at her heart. She launched herself at them, attacking with a flurry of vicious moves, knocking their weapons from their hands as fast as she could with a stunning series of kicks and punches.

She knocked the final gun away—but the moment she thought she was safe, the leader slammed his billy club across her face and she dropped to the ground. In a frenzy, the cops began to beat her mercilessly.

Inside the Bronze, the Potentials were gathering, moving in on the guy with the machine gun, but not quite daring to do anything to alarm him.

"Trust me," Machine Gun Guy said. "Best thing you can do is wait here."

Dawn said to the girls, "Don't listen to him. He won't hurt us." in a loud, defiant voice, announced, "I'll just go borrow their phone."

The cop raised his weapon and fired it into one of the

hanging lamp globes. It exploded all over the dance floor.

Dawn froze. The Potentials took cover.

The music stopped.

"Best thing you can do is wait here," the cop said.

The girls surrounded him as Kennedy told the guy, "You're going to have to shoot us all to stop us."

"Doesn't really bother me," he told them. "*Back up.*"

But the girls were crowding in, getting in his face.

"No," Amanda said, finding her power.

He was startled.

"What?"

"You're not in charge here," Kenny informed him.

Amanda said, "We are."

He turned toward her, fully prepared to shoot. But Kennedy move lightning-fast, grabbing the barrel of the gun and ramming the butt of it into his jaw.

He reeled back, swinging wildly at her. The guy went flying. As she rushed him, Amanda got behind him. Pool cue in hand, she whacked him over the head with it. He went flying.

Then all the girls went into Berserker mode, seizing the power, taking the hill, rocking and rolling the bad guys like it was 1999; Yeah, baby, yeah!

They'd walked in with a Slayer and thy were not going to take crap from anyone.

The cops beat Faith with their clubs. She was on the ground, taking it. Then she shot out a leg, swiping one her assailants off his feet. She jumped up, ramming her knee hard into the face of another one. A third rushed her; she spun and slammed him against the alley wall.

Then she faced the leader again, aware that The First pig had gotten to his feet and was behind her. Without even looking at him, she made a fist and smashed in the face. He was down, round two, and she circled the leader, getting ready to rumble.

And they pounced, totally going at it, all scrappy and brutal. Dirty cops and dirtier fighting; Faith was into it—head slams to the cement, gut punches, no holds barred. The battle took them to center of the club as Amanda and Kennedy rushed outside and hauled the two cops off Faith. It was a total melee.

And of course Faith was winning.

Jerks couldn't handle that; three of them grabbed her from behind and peeled her off their buddy.

Faith, bloodied but far from beaten, watched as the leader rushed to help the guys being attacked by her girls, Amanda and Kennedy. She smiled, got to her feet, and kicked him as hard in the head as she cold.

Kennedy kneed her boy in the stomach, grabbed his club from his hand, and whacked him over the head.

Amanda shoved her cop backward into a small stack of crates. She towered over him, landing a foot on his chest, and, grinning like an Amazon, dropped another crate on his face.

"That was kinda cool," she exulted.

Then Faith slammed the leader back, whipped around, and punched the very last man standing in the head. She was on the leader, in his face, grinning at him. She pressed his club into his neck.

"You know, when you've been locked up in prison for three years, you end up forgetting how good something things feel, till you get out."

As he found his fear gene, she drawled, "Then it all comes rushing back."

"Faith," Kennedy warned, afraid she was going to go to far.

"Don't worry," Faith told her. "I'm not going to hurt him."

She dropped the club, grabbed the dirtbag's head, and slammed it into the wall. As he slumped to the ground, she said cheerfully, "I'm sorry. Did that hurt?"

"Faith?" It was Buffy, arriving just after the nick, as more girls spilled out of the Bronze and Faith was adjusting her clothes.

"What are you doing?" Buffy asked, all school-teacher. Pissed-off schoolteacher.

"Just blowing off steam," Faith said easily. "Well, it started out that way."

They traded looks—*pow, ka-pow!*—and then Buffy said, "Girls, go home I want to talk to Faith for a minute."

"Buffy," Dawn said, stepping forward to explain. "We were—"

"Dawn, you too," Buffy ordered her. "Go on."

As the girls complied, Buffy came over to Faith.

"What is this?" she demanded, big blue eyes flashing.

Faith shrugged. "They needed a break. They were running themselves into the ground. Things just got of hand."

"Taking a break off is one thing. I get blowing off steam, but they were *fighting*," Buffy said angrily. "And those girls are *drunk*. What were you thinking?"

Faith was not about to justify herself to Buffy. "It

seemed like a good idea at the time."

"What if someone had gotten hurt?" Buffy was practically shouting.

"They didn't," she returned.

"Faith. I need to know those girls are going to be safe when I'm not there," Buffy said.

"No one got hurt, B!" Faith was so tired of her stuff. "Look, you don't even know these girls. Maybe you need to have a little more confidence in them, let them get down and dirty, mess up sometimes. How the hell else are they going to learn?"

"It's one thing to learn from your mistakes," Buffy insisted. "But you don't throw *children* into—"

"They're not children," Faith said.

"That's really not the point." She turned on her heel and stomped off, heading after the girls.

"What about the vineyard?" Faith shot at her.

Buffy froze. Turned around.

"What?"

Faith knew she'd gotten her where she lived; decided to visit with her there awhile. "How safe were they when you dragged them off to meet Caleb? How safe was Rona? Or Amanda? Or Molly?"

Buffy slugged her as hard as she could, and Faith went down. She didn't fight back, just looked Buffy in the eye.

And Buffy turned and walked away, leaving her there.

The bike was a monster; Spike rode it like a rebel. Bad man, on a bad machine. Dru would be calling him

"Daddy" by now.

Except for the bit about Andrew on the back, in Dawn's old football helmet.

Spike was focusing on the road, but Andrew was focusing on the adventure. He said, "You sure you don't want to stop and pick up some burgers or something? You know, road trip food?"

"It's not a road trip," Spike growled at him. "It's a covert operation."

"Right." Andrew nodded. "Right. Gotcha."

They drove in silence for another beat.

"I bet even covert operatives eat curly fries," Andrew ventured. "They're really good."

There was a moment. Then Spike gave a little. "Not as good as those onion blossom things."

"I love those!" Andrew cried.

"Yeah, me, too," Spike allowed.

"It's an onion, yet it's a flower," Andrew murmured appreciatively. "I don't understand how such a thing is possible."

But Spike knew. "See, the genius is, if you soak it in ice water for an hour or so, it holds its shape. Then you deep fry it root-side-up for about five minutes."

"Masterful," Andrew crooned.

"Yeah." Spike was wistful, too. Then he realized what he was doing and said, "If you tell anyone we had this conversation, I'll bite you."

"Okay," Andrew said.

They kept driving. . . .

Faith stood on the porch, looking out into the street.

She was smoking, clearly trying to cool off.

A man approached her, quite the hottie, and asked her, "Big meeting started yet?"

Not looking at him she said, "God, I hope so."

"Faith," he said, evidently realizing who she was.

She looked at him again. "You must be Principal Wood," she said. "Heard a lot about you."

"It hasn't really started, has it?" He asked her. "I hate being late."

She shrugged. "Troops are still gathering. You're safe."

He didn't go inside. Instead, he looked her over and said, "Someone banged you up pretty good."

"Yeah. Cops. Mostly," she added dryly.

"Mostly?"

She touched her jaw. "This one was from someone who just thinks she's a cop." She touched it. "It's my favorite of all my current bruises." Faith checked him out, gestured. "Someone banged you up pretty good, too."

"I have no favorite bruises," he drawled. "I love them all the same."

There was silence. Then he said, "So someone thinks she's a cop, huh? You're not gonna have to, like, ice her now or something, are you?" As she raised her eyebrow, he added, "I don't know a lot about how prison works."

She smiled at his dorkiness.

"I'm not going to kill her. I wanted to. But I didn't. And by the way, bully for me, since no one else said it."

"For not killing Buffy," he finished for her.

"It's this new thing I'm trying," she said coolly.

He scrutinized her for a moment. "She told me about you."

"Believe every word."

"So what changed?" As she looked questioningly at him, he elaborated, "Why didn't you fight back?"

"Other things matter more," she replied, shrugging.

He kept studying her. "I think that's not all."

"You do?"

"I do. You look like . . . I think you're worried about her."

She favored him with a sour smile. "I think you need to brush up on your Faith-and-Buffy history."

"Okay, you say so." He paused. "It's just . . . I read people pretty well. It's a thing I do."

"You read people," she echoed. At his nod, she said, "You live around here, right?"

He was caught off guard. "Uh, no, I mean center of town, really, but . . ."

"Where'd you park?"

"I walked," he told her, even more confused.

She moved a little closer, nothing too obvious, but enough to make him a little nervous.

"Yeah. I noticed. Interesting. Long way to walk. Especially in a place like Sunnydale." Then she moved in for the confrontation. "This town, walking anywhere after dark is like an extreme sport. Someone who didn't know you very well might think you were out looking for a fight or something."

He gave his head a little "no-way" shake. "You've known me exactly fifty-three seconds."

Faith stood back, nodded, and smiled.

"Just saying, maybe you've got bigger issues than what's wrong with B." She gave him a little look. "I read people too."

As they regarded each other, headlights swept over them, car in the driveway.

"Xander's home," Faith said.

They were off the hog and in the Gilroy Mission. It was dark and very Spanish adobe, and as they crept down the hall, Andrew murmured, "No one's here. These kind of places make me feel funny inside."

"How about that," Spike drawled. "You and me got something else in common after all."

Perhaps sensing a bonding opportunity, Andrew moved into confessional mode. "This one time, when I was in Sunday school, I woke up later, so my mom made me skip breakfast, and I was really hungry; so I told the teacher I had to go to the bathroom, but I really broke into the supply cabinet and ate a whole package of communion wafers."

Spike smile to himself. "Yeah? Good on you, boy."

"But then I got sick for two days . . ."

A side door slammed opened and a dark, hooded figure rushed them, tackling Andrew.

"Spike!" Andrew cried.

Spike leaped, throwing the hooded figure off Andrew. Andrew fell against the wall as the hooded figure swung at Spike hard enough to stumble; then Andrew kicked out his feet and used them to grab hold of the figure's feet.

Their attacker went down; his hood came off and Spike grabbed him by the neck slamming him, still on the floor, against the wall.

Spike pushed him into the light.

He was just a man, a middle-aged, terrorized man wearing the clerical collar of a Catholic priest . . . and a mark burned into his cheek.

Caleb's mark.

The priest closed his eyes and began to pray, then opened them again and said to Spike. "Please. Do it quickly."

He waited for death.

Nothing happened.

The man said, "You're not going to . . . ?"

Spike crouched down so that he was face-to-face with communion wafer man, and said, "Not without us having a good death-bed chat." He said in a menacing voice, "Tell me about the tat."

The priest covered the mark; he shook his head, too terrified to talk.

Spike glowered at him. "Are you part of Caleb's faction?"

"No! No!" the priest cried.

"Then tell me what happened," Spike pressured him, as the man got more and more frightened, if that were possible.

"I—I can't," he said.

"'Can't' is a four-letter word," Andrew interjected. He stood behind Spike, hands on hips, and said, "I'm Andrew. I'll be your 'bad cop' this evening. You better start singing or my associate here—"

Ignoring Andrew, Spike said, "We're trying to fight him. Caleb. We need your help."

The priest let out a small, bitter laugh.

"You can't fight him. You can't stop him. You can only . . . run."

Andrew came back in. "'Run' is a three-letter word."

Spike glared at Andrew, who shrugged, and Spike returned to his regularly scheduled interrogation.

"Talk."

The priest thought a moment. Then he said, "I'll do better. I'll show you."

He rose and led them around a corner, where he picked up a lighted torch from a stand. As he they walked down the corridor, he said, "One night, some time ago, a man arrived at our doors."

"And you said, 'C'mon in, do some damage,'" Spike drawled.

"We are a benevolent order, and yes, we welcomed him," the priest said. "We offered to feed him."

They reached the end of the corridor. To Spike's surprise, the man pushed the wall and a secret room fwommed into view.

"But he had come for something else," the priest said.

They entered the small dark room. It was covered with tapestries, very religious-like, reminded Spike of Europe. Back in the day, he'd been sorry he'd missed the Inquisition.

"He made his way here, to the inner sanctum," the man continued. "He was excited, talking the whole time. About destiny, that sort of thing. We followed him here."

"Yeah, we hear he's a smooth talker," Spike drawled.

"He revealed something we didn't even know was here. Before our time."

The priest removed a framed tapestry about three foot-square from the wall. Behind it hung an ancient-looking stone panel covered with patterns and strange words.

"He read it. And he didn't like what it said," he told Spike and Andrew. "His temper . . . he was like . . . he was the purest evil I have ever seen." He touched his cheek, and his gaze became unfocused. "He heated his ring against a lighter, pressed it against me. And then I . . . I ran. And hid. And listened to the others die." His voice broke.

"Running away," Andrew picked up. "It saved your life." Then he realized that Spike was reading the words on the stone tablet. "What does it say?"

"'It is not for thee,'" Spike read. "It is for her alone to wield."

Trailing after Willow and Anya, Xander entered Buffy's house. In the living room, about thirty people stared back at him as he caught sight of a hastily-made welcome-home banner draped across the living room. Not in yellow crayon, but he understood the sentiment. Though not loving the spotlight, he was touched.

His Dawnie rushed forward and gave him a huge hug. Then Faith came in, too, and Wood.

"We didn't have time to do more," Kennedy told him. "You have to pretend there's a big party here."

"That's fine, actually," he quipped. "Parties in this

house . . . I usually end up having to rebuild something."

Amanda smiled at him. "I was thinking of smashing a window just to make you feel at home, but then I thought, you know, no. Also, Dawn wouldn't let me."

Xander smiled and opened his mouth to speak, but Buffy beat him to the punch, saying, "Welcome home, Xand," as she came down the stairs. She was friendly, but more business than happiness, and she continued on, saying, "I wanted you to be here for this. I think you're going to be interested in what I found out."

This was news to Willow. She checked Giles out. He, too, looked confused and out of the loop-y.

Buffy continued. "It's about the wine cellar."

Uh-oh.

Willow looked up, caught Dawn looking back. They exchanged a look, both concerned about where this was going. . . .

"I know that night was difficult," Buffy said. "For all of us. But I've figured out some things about the place, and I realize now what we have to do." She looked around the group, taking a moment. Then she said, "We're going back in."

They all just gaped at her.

"Listen," she said urgently, "I know what you're thinking, scary place where good guys go boom, I get it. I do." She looked at them all. "But I had a little visit today at the school from Caleb.

"I'm fine," she added. "I mean, it wasn't fun, but I'm fine. I'm better than fine. I figured something out. He kept making all this noise about the school."

Robin asked, "Is it the Seal again?"

"Do we need to try shutting it again?" Willow asked.

"Andrew's got plenty of tears left in him," Anya drawled. "Just tell him they cancelled *Stargate*."

"No," Buffy said emphatically. "That's just it. We've spent so much time being worried about the Hellmouth and the Seal . . . why isn't Caleb guarding them? Why doesn't he have someone there protecting it?"

No one answered.

She pushed her case. "Why is he camped out at the vineyard? The bad guys always go where the power is." She gazed around the room for agreement, but everyone was still just listening. "If the Seal was so important to Caleb and The First, they'd be there right now. They're protecting the vineyard. Or something *at* the vineyard.

"I say it's their power."

She waited. Still no one spoke, so she added, "And I saw it's time we go take it away from them."

Not a single person moved. No one spoke . . . until from behind Buffy, Faith drawled, "Or in the alternative, how about . . . we don't."

Buffy whirled around, looking at Faith in surprise.

"It's a neat theory, B. But I'm not going back in that place, not without proof," Faith told her. And neither should you."

She gestured to the Potentials. "And neither should they."

Buffy took a couple steps back in her tone of command. "I'm not saying it'll be easy . . ."

"I think Faith had the floor," Robin said. Buffy looked at him, stung.

"Maybe it'll end okay, the way you want to play it," Faith said. "But maybe it won't. And right now . . . right now I don't think I want you playing the odds. Not with my coin."

"Did you come here to fight?" Buffy accused her.

"Listen. We're fighters. All of us. But you gotta give me something *to* fight. Something real. Not . . ." She trailed off, looking for a word.

Giles supplied it:

"Windmills," he said quietly.

"There is something there," Buffy bit off.

"Maybe. But we don't know that for sure. You're asking a hell of a lot," Giles told her, gazing at her. His gaze was firm, mingled perhaps with some sorrow. But he was going to stand his ground. It was evident in his manner, and his tone.

"Too much," Robin added.

Buffy was taken aback. Way aback.

"I don't understand," she said. "Seven years I've kept us safe by doing this, exactly this, making the hard decisions." She looked around the room. "Suddenly you're all acting like you don't trust me."

"But didn't you just tell me today that you don't feel like you can trust us?" Giles asked her. "Maybe there's something going on that we need to address."

"Is this why you sent Spike away?" she half-shouted at him. "To ambush me?"

Rona said quietly, "You know, I'm sick of your deal with this Spike guy. This isn't about Spike. This is about you. You're being reckless."

Buffy stared at her. "What?"

Rona began to find her voice. A lot of anger had been smoldering, and it began to come out. "You are. I don't even know you, and I can tell. You're so obsessed with beating this Caleb that you're willing to jump into any plan without thinking."

"That's not what I'm doing!" Buffy protested.

Kennedy jumped up and moved toward Buffy. "Well, that's how it feels to us! People are dying! *We* are dying."

Willow got between them, acting as a barrier between Kennedy and the object of her anger.

"Kennedy," Willow warned her, and Buffy was grateful for the support.

"Why are you always standing up for her?" Kennedy demanded.

"I'm not," Willow said softly. She said to Buffy, "Everything that's happened . . . I'm worried about your judgment."

Shaken, Buffy regrouped. She looked at all the faces, and tried to make them see her point.

"Look, I wish this could be a democracy. I really do. But democracies don't win battles. It's a hard truth, but there has to be a single voice. You need me to issue orders and be reckless sometimes and not take your feelings into account." A beat, and then, "You need someone to lead you."

"And it's automatically you." Anya was hostile. "You really do think you're better than we are."

"No," Buffy insisted. "I—"

"But we don't know, do we? That you're actually better. You came into the world with certain advantages, sure, that's the legacy. But you didn't earn them.

You didn't work for them. You never had someone come to you and say, Here, you deserve these more than anyone else. They were just . . . handed to you.

And that doesn't make you better than us. It makes you luckier than us."

"I've gotten you this far," Buffy said.

"Not without a price," Xander cut in.

Buffy was wounded. "Xander . . ."

"I'm trying to see your point here," he said, "but I guess it must be a little to my left, because I just can't."

"Look, we can talk strategy," Buffy offered. "I'm willing to hear suggestions on how to break it down, but this is the plan. We have to be together on this or we *will* fail again."

Giles was irate. "Well, I think we've clearly demonstrated we're *not* together on this . . ."

"Which is why you have to fall in line!" she shouted at him. Then, composing herself, she said, "I'm still in charge here."

"And why is that, exactly?" Rona charged.

"Because I'm the Slayer," Buffy shot back.

Rona slid her glance in another direction.

"And isn't Faith a Slayer too?"

Everyone turned to Faith, who started and said, "Ka-wha? Whoa, whoa, whoa, *so* not what I meant." She managed a smile. "I'm not the in-charge chick. I just think B here needs to chill out for a bit, take a siesta maybe, but I'm not the one you want."

They kept looking at her.

"Maybe we need a vote," Kennedy announced. "To see who wants Faith to have a turn in charge."

"No," Buffy said. "You don't get to vote until I've had time to get everybody drunk and pal around a bunch! See, I didn't get this was a popularity contest. I think I should have equal time to bake them cookies, braid their hair . . ."

". . . learn their names," Faith said.

Buffy was seething. "Oh, you're just loving this, aren't you!"

"You have no idea what I'm feeling!" Faith blasted her.

Buffy gestured expansively around herself. She was exhausted, and angry, and aware that she was in a battle for lives. Lots of lives.

"Come in and just take everything I have! You've tried that before." She glared at Faith, who had tried to kill her mother, and slept with her boyfriend, nearly murdered Angel, and fought her, Buffy to the death.

"You tell them about that? Tell they how you used to kill people for fun? Did they think that was nifty?"

"Buffy, that's enough!" Giles thundered.

Faith got right up close. "I didn't come here to take anything away from you, but I'm not going to be your little lap dog, either. I came here to beat the other guy. To do right, however it works. I don't know if I can lead, but the real question is . . . can you follow?"

Both sides rested. The debate was over.

"So we vote," Robin said.

I can't believe this. I can't let this happen, Buffy thought wretchedly "Wait. Just . . . guys . . ." she pleaded. She looked to Willow, Xander . . . neither of whom could meet her gaze.

Buffy shook her head as fresh tears welled. "I can't. I can't watch you throw away everything you've . . . I know I'm right on this. I just need a little fai—" She found another way to say it.

"I can't just stay here and watch her lead you into some disaster."

Dawn came to her sister then, and tenderly kissed her on the cheek. Her eyes filled as she said brokenly, "Then you can't stay here."

Everyone was stunned.

"Look, I love you," Dawn said, crying. "But you were right. We have to be together on this. You can't be a part of it. So . . . I need you to . . . leave."

The final betrayal.

Oh, my God.

No one took her side. No one spoke up for her.

No one asked her to stay.

So Buffy the Vampire Slayer turned and walked out the front door.

Rona sang snidely, "'*Ding dong the witch is dead.*'"

Dawn whirled on her with tears in her eyes and said, with more grief and anger than she had felt even upon learning she was the Key. "*Shut your mouth.*"

Faith came after Buffy. Though the other Slayer wouldn't even look at her, Faith had to say what she had to say. She felt for Buffy; *huh, never would have seen* that *coming, never would have realized that when they were talking about losing confidence in her that would have meant they had more . . . faith in Faith.*

But Buffy . . . she's the one who's all dressed up

with nowhere to go. She's a freaking' Ferrari nobody wants to drive.

"Look, I swear I didn't want it to go this way."

"Don't," Buffy said shortly.

"I mean it," Faith pressed, "I'm . . ."

And then shut her mouth, because she realized that Buffy was trying not to cry.

"Don't be afraid . . . to lead them," Buffy said in a mangled voice. "Whether you wanted it or not, their lives are yours. It's going to get harder. Protect them. But . . . *lead* them."

Buffy finally turned and looked at Faith. Her face was statue-cold, just like stone, but the tears were streaming down her face. Faith knew enough not to speak, and she held the gaze. Hey, sisterhood was powerful, and when had they ever been sisters?

But they were both Slayers.

They both had the Power.

She gave Buffy a short nod, and headed back into the house.

Buffy walked alone. The town was deserted, doors left open; abandoned belongings strewn on lawns. Everyone was gone.

Sunnydale had fallen . . . or would, soon.

Very soon.

And she appeared to be powerless to prevent it from happening.

Chapter Twenty: "End of Days"

Hours had passed since Buffy's warriors, her most trusted friends, and her only sister had all turned on her.

The room was chaos, everyone talking at once—Giles, Anya, Kennedy, Vi, Caridad; much total panic, and Faith said, "Okay, you guys, let's not freak out."

Kennedy, scrappy as always, said, "I'm not. All I'm saying is that now that Buffy's not here, we finally have some say in how and when we lose our necks."

A ripple of fear went through the Potentials.

Robin suggested to Kennedy, "Maybe you don't have to be so blunt about the losing of the necks . . ."

Anya waved her hand. "Let the woman speak the truth. We're all on death's doorstep, repeatedly ringing the bell, like maniacal Girl Scouts intent on making quota."

Xander said to her, "I'm thinking maybe not everyone should have a say here." She rolled her eyes at him, irritated.

Giles spoke up. "What we need to do is figure out how to have constructive dialogue without going completely mad . . ."

Amanda shyly raised her hand. "Do you know Parliamentary Procedure? Because that's a convenient way of organizing verbal—"

Kennedy and Robin spoke at the same time, Kennedy arguing, "I just wonder if those of us who've been here longer should have more of a say," at the same time that Robin ventured, "Maybe if we break down into smaller groups, this wouldn't be so chaotic. What do you think, Faith?"

"When I was involved with Model UN," Amanda continued doggedly, we found Parliamentary Procedure to be a total life saver. For example, once when I was Uruguay . . ."

Giles caught Dawn's eye, saw the stricken look on her face. As the debate continued around them, he said to her, "She's going to be okay. It—it's all for the best."

"Yeah," she said wretchedly. "But then, why do I feel like this?"

He gave her a sympathetic hug—short, and mostly British, though tinged with some warmth.

"Everything's going to be all right," he promised.

"I hope so."

But it was hard to believe that, as the arguing swirled around them.

"I hear what you're saying," Faith began, as

Kennedy half-shouted, "Shouldn't we get down to business and start talking about our game plan? We don't have all the time in the world here. Or maybe we do . . . but that doesn't mean much any more."

"You guys?" Willow called earnestly. "You guys? I think we're wasting our time arguing about how to argue."

Amanda tried again. "Why don't we—"

Rona glared at her. "Girl, don't you mention Parliamentary Procedure again."

"I second that," Dawn said.

Faith was quiet, steady, and wrested back her leadership position "Everyone listen to me," she said. "Chill."

And then did. They all looked to her. It was quiet. Her voice had calmed them.

"It's been a long night, and I don't know about you, but I'm wiped. Why don't we all catch some sleep and figure all this out in the morning?"

Kennedy was shocked. "Do we really have time to waste—"

Still calm, Faith continued, "Look, I understand you guys are wicked stressed."

The redheaded Vi nodded emphatically.

"Frankly?" Faith said. "Our situation blows. But we've got to stay cool. That's the only way we're going to get through this." She looked around the group. "Can everyone handle that?"

The group was coming down off the hysteria; they were settling down; they were regrouping.

Under a new leader.

"Yeah, yeah," Vi said. "We'll get some rest and tomorrow, this won't seem so—"

Suddenly the house pitched into darkness.

Vi screamed

And it was knee-deep in the hooplah all over again, complete and total panic as the girls freaked out.

Amanda shouted, "Vi, be quiet!"

"What happened?" Vi asked querulously.

"The lights went out?" Rona asked, all wise-ass.

"I'll get some candles," Amanda said.

"I'll check the fuse box," Kennedy added.

"Don't bother." Faith had moved to the window, and was peering outside. "All the lights on the whole street just went out."

"Which means?" Rona demanded.

Faith was grim. "That everyone from the power company has gotten the hell out of Sunnydale."

There was a moment of silence.

Then Vi said, "I think I'm freaking out."

Buffy felt like a floating piece of ice as she walked along the street. Very cold, very detached from anything.

She walked down the middle of the street. The lights were all out. Door were slung open, houses abandoned. Across the way, a family was packing their belongings into their car and getting the hell out of Dodge.

Buffy chose a small house and walked up to the door.

CRACK!

The door swung open as she broke and entered into the dark, still house.

She took a couple steps in, her face still blank. A floorboard creaked.

Then a man's voiced shouted, "Don't move!"

Buffy didn't flinch, but she did turn around.

The man had a shotgun aimed at her head, but his hands were shaking so badly that he probably wouldn't even hit her at this close range. His bulging eyes believed sleep deprivation and paranoia.

"Get out of my house!" he shouted.

"Hey," she replied in a flat, dull voice.

Then, incredibly quickly, she seized the gun and tossed it on the couch.

"I thought this place would be empty," she said by way of apology. "Everyone has left town. You know, you really should leave."

He blustered at her. "You can't just kick me out of my own house!"

"It's not your house," she said. "It's not your town. Not anymore."

As Buffy turned toward the kitchen, he moved out of her way. Taking the shotgun with her, she opened the refrigerator door—no light went on—and looked for something to eat.

"Hey," she said, do you have any Tab?"

But the man had gone, fleeing into the night. . . .

Spike and Andrew were waiting out the light, and it was boring, boring, boring. Andrew was doing his best to entertain himself but Spike was just not cooperating.

They were sitting in the secret room in the mission, the bare walls covered by tapestries.

Inspiration!

"All right," Andrew began, "I spy with my little eye something that begins . . . with a . . . *T*." *Hah!*

"Tapestry," Spike said without a beat. He was slumped against the wall with his head in his hands, a total Gloomy Gus.

Nevertheless, Andrew was impressed. "Hey, good one. How did you—"

"Tapestries are the only things in the whole bloody room," Spike bit off.

Andrew smiled, feeling very wise. "Ah, so say you . . . but I say . . . look deeper."

"I'll look deep in your jugular, s'what I'll look deep at."

"Don't spazz out," Andrew replied anxiously. Then he ventured, "Rock paper scissors?"

Spike stared at him.

"What is wrong with you?" Spike demanded. "Don't you understand what's happening here?"

"Uh, yeah," Andrew replied, as in "no duh." "We're waiting till it's night again so you can ride on the motorcycle without exploding."

Spike slammed the floor with his fist. "And every minute we're stuck here, the Slayer's back there, facing hell knows what."

"You're worried about her, "Andrew said. "Come on, what's the worst thing that could happen to her?" A beat, and then he felt a little ill as he said, "Wow, I'm imagining something really horrible. How about you?"

"All right," Spike groused. "I'll play if you want."

Andrew was thrilled. "You will?"

"It's either that or bash my head repeatedly against this wall," Spike muttered.

"Okay," Andrew said excitedly. "Let's see . . . let's see . . ."

He scanned the room, which was bare except for tapestries, and said, "I spy with my little eye something that begins with a . . . *Y*!"

Spike scowled as he studied the room. "A *Y*? There's nothing here that—"

Andrew crowed, "*Yet* another tapestry!"

Spike sighed heavily. "Should have picked the bashing." Then he returned to his regularly scheduled worrying about Buffy.

Faith had created command central in Buffy's basement. The room was lit with battery-powered emergency rooms; the Big Board stood behind Faith and the troops. There were fighting dummies nearby, and in the forefront, the soldiers sitting in a circle: Willow, Dawn, Giles, Anya, Robin, Kennedy, Caridad, Amanda, Vi, and many more Potentials.

And Xander wearing an eye patch. He had become, for Faith a symbol that nothing was as it should be. Everything was confused and messed up. She was overwhelmed, trying to maintain control of a very large group of scared and confused people.

"So what do we know?" Faith asked.

Xander replied, "We know we're basically the last humans left in Sunnydale."

"And that, like, all the evil in town wants us dead," Caridad added.

Vi was scared. She murmured, "I don't want to die."

Don't worry," Anya said, quietly comforting. "It's far more likely that you'll stay alive long enough to watch most of your friends die first." Missing Vi's stricken look, she patted her on the back. "*Then* you'll die."

Kennedy said to Faith. "We also know that Caleb told Buffy that everything's going down at the Seal. I think we should head—"

"Let's not get ahead of ourselves," Faith interrupted, as she looked to the group at large.

"We know we've got a lot of enemies," she said. "We'll start there."

Kennedy moved back in. "Faith, I'm sorry, don't you think we should—"

"I got this," Faith dismissed her. "So, let's go over our Rogues Gallery. Who exactly do we got here?" She tapped the Big Board.

"There's The First," Dawn said, "who we can't touch."

Xander added, "And our friend, Mr. Reverend I-Hate-Women."

"Who's basically untouchable," Anya pointed out.

"And the 'Roid-rage Vamps, who are pretty much the worst," Dawn added, "and the . . ."

"Bringers," Faith said decisively. "I think they're our weakest link."

Giles frowned, looking concerned. "Are you saying we should think about attacking the Bringers?"

"Maybe." Not so decisive, Faith shrugged. "Okay, what if we kidnap one."

"And what, hold it for ransom?" Kennedy asked, her tone hostile, accent on the attitude.

Xander gestured. "I'll get the magazines and start ripping out letters now. 'Dear The First, if you want your Bringer back . . . well, we will be surprised because you have three million other ones, so please disregard this letter. Yours sincerely . . .'"

"I'm saying," Faith said, "we think about getting us a Bringer and making it talk. Get some info on The First and Caleb that way."

Dawn liked that. That was a good idea. Others were hopeful, agreeable . . . incredulous.

"I'm on board," Dawn announced.

Robin wasn't sure. "How do you think we should capture one?" he asked. "If they don't want to be found . . ."

"Okay," Kennedy interrupted, more forcefully this time. She gestured with her hand as she spoke, glancing at the others in the eerie, flat light. "I'm not sure that this is such a good idea. Why try to get information when we already know about the Seal? Why don't we send a team to the high school, do some recon, and then—"

"No," Faith said, closing the matter.

"Just like that," Kennedy said hotly. "You're not even listening."

Willow put her hand on Kennedy's arm and murmured, "Sweetie, you're pushing too hard."

Kennedy shrugged her off as she glared at Faith. "I

thought things would be different now, but you keep shutting me down."

Faith dealt it right back, not skimping on the harsh. "Things are different. Because, now? I'm your boss."

Faith stood.

Power on.

"Look, you guys, I'm not Buffy. I'm not the one who's been on your asses all this time. But I'm not one of you anymore, either. I'm your leader. I didn't ask to do this. And honestly? I didn't want to. But now I'm in charge. Which means I go first and I make the rules and the rest of you follow after me. Is that clear?

"So back the hell off, Kennedy, and let me do my job."

Off Kennedy's stunned look, she said, "Alright?"

Sullenly, Kennedy gestured and said, "Aye aye, captain."

Faith turned to the others. "Okay. Let's get down to business."

Secret chamber at the vineyard, just like in the mission . . . only not just like, because here . . . something Caleb and The First wanted.

In the torchlight, buzz saws whined and sparked; hammer clanged. Dust danced in the flickering light. Bringers toiled while Caleb and The First looked on, like devils watching the damned labor in hell.

Wearing her Buffy guise, The First said to Caleb, "I'd hoped you'd give me some better news."

"And I wish I had some," he said sincerely.

They watched for a few more minutes, and then

The First asked, "Is this going to do anything? Or is all of this just to make the Bringers sweat?" She pondered that. "Do the Bringers sweat?"

"Actually, I think they pant," Caleb told her. "Like dogs." He moved his shoulders and gave his head a shake. "And, I don't know if this is doing any good. But we've got to try everything. What's a prophesy got on brute strength?"

The Slayer said, "You realize what will happen if the Slayer and her girls get it, don't' you?"

They won't. Caleb's eyes flashed.

"That's right. They won't." The First turned, walking away, speaking to Caleb without so much as glancing at him. "Because you're going to kill them and everyone they know."

Caleb smiled, liking that.

Liking that very much, as he murmured, "Hallelujah."

Down the alley Kennedy gave a scuffed, pissed-off kick to a garbage can. Hands in pockets, glowering . . . and distracted.

Without warning, three Bringers leaped from the darkness, one of them grabbing Kennedy from behind. She fell to her knees; the knife edge pressed sharply against her cheek and then—

The second Bringer staggered back, knife clattering to the cement . . .

. . . as Giles yanked him back with a lasso he had just thrown around his neck.

Then the Bringer lunged at Kennedy as Caridad burst from the darkness and gave it a solid kick to the temple, while Amanda and a Potential named Isabella erupted from the darkness, slammed their fists into the third Bringer, and Isabella stabbed him in the gut. He went down, dead.

Kennedy picked up the first Bringer's knife as the second one tackled her, throwing her to the ground; solid guy, not like the first, and his breath was foul. She struggled as he got his hands around her neck, and then his hands lost their strength as she stabbed him in the chest.

She wrenched out the blade and wiped it on her jeans.

She said to the others, "I've never been the bait before. That was . . . actually kind of scary," she admitted.

Caridad reminded her, "We had your back."

Giles tossed the end of the lasso to Kennedy, telling her, "You did well. Your performance as a disgruntled minion was spot on."

She pulled the rope tight, wrapping the slack around her arm. "I'm Method." She smiled. "Let's get this back to the Captain.

The triumphant posse walked off into the moonlight.

One for us, Kennedy thought. *Finally.*

The kitchen glowed by hurricane lamps, casting campfire faces on Anya, Amanda, and a couple of the other girls as Dawn sat anxiously with them. She didn't know what the others were doing to the Bringer down in the basement. She did know that he had to talk, no matter how much he didn't want to, because she knew how vicious Faith could be and she had seen firsthand what kid of a beating Principal Wood had given Spike. She was very grateful to the monks who had created her for giving her happy family memories. But these were not going to be happy memories, ever. Dawn was not battle-hardened, no matter how battle-weary she was.

The sound of heavy footsteps on the stairs alerted her to the fact that the interrogation crew was on its way up. She steadied herself for news.

"Hey!" she said to Giles as he walked into the kitchen. "So?"

"The Bringer's dumb," he replied, downcast.

Anya rolled her eyes. "And you were expecting, what? A Rhodes Scholar?"

"Dumb as in mute," Giles replied, not without patience.. "Dumb is a politically incorrect and out-dated term that belies my youth in the Mesozoic Era."

"Someone ripped out its tongue," Faith elaborated.

"Oh, gross!" Amanda cried.

Xander moved to the counter and said with a pirate swagger, "Hey, whoa there, sweet cakes. Missing body parts can look pretty awesome." A beat, and then, "But this was totally gross."

"Hey," Dawn piped up, "I've been reading this old Turkish spell book. There's an old conjuration that the ancient Turks used to communicate with the dying . . ."

Willow nodded thoughtfully. "Oh, yeah. I think I've read a translation of that."

"There's a translation?" Dawn cried. "Oh, great! I'm reading like two words of Turkish a night when I could be . . ." She took a deep breath as the others looked on, mildly amused. "Okay, I'm over it."

She looked at the group. "So the spell is for communicating with people who can't talk. Like when a person is dying and can't speak anymore, this spell would allow them to say their good-byes or, y'know, gripe about how nobody ever came to visit." Then, specifically to Willow, she asked, "Do you think this'll help with Mr. No-Tongue?"

Willow considered. "It should work, yeah . . . if we transmute the Bringer's internal synapses into sound waves . . . yep, I think so. I'll just need to get together some ingredients. It shouldn't take too long."

Leader Faith was good with that. She moved her head, saying, "Well, all right, cool. While Willow's doing that, why don't the rest of—"

"We're ba-ack!" Andrew sang from the foyer as the entry door slammed shut.

He and Spike appeared in the dining room, Spike first, and as Faith saw him, she thought, *Uh-oh, here we go*.

"Hey," Spike said by way of greeting.

Andrew was full of vinegar as he jabbered a mile a minute. "Hi, everybody. I missed you guys a lot. Sorry we took so long getting back from our mission-mission but we had to wait out the sun and—" He brightened even more brightly at the sight of Xander's eye patch. "Oh, cool, very Col. Nick Fury! You're lookin' good!"

"*Seeing* slightly less good," Xander said, with a touch of warmth in his voice. Andrew was in many ways a reflection of the geek that had been Xander back in the day. He thought wistfully of Jesse, the friend he had lost early on to the vampires. "But, thanks."

"Well, I think we had a very successful trip," Andrew prattled on to everyone who had ears to hear. "We rode on Spike's 'hog,' which was very cool, and we played some amusing games, and oh, yeah, we've got some information—but do you know what? I really need to urinate."

With that, he dashed off toward the bathroom.

"He's a breath of fresh air, isn't he?" Spike said archly. "Thank God I don't breathe. So, I think we got a lead." He looked around. "Where's Buffy?"

Dawn said neutrally, "She's not here right now."

Spike took that in, said, "When's she get back?"

Nobody spoke. Faith got ready to rumble, if rumbling was going to be necessary; everyone was else was jittery, and hey, no surprise there . . .

"What, she finally ran off and joined the circus?" he asked jovially. "Always though she'd be genius at the old knife-throw . . ."

Then, sensing that no one else was moving with him to the land of whimsy, Spike demanded, "Where is she?"

Willow looked like she was going to throw down, so Faith kept her mouth shut.

Sure enough, the Wicca waded right in.

"While you were gone, we all got together and talked out the disagreements we've been having. And eventually, after some discussion . . . Buffy decided that it would be best for all of us if she took a little time off. A little breather," she finished lamely.

Faith ticked her glance to Spike, who said evenly,

"I see. Uh-huh." He gave her a hard look, and Willow looked away. "Been practicing that li'l speech long, have you?" He regarded the group at large.

"So. Buffy took some time off, right in the middle of an apocalypse. And it was her decision?" he pressed, gazing at them all.

Heads were hung in shame.

"Well, we all decided," Xander said, likewise stepping up.

"Yeah, *you* all decided," Spike echoed.

He paced, smiling strangely, then faced them all, "You sad, sad, ungrateful *traitors*. Who do you think you are?"

Looking stricken, Willow murmured, "We're her friends. We only want—"

"That's ballsy of you," Spike interrupted. "You're her friend and you betray her like this?"

Giles moved forward. "You don't understand."

"You know, think I do," Spike shot back. He sneered at Giles and said, "Rupert. You used to be the big man, didn't you? The teacher all full of wisdom. And now she's surpassed you, and you can't handle it."

Spike's seething gaze took them all in.

"She's saved your lives again and again. She's died for you. And this is how you thank her? This is how—"

Okay, my ups, Faith thought. She stepped in front of him, cutting him off and said, "Hey, why don't you take it down a notch or two? The time for giving speeches is over, Bat-boy."

He took a step closer to her, pissed, threatening. "Is that right?"

"Yeah," she said, unafraid. "That's right. Save you lack of breath."

"All right," he drawled, and hauled off and punched her in the jaw. It caught her off-guard, even though it shouldn't have; she fell against the counter and the others backed away—if this had been a Western, the piano player and the saloon girls would be cowering behind the bar. . . .

As Faith touched her jaw, a smile spread over her face.

"You're pretty sweet on her, aren't you?"

Using the kitchen counter as her leverage point, Faith kicked up both legs, cracking Spike in the face.

"Well, I think it's cute."

He hit her back, hard, and she returned the favor with equal forced.

"The way she's got you whipped," Faith continued, with a tremendous kick that sent him flying onto his back. She jumped on him, hitting him in the face, again and again, brutally; but he threw her off him and threw her to the wall, got right in her face; he was shaking with fury.

"Finally got what you always wanted, didn't you?" Silently she stared at him and he knocked her head back, hard. "Where is she?"

"I don't know," Faith replied.

She wrenched out his grasp and kicked him in the gut, readying for his returning blow.

But he threw up his hands in disgust and turned away from her. Headed out toward the kitchen doorway.

No one could look at him.

And he left the building.

In more ways than one.

There's nothing to be done for it now, Willow reminded herself, as she prepared to start the Turkish spell for the dying. But it unnerved her to realize that Spike was gone, and Spike was angry. Like the others, she couldn't trust him, and she had no idea what he was off doing. It unsettled her. There was already so much to worry about . . .

In the basement, the Bringer was sitting awkwardly on the floor, his arms above his head, wrists manacled in Spike's old chains. Candles illuminated the room. Kennedy, Giles, Andrew, and Xander stood watch slightly behind her. Turkish incense thickened the tension, and Kennedy looked like she was about ready to pop.

Willow said in Turkish, "*You are getting very sleepy. Very, very sleepy. I do not have a pocket watch but then again, you do not have eyes. Speak to us.*"

She closed the book, waited; nothing happened.

In a stage whisper, Andrew said, "Maybe you should let me rough him up a little."

"Andrew!" Xander and Kennedy admonished him. "Quiet."

Willow was perplexed. "I don't know, you guys," she said. "That should have worked."

Giles thought, and then he suggested, "Perhaps you should try again. Sometimes your conjugations are a little unusual . . ."

Then Andrew murmured, "I am a drone in the mind that is evil. . . ."

Annoyed, Xander snapped, "Could you just shut up?"

Andrew ignored him. "I say, I am a part of the Great Darkness . . ."

"Somebody needs a reality check," Kennedy said, equally annoyed.

"And a muzzle," Xander volleyed.

Then Giles began to connect the dots.

"Wait," he said. He looked at the Bringer, then at Andrew.

The picture popped into perspective: Andrew was serving as a conduit for the Bringer.

Andrew droned on, "I am only a fragment of The We. We work as one to serve The First."

Willow faced Andrew and then the Bringer. "Okay, well," she said, taking a breath, "what are you, The We, doing for The First?"

Everyone listened carefully as Andrew/The We replied, "We work to prepare for the inevitable battle."

Then Kennedy shot forward, getting right in the Bringer's face. She pulled the Bringer's knife from her belt and pressed it to the Bringer's neck. Willow was not happy with the aggression, but said nothing.

"How? Tell me exactly what the Bringers are doing," Kennedy insisted.

"Kennedy, he can't see the knife," Giles said, objecting.

Andrew/The We said calmly, "We can feel the knife."

"Kennedy" Giles requested, holding out his hand. She reluctantly yielded the weapon.

Andrew continued, "We attend to the needs of infinite Evil. We exterminate girls and destroy the legacy of Slayer. We build an arsenal beneath the dirt. We obey the commands of our teacher Caleb. We protect . . ."

"Wait," Xander said, his ears at fully 50% capacity above, well, nothing, but wishing that extra-credit on the senses beyond eyesight would kick in. "Go back to that dirt thing."

"We build weapons for the coming war," Andrew said.

"Can you do better specificity-wise than 'under the dirt?'" Anya asked.

"At the farthest edge of town," Andrew said conversationally. Then he was back in evil minion mode. "We are everywhere. We are like the ocean's waves. We watch your efforts and are not scared. We will laugh at you as you die."

Then without warning, Giles slashed the Bringer's knife across its throat. The Bringer gasped, sucking air through its wound for a moment, and died.

"What the bananas!" Andrew cried, fully Andrew again. He glared at Giles as he clutched his throat. "Okay, it is so lucky for you that you didn't just magically decapitate me," he said.

"We got something here," Giles said briskly. "Let's get Faith in on this."

They trooped up the stairs, Andrew last.

"Xander, if you'll grab some maps, we can start narrowing this down. We need subterranean space with an area larger enough for an armory."

Andrew groaned importantly, "Ooh, I feel used and violated and I need a lozenge."

Buffy was lying on the stranger's bed, not in it; moonlight streamed in from the window and the shotgun was at her side.

Someone knocked on the front door. Buffy didn't even react. The knocked was persistent, and the door opened, and she didn't have the wherewithal to do anything more than nothing.

Footsteps, coming her way.

Then his voice.

"There you are," Spike said, striding in. He was filled with energy; just looking at him exhausted her.

And yet . . .

"Do you realize I could just walk in here, no invite needed? This town really is theirs now, isn't it?"

She looked at him and he nodded sharply, saying, "I heard. I was over there. That bitch."

Buffy shook her head.

"She's all smiles and *reformation* when you're on your feet. Minute you're down? She's all about the kicking, isn't that right?" Spike spat. "Makes me want to—"

Beyond tired, Buffy said, "It wasn't just Faith. It was all of them and it's not like they were wrong. Now, please." So very tired. "Leave."

Spike didn't budge. Spike had news.

News he had not shared with the treacherous bunch living in Buffy's house while she camped out like a mongrel.

"This'll change your tune," he said excitedly. "I came here 'cause I got something to tell you. You're right. You've been right since the beginning."

He looked at her triumphantly, but she was still drawing a blank.

"Caleb *is* protecting something from you," he announced expansively. "And I think you were spot on all the way. I think it's at the vineyard."

He looked at her with great expectations.

"So?" he asked leadingly. He kept waiting. "You were right." Another beat. "Buffy."

She shook her head. "I don't feel very right," she confessed. "They blame me for stuff, and honestly? I can't say they're wrong."

Spike gazed at her; he crouched by the bed and said, "You're not fooling me. You're not a quitter."

But she was utterly defeated. "Watch me."

"Buffy, no," he said, as if he could somehow transmit his strength to her. "You were their leader and you still are. This isn't something that you gave up. It's something that they took."

"And the difference is?" she asked dully.

He grinned his feral Spike grin.

"We can take it back."

"No," Buffy said, sitting on the bed.

He was taken aback. "No?"

"No."

"You mean no, as in, eventually?"

She smiled thinly. "You really have trouble with that word, don't you?"

He frowned, regarded her, gave his head a shake.

"I don't understand. I don't understand you one bit."

"I've actually been aware of that for some time," she said drolly.

"You can get them back," Spike enunciated with care, as if she were a bit thick.

"Can, maybe." She looked at him with questions in her eyes. "Should? I don't know. I'm so tired . . ."

"They need you!" Spike insisted.

It was what she wanted to hear, but she wouldn't admit it. "Well, I—"

"It's bloody chaos over there without you!"

"It is?" Despite herself, her voice rose.

"Yeah, yeah, it's, uh . . . there's junk, food cartons, sleeping bags not rolled up. Everyone's very scared and uh, unkempt . . ." He trailed off.

"Sounds dire," she said ironically.

"Look, I didn't see a lot," he grumbled. "I came, hit Faith a bunch of times, and left."

She perked up a bit. "Really?" Then she caught herself and said, "I mean, I'm not glad of that . . ."

"Say the word and she's a footnote in history," he promised her loyally. "I'll make it look like a painful accident . . ."

"That's my problem," Buffy told him, growing anxious. "I say the word, some girl dies. Every time."

"There's always casualties in a war," Spike remarked.

"Casualties," she echoed. "It sounds so casual. These are girls. That I got killed." As she looked at him, she continued, "I've been thinking a lot . . ."

"Okay, first mistake," he drawled.

"And I can't fault them for kicking me out," she admitted, searching herself, finding herself wanting. "I've just cut myself off from them, all of them. 'Cause I knew I was going to lose some of them, and I didn't want to . . ."

Distressed, she rose.

"You know what?" she said to him. "I'm still making excuses. I've *always* cut myself off, I've always . . . being the Slayer made me different, but it's my fault I stayed that way. People try to connect to me but I just . . . I slip away."

She paused, looking to him for confirmation. When he remained silent, she pressed, "You should know."

"I seem to recall a certain amount of connecting," he told her.

"Please, Spike," she said. "We never got close. That's why you wanted me. 'Cause I was unattainable."

He stood, really looking at her, and said, "You think that's all it was?"

She hesitated. "I don't want to go over the . . ."

"No," he interrupted. "Hold on here. I've hummed along to your pity ditty; I think *I* should have the mic for a bit."

She dropped down onto the bed, looking wearily up at him.

"Fine," she said. "The stage is yours. Cheer me up."

"You're insufferable." He shook his head.

"Thank you," she said. "That helped."

"I'm not trying to cheer you up!"

"Well, what are you trying to say?" she demanded.

"I don't know." He huffed in just the way he did; paced a little, looked frustrated and confused. "I'll know when I'm doing saying it. Something pissed me off and I just . . . Unattainable! That's it?"

Shrugging, she said, "Okay, I'm attainable. I'm an attanathon. Can I sleep now?"

"You listen to me," he said quietly. "I've been alive a lot longer than you, and dead a lot longer than that. I've seen things you couldn't imagine, and one things I'd prefer you didn't. I don't exactly have a reputation for being a thinker; I follow my blood, which does not always rush in the direction of my head. So I've made a lot of mistakes. A lot of wrong bloody calls."

He squatted before her as she sat on the bed. "A hundred plus years, only one thing I've ever been sure of: you."

He moved to touched her face; she misunderstood and began to turn away, but he put his hand to her cheek, and urged her to listen, to see, what was in his heart.

In his soul.

"Look at me. I'm not asking you for anything. When I tell you that I love you, it's not because I want you, or 'cause I can have you. It has nothing to do with me."

His voice astonished her, moved her, as she listened.

"I love what you are, what you do, how you try. I've seen your strength, and your kindness. I've seen the best and the worst of you, and I understand with perfect clarity exactly what you are.

"You're one hell of a woman."

Buffy was silently crying; he could only smile at her kindly, containing his own emotions.

"You're the one, Buffy."

Softly, she said, "I don't . . . I don't want to be the one."

"I don't want to be this good-looking and athletic," he riposted. "We all have our crosses to bear."

She smiled a little.

"No you get some rest," he ordered her, rising. "I'll check in before first light You can decide how you want—"

"Spike?" Her voice was barely above a whisper; he turned.

"Could you . . . stay here?" she asked.

They regarded one another silently.

"Sure," he said, taking off his coat and moving to an armchair. He started moving the former occupants' clothes off it. "That diabolical torture device, the Comfy Chair, do me fine—".

"No. I mean . . . here." Her voice cracked. She looked down uncertainly. "Would you just . . . hold me?"

No more words.

A look, a moment, a soft inhalation, and a wish . . .

He came to her then, and wrapped her in his arms. She put her head down on his chest.

No more words.

* * *

Faith was tired of the leader gig. Hadn't wanted it, wasn't dealing all that well with it. All she wanted to do was sleep.

She and Giles were standing in the doorway to Buffy's old bedroom. Giles was showing her a section of a map as they planned some forays to search for the armory and no doubt kick some Bringer butt.

"Sewer tunnel on the north side's closest, so guess we'll start there."

"That sounds fine. What time should I tell everyone?" he asked.

She didn't know. "How about around seven?" Then, catching herself, she said, "Seven sharp. So tomorrow, we fight."

"Tomorrow," he concurred. "Good night, Faith." He turned, turned back. "And Faith?"

"Yeah?" she asked dully.

He smiled gently. "You're doing just fine."

She smiled a small, grateful smile.

Then she turned into the bedroom.

And The First was there, with a little surprise: he was appearing to her as Mayor Wilkins, the man/semi-demon who had taken her in . . . and had her kill her first human being, the vulcanologist who might have blown the mayor's big plans for becoming a full-blown demon on Ascension Day.

"I'd say better than 'fine,'" he drawled. "I'd say you're doing a bang-up job."

She was totally rattled, but she tried not to show it.

"Get out," she said harshly.

He was his old amiable, evil self as he chuckled

and said, "Well, gosh, I think a 'hello' or 'nice to see you' might be a little more welcome. It's the end of humanity, Faith, not the end of courtesy."

"You're wasting your time," Faith informed him. "I know who you are. *What* you are."

He gazed at her. "Nobody's explained to you how this works, have they?" He paced a little, as if searching how to put it. "You see, I am part of The First, as you kids call it, but I'm also Richard Wilkins the Third. Late mayor . . . and founder . . . of Sunnydale."

She pulled in, not reacting . . . but still listening.

"Here," he offered. "I'll prove it to you. Ask me a question only I would know the answer to. Something like . . ." He thought a moment. ". . . where did I hide the moon pies in my office, or who was my favorite character in *Little Women*?" He paused. "We never got that far, did we." A beat. "Meg."

He threw his hands up in a 'can you believe it!' gesture.

"I know! Most people guess Beth. But Meg was a such a proper young lady. Remember when Jo burned your hair?"

Faith kept herself cold, kept herself distant. "I know what you're doing. It's not going to work." She shrugged. "But feel free to keep talking. Hell, I could listen to you yap all night."

He wagged a finger at her, giving her a parental frown. "Hey, hey, hey . . . *language*. You're a leader now. You keep throwing the "H-E-double hockey sticks" around, pretty soon these girls are going to pick up on it. Then what?"

"You let me worry about the girls," she said icily.

"Of course. Of course." He added, giving her a confidential smile, "You're doing a great job with them, by the way. Much better than Buffy ever did. You were smart to kick her out."

Faith was taken aback. "That's not what we . . . Buffy got them this far."

He scoffed. "Why are you protecting her? You think she cares about you?"

Faith didn't say a word.

"She nearly killed you, Faith," he reminded her.

"It's different now," she murmured.

"No matter what you do, Buffy will always see you as a killer, not as a person. And now you have what she so desperately wants—the respect of these girls."

He came closer to what was under Faith's surface. . . .

"All she needs is an excuse, and she'll finish what she stared when she stuck that knife in your belly." He paused and added, "Stay on guard, Faith. Buffy's dangerous. If you're not careful, she'll destroy you.

"I'm just saying," he added pleasantly. "It all comes down to love."

They were squaring off; she braced herself, knowing The First was going to try to work her, hurt her, throw her off balance.

Deep down, you've always wanted Buffy to accept you, to love you, even." He raised his brows. "Why do you think that is?"

"You a shrink now?" she asked sullenly.

"You keep looking for love and acceptance from

these people, these 'friends' of yours," he pointed out, sounded very reasonable, very kind. "But you're never going to find it. The truth is, nobody will ever love you." He smiled at her. "Not the way I love you."

"Get out," she spat, balling her fists. He was getting to her; she couldn't deny that.

"They'll forever see you as a killer," he added, still pleasant.

"I said get out!"

"I'll always be with you, firecracker." His tone was fatherly, gentle, and filled with the love that she wanted. "In everything you do."

Dear God, the love that she wanted . . .

. . . and then he disappeared.

Then a voice behind her said, "Faith?"

She whirled around to find Robin there. He put his hand on her shoulder; she shook it off and moved away.

"Shouldn't sneak up like that," she said. "Almost took your head off."

"Sorry," he said. "I knocked . . ."

"What'd you see?" she demanded.

He gestured to the room, then to her. "Just you looking spooked. What happened?"

She tried to let it go, but she was still shaken. "Nothing," she insisted. "Forget it." Then she remembered he'd come in for a reason, and that she was on point, and said, "What's up?"

"I was just going to fill you in our weapons status," he told her.

"So, fill," she said brightly. "Go."

"We need more," he said frankly. Then he titled his head, scrutinizing her. "You sure you're all right?:

Her temper flared, and she knew why, but it was none of his business. "What?" she threw at him, mean as a punch. "You want to rap about my problems?" Her voice raised. "You hopin' to be the guy who puts the pal in principal for me?"

He stayed calm, though not entirely unaffected, as he said to her, "Okay, I came up to talk weapons. I see you, you look kind of upset, and I ask you if you're okay. Where exactly did I go wrong?"

She processed that and stepped down from phasers on kill. "Sorry. I just don't know what I'm doing . . . I just . . ."

"I'll leave you alone," he said thoughtfully. "Didn't mean to intrude."

As he turned to go, she blurted out, "It was The First."

He turned back and looked at her, then entered the room and shut the door.

"You're really in the game now," he said. "The First doesn't show unless it thinks you really matter."

"Lucky me," she drawled. "I'm a player."

They sat down on the bed side by side, and she held up a shaking hand. "Man," she said. "Look at that. That really got me. I mean, demons, vampires, women in the penitentiary system, none of those make me freak."

"But that's what The First does," Robin explained. "Finds your Achilles heel.

"Naw. It just talked to me." She made a face. "It does a heel thing too?"

"It's a phrase." He didn't sound at all patronizing. "Your weak spot."

"Ah. The school thing." She nodded. "I was kind of absent that decade."

They shared a smile, put some closure on the tension, moved on. It was actually kind of nice, as far as Faith was concerned.

"So who was it . . . The First?" Robin asked her.

She stirred. "He was . . . like, an old boss of mine."

"Just a boss?" He was noncommittal in his surprise. "And seeing him makes you shake like that?" A beat, and then, "Wouldn't give you a raise, huh?"

"Yeah, right." She smiled weakly. "Nah." Took a breath. "I know it sounds retarded, but he was like a dad to me."

"Oh." Then he said to her, in deep confidence, "It was my mother. When it came to me. And I mean, it *was* her. Right down the perfume: patchouli and lilac."

Faith heard the hurt in his voice and looked into his eyes.

"Sorry," she said.

"Yeah." He was, too.

"I'm just pissed at myself," she admitted, shifting again. "I knew it was a trick . . ."

"So did I," he reminded her. "And I still wanted my mama to hold me like a little baby." Off her amused look, he added, "In a manly way. Of course."

"Of course."

He said, "Nobody wants to be alone, Faith. We all want someone who cares. To be touched that way. The First may deal in figments, but the wanting is real."

The look they shared . . . intense. *We get each other*, Faith thought, seeing him in a different way. *We get the need in each other*.

"Hitting things and a whole lotta Jack D dulls it some," she drawled.

He did not back off, did not back down. He was quite the man.

"Among other things," he said.

She smiled bigtime at that. Then she said, "When it came to you, did The First tell you the truth?"

"Yes," he said simply.

Faith considered that. Then she told him, "It said that we've got to watch out for Buffy. That Buffy's dangerous." She gazed at him, pretty damn troubled.

"What do you think?" he asked her

She shook her head. "Could be. We've given B a mighty reason to be pissed off.

"The messed-up thing?" she added, going for it. "The First is telling me to worry about her, and I just wish she was here. In a couple of hours, I'm leading these girls into some serious crap. And she's the only one—"

"She's not the only one," Robin reminded her firmly. "You're a Slayer, too. And I think you're a leader."

She gave it up. "I'm an ex-con that didn't finish high school.

He gave her a sad smile. "I'm the principal of a school that *nobody* finished. And I'm totally out of my league in this."

"I hear otherwise," Faith said, giving him a look.

That flattered him, and threw him off; he regained his composure and said, "So, tomorrow . . ."

"Forget about tomorrow," she told him. "This is tonight." She put a hand on his arm, let her touch linger there for a moment, gazed up at him and said softly, "Been a while. Am I out of line?"

"Hey, you're the leader." His voice was husky.

She kissed him. Held his face between her hands and kissed him hard, pressing him back down onto the mattress. Faith, the one who burned bright, the flame, the comet. She straddled him, came up for air so she could burn hotter, longer, and said to him, "Kiss me."

He did. Deep, hard. He slid his hands under her T-shirt and caressed the bare length of her back, the muscles, the scars.

She began to undress him . . .

. . . let there be fire . . .

Willow went into her room to put the troops to bed for the night, dressing in a tank top and jammie shorts. She was looking at one of Giles's maps.

"Okay, guys," she said, studying the map, "Giles said that Faith said that we should be ready to go early in the—"

She blinked. The only person in the room was Kennedy in a beautiful gown, lying under the sheets. One of her exquisite, muscular legs was revealed. Candles glowed, bronzing her with a glow.

With a catch in her voice, Willow asked, "What happened to the girls?"

Kennedy peered through her lashes and murmured, "Looks like there's only one girl here. "

Willow raised her brows. "But what about the other ones, with their sleeping bags and their headgear and their snoring and . . ." She smiled big. She smiled radiant. She smiled like an Amazon on the night before the big battle. "They're not here."

Kennedy's mouth curved into a bow.

"Nope."

Willow shut the door.

"That's nice."

She went over to the bed and sat on the edge near Kennedy, and kissed her lightly on the lips.

"Nice and necessary," Kennedy teased. "Our foreplay was threatening to turn into twelve-play."

She kissed Willow back; then she took the map from Willow's hand and dropped it to the floor. Pulled the Wicca close and said, "C'mere."

Willow slid under the sheets, then turned away. Kennedy spooned her, kissing her neck, and asked, "Something not right?"

"No, no, I just . . ." Willow took a breath. "I guess I'm kind of scared."

Kennedy got that. "It's probably too stupid to ask why, huh? Death, war, apocalypse . . ."

"Me," Willow admitted. As Kennedy looked at her tenderly, she gently pushed a strand of hair off her face.

"I'm scared if we . . . then I'll . . . and then . . ."

"And then, isn't that the good part?" Kennedy asked.

"Yeah, good." Willow nodded earnestly in her Willow way. "Good feeling. But also . . ."

"Bad stuff like unrestrained moaning and screaming with joy?" Kennedy joshed her.

Willow looked abashed. "Well, yeah, sort of. Yeah, with the unrestrained of it. I've been in a place where I kind of should be restrained. I've been controlling myself and if I get out of control . . . if I let myself go, I could just . . . go."

"You're worried you're going to turn into Big Bad Willow."

"It's not stupid," Willow pointed out. "When we kissed, I turned into a—a Warren." She was stricken.

"It's not stupid," Kennedy agreed, "but it's not going to happen. C'mon . . ."

Willow gazed uncertainly at her, and Kennedy said, "Am I doing that thing? Am I pushing too hard?"

"I don't know," Willow told her honestly.

"I guess I just want you to know that you're safe with me," Kennedy said. "I'll keep you safe. You can float around and I'll tether you down."

"You'll be, like, my kite string?" Willow asked her, breathy, beginning to relax.

"You be a kite and I'll be your kite string, okay?" Kennedy said.

"Okay," Willow said, and their kisses turned passionate; Willow let go . . . let go . . . abandoning herself to the moment, to Kennedy.

How the Potentials could sleep through all the racket

going on upstairs was beyond Anya. She and Xander sat on the counter, eating ice cream, but for heaven's sake . . .

"They could have a little respect, you know," Anya said crabbily.

"Mmm," Xander said noncommittally.

"I mean, they should at least acknowledge the possibility that some people might not want to listen to an a cappella concert of moaning and groaning."

Xander took a spoon from her and ate a bite.

"Mmm," he said again.

"It's disgusting, is what it is."

He handed her back the spoon. "Little jealous, eh?"

"Well of course! A lot jealous. If you and I are done having sex, I think everyone else should just knock it off . . ."

In the night: the comfort, the passion before the battle, before death took all the life away:

In the arms of the angels . . .

Faith and Robin in pure need, pure passion . . . he took over, took the lead, made her follow. . . .

Willow and Kennedy, abandoning . . . Kennedy licking Willow with her pierced tongue, making her let go, making her soar into the night sky. . . .

Xander and Anya on the floor, still clothed, she on top, not done yet, oh, not yet, not yet. . . .

And Buffy and Spike.

The lovers.

She was asleep in his arms. He kept vigil, watching her, stroking her hair, infinitely gentle. He leaned down and pressed his lips against her forehead.

May you find . . . some comfort . . .

"I envy them," The First said to Caleb as they walked together in the vineyard. She had put on the face of Buffy. "Isn't that the strangest thing?"

"Well, it does throw me a tad," he admitted. "They're just, well, they're barely more than animals, feeding off each other's flesh. It's nauseating.

He came forward, toward her. "But you, you're everywhere. You're in the hearts of little children, in the souls of the rich; you're the fire that makes people kill and hate, the cleansing fire that will cure the world of weakness. They're just sinners.

"You are sin."

The First smiled enigmatically. "I do like your sermons."

"And you're in me," he told her. "Gave me strength no man can have."

"You're the only man strong enough to be my vessel," she told him. "And I know you feel me, but I . . . I know why they grab at each other. To feel. I want to feel."

She grew heated. "I want to put my hands around an innocent neck and feel it crack. I want to bite off a young girl's face and feel the skin and gristle slither down my throat."

Caleb was moved. "Now that is truly poetical," he told her.

"We have to kill them," The First insisted.

He nodded. "We are."

"We have to do it faster.

"Amen."

Morning broke, the fearful phantoms . . . solid and real; but the tenderness, too, as Buffy opened her eyes and gazed at Spike asleep in her arms. Peaceful, a boy again. She gazed at him, a girl again, a lover, a mother, a sister. Someone powerfully connected to William, who might, soon, have to watch his true love die. . . .

At Checkpoint Revello, the Potentials were dressed for action. Kennedy and Miss Kite were listening. Everyone was listening . . .

. . . to Andrew, who had on a pith helmet and reminded Faith pretty much of Joxer on *Xena*, although he had something of far more substance to tell them than Joxer ever shared with X.

"So it turned out that all these stone tablets basically said the same thing: The First and Caleb are trying to protect something. We don't know exactly what, but it's something powerful and they don't want the Slayers to get it. I'm thinking it could be a weapon and if we are looking for an arsenal—"

"You're not coming," Faith told him flat out.

"If *one* is looking for an arsenal," he immediately corrected, "well, what better place to find a—"

"Weapon," Faith concluded. "Okay, got it. Good. Good thinking, Andrew," she added, trying to remember her leadership duties.

"It's a pleasure, Faith," he beamed. "Back to you."

She turned to Giles, Willow, Dawn, and Xander.

"I need you four to suss out the low-down on B. I don't want you talking to her, getting in her way, or, for that matter, letting her know you're there. Just do a little recon."

Robin asked her, "Where do you want me, Faith?"

"By your phone. I'll call you when I need you."

Her tone was cold, impersonal, as if they had not spent the entire night setting the room ablaze. He heard it, and realized he had been a one-night stand. Nothing more. Nothing there.

Nothing there at all.

Dawn asked anxiously, "What are we looking for, I mean, is there some reason we should . . . spy on Buffy?"

"We're just making sure she's okay," Faith answered, trailing off for a moment. Then she gaped at the large group of Potentials. "Those of you who are coming with me to the arsenal, you know who you are."

Kennedy, Vi, Caridad, Amanda, and others . . . including Kennedy, who pulled Willow's hand up to her lips and gave it a little kiss.

"Everybody ready?" Faith asked. Getting affirmatives, she said "Let's do this thing."

Oooh, just like Princess Leia, Andrew thought dreamily.

Who is't? Oh, it is my lady, it is my love . . .

Spike drowsed, smiling, and reached for Buffy.

But she wasn't there.

She had left him a note; soberly, he opened it and began to read.

Walking in the vineyard with the one I love . . .

Caleb and The First strolled among the barrels of wine, as Caleb told her, "It shouldn't be long now. Prophesies say one thing . . . but brute strength says another. We'll get it out." He added, "We're almost there."

The First, wearing Buffy, smiled at him and said, "Yes, that's true. Now rouse the Bringers, get them back to work—"

As if on cue, something came thump, thumping down the stairs.

It was a Bringer, dead, the corpse rolling to a stop at Caleb's feet.

"Hey," came a voice from the top of the stairs.

It was Buffy. The real one.

The Slayer.

As she looked down on them, she said, "I hear you've got something of mine."

She charged down the stairs and faced off with Caleb, tense, taut, every nerve on a wire. He, however, remained his affable, casual self.

"Well," he drawled, "if it ain't the prodigal Slayer . . ."

"So where's it at?" she demanded. "I'm going to find it sooner or later."

Her gaze darted around the room, looking for Potential hiding places. He smiled, knowing there were lots of them, and stepped closer to her.

"No, you're not," he riposted. "I lay a hand on you and you're just a dead little girl." *And a dirty one at that. Filthiest ever created . . .*

"So, lay a hand on me," she said, lifting her chin, powering on her Slayer attack mode. "If you can."

And his fist shot forward; he was going to give her one hell of a punch . . .

. . . but she bent back, far, much farther he could have even anticipated . . . and his fist went right over her head. She pivoted, turning out of his way as he staggered forward, his momentum unchecked. He swung again at her; this time she ducked and slid past him head-first, like a ballplayer going home . . .

He was furious.

She got to her feet, turned, and then . . .

. . . he charged at her, crouching low to get her in the gut . . . but she leaped straight up, onto a barrel.

She ran the length of the casks; she was as agile as a high-jumper, scanning the room, looking for *it*. Caleb gave chase, lunging at her ankles, and missed.

Barrels crashed down on him, wine flowing everywhere . . . and he rose again, hallelujah, and he was gonna get this Jezebel and cut her to ribbons . . .

. . . if he could find her . . .

Then he saw her sitting on top of a barrel, went toward her, then whip-turned around and saw another Buffy behind him.

The Buffy on top of the barrel was The First, who said, "Caleb, this is getting embarrassing."

So he flung himself at the other Buffy, and missed her. He hit the ground hard.

"Do you have to look like that?" he asked The First.

"Will you concentrate?" she shot back.

"It's just a little confusing," he argued.

"Fine. Go! Kill!" she commanded.

And then she disappeared.

Caleb turned on Buffy.

Who knew half my life would be spent in sewers, and not fighting crocs? Faith thought ironically, as the flashlight beams bounced off the slimy walls. Water dripped. It was dank, chilly, and stinky. Kind of like Boston.

Amanda looked around, excited but nervous, and chattering to prove it.

"Do you think there's rats down here? This one summer my cousin and I dissected this dead rat we found in the basement. It was so creepy, oh boy . . ."

"Amanda," Kennedy warned.

They walked on in silence, the nervous hysteria abating.

"Everybody stop," Faith ordered. "I think we found it."

They pointed their flashlights in the direction she indicated.

Yeah, baby.

It was an arsenal indeed, a glittering trove of swords and axes about twenty feet away, gleaming very yo-ho-ho in the murky tunnel.

"Look at all this," Kennedy said, shining her flashlight all over it.

They advanced.

"I don't get it," Vi ventured cautiously. "Why'd they abandon all this stuff?"

"Maybe 'cause they didn't," Faith said.

And suddenly Bringers attacked, dropping down like ninjas with their knives flashing, their ugly, weird faces contorted with effort.

The fighting commenced.

The fighting continued . . . or didn't, as Caleb had still not managed to connect with Buffy. He was getting righteously indignant; the place was redolent of sweaty Preacher Man, as he swung and she dodged, jabbed and she dodged.

Then he chased her; she ran backward until she ran up against a cement post, and his face was right in hers.

Yes, yes, he thought, thrilled. *I have you now, whore!*

He swung.

She dodged.

His almighty punch connected to the cement. It hurt like hell . . . and it was like Samson and the pillars as the post started to crumble.

He seethed. He would see her dead, see her in hell, put an end to this here, now . . . he tried to grab her; she feigned left and too late, he realized she had tricked him . . . she jumped back on the wine barrels and so help him, if he had had a grenade, or another bomb . . .

Not long now, he promised himself.

He began to yank barrels from under her feet; she

reached up to a ceiling beam and swung herself to safety.

Wretched, red-faced, and angry, he said to her, "You whore."

"You know," Buffy said, "you really should watch your language. Someone who didn't know you might think you were a woman-hating prick."

Furious, he grabbed another barrel . . . and threw it at her.

His aim was perfect, smashing into her and knocking her backward—but her legs held the beam like a trapeze and she flung herself into the air, landing on the ground.

As she gained her footing, she saw a small copper trap door in the floor.

She ran toward it, sliding along the wine-drenched cement on her knees, pulling it open . . .

Caleb lunged at her, but it was too late. Buffy dove head-first through the trap door as Caleb raced after her, knocking barrels over, crushing them and landing on top of the wreckage, heaped on top of the trap door.

Beneath it, Buffy tumbled alongside the ladder, landing in a heap on the cement floor.

Faith ran, stabbing another Bringer in the back; as she pushed the corpse out of her way, she freed Vi just in the nick.

Amanda shot Legolas-style with her crossbow, except Legolas didn't tend to miss; as the Bringer charged her, she realized she was out of bolts; she ran kamikaze-style at the ol' no-eyes with a wild battle cry.

Vi and Kennedy tag-teamed against a pair of Bringers; and Faith whipped around to find not her dream date, but another damned Bringer . . .

They fought. They fought some more. They fought the most and then . . .

. . . all the Bringers were dead.

Well, Faith thought; and then, *well* again, because she didn't know what else to think.

"Is that it? Vi said. "I mean, not that that wasn't fun, but . . . *eight* Bringers?

That's what I was gonna think next, Faith thought.

They pawed through weapons. There just wasn't much there.

"Isn't this supposed to be the major leagues?" Vi said.

That next.

Vi came from around the corner, reporting in.

"There's not much here, actually. Not really a full arsenal, more of a just an . . ."

"Arse?" Amanda queried. She chuckled to herself. "Heh heh. Good one."

Okay, that *I was not going to think*, Faith thought.

"Yo, Faith, check this out," Kennedy called.

As Buffy unsteadily got to her feet, she looked around at the walls of rough stone, registered that she had fallen somewhere hidden, somewhere secret—like a holy of holies; the beating heart of the place that was The First domain . . . or rather, the place that The First wished was its domain.

Then she realized with a start that she had found it.

I have something of yours . . .

. . . and this is it. And he was right: It is mine.

Her heart pounded. Her breathing became shallow. She reached out a hand as she stared in awe and wondered.

Mine.

Waiting, for me . . . for eons.

It was a scythe, buried to its hilt in stone like King Arthur's sword, but round and circular like the moon . . . like the shape of a pregnant woman. A scythe, ultimate symbol of woman, and womanhood. Of the power only a woman could wield.

The Power . . . of the Slayer.

The stone in which it was encased had been chipped and blackened; but it was clear that Caleb and the other minions of The First had been unable to pry it loose.

Yes. It was a moment. Her moment. Her first smile, in a very, very long time.

Faith and the others joined Kennedy, gazing where her flashlight beam had penetrated the gloom.

There was a metal box on the ground.

Eureka, Faith thought happily, and raced toward it. She smashed the lock off with her boot and knelt before it, throwing back the lid.

A bomb!

It lay inside, the timer counting down:

6 . . .

5 . . .

"Everybody get down!" she shouted.

4 . . .

3 . . .

2 . . .

Chapter Twenty-One:
"End of Days"

Faith dove as she shouted, "Get down!"

And the bomb exploded.

In the secret chamber, Buffy stood in awe. The scythe, embedded in rock, called to her in a language of the heart, and the soul; she knew it belonged to her, didn't know how she knew that. But she had a deep sense of coming back, of coming home, of being here for the very purpose of claiming that weapon.

She walked forward, reaching out a hand . . .

. . . just as Caleb dropped down her, landing on his feet with a wry smile on his face.

She whirled to face him; as he approached, she did not break her stride.

"So? You found it," he said. He shrugged.

"Because the question now, girly girl, is: can you pry that out of solid rock before . . ."

She gripped the scythe's hand and, as easily as pulling a knife from butter, pulled it from the rock.

Caleb stopped short as Buffy looked at him, and said, "Darn."

The scythe felt good in her hand; it felt right.

It felt hers.

Blocking Buffy's only way out, he said, "Now, before you go hurting yourself, why don't you do yourself a courtesy . . ." He stepped forward, hand out ". . . and hand it over now."

"Yeah? You want it?"

She flipped the scythe over in her hand, as if she'd done it a thousand times. Now the weapon was pointed straight at her enemy's throat.

"In the head or the gut?" she added.

He stayed calm which was impressive. "You don't even know what you've got there."

"I know you're backing away," Buffy drawled.

She sidestepped around him. He kept his distance, and Buffy felt a thrill. He was genuinely afraid.

So he went for the attitude.

"You think wielding some two-side doodad's going to make a difference?"

Then, in her Buffy voice, The First said, "Let her go, Caleb."

She was standing behind Caleb, gaze on the Slayer . . . and on the scythe in her grasp.

"I said, let her go."

Caleb also kept his gaze fixed on Buffy and the

scythe. "I let her go, she slices me open with that thing."

"No, she doesn't," The First informed them both. "She hasn't got time. She's got friends, and her friends are in trouble."

Buffy's gaze ticked from Caleb to The First as her mirror image said helpfully, "Faith go boom."

Caleb shook his head. "I'm not letting her out of here with that thing."

"Sure you are," The First said pleasantly, "and then you're coming for it later." To Buffy: "When she's got her back turned."

He was incredulous. "After all the work we did to free it?"

The First got firmer with him as she replied, "It's hers *for now*. Let her go."

Seething, Caleb stepped out of Buffy's way . . . and then she leaped straight up, catching the edge of the trap-door opening above her—making the point that Caleb had not been in her way at all.

Still one-handed, she swung herself up the opening . . . and got the hell out of there.

Aftermath.

Death.

Smoke and dust choked the sewer; chunks of brick and cement crashed down from the ceiling like more bombs, like a fusillade. Beams dangled at grotesque angles; metal groaned; water rushed alarmingly from some distance away as girls wept and screamed in pain. It was loud and dark and twisted and horrible, stinking of mud and blood and very, very broken bodies.

Around her, her comrades in arms lay dead, eyes open as if in shock; and Amanda crawled out from beneath bodies and half-stood, bleeding, and terrified.

"Hey!" Her voice shook. "Hey, Faith! Anybody?" Her voice rose in shrill panic. "Is anybody here?"

"Me." It was Caridad, also banged up, also alive.

They moved on together, passing through the destruction, smoke, and twisted metal, slogging back toward the main section of the sewer.

"Hello?" Caridad called through the noise. "Anyone?"

Then Amanda put her arm on a survivor . . . Vi, who was coughing hard as she struggled to her feet, cradling her arm.

"I . . . I'm here," she said, coughing.

Other girls called out, but their voices were swallowed by the cacophony, terror and confusion reigning over all.

The trio pushed on, Caridad asked, "Who else we got?"

"Dunno," Amanda told her, then to Vi, "You okay?"

Vi said, "I think my arm is broken." As Amanda pointed to two dead Potentials, the redhead added, "Guess I'm lucky."

Then Kennedy joined them, limping and bloody; she asked, "Where's Faith?"

"I don't know," Vi said anxiously.

"Find her," Kennedy ordered.

"Maybe we should get the hell out of this place," Caridad pleaded, looking fearfully around.

"Find her!" Kennedy bellowed.

Three Potentials found her, pulling her dripping body from the water. Looking on, Vi, murmured, "Oh, God."

"Is she alive?" Kennedy demanded.

Amanda touched their leader gently, reporting, "Breathing. Pulse."

"We gotta get her out of here," Caridad said.

Vi looked around and asked shrilly, "Which was is out?"

Amanda gave her head a little shake. "There's other girls. There's more than Faith. We don't even know how many of us are still . . ."

A feral growl cut short her sentence; as one, the girls turned to face the source of the sound as it echoed through the darkness, but they could see nothing but smoke whirling in darkness.

Vi swallowed hard. "It could have been grinding metal. It could have been . . ."

The growl was louder this time.

Her gaze steely, Kennedy lifted her chin, and said, "No. It's one of them."

"That's not possible," Caridad murmured.

"How'd it get in here?" Amanda asked.

Vi looked at Kennedy. "Plans?"

"Run!" Kennedy ordered them.

They moved like a single being, racing through the tunnel, other Potentials moving into their group like wild animals fleeing a rogue elephant. Kennedy led the ones who could move, who were in team guiding the ones carrying Faith . . . all was chaos, fear, shouting—

"This isn't the way!" Vi protested.

"Yes, it is!" Kennedy bellowed at her.

"We're heading in the wrong direction!" Caridad insisted.

"No!" Kennedy cried. "This is it!" Then, less sure, she said, "It's just . . . it looks different . . ." She reached a pile of debris—fallen pipes and bricks, cluttering their egress. "Cut the chatter! Up and over it!" she ordered. "Wounded first! Let's go!"

Kennedy half-helped, half-shoved Vi up the pile. Vi climbed up on some of the debris, peeking over just as an Ubervamp popped up.

She screamed and fell back; in the panic, she scrambled back to the group, Kennedy grabbing hold of her and yanking her into the cluster of Potentials.

"Group together!" Kennedy told them. "Form a circle. Nobody panic. It's all of us, one of him." She pointed at the pile of debris. "And he's gotta get over that. We can take one of these things.

"Remember the training. Everybody get read—"

Before she could finish the sentence, a second Ubervamp jumped Kennedy from behind.

Andrew was in the living room and he would have felt like an American G.I. passing out silk stockings and chocolate bars, if he had been into those boring old war movies where everyone wore khaki; as it was, he was a sort of chick magnet—or at least, his duffel bags were chick magnets. Lucky duffel bags.

"It was pretty exciting," he told the Potentials as they pawed through the goodies. "A whole grocery store, abandoned. Food lying around everywhere. The produce was on its way to funky town, but the other stuff was just . . ."

"Oh, for god's sake!" Giles shouted.

"Hi, Mr. Giles," Andrew said, somewhere between a grimace and a smile. "Okay, I did a little looting, which is technically unethical, but these girls need to eat . . ."

"Andrew," Giles said impatiently as he came forward and glanced down at the food items spilling from the bags. "Things are getting very dire around here, and we've got more important things to worry about than . . . ooh! Jaffa Cakes!" He started going through the groceries, just like the girls.

"The apples still looked pretty good," Andrew announced, "so everyone make sure they check those out."

Then the Buffy patrol returned; Anya, Xander, Willow, and Dawn, and Giles swallowed down his Jaffa Cake as she asked, "Did you find Buffy?"

"No," Xander told him, frustrated.

"But you did that spell with the little lights," Andrew pointed out. "The locator."

"It crapped out on us," Anya said.

"No, it didn't . . . exactly," Dawn reported.

"It just took us to an empty house," Willow explained to Giles, sad and worried. "She must have moved on already."

Giles took that in. Then he said, "Well, I'm afraid

there's rather worse news here."

He glanced toward the Potentials, then led the core group off to the side for more privacy. Andrew was there.

"Faith hasn't returned with the other girls," Giles informed them. "Something's gone wrong."

Andrew nodded soberly. "I've been keeping morale up, because that's important."

"We have to go to her," Willow said.

Xander nodded. "Guess so."

"Yes," Andrew said firmly. Then, "I'll stay here, keep working on that morale thing."

In the sewer, as the second Ubervamp attacked Kennedy, she instinctively flipped him over her shoulder as she screamed bloody murder.

A third crashed the party and scrambled up a tilted metal beam atop the pile; it crouched atop the beam like a huge bird of prey, eyeing the Potentials, hissing at them.

The girls backed away as Caridad shouted, "Weapons! Over there!"

The three Turok-han poured over the debris, lunging as one upon the tight cluster of girls. The Potentials ran for their lives; Amanda raced ahead, then turned back.

The three monsters converged on one of the newer girls, grabbed her, began ripping her apart with animalistic brutality and speed; horrified, Amanda couldn't stop watching, couldn't stop them, couldn't stop . . .

Caridad grabbed hold of her and pulled her along.

Kennedy grabbed up one of the Bringers' weapons on the mucky floor of the sewer and held it up, protecting the others, poised to meet the enemy. The Ubervamps, their mouths dripping gore, rushed the girls, backing them up against the wall.

The first Turok-han ripped her blade from Kennedy's hand, slapped a long-fingered hand around her throat, and lifted her off the ground as if she were weightless.

Oh, God, Willow. Willow, I love you, Kennedy thought wildly, preparing herself for death. She was beginning to suffocate, and she hoped to God she went out that way.

Then a loud crash of cement, mortar and dust startled the creature as a metal grate behind Kennedy collapsed. Light streamed in from the hole above.

It was Buffy, surrounded by light, and holding her scythe.

The Turok-han dropped Kennedy and lunged for Buffy. Buffy, holding the scythe by its handle, punched it in the throat with the scythe's blade; the blade sliced right through its neck in one solid motion.

Decapitated, the supervampire dusted.

The second and third Ubervamps rushed Buffy from behind; Buffy spun and staked the second Ubervamp with the handle of the scythe, pushing through his stone-hard breastbone and into his heart.

With a roar of fury, that vampire dusted too.

The third grabbed her and hurled her hard onto the metal grate, then jumped her. Buffy rolled backward, out of its reach, then flipped the scythe into position as she got to its feet. Facing the Turok-han, she was in perfect position to cut off its head with the scythe, swinging it like an axe.

It, too, dusted instantly.

Battle over, Buffy looked below her from the pile of rubble to see the Potentials staring up and her with awe and reverence. Cathedral-like streams of light backlit her, adding an aura of holiness to her heroic stance.

"Get the wounded," she said. "We're leaving."

Kennedy ventured, "Are there more?"

"There's always more," Buffy retorted. "Let's move."

The wounded were transported back to Revello Drive; everyone else got back on their own steam. Dawn bandaged injuries while three unconscious girl lay on make-shift pallets. Buffy bent over a girl with a terrible wound; the Slayer was trying to staunch the wound with her bare hand.

"Willow,' c'mere,' she said. "This girl's losing blood."

Willow brought a cloth and pressed it hard over the wound. "Got it," she said.

Buffy rose, surveying the scene, then wiped her bloody hands on a blanket on the floor. Then she hefted up her scythe.

The front door opened, and Giles and Xander brought Faith in. She was unconscious; and Buffy stepped over to join the two men who were carrying her fallen comrade.

"The room upstairs is ready for her," Buffy said.

Giles nodded. "Good."

Xander said, "Hope we're in time."

Kennedy and Amanda trailed in after the cortege, faces pinched with weariness and exhaustion; their bodies were covered with injuries. Kennedy's neck had been bandaged in the field.

"Is she okay?" Amanda asked. "Is she going to be okay?"

"I'm sure she'll be fine," Kennedy soothed. "Right?" she asked Buffy, as Giles and Xander carried Faith upstairs.

Buffy stopped in the entryway with the girls, saying to Xander, "I'll be up in a second."

"Careful," Xander's voice trailed downstairs.

"Watch her head," Giles continued.

Buffy looked up after them, watching, worrying, trying to tamp it down while she dealt with what—or who—was in front of her—wounded, frightened, worried warriors, home from battle.

"You guys heal fast, right?" Kennedy asked. "You Slayers?"

"Yeah," she said absently.

"So, she'll be okay?" Kennedy pressed.

"I don't know," Buffy told her honestly. Now was not the time to lie about things. Morale or no, they had to know what was going on.

Caridad gestured to Buffy's weapon and said, "What's with the scythe?"

"I took it from Caleb," Buffy said, unable to stop looking up the stairs. "Might be important."

"Let's hope," Vi murmured.

Amanda blurted, "I think we got punished."

That got Buffy's attention. She looked at Amanda and said, "What?"

Kennedy dipped her head. "We . . . we followed her, and it was . . ."

"It didn't work out," Vi finished lamely.

Buffy shook her head. "That wasn't her fault. It was a trap. I could have fallen for it as easily as her."

Caridad took that in. "So . . . are you . . . are you, like, *back*?"

Buffy realized she hadn't thought that far. She said, "I don't know. I guess I'm . . . not leaving."

Kennedy clearly liked that answer as she nodded, satisfied. Then she pushed on like the Amazon she was and said, "So . . . we got a plan now or anything?"

Buffy headed upstairs, calling back, "Yeah, there's a plan. Get ready. Time's up."

As she continued up, she heard Amanda murmuring, "I still think we got punished."

She went into her old room, to see Xander and Giles tending to Faith. Three more Potentials stood watching, moving out of Buffy's way as she came into the room.

"Is she breathing okay?" Xander asked.

Giles nodded. "Still not conscious, though."

Emotion welled up inside Buffy . . . *Oh, my God, she might die, she might be dying right now . . . Faith . . .* but she steeled herself and said, "We've still got work to do."

She caught Giles's eye; he rose and followed her into Willow's room. A Potential got Willow and brought her in, leaving the three of them alone to examine the scythe.

"I think it's . . . maybe some kind of scythe?" Buffy said, every inch the general as Willow and Giles examined it. "Only thing I know for sure is, it made Caleb back off in a hurry."

"So it's true. Scythe matters," Willow quipped.

Giles tried very hard to ignore that, and continued examining the weapon.

"It's really quite ingenious," he said.

"Kills strong bodies three way," Buffy agreed.

"And you say you sense something when you hold it?" Willow asked.

"Not much," Buffy replied, gazing first at it, and then at the Wicca. "Just . . . it's strong. And I knew it belonged to me. I mean, I just *knew* it."

Giles considered that. "So in addition to being ancient, it's clearly mystical."

"Yeah," Buffy said with a tinge of irony. "I figured that when I King-Arthur'ed it out of that stone."

"Sounds like maybe some kind of traditional Slayer weapon?" Willow suggested.

That clearly struck Giles as odd; he frowned and said, "It's hard to imagine something like that could exist without my having heard of it."

"Yeah, well, the good guys aren't traditionally known for their communication skills." Buffy made of avoiding eye contact with Giles, and he sucked it up.

They moved on.

"Right," he said. "Is there any chance it's something besides a tool to kill things?"

Buffy shrugged. "The First's guys were clearly trying to get it out of that stone," she said. "It's not just some tool. It's important. Find out whatever you can: who made it, why. And when. Does it have a name? And, I dunno, a credit report? Find out *fast*."

"We'll start immediately," he promised her.

"Don't worry, Buff," Willow soothed her, smiling gently. "We'll find out everything there is to know."

"Thanks," Buffy told her genuinely. She looked at the strange scythe, and her heart pounded in her chest as she felt, again, the odd connection between herself and it. "Because right now, this thing's all we've got going for us."

Downstairs, Anya and Andrew were nursing the wounded, Andrew tying a bandage around a girls shoulder with strips torn from a flowered bed sheet.

He wrinkled his nose and said, "I liked the real bandages better. This bed sheet is awfully festive."

Anya looked on, nodding, saying, "I know. They're all going to look like mortally wounded Easter baskets."

"What?" the patient asked, alarmed.

Anya took a hefty swig from a bottle of Scotch.

"Hey!" Andrew frowned at her. "We're supposed to use that to sterilize wounds. Mr. Giles said!"

"Oh, what does it matter?" she asked rhetorically, rolling her eyes.

"Hmm, good point," Andrew murmured.

She handed him the bottle, saying, Giles knows his single-malt antiseptics."

Andrew drank, coughed, and scrunched up his

face, handing it back to her. "Bleahh. Everything is horrible."

"Yup." Anya cradled the bottle. "Many of these girls will die. Slaughter house is what it is."

Their patient was even more alarmed, "What?"

Anya said to her kindly, "Trying to talk will just kill you sooner."

Andrew huffed. "We need supplies. And not just bandages and junk. These girls need stitches and pain killers."

"And I could use a cookie," Anya put in. Then she straightened and said, "But I'm not making reckless wishes."

Then Andrew brightened. "No! We can do it! The hospital!" He was amazed by his own brilliance. "It's gotta be all abandoned like the grocery story was. Stuff just lying there for the taking." He looked into the distance, a bust of Alexander the Great, or maybe Alfred J. Newman. "I'm going in," he announced.

Anya raised her brows. "You are?"

"And you're coming with me!" he informed her excitedly.

"I am?"

He blushed a little, although heroically. "Well, I think you should drive 'cause that Scotch made me a little dizzy."

Anya rose. "I'll get Kennedy to watch these girls. She's tough. Imminent death won't bother her."

As the two began to leave, their patient called mournfully after them, "What?"

* * *

It was Buffy and Xander, in the kitchen, and they were not playing Clue. They were, essentially, saying good-bye. Or at least, she was trying to.

"You got it?" Buffy asked him firmly.

He half-raised his hand in that "hold on a minute" way of his. She knew his every gesture, the nuance of his voice; plus, she had seen him do the Snoopy Dance and heard him sing in Hindi.

"Wait," he said. "I'm not to the 'got it' place yet. I'm still in the neighborhood of 'you've got to be kidding.'"

She was adamant. "You know it's for the good."

"I don't." He looked at her, hard. "Buffy, do you get that if I do this, that's it for me for this fight?" As she gazed back at him, he said, "I feel like you're putting me out to pasture."

"Of course I'm not putting you out to pasture," she insisted. Then she said, half to herself, "What does that even mean?"

He cocked his head, sighed, searched for a way to put it. "Oh, you know, it's like, when a cow gets old and loses an eye or its ability to be milked, the farmer takes it and puts it in a different pasture where it won't have to . . . fight . . . with priests. . . ."

Realizing he had vagued out, he said, "You don't have to protect me."

"I'm not."

"I got hurt," he continued. "But I'm not done. I can still fight."

She nodded strenuously, her eyes big and wide. "I know. That's why you're doing this. I need someone I can count on. No matter what happens."

"I just . . ." His voice dropped. He regarded his friend, and his voice shook with emotion. "I just . . . always thought I'd be here for the end with you," he said.

She scowled. "Hey!"

"Not that this is the end," he added quickly.

"Thanks a *lot,* she mugged.

"No, no, no, no," he sweated, "I mean 'end' in a heroic, uplifting way." A beat. "I'm still optimistic! You're just thrown off by this gritty-lookin' eye patch." He preened a little.

She smiled reassuringly, loving him in that moment. As in all moments. "I know what you meant."

"I should be at your side. That's all I'm saying."

"You will be," she said feelingly. She gazed at him. "You're my strength, Xander. I never would have made it this far without you."

Her words moved him, but he was macho as she continued, "I trust you with my life. That's why I need you to do this for me."

Her words finally sank in. He surrendered.

"Okay."

Then she lightened it up. "Also, you can't shoot a bow and arrow anymore and every time you swing a sword I worry you're gonna break one of our good lamps."

"Hey!"

As Buffy started to walk out of the kitchen, she called back over her shoulder, "Don't look at me. You're the one who said I'm going to die."

"I didn't say you're going to die. I . . . I *implied* you're going to die. Totally different."

Buffy shrugged. "Yeah, okay, sure."

Xander trailed after her. "Besides . . . if you die, I'll just bring you back to life." He paused and added softly, "It's what I do."

Willow and Giles worked in Willow's room, Giles reading the moldy bound books, Willow on the laptop. Her fingers were flying, and Giles was reading fast. The scythe was like a third person in the room, a silent sentinel with its secrets locked away . . . and the power in it thrumming eagerly, to be used by the Slayer.

Then Willow found something. "Okay," she said, looking at the screen, "before the vineyard was just you know, a vineyard? It was a monastery."

She glanced over at the scythe. "It could have been put there there. Creepy monks, messing with powers they don't understand?"

Giles frowned thoughtfully and shook his head. "No. It's far older. Pre-Christian."

"Well, I found a reference to stories the monks used to tell about something older . . . like, maybe some kind of pagan temple."

That intrigued Giles.

"Native American?"

"No." She thought a moment, glanced again at the screen, then back at him. "Maybe we're coming at this the wrong way. Maybe we need to research the weapon itself." She gestured. "I mean, look . . . maybe it's the Axe of Dekeron . . ." She read off the monitor ". . . said to have been forged in Hell itself. Lost since the Children's Crusade, where it killed a lot of . . . children." She looked up. "I hope that's not it."

Giles gestured with his book. "I've found references to the Sword of Moskva, and the Reaper of the Tigris." He was frustrated. "I don't see how we're going to narrow this down. There's never a clear enough illustration."

He slammed his tomey volume shut. "Damn. We're running out of time and we've nothing useful."

Willow got up and crossed to the scythe, warily lifting it up. She examined it.

"It doesn't have any markings," she said. "Would it be so hard to include a little sticker? 'Hello, my name is the Blank of Blankthuselah, consult operating instructions before wielding."

She closed her eyes, moving into a meditative state, searching for the scythe's vibratory plane.

"Willow?" he asked. "Do you feel the power Buffy talked about?"

She opened her eyes. "Gotta say no. Must be a Slayer thing."

"Tapping into some magicks might help with that," Giles ventured.

"It might," she agreed. "But this . . . thing . . ." She sighed. "I mean, if Caleb is scared of it, it's something pretty dangerous, and tapping into that . . ."

She put the scythe down, a little afraid of it.

"Willow," Giles said gently, feeling protective of her, "you know there's a way to do it without endangering yourself. Drawing positive power from the earth, the power that connects everything . . ."

"I know," she said wistfully. "And when I was in England, I got it. But here . . . I can't do it. If I tried something big, I just know I'd change and then it's all black hair and veins and lightning bolts." She flushed with shame. "I mean, I can barely do the locator spells without getting dark roots."

"But if it's necessary?" he urged, trying to be careful of her, yet needed to convey to her the urgency of their situation.

She looked at him straight on. "Giles, honestly, I don't know."

"Do what you can, Willow. That's all any of us can do."

"I guess so." She went back to the computer and studied the screen again. "Man, none of these sound right." She pointed. "Look at this, something just called *m* with a question mark. What the heck is that?"

"I can't imagine," he began, then blinked and said, "Wait, let me see." He leaned over the keyboard. "That's not a question mark. That's the International Phonetic Alphabet sign for a glottal stop. It's a sort of gulpy noise." He nodded to himself. "I'm remembering something here . . . hieroglyphs. Hieroglyphs stand for sets of consonants, as you know."

"Yes, absolutely," she replied, although she doubted .0001% of the population knew that; she certainly hadn't.

"The consonants *m* plus glottal stop are repre-

sented by a little picture commonly thought to repre-
sent a sickle or scythe."

He was getting into it now, going into a full Giles
deal. Only as a Watcher and on *Jeopardy!* could so
much trivial information prove so useful.

"It appears in thousands of carvings, in Egypt and
throughout the ancient world."

"Carvings?" Willow echoed, looking at him. She
could feel the tumblers beginning to line up, the sense
to become . . . sensible. "Like you'd have on a pagan
temple?"

"Let go back, see what else we can find out about
that temples," Giles said, as he picked up the scythe.

"A scythe is a symbol of death," he mused. "Find
out where these pagans buried their dead."

Dawn was on the dawn patrol, with Xander in the front
seat in the driveway, only it was still night.

She was rooting around in the weapons bag and
Xander was pretending to help look, feeling noble and
nefarious at the same time.

"Xander, my crossbow is not out here," she
kevtched. "I told you, I don't leave crossbows around
all willy-nilly." A beat. "Not since that time with Miss
Kitty Fantastico."

Xander grumped, "Did you know I have to take a
driver's test every year now?"

"Because you're old?" Dawn asked, still rooting.

"No," he said patiently, "because of my eye. It's a
whole state law. They don't trust my depth perception
anymore."

"That sucks," she said, distracted.

He got out of the car and walked around to the open door next to Dawn.

"You know what's even worse? All the stupid 'It's all fun and games until someone loses an eye' jokes." He mocked up a voice. "'I guess the fun and games are over, eh, Xander?'"

"Giles was just having fun with you," Dawn insisted.

"That's not the point!" he shot back. "It's an obvious joke. It's be like if someone called me a Cyclops."

She burst into laughter. "Oh, right! I didn't even . . ." Then she saw his displeased expression and caught herself. "That's not funny at all."

"I mean, give me an 'eye of the beholder' joke or an 'eye for an eye' joke or maybe even a weird postmodern 'I, Claudius' joke." He frowned at her. "It's about standards, Dawn. Just be creative."

"I know." She got up out of the car, ostensibly to go back into the house to get her crossbow. "You know, everyone is still a little on guard around you," she said. "Give them time."

She turned around, back to Xander, to shut the door.

"Before you know it, they'll be—"

And that was when he did it: he clamped a handkerchief over her nose and mouth, holding it as she tried to scream, as she struggled; then breaking her fall as she went limp and unconscious.

He put her in the car, put that sucker in reverse,

and flew out of their like a bat . . . a one-eyed bat . . . from Sunnydale.

Down in the cellar, Caleb was throwing a tantrum, as only an insanely evil superstrong person could throw: couple of dead Bringers, and he was heaving wine barrels everywhere. They were crashing on either side of The First, who was wearing her Buffy face, and she hardly blinked.

"Not that I care personally," she said, "But you're wasting a lot of robust, full-bodied Merlot."

Smashed barrels lay on the floor, and a broken chair. He was out of breath, but still brimming with righteous indignation.

"Why did you let her go?" he demanded. "You know I could take that girl in a fight."

"We'll get her. Calm down," The First told him.

"I'm calm. You should see me when I get angry," he bit off.

"She's powerful now," The First drawled. "And you're weak."

He glared at her, flexing his hands, pulling back his mouth in a tight frown. "All of a sudden, I'm getting less calm."

"Face it," she said. "Your strength is waning. It's been a while since we merged."

Caleb looked around, nodded. "Suppose you're right. Okay, let's do. it."

She rolled her eyes. "Boy, you really know how to romance a girl. No flowers, no dinner, no tour of the rectory . . . just, 'let's do it.' Help me. My knees are weak."

He gave her a look. "Watch what you say now. You're starting to sound like *her*. This is a sacred experience for me."

"Oh, for me as well," she assured him. Then she sighed and added, "When this is over . . . when our armies spring forth and our will sweeps the world—I'll be able to enter every man, woman, and child on the face of this Earth."

She gave him a lustful, seductive look.

"Just as I can enter you?"

Pleased with her attention, he asked, "Are you trying to make me jealous?"

Her demeanor changed; she became deadly serious as she rejoined, "I'm trying to make you a god."

Then as Caleb watched, The First shot out of its form as Buffy; becoming its true self—malevolent, magnificent, a red demon of huge power and majesty.

It rose to the top of the room mushrooming in size and sizzling with distilled evil; and he whispered, in total rapture and awe, "I am thy humble servant."

And it dove into Caleb's body, filling him.

It was violent, voluptuous, transcendent. He shook with the fullness of it, the drive and the sound and the fury, fall to his knees . . . oh, glory, hallelujah, he *was* a god . . .

His head lowered in worship, in the prayer of it; then slowly he lifted his head, the shadows churning inside his until even his eyes were black, and he said, "And I am ready to serve thee."

He rose and presented himself . . . a figure of power.

* * *

Faith's Slayer-sized restorative powers had started to work, and though she looked like a beaten-up side of beef, she was able to sit up in bed and test out the scythe when Buffy took it to her. Her eyes were closed; she was lost in reverie, as Buffy stood by the bed, watching.

"You feel it too, don't you," Buffy said, as Faith opened her eyes.

The dark-haired Slayer grunted. "Damn. And *damn*. That's something."

"I know," Buffy said.

"It's old. Strong. And it feels like . . . like it's mine," she finished, a slight mixture of shame and resentment in her voice. "So I guess that means it's yours."

"It belongs to the Slayer," Buffy corrected her.

Faith shrugged. "Slayer in Charge. Which I'm guessing is you."

Buffy sat on the edge of the bed. "I honestly don't know," she admitted. "Does it matter?"

Ever Five-by-Five Girl, Faith replied, "Never mattered to me. But somebody has to lead." She perked up. "Let's vote for Chao-Ahn! Harder to lead people into a death-trap if you don't speak English."

"It's not your fault," Buffy insisted.

Faith gave her her patented tough-woman stare. "Really not looking for forgiveness. What do you want me to say? I blew it."

"You didn't blow it," Buffy repeated.

Faith laughed shortly; her ringed, swollen eyes

were haunted, her bloody mouth stretched back in pain. "Tell that to the—"

"People die. You lead them into battle, they die. No matter how smart you are, or how ready, war is about death. Needless, stupid death."

Faith looked at Buffy for a moment, and then she said, "So here's the laugh-riot. My whole life, I've been a loner."

She fell silent; confused, Buffy said, "Was that the funny part? Did I miss . . . ?"

Faith said with effort, "I'm trying to . . ."

"No, no. Sorry." Buffy inclined her head. "Go."

Taking another moment, Faith started over . . . and did not flinch. She went through her thoughts, and not around them. Not this time.

Not this close to death.

"No ties, no buddies, no relationships that lasted longer than . . . well, I guess Robin lasted pretty long." Her eyes gleamed with mischief. "Boy's got stamina."

Buffy's eyes got wide. "Principal Wood? And you? And on my . . ." Gingerly she rose from the bed, and took a step away from it.

Faith cocked her head. "Don't tell me *you* two got wriggly . . ."

"No, no!" Buffy said, flustered. "We're just good friends." She hesitated. "Or . . . mortal enemies, depending on which day of the . . ." She looked back at Faith. "Is *this* the funny part?"

"Okay, the point?" Faith said. "Me, by myself all the time, and looking at you, everything you have, and . . . I don't know, jealous. And there I am, everybody looking to me, trusting me to lead them . . ." Her eyes softened, and the haunted look came back. "I never felt more alone in my life."

Buffy gazed at her, felt such a connection, yet still felt the distance—she and Faith, what an unlikely pair,

"Yeah," she said.

"And that's you every day, isn't it?" Faith pressed.

Someone understands. Someone gets this gig. Oh, Faith . . .

"I love my friends," she said, "and I'm grateful for them, but yeah. That's the price. Being the Slayer."

"There's only supposed to be one." Faith looked at her questioningly. "Maybe that's why you and I can never get along. We're not supposed to exit together."

"Also, you went evil and were killing people," Buffy reminded her helpfully.

Faith nodded thoughtfully. "Good point. Also a factor."

"But you're right," Buffy said. " I mean, I guess everyone's alone, but . . . being a Slayer. There's a burden we can't share."

"And no one else can feel it." A beat, and then Faith grinned and said, "Thank God we're hot chicks with super powers."

"Takes the edge off," Buffy agreed.

"Just comforting," Faith added.

"Uh huh."

She left Faith then, and was going downstairs with the scythe in her hand, to find Spike coming through the front door. She wasn't certain how he would feel, since she had, essentially, split on him with just a scribbled note of explanation. But there was a flash of joy on his face that he could not conceal, and she warmed to him, relieved.

"Honey, you're home," he said in a slightly low tone, so as to not wake the sleeping girls.

"Yeah." She nodded, smiled.

"And you did it. Fulfilled your mission, found the holy grail, or the holy hand grenade, or whatever the hell that is."

"Right now we're going with scythe." She showed it to him. "You like?"

He looked it over, taking its measure, and replied, "Pointy and wooden is not exactly the look I want to know better, but it does have flair. I can see how a girl would ditch a guy for one of these."

"I'm sorry about that," she said sincerely.

She headed to the back space between the kitchen and the living room; he followed.

"Doesn't matter," he drawled. "You're back in the bosom, all's forgiven, and last night was just a glitch. A little cold comfort from the cellar dweller, let's don't make a thing out of it."

That took her a bit aback, but she said, "Great. I got work to do."

"Another solo mission, of course," he said leadingly.

She turned, annoyed. "Yes, it is."

He straightened slightly, rushed with, "It's fine. Don't have to get shirty about it."

"I'm not shirty!" she insisted. "What even *is* shirty? That's not a word."

He was not annoyed, he was calm. "All right, all right," he soothed. "Big secret mission. It's fine."

"It's not a secret." She backed up. "I mean, it is, but that's the point of the mission: find the secret. This was forged by . . . we don't know, something about a tomb on unconsecrated ground. I have to find out what this is. Why I have it."

He listened, accepted, moved on. "And this is the thing Preacher Man was so anxious to keep out of your mitts."

"That it is," Buffy concurred.

"Well, maybe I'll swung by his place while you go," Spike offered, "make sure he's sitting tight."

"Great," Buffy said brightly.

A beat, and then he headed for the kitchen door and she turned to go out the front. Then she turned and went after him, calling out, "You're a dope!"

He turned, baffled. "I'm what?"

"You're a dope, and a bonehead, and . . . and you're shirty."

He could only stare at her. "Have you gone *completely* Carrot-top?"

She held up the scythe, and ranted sotto voce: "You see this? This may actually help me fight my war. It may be the key to everything, and the reason I'm holding it is 'cause of you. Because of last night, the strength you gave me. I'm tired of defensiveness and weird mixed signals. I've got Faith for that."

She took a breath. "Let's just get to the truth. I don't know how you feel about last night, but I'm not gonna—"

"Terrified," he said.

She stepped. *Okay. Honest. Real. Oh, my God, we're doing this.*

"Of what?" she asked him.

"Last night was . . ." He looked down, gave his head a shake, closed his eyes. "God, I'm such a jerk. I can't do this."

"Spike . . ." she urged.

He couldn't look at her, but he could tell her.

"It was the best night of my life."

Then he did look at her, his eyes welling up defiantly, as he pointed at the scythe. "If you poke fun at me you bloody well better use that 'cause I couldn't bear it. It may not mean that much to you . . ."

"I just told you that it did," she murmured.

"I know, I hear you say it, but . . ." He made himself go on, his voice choking with emotion. "I've lived for sodding ever, Buffy, I've done everything—I've done things with you I can't even *spell*, but I've never . . . been close. To anyone, least of all you . . . until last night.

"All I did was hold you, and watch you sleep, and it was the best night of my life. So, I'm, yeah . . . terrified."

She came closer, said quietly, "You don't have to be."

He gazed down at her, hopeful, a bit guarded, daring to ask, "Were you there with me?"

"I was." She gazed back up at him.

There was a moment. Their moment.

Theirs . . . and no one else's.

"What does that mean?" he asked her.

"I don't know." Her voice betrayed her fragility, her own fear. "Does it have to mean something?"

The spell was broken, albeit slightly; he backed off, not hurt so much as a wee bit detached. "No," he said. Then, "Not right now."

"Maybe," she said, "when—"

"No," he said, a firm grip on the magic of this moment, this bond, "Let's just leave it."

"'Kay," she said.

He smiled at her. "We'll go be heroes."

Then he did.

Buffy watched him go.

The Sunnydale Hospital was like a morgue . . . or not, because there weren't any dead bodies lying around. No one was lying around. It was deserted. Folders were heaped and tumbled off the nurse's station, doors hung open.

Anya and Andrew each carried the colorful matching pillowcases from the bandage sheet set. They were half-full; and Andrew thought wistfully about caches of Halloween candy long devoured, and wished he were, like sixteen again and life was carefree . . . except for getting beaten up everyday at school and having head flushed in the toilet.

"Okay," he said to Anya, leading their raiding party, "so if the supply closet on this floor is exactly above the last one, it should . . . be . . . here!"

And it was! The door was even marked, "Supplies."

"Yes," Anya said. "That is consistent with the six floors we already did."

He opened the magic door and peered inside. "Oooh!" he cried. "This one has oxygen tanks!" .

Anya said, "They'd only be useful if something big was attacking and then we could throw one down their throat and blow 'em up like Roy Scheider did with the shark in *Jaws*.

He gaped at her and thought in Mehico-an, *Ay, que mujer! Ay, Chihuahua!*

"You are the perfect woman," he said adoringly.

Looking pleased, she inclined her head. "I've often thought so." She gestured to the supply closet. "Wanna rob?"

"Let's rob!" he cried gleefully.

Close together, they took: "Gauze and alcohol and tape and sutures in case we need to get stitchy with it," Andrew said. "Oh, and there's a box full of ointments." He looked at the label, nodding with recognition. "I used one of these on a rash once."

"Show me," she told him.

He sure would! "Well, it's healed up, but it was sort of red and crusty with little itchy places—"

"Show me the box full of ointments, you little freak."

Andrew handed the box to her and she dumped it all out into her pillowcase, saying, "Get cotton packing for the biggest wounds."

Ewww.

He looked at her. "This is going to be bad, isn't it?"

Her expression was almost pitying. "Yeah."

"So how come you're here?" he asked her. "I mean, you could just go, right?"

"Yeah, I did before," she told him.

"Before what?"

"There was this other apocalypse this one time," she elaborated, "and I took off. But this time . . ." She shrugged as if to say, *Here I am.*

"What's different?" he asked.

She thought about that. Well, I was kind of new to being around humans before. And now I've seen a lot more, gotten to know people, seen what they're capable of, and I realize now that they're just so . . . amazingly screwed up!" she said, her voice rising. "I mean, so really, really screwed up in a monumental fashion!"

"Oh." He was bewildered.

It was as if someone had opened up at the gates at the racetrack as she plunged on ahead. "They have no purpose that unites them so they drift around, blundering through life until they die. Which they *know* is coming and yet every single one of them is surprised when it happens to them. They're incapable of thinking beyond what they want at that moment. They kill *each other*, which is *clearly* insane . . .

" . . . but here's the thing. When it's something real, they fight. I mean, they're lame morons to keep fighting, but they do. They . . . they never quit. And so . . ." She took a deep breath and let it all out. "And so I guess I'll fight too."

"That was kind of beautiful," Andrew said dreamily. "You love humans."

"No, I don't," she snapped.

"Yes, you do," he jabbed. "You luuuuuve them."

"Stop it!" Her eyes flashed. "I don't love them and I'll kill you if you tell anybody."

"I won't tell anybody." His voice fell. "Won't get a chance to, anyway."

She avoided his gaze. "I don't know. You might survive."

Andrew shook his head. "No, *you* might survive. You can handle a weapon. You've been in this world for, like, a thousand years. I'm not so . . . I don't think I'll be okay," he said frankly. Then he moved his shoulders sweetly, stoically

"I'm cool with it," he told her. "I think I'd like to finish out as one of those lame humans trying to do what's right."

"Yeah." She was sympathetic and honest.

And then Andrew said, "Wheelchair fight?"

Wheelchair fight.

A cemetery.

A Slayer.

A scythe.

Panama.

Buffy walked through the clean, well-kept grave-yard, past the many headstones she knew so well . . . and then she got to the place where those who had died in less than good graces had been stashed; down among the weeds and thistles. The gravestones were tilted, sparse, forgotten.

She looked around, and finally spotted a tomb,

Egyptian-looking in design.

She tried to find a way to open the door, then finally gave up and pushed it down, sending up a plume of dust that swirled and eddied like a ghost before it dissipated.

She entered cautiously, amazed at the thick layers of dust coating the walls, thinking vaguely of mummy movies and wondering what weird context Andrew would put this in.

"I'd forgotten," a voice echoed in the dark.

Buffy whirled around, her scythe at the ready.

An old woman sat on a throne of dust, her clothes so old and faded they appeared to be made of dust as well. Her face was sepia, her eyes . . . ancient.

"I'd forgotten how young you would be," she said. "It comes from the waiting. The mind plays tricks."

Buffy walked toward her, and the woman gestured to the scythe. "I see you found our weapon."

"Who are you?" Buffy asked cautiously, half-expecting her to turn into The First.

"One of many." The woman closed her eyes, opened them, looked far off through time, so much, so very much, but distant memory. "Well, time was. Now I'm alone in the world." She ticked her gaze toward Buffy. "I'd gamble you know what that's like."

She stood, approached Buffy, who stiffened and went on the defensive.

"Don't worry," the woman said. "You hit me, I'd just about crack in half. But then . . ." She scrutinized the scythe, keeping a respectful distance. "You have been doing some killing lately. And you're going to do a lot more. Not a wonder you're so anxious."

"So, who are you?" Buffy demanded impatiently. "Some kind of ghost?"

"Nope." The woman smiled faintly. "I'm as real as you are. Just . . . well, put it this way. I look good for my age." She said again, "I've been waiting."

She held out her hand, and waited. Buffy felt compelled to hand her the scythe. The woman hefted it appreciatively, and examined it.

"You pulled it out of the rock. I was one of those who put it there, and don't think *that* was easy." She smiled more fully.

"What is it?" Buffy pushed.

"Weapon," the woman replied, as is if it should be obvious. "A scythe. We forged it in secrecy, for one like you who . . ."

She stopped and smiled at Buffy, still holding the scythe. She looked like a Tarot card, wonderful and old and mystical.

"I'm sorry," she said. "What's your name?"

"Buffy."

The woman insisted, "No, really."

Buffy shrugged.

"Buffy." The woman tested her name out on her tongue. Then she proceeded. "We kept it hidden from the Shadow Men, who—"

Buffy nodded sharply and lifted her chin. "Yeah. Met them. Didn't care for 'em."

The woman looked at Buffy with new respect, and handed the scythe back to her.

"Yes," the woman said. "Then you know. And they

became the Watchers, and the Watchers watched the Slayers." She raised her brows and said proudly, "But we were watching them."

"Oh!" Buffy blurted, surprised. "So you're like . . . what are you?"

"Guardians," the woman said. "Women who want to help and protect you. This . . ." She gestured to the scythe ". . . was forged, centuries ago, by us. Halfway around the world."

Buffy glanced around. "Hence, the Luxor casino theme."

"Forged there, it was put to use right here," the woman continued. "Only once, to kill the last pure demon that walked upon the earth. The rest were already driven under.

"And then there were men here, and then there were monks. And the first men died and were sent away, and then there was a town."

She looked at Buffy. "And now there is you. And the scythe remained hidden."

Buffy took that in as best she could, although she was really only interested in the bottom line: "Does this mean I can win?"

The woman shrugged. "That's really up to you. This . . ." she reached out, running a finger along the flat side of the scythe. ". . . is a powerful weapon."

"Yes," Buffy said.

"But you already have weapons," the woman continued.

"Oh." Not what Buffy was expecting to hear.

"Use it wisely," the woman said, "and perhaps you

can beat back the rising dark. One way or the other, it can only mean an end is truly near."

Then, just as she finished speaking, two hands reached in from the darkness behind her, and with blinding speed, snapped her neck.

She fell to the ground, dead.

Caleb stepped forward, over the body. He said pleasantly, "I'm sorry. I didn't catch that last part on account of her neck snapping and all. Did she say the end is 'near' or '*here*'?"

High desert, high moon, and Xander was *fahrin' fahrin' auf der Autobahn* . . .

. . . when Dawnie made moanie noises.

Xander said, "Dawn, you awake?"

She squinted around, took in their black surroundings, looked at him. "What the hell happened?"

"Um . . . thought you might say that." He grimaced.

She grimaced back, angrily. "Actually, I meant to say, 'what the *hell* happened?'"

"It was chloroform." He felt just sick about it.

"Color forms? What?"

"Chloroform. Are you still loopy?"

"Sorry about that," she said, dry as toast. "Someone knocked me out with *chloroform*. Xander! Talk to me! Where are we going?"

"Away," he said simply.

Then he handed her a sealed envelope.

She opened it.

Dearest Dawn,

*Don't be angry with Xander. He
did what I told him to do. This isn't
the place for either of you right now.
Please know that I love you and that everything I do is for you. I promised once to
show you this beautiful world, and I'm
gong to do everything I can to make that*

ZZZZZZZZot!

Xander went rigid behind the wheel and slumped.

Dawn put down her stun gun, which she had slipped from her weapons bag while reading Buffy's note, and put her foot on the brake.

The note, she tossed into the back seat.

Then she pulled over, got out, dragged Xander over to her side of the car, walked around, slid in, hung a U, and went home.

As Buffy processed that Caleb was in the tomb with her, and that he had just killed the old Guardian, he grabbed the scythe and tried to yank it away from her, as simply as he had broken the woman's neck.

Buffy recovered, shaking off her astonishment, and whacked him in the side of the head with the handle end, moved to the other side and whacked him again, and went for a third time, three-times-fast.

Reeling, he let go of the scythe, and Buffy leaped back.

He rushed her, punching a column so hard that it dusted like a vampire.

"You're not slipping out of this fight, girl," he said

exultantly. "Don't you see? You can't stop me. I can just keep coming back for more." He grinned. "Like being reborn."

She lunged at him with scythe; he ducked. She pressed her advantage, swinging and thrusting. He dodged each parry with amused ease.

Then he smiled broadly and stood upright, presenting her with a target . . . and she swung hard at his neck; without looking, he shot a hand up and caught the blade in mid-swing, stopping it cold.

With the other hand, he punched Buffy so hard she went flying across the tomb and smacked the far wall, sending up dust as she fell to the ground . . . dropping the scythe.

They both raced for it . . . and Caleb got to it first.

But he couldn't keep it—she kicked the scythe from his hand and caught it in the same motion. Then she spun, clipping him behind the knees with the weapon's shaft and lifting him off his feet. He went crashing to the dusty floor.

Now, she thought, as she spun the scythe, stake-end first, and thrust it straight to Caleb's throat.

He caught it an inch before his face, twisting the scythe hard, sideways, sending Buffy flipping over: it was her turn for a smackdown.

Caleb seized the moment and jumped to his feet; Buffy staggered to hers, and he punched her in the face. She staggered back, and Caleb began to pummel her like a punching bag, each blow nearly enough to take her head clean off.

It hurt; each blow took something out of her.

Although she tried to defend herself with the scythe, she wasn't making it.

"I gave you ample warning," he reminded her. "I told you not to interfere. And you chose not to heed. But you know what?"

His last word was punctuated by a blow so hard that it hurled Buffy right through a stone column. Dust plumed everywhere, and she sank into it, began to sink into herself . . .

"I was kinda hoping it would go this way," he finished, smirking.

Then, with a grand gesture, he arced the scythe up over her head, and—

"Hey," said a male voice.

It as a voice Buffy knew.

A voice she loved.

And the owner of that voice rammed his fist into Caleb's face and sent him spinning across the tomb. Dazed, he dropped the scythe, and it clattered to the ground.

Buffy squinted up. Not a dream.

Angel.

He loomed over her, hand held out. She took it, and he lifted her to her feet.

"I was never much for preachers," he told her.

"Angel." She could scarcely believe that he was here. But he was, and he had just saved her life.

"You look good," he said to her.

"You look timely," she said. "And also good."

"Heard maybe you needed a hand." He grinned.

Then Caleb got to his feet, and Angel moved in for

the kill. But Buffy placed a restraining hand on Angel's arm, and he glanced at her with an understanding expression.

This one of those things you just have to finish yourself?" he asked.

She nodded. "Really kind of is."

Livid, Caleb advanced as Buffy plucked the scythe up and stood her ground; he rushed her, raining down a series of lightning-bolt blows on her.

She blocked each and every one of them with the shaft of the scythe.

Angel leaned up against a wall, enjoying the show.

"You're so gonna lose," Angel called to Caleb. "She does this thing where . . ."

She dodged Caleb with a blurry-fast move.

"Oooh, yeah." Angel's pleasure was almost sensual. "I've missed watching this."

She swung the blade end of the scythe at her enemy; as before, he caught it again. But this time he shoved it back at her. She twisted out of the way, the stake end barely missing her as it imbedded in the wall behind her.

The Slayer pulled it free, then lowered it down, and in one brutal motion, ripped it straight up—gutting Caleb from below.

She retracted the blade, and Caleb fell to the floor, raising dust, looking very dead.

"See?" Buffy said to Angel. Then she took a step back, exhausted and unsteady. "Under control."

She walked into him, and as he steadied her, said, "Well, at least tell me you're glad to see me."

As worn down as she could be, she gathered herself inside his embrace, hugging him, letting go of the scythe and putting both arms around him; they stood together for a long, quiet moment.

Then she pulled back, looking him in the eyes, and kissed him. Tenderly, at first, but then it built, a long kiss that spoke of years of yearning, and not having, and this solid moment laced with death . . .

And as they kissed, Spike watched from the shadows, stunned.

And a voice—Buffy's own—said from behind him, "That *bitch*."

Chapter Twenty-Two: "Chosen"

In the Egyptian tomb, more with the kissage as Angel and Buffy held each other; champions share passions others can only dream of, and their kiss could easily have moved a mountain . . . or sent the world straight to hell.

"Well," Angel said, as finally, reluctantly, they ended the kiss, "I guess that qualified as 'happy to see me.'"

Her eyes shone with the joy of his presence. "Angel, what are you doing . . . no. Don't even. I just want to bask.

They looked at each other, warm and giddy. The smile was still on Buffy's lip as she continued, "Okay. I'm basked. What are you doing here?"

He smiled back at her. "Not saving the damsel in distress, that's for sure."

"You know me," she told him. "Not big with the damseling."

He turned away, saying, "Got your share of distress, though."

"And then some," she agreed. "You heard.

Angel retrieved an accordion file from the corner. He wasn't about to tell her that it was the same file dead Lilah had tempted him with to get him to accept the "gift" of the Wolfram & Hart operation in Los Angeles—and that he had initially turned it down. Buffy's fate he had thought to leave to her; he had bitten into the apple for Connor's sake. Like a fairy tale prince, his son was going to be raised by good, kind strangers . . . only in this case, Connor would never remember that he had been born to vampire parents, that he had been raised in a hell dimension by a man so twisted he had committed suicide so that Connor would think Angel had killed him.

Connor had helped conceive Jasmine, who offered the world utopia . . . with strings. One of those strings being Connor's complicity in the death of an innocent. . . .

None of this was what he said about his Sunnydale file.

Instead, partly to distract her, he said "I got coverage on the whole thing. Very gripping, needs a first act."

She shook her head. "You *have* to leave L.A."

He looked up from the file and said, "It's The First. Right? The First Evil. The power that tried to convince me to kill myself."

"Yeah." She nodded. "It's gotten a little more

ambitious since then. It's raising an army."

Angel considered. "Well, it failed once, and I'm here to tell you that—"

Just then, something hit Angel in the back of the head so hard that he went soaring across the room. He landed in the dust face-first, slamming to a stop against a wall.

It was Caleb, eyes black, ebony blood dripping like tears from them, and from his nose and mouth.

"You ready to finish this, bitch?" His voice was otherworldly, coming from everywhere.

Then he rushed her, swinging at her. She blocked with the scythe. His movements were halting, but his strength was greater than ever.

She stumbled back.

"Okay," she said sarcastically, "how many times do I have to kill you? Ballpark figure."

"You understand nothing!" he cried in reverbo-rama.

He came at her; they fought—lunge, parry, riposte—as he shouted at her, "You think you have power over me? I am everything. Everywhere!"

"Speech getting old," she informed him

"Stupid girl!" He was a wild . . . entity as he came at her. "You'll never stop me. You don't have the b—"

As he was saying it, she arced the scythe back and swung it up right between his legs.

"Well, who does nowadays?" she asked him.

A moment, and she used both hands to rip the blade upwards. His dark blood splattered her face as she finished the job.

One half of Caleb toppled to the right, and one half

to the left. Praise God Almighty, he was torn asunder.

Angel got to his feet, spinning around, furious, as he said, "Okay, now I'm pissed. Where is he?"

Buffy pointed to a spot on the floor to the left. Angel looked. Then a spot on the floor to her right. He looked. Then he looked back at her, impressed, and she smiled girlishly.

"He had to split." She snorted with dorkish laughter, and Angel just shook his head. "I'm sorry," she said, quelling herself. "I just, ahh . . . I haven't had a good pun in a while."

"That would still be the case," he darted at her.

She feigned being insulted. "Hey! My kill, my word play."

He reached to the sky. "I'm out of line."

Well, I'm still glad you're here," she said adoringly.

From the shadows, Spike watched, his world shattering. The First murmured to him, "Yeah, she needs you real bad."

He thought of how he had shown her his heart; truth time on the way out the door, bein' terrified. Blowing up his barriers, letting her in and then . . . of course. Of course.

Angel.

As Spike looked on, Angel went into his expandable files and yanked out some papers, handing them to Buffy. She looked them over, nodding to him as she said, "I'll have the guys run through this, see if there's anything new." She looked up at him. "Reliable source?"

"Not remotely," Angel assured her.

She took a breath. "Well, any port in an apocalypse."

"I brought you something else as well."

He pulled out a tremendously gaudy amulet and held it out to Buffy, whose eyes widened at the sheer tackiness of it. Least, that was Spike's best guess; he felt that he didn't know this girl.

Ah, c'mon, mate. Sure you do. This is exactly what you expected.

"I can already tell you, I don't have anything that goes with this," Buffy said to Angel.

"It's not for you," Angel told her.

She and Spike both were surprised. As she looked up at Angel and said, "'Splainy?"

Angel shook his head. "I don't know everything. It's very powerful and probably very dangerous. Has a purifying power . . . or a cleansing power . . ." He glanced at it ". . . or possibly scrubbing bubbles. The translation is . . . anyway, it bestows strength, worn by the right person."

Buffy pondered that. "And the right person is . . . ?"

"Someone ensouled. But stronger than human. A champion." A beat. "As in me."

She gestured to herself. "Or me."

"No," he said firmly. "I don't know nearly enough about this to risk you wearing it. Besides . . ." He grinned faintly. "You've already got that cool axe-thing."

She gave the scythe a bit of a pat and said, "So you're going to be with me in this."

"Shoulder to shoulder," Angel told her. "I'm yours."

Bloody moron, Spike cursed himself. *Blinkin, soddin' fool . . .*

And he left the tomb, left the lovers, got the hell out of there and off again into the world without her, world he knew so well . . .

. . . Hell.

Buffy looked at Angel warmly and said, "No."

Angel frowned. "No, what?"

"No, you're not going to be in this fight," she said.

She turned to go; he followed, displeased. He stopped her near the entrance and said, "Why the hell not?"

"Because I can't risk you," she told him calmly.

He was confused. "You need me in this."

"No." She shook her head. "I need you gone."

Yet more confused. "Why?"

She took a moment to collect her thoughts. "If I lose . . . if this gets past Sunnydale, then it's days—or hours—before the rest of the world goes. I need a second front, and I need you to run it."

"If I'm here we have a better shot at capping this thing," he insisted. He gestured to the papers in her hands. "I've read the files—"

"I've lived the files," she interjected, "and I . . . if I can't win this . . ." She gazed at him, her eyes clear, her voice steady. "It's my fight, Angel. It might be my last. But it's mine."

He looked at her, and she knew there was a whole

lot he wanted to say. And she also knew he wasn't going to say it.

Which was a good thing. Because she wanted Angel here. She needed Angel here. But she could not have him here.

"Okay," he said, "that's one reason. What's the other?"

"There is no other," she replied, but . . . there was. There was . . .

She went outside into the graveyard, not knowing so much as feeling that there was.

"Is it Spike?"

How does he know?

She stopped and turned, not overly anxious to look him in the eye as he approached. Her heart began to pound. She felt on the verge of something, standing on a very different kind of threshold.

"You're not telling me something," Angel insisted. "And . . . his scent." He gestured toward her body. "I remember it pretty well."

She reddened; the nape of her neck was prickling. Everyone was into truth so much these days. "You vampires," she said, trying to deflect, "did anybody ever tell you that the whole smelling everybody thing is a little gross?"

Angel asked her point-blank. "Is he your boyfriend?"

She raised a brow. "Is that your business?"

"Are you in love with him?"

That, she couldn't answer. She looked down, away . . . anywhere but at him. Angel, her lost love, her soulmate . . . and she couldn't answer him.

"Maybe I'm out of line," he began, "but this is kind of a curve ball for me. We *are* talking about Spike here."

"It's different," Buffy said. "He's different. He has a soul now."

"Oh." Angel was astonished. "Well."

"What?" she asked.

"No, no, that's great." He muttered, "Everybody's got a soul now."

Buffy frowned at him. "What, are you pissed?"

"No, it's great," he insisted, eyes wide and honest. "One for our side."

"He'll make a difference," she said, feeling as though she were vouching for Spike, as if she had to defend why she . . . why he and she . . .

He muttered on, "You know, I started it." He looked at her. "The whole . . . having a soul. Before it was all the 'cool new thing' . . ."

She blinked in amazement. "Oh, my god, are you twelve?"

He glowered, "I'm getting the brush off for Captain Peroxide, it doesn't bring out the champion in me," he informed her coolly.

"It's not the brushoff," she insisted, then added, "Having both of you here would be . . ." Confused, she searched for the word. "Confusing."

He remained glowering and added skeptical to his facial repertoire. "For who?"

"Everybody!" she insisted. "Why are you so . . . are you going to come by and get all Dawson on me every time I have a boyfriend?"

"Aha!" He pointed at her. "Boyfriend!"

"He's not! But . . ." She thought about it. "He is in my heart."

"That'll end well," he drawled.

"And what was the highlight of our relationship?" she demanded heatedly. "The time you broke up with me or the time I killed you?"

He backed down, the fight going out of both of them. She leaned against a sarcophagus, placing the file atop it.

"I'm well aware of my stellar history with guys, and now I don't see fat grandchildren in the offing with Spike, but . . . I don't think that matters right now." She thought a moment, came to some budding conclusions . . .

"You know, in the midst of all this . . . insanity, a couple of things are actually starting to make sense. And the guy thing . . ."

He joined her, also leaning on the crypt.

"You know, I've always figured there was something wrong with me," she told him, "'cause I never made it work. But maybe . . . I'm not supposed to."

Food for thought; he chewed on it, and then said, "Because you're the Slayer?"

"Because . . ." She thought hard. "Okay." Gazed at him. "I'm cookie dough."

He gave his head a shake. "Yet another curveball."

"I'm not done baking yet." She moved her shoulders. "I'm not finished becoming . . . whoever the hell it is I'm going to turn out to be. I've been looking for someone to make me feel whole, and maybe I just need to *be* whole."

Her tone was wistful, hopeful, and determined. "I make it through this, maybe one day I turn around realize I'm ready. I'm cookies. And then if I want someone to eat me . . . or, to enjoy warm, delicious cookie-me, then that's fine. That'll be then. When I'm done," she finished. She looked up at him to gauge his reaction.

He said, "Any thoughts on who might enjoy . . ." He frowned uncomfortably. "Do I have to go with the cookie analogy?"

She replied, "I don't really think that far ahead. That's kind of the point."

"I get it," he said. After a moment, he handed her the amulet. "I'll start working on a second front. Make sure I don't have to use it."

His hand was on hers; he turned to go, and she gave his hand a little tug.

"Angel, I . . . do," she said. "Sometimes." She swallowed down some big emotion and said, "Think that far ahead."

He stopped and smiled a bit as she added, "We both have our lives, but sometimes . . ."

"Sometimes is something," he finished for her.

"It'd be a long time coming." She looked excited, as if she were beginning to realize something. "Years, if ever."

He walked backward into the dark, smiling at her.

"I ain't gettin' any older."

He disappeared into the shadows, and she watched

him go, remembering when they first met. He would glide away like that and disappear.

But he always came back. I thought he was gone forever from my life, and yet, here he is again . . .

Or rather, here he was again . . . I may die soon, and I will never see his face on this Earth . . .

She went home, walked through the front door and found . . . *Dawn?*

Her little sister glared at her; Buffy, in turn, gazed over at Xander, who looked pained and sheepish. Anya was rubbing his head; Giles and Willow were there too.

As Buffy looked back at her sister, Dawn silently kicked her in the shin.

Buffy said, "Ow."

"Dumbass," Dawn growled at her.

Buffy looked over at Xander, who simply threw up his hands and said, "Don't look at me. This is a Summers thing. It's all very violent."

Buffy said to Dawn, "You get killed, I'm telling."

And that was that.

Sensing the change in cabin pressure, Willow asked, "Did you find out anything about the scythe?"

Buffy seized the preening opportunity with glee. "I found out it slices, dices, and makes julienne Preacher."

"Caleb?" Giles asked, actually excited despite being British.

"I cut him in half," Buffy affirmed. "I'm not going to lie. It was pretty neat."

Well, all right!" Willow cried.

"He had that coming," Anya concurred.

"Party in my eye-socket and everyone's invited!" Xander yelled, then winced and said, "Sometimes I shouldn't say words."

Buffy waggled the scythe and said, "I did find out some history on this puppy. I'll fill you in. And I got some files, might be helpful." She handed them to Giles. "And . . . this." She held out the amulet. "Supposed to be powerful, don't know much more."

Giles looked at the bounty and asked, "Where'd you get all this?"

"Angel," she said.

"Angel?" Dawn echoed.

Giles asked, "He's here?"

"I sent him back to L.A.," Buffy said. "To prepare." She headed out toward the basement, turning back to add, "If we fail."

Xander cocked a brow at her. "Operative word 'if.'"

Anya added, "Operative word 'fail.'"

Dawn chirruped, "Or, operative word 'Wheee!'" Lowered it, cricketed, "Nobody gets me."

Buffy went downstairs to the basement. Spike was sitting in the moonlight, shirtless, looking off.

"So where's Tall, Dark, and Forehead?" he asked her.

"Let me guess," Buffy said. "You can smell him."

He tilted his head, appraising her as he said, "Yeah, that; and I also used my heightened vampire eyeballs to watch you kissing him."

Oh, God . . .

She felt terrible.

"It was a . . . hello," she said. "I was surprised."

He gave her a look. "Most people don't use their tongues to say hello. Or, I guess they do, but . . ."

"There was no tongues," she said quickly. Then, "Besides, he's gone."

"Just popped round for a quickie, then?" His voice was harsh.

"Good, *good*," she said sarcastically. "I haven't had quite enough jealous vampire crap!"

"He wears lifts, you know."

She shook her head tiredly. "One of these days I'm just going to put you two in a room and let you rassle it out."

"No problem at this end."

"There could maybe be oil of some kind involved," she said, warming up to the idea.

He cut her off. "Where's the trinket?"

She paused. "The who-ket?"

"The pretty necklace your sweetie-bear gave you. The one with all the power." He gazed at her very calmly. "I believe it's mine now."

"How do you figure?"

"'Someone with a soul, but more than human,'" he quoted her. "Angel meant to wear it, that means I'm the qualified party."

"It's volatile," Buffy told him. "We don't know . . ."

"You need someone strong to bear it, then," he informed her. He drawled, "You were planning on giving it to Andrew?"

She hesitated. "Angel said . . . this amulet is meant to be worn by a champion."

He deflated . . . until she held it out to him, and he understood: She was calling him a champion.

"Been called a lot of things in my time," he said.

"I want you to be careful," she said gently.

He smirked with self-referential irony. "You're talking to the wrong guy, love." He felt it. "This *is* powerful."

A beat, as he turned it over in his hand.

"Faith's still got my room," she murmured.

He frowned at her. "Well, you're not staying here! Can't buy me off with shiny beads and sweet talk. You've got Angel breath."

She looked down, accepting his decision.

"Won't just let you whack me back and forth like a rubber ball. I've got my pride, you know."

She got up and started to go.

"I understand," she murmured.

He moved quickly to block her. "Clearly you don't," he said, "since that whole 'having my pride' thing was a smokescreen."

She exhaled, very relieved. "Oh, thank God."

He joined in the relief effort, saying, "I don't know what I would have done if you'd gone up those stairs."

She touched his face with great tenderness. "Let's not find out."

They slept spoon style again, Buffy wrapped in Spike's arms, facing away from him. He slept; she could not.

She looked at his hand, resting on the bed in front

of her, running her hand along it. After a moment, he rolled over, and Buffy took the chance to sit up. Got up, and crossed to the window, looked out on the world bathed in moonlight.

"Pretty, ain't it?" Caleb said right beside her.

She started, then recovered, reminding herself it was The First. "You're not him," she said.

"No, you killed him right and proper," he answered. "Terrible loss." He pulled a sad face. "This man was my good right arm. 'Course, it doesn't pain me too much. Don't need an arm." He smiled broadly. "Got an army."

Buffy rolled her eyes. "An army of vampires. However will I fight a bunch of . . . oh, *right!* I've been doing that for years!"

"Every day our numbers swell, he boasted. Then he sneered at her. "But then you do have an army of your own. Some thirty-odd pimply-faced girls who don't know the pointy end of a stake." He thought a moment. "Maybe I should call this off?"

Buffy asked, "Have you ever considered a cool name?" Since you're incorporeal and basically power-less you could call yourself 'The Taunter.' Strikes fear . . ."

"I will overrun this earth," The First proclaimed.

"You know how many people have said that to me?" Buffy shot back.

"I do," he assured her. "Since they all had a small part of me in them. Whereas I have all of me in me, so I like my chances somewhat better." His voice rose as if it were seeking the vulnerable, thin places in her soul to pour in his poison, and let it rot her from the inside out.

"And when my army outnumbers the humans on this earth, the scales will tip and I will be made flesh."

"Talk on," Buffy taunted. "I'm not afraid of you."

"Then why aren't you asleep in your dead lover's arms?"

His expression was cagey, his point . . . well taken . . . as she looked over at Spike and had no answer.

"'Cause he can't help you. Nor Faith, nor your friends. Certainly not your little wannaslay brigade. None of those girlies will ever know real power unless you're dead. You know the drill."

Then Caleb morphed into Buffy herself and came in close, as close as possible, voice carrying truth.

"Into every generation, a Slayer is born. One girl in the all the world. She alone will have the strength and skill to fight the . . . well, there's that word again. What you are. How you'll die. Alone."

She took that in, said nothing for a moment, and then:

"You're right."

The First was bemused. "Mmm. Not your best."

From across the room, Spike moved on his cot and cried out, "I'm drowning in footwear." His eyes flew open. He glanced at her and said, "Weird dream." When she didn't reply, he frowned at her and said, "Buffy? Is something wrong?"

"No," she said, then, "Yes. I just realized something." She stared at him as the steadiest calm she had ever experienced mingled with her warrior's blood. She was serene and highly charged at the same time.

Then she said, "We're going to win."

The sun had risen by the time the core group assembled in her bedroom. Faith was there, too, working out the kinks in her neck and arms, testing her strength as Buffy finished explaining her plan and said, "Well? What do you think?"

Xander went first, wading slowly as he said, "That depends." Then he said sincerely, "Are you *kidding*?"

She frowned. "You don't think it's a good idea?"

"It's pretty radical, B," Faith concurred.

"It's a lot more than that," Giles said. "Buffy, what you're talking about flies in the face of everything we've ever—that every generation—has ever done in the fight against evil." He smiled broadly. "I think it's bloody brilliant."

"You mean that?" Buffy asked.

"If you want my opinion," he said shrugging.

"I really do," she said warmly.

"Whoa, hey, not to poop on the party," Willow said, knitting her brows with earnest Willow concern. "But I'm the guy who's going to have to pull this off."

"It is *beaucoup d'mojo*," Faith drawled.

"Is it even possible?" Dawn asked.

Giles was getting excited. "I believe it is, if what Buffy has told about this weapon is true."

"Not to careen back to the *me* subject," Willow said, "but . . . I'm . . . this is beyond anything I've ever done. This is total loss of control, and not in a nice, wholesome, my-girl-friend has-a-pierced-tongue way."

Buffy regarded her friend soberly, and told her frankly, "I wouldn't ask if I didn't think you could do it."

Willow fretted still. "I'm just not sure I'm stable enough to—"

"Oh, sure ya are," Anya reassured the Wicca, giving her a little wave. "You're as stable as the molecules in Mister Fantastic's uniform, am I right?"

Xander grimaced. "Oh, you just couldn't have picked a worse example."

Giles took over. "You're going to do this, Willow. Get the coven on the line, see how they can help. I'll—"

"Oh!" Dawn cried; then, as everyone looked at her, muttered, "Pierced tongue."

Unnerved, Buffy quickly said, "Dawn should do a research thing."

"Yes," Giles said to Dawn. "You—"

"It's cool," she said. "Watcher Junior to the library." As she went, she said to Buffy, "You get to save the world, I get more homework."

As she got up to leave, Buffy said to her, "You could have been in Oxnard . . ."

"I'll start digging up my sources," Giles pondered. He looked up at the group. "Literally, actually; there's one or two people I need to talk to who are dead."

Anya said to Xander, "Come on. Let's go assemble the cannon fodder."

"We're not calling them that," Xander remonstrated her as he stood up.

She gave him a "no kidding" look and said, "Not to their faces. What am I, insensitive?"

"Willow . . . ," Buffy said, turning next to the Wicca.

Willow looked at the scythe. "I'm going to need to run an energy scan on that puppy. To start with."

Faith gave Buffy a mocking grin. "Sure you're ready to give it up?"

Without another word, Buffy handed the scythe to Willow.

Later on that morning, Buffy spoke to the assembled Potentials. She paced as she spoke, and she could feel the tension in the room. Not all the girls were glad she was back, and some of the newbies didn't trust her at all.

"I hate this," she began. "I hate being here. I hate that you have to be here. I hate that there's evil, that it's growing, and I hate that I was Chosen to fight it.

"I wish, a whole lot of the time, that I hadn't been." She flashed them a wry smile. "I know a lot of you wish I hadn't been, either."

Kennedy and Vi smiled a bit; others looked embarrassed.

"But this isn't about wishes," she went on, looking at their faces, seeing how young they were, how frightened. "This is about choices. I never had one. I was Chosen. And I accept that. I'm not asking you to accept anything. I'm asking you to make your own choice. I believe we can beat this evil—not when it comes, not after its army is ready, but now. Tomorrow morning I'm opening the Seal. I'm going down into the Hellmouth and I'm gong to finish it once and for all."

They shifted, some gasping, others shaking their heads: *Another stupidly aggressive plan of Buffy's. She's going to get herself killed.*

"I've got strong allies: warriors, charms, sorcerers, and I'll need them all. But I'll also need you. Every single one of you."

She looked at each one in turn. She memorized their faces. She read their hearts. "So now you're asking yourself, 'What makes this different? What makes us anything more than a bunch of girls getting picked off one by one?'

"It's true none of you has the power Faith and I have. I think both of us would have to die for a new Slayer to be called, and we can't even be sure that girl is in this room. That's the rule. So here's the part where you make a choice."

While Buffy addressed the troops, Faith and Robin toiled in the high school basement, moving something big and metal in front of a grate. Robin was assimilating what Faith had told him about Buffy's plan, and he was dubious.

"It's a hell of a risky idea," he said.

"Buffy's wacky that way," she replied.

"There's one more vent right by the stairs," he continued. They headed for it. "We block that, they've got no sewer access. It should drive them up into the school proper."

"That's assuming they get past us," Faith drawled.

He gave his head a little shake. "Which, no offense, I am."

She grinned at him, "Come on. You gotta have a little faith."

"Think I've had my share, thanks," he said sardonically.

"Well, I trundled right into that, didn't I?" she replied, with a very small wince. "Look, I'm sorry if it seemed like I was blowing you off the other day. I was just trying to, you know, blow you off."

They started covering the vent by the stairs with stuff.

"I figured that out all by myself," he told her.

"It's nothing personal." She grunted as she did the heavy lifting. "It's just, after I get bouncy with a guy, there's not a whole lot more I need to know about him."

"That's bleak."

"Way of the world," she bit off.

"Good to know. For a second there, I was mistaking it for more defensive, isolationist Slayer crap."

"And he comes out swinging," she mugged.

"There is a whole world you don't even know about," he told her, "and a lot of the men in it are pretty decent guys. They'd surprise you."

"Guy looks at me, let's just say his priorities shift."

He raised his brows, surprised by her words. "'Cause you're so hot?"

"Is what it is, yo."

"Please," Robin said, "I'm *much* prettier than

you."

Faith started in open-mouthed, Victorian shock, putting a hand to her chest.

"And for the record," he continued, "our little encounter didn't exactly change my world."

"You're tripping!" she cried. "That was rock 'em sock 'em!"

He added dismissively, "Oh, it was nice enough . . . you're very enthused. With a little more experience, I think you'll really—"

"Dude!" she cried. "I got mad skills!"

"No. Of course." He gestured to their lovely piles of crap. "Let's finish up."

"Hell with that," Faith said. "We're going again! You're going to learn a little respect here, pal." She started pulling off her shirt,

Robin stopped her. "Faith. Make me a deal. We live through this, you give me the chance to surprise you."

She narrowed her eyes suspiciously. "Well, what would be the surprise?"

"You *do* know the meaning of the word, right? He sounded amused . . . at her expense.

"Fine," she shot back. "Deal."

"Good enough," he told her.

They started to move the junk some more.

"No way are you prettier than me," Faith muttered.

"Little bit," he teased.

The day flew by as Willow labored over her books of shadows and incantations. Kennedy sat like a beautiful incarnation of the Goddess among the books, papers, and mystical objects . . . and the scythe.

"I really wish she hadn't said that about me," Willow murmured.

"What, the thing Buffy said?" Kennedy asked. "I think it's true."

Willow made hapless face. "Eheh."

"I'll be with you. To keep you grounded," said the kite string.

Willow made a spear-jab motion and said, with all sincerity, "You may have to keep me stabbed . . . if I . . . go to the bad place."

Kennedy inhaled, looked dizzy, looked scared. "You're saying I might have to kill you."

"I am," Willow agreed.

Willow's girl snapped, "Bite me."

"I will. I mean, I do. Mean it." Willow was very, very sincere. "If I go south, you have to protect the others."

"It's not going to happen," Kennedy insisted.

The Wicca had to make her understand "The darkest place I've ever been . . . this is what lies beyond that. This is too important for me to . . ."

". . . Buffy believes in you," Kennedy reminded her.

Willow sighed. "You know Buffy: Sweet girl, not that bright."

"Hey." Kennedy leaned toward her, as if by closing the space between them, she could force Willow to really hear what she had to say. "I'm the first to call her out when she's not making sense. In fact, this may have escaped your keen notice, but I'm kind of a brat.

I've sort of always gotten my way. So you're going to make it through this, no matter how dark it gets. Because . . ."

Her eyes misted, and she came to Willow, then.

". . . you're my way."

They kissed, and Willow drew sustenance from the kiss, and some hope. She never wanted that kiss to end.

When it did, she said, "I better go over it again."

And the day had flown by for Giles, who sat at the dining room table with Xander, books and plans strewn about. Amanda and other Potentials looked on, tired but engrossed.

"I've gotten turned around," Giles said. "You're here."

"By the pillar, yeah," Xander told him. "I'm protecting this area."

"That puts me here." Giles pointed. "By the door. Demons around the perimeter. Right. So I open the door."

Andrew sat at the table as well. He was wearing his red DM cloak, hood up, consulting his GURPS and his personal notes from his many, many-many years of serious gaming.

"You go through the door," He told Giles. "You are confronted by Trogdor the Burninator."

Giles was pissed off. "Bugger all. Fight." He rolled the ten-sided dice.

Andrew checked his score. "Adios to five hit points," he informed Giles. "Trogdor has badly wounded you."

"What about my bag of illusions?" Giles demanded hotly.

"Illusions? Against a burninator?" He chuckled. "Silly, silly British man."

Amanda piped up, "I invoke a time flux on Trogdor."

Andrew was piqued. "Step down, girlfriend, you can't just—"

"Nine level sorcerer, *and* I carry the emerald chalice. Trogdor is frozen in time. Deal with it," Amanda crowed.

Xander brightened. "Smackdown on red riding hood! This could get ugly."

"Could it possibly get uglier?" Giles moaned. "I used to be a highly respected Watcher. Now I'm a wounded dwarf with the mystical strength of a doily." He rubbed his eyes. "I wish I could just sleep."

Amanda broke character for a moment and said, "What kind of a person could sleep on a night like this?"

Xander fondly regarded his ex-fiancée, current . . . current whatever, and patted her head as she snored away, her head on the table.

"Only the crazy ones," he said, with great affection.

Upstairs Dawn counted coup as she regaled the young Potentials with tales of the Slayer. Some were in sleeping bags, and some where just hanging out at her feet; all were rapt.

She said, "And the Master grabbed Buffy from behind and bit her. She tired to move but he was too strong. He fed on her blood and he tossed her in the water, cackling insanely as the bubbles rose around her and she slowly drowned to death."

Vi was freaking. "Do you have any *other* stories?

Dawn made a "hold-on" gesture and said, "She gets up again. It's very romantic." She looked at all the Potentials. "Guys, you gotta stop worrying. It's Buffy. She always saves the day."

What will this day bring? Buffy thought, as she stood on the front porch and gazed into the blackness. *Will we actually pull this off?*

Some say the world will end in fire, Spike mused, as he stared down at the amulet. *Am I the champion meant to wear this? If I wasn't, I am, now.*

I have to be, now.

Then he became aware of eyes on him, and looked up. It was Buffy, beautiful and brave; his girl, whether or not he was her man; she was the Chosen One, and oh, God, he would choose her a million times over another night. Another sunset. Another lifetime.

In fire, then.

Sunnydale High School: the last stand, the last battle, the last day as the sun finally rose and rose too fast.

Robin led the girls into the empty corridors of the building. He stopped at the big space at the bottom of the stairs.

"Welcome to Sunnydale High," he told them in a booming voice. "There's no running in the halls, no yelling, and no gum. Apart from that, we have only one rule."

He stopped and turned.

"If they move, kill them."

Buffy began to move her warriors into position as she announced, "Potentials are in the basement. Follow Faith and Spike."

As they began to leave, Xander called, "If you have to go to the bathroom, it's on the left. If you don't have to go to the bathroom, picture what you're about to face. Better to go *now*."

Robin turned to Willow and said, "Willow, my office is through there."

"It's right over the Seal," Buffy reminded her.

"I'll start getting you set up," Kennedy said to her mate.

"Thanks," Willow murmured gratefully.

"Okay, civilians." Robin gestured as he spoke. "The vampires get upstairs, we have three areas they could get through to another building and down into the sewers.

"Down the hall in the atrium; the north hall here; and the primary target, through the lounge to the science building. Odds are, most of them will head there. Easy to find, big, no sunlight."

Giles spoke up. "Teams of two, then, and I suggest you and I take the lounge."

"I concur," Robin replied.

"Xander, I want you with Dawn," Buffy said.

"I concur," Xander said.

"We'll take the atrium," Dawn announced.

"So that leaves me and the dungeon master in the north hall," Anya concluded.

Andrew was peaking. "We will defend it with our very lives."

"Yes," Anya put in, "we'll defend it with his very life."

"Don't be afraid to use him as a human shield," Xander told her.

"Good. Yes. Thanks," Anya said.

"And I just want to say how proud I am to die for this really special cause with you guys," Andrew said. "There's some people I'd like to thank, both good and evil . . ."

He was holding a paper, which he now unfolded, and began to read. "A shout out to my brother, Tucker, who gave me the inspiration to summon demons, and also—"

"Nobody cares, ya little monkey," Anya said, not without affection, as she dragged him off.

Robin left, too, and Dawn announced, "I'm going to check out our filed of engagement."

She started down the hall. Buffy followed.

"Dawn."

"No." Dawn turned back, not waiting for Buffy to speak. In a choked voice, she said, "Anything you say is going to sound like good-bye."

Resolutely, she turned back around, and left. Buffy silently watched her, working hard not to lose it, for if there was going to be a moment when she would falter, this was it.

She made it through.

Then she turned back around and joined the group.

The Four: Buffy, Giles, Willow, and Xander.

Us. The originals, Buffy thought. *Everyone else came later. These are my comrades, my dearest friends. I am the Slayer who did not walk alone.*

They kept me in their pocket, only I didn't realize it . . . until almost too late.

The Four.

The Slayer, the Watcher, the Witch, and the One Who Saw.

"So," Buffy said, taking on chipper. "What do you guys wanna do tomorrow?"

Willow considered. "Nothing strenuous."

"Mini-golf is always the first thing that comes to mind," Xander said, weighing in.

Giles looked mildly disappointed. "Well, I think we can do better than that."

"I'm pretty much thinking about shopping. As usual," Buffy announced.

"There's an Agnes B. in the new mall!" Willow told her excitedly.

"I could use a few items," Xander said.

"Well, no, aren't we going to discuss this?" Giles asked. "We're saving the world to go to the mall?"

"I'm having a wicked shoe craving," Buffy said.

"Aren't you on the patch?" Xander asked her.

Willow shook her head sadly. "Those never work."

"And I'm just here, invisible to the eye, not having any say . . ." Giles whined.

And the three younger champions headed off, leaving the older one to watch them.

"See, it's the eye-patch thing," Xander groused.

"Right," Buffy said, "do you go with the full black secret agent look—

"Or the puffy shirt pirate-slash-poet feel," Willow suggested. "Sensitive yet manly . . ."

"Now you're getting a little renaissance fair on me," Xander told her.

"It's fine line," Buffy admitted.

Giles turned away from them.

"The earth is *definitely* doomed."

Then the three peeled off from each other, Willow first, then Xander, much with the cazh chatter as they would have, any other day . . .

. . . and Buffy was alone . . . with memories, with voices:

Xander: "Oh, me and Buffy go waaaay back. Old friends. Very close."

Cordelia: "If you hang with me and mine, you'll be accepted in no time."

Willow: "Do you want me to move?"

Giles: "I'd much rather be home with a cup of Bovril and a good book. . . ."

Angel: "Let's just say I'm a friend. . . ."

Then she was in the basement at the end of the hall, where Spike was waiting.

"Time to go to work, love," he said.

He gestured to the Potentials. Some were crowded outside the Seal chamber because there was not enough room inside. But they parted respectfully for Buffy. Her gaze ticked toward a few of them. They were so brave, and yet so terrified. Maintaining their control so well . . . she was so proud of them. She wanted to save them, all of them, not lose a single one, ever. For no one to die, ever, in the world. . . .

She moved into the room and stood beside the Seal, next to Faith, who held out Andrew's mystical knife.

"You're first, B," Faith said.

Buffy took the knife, cut her hand, and let her blood drip onto the Seal. Faith took the knife and said, "Pucker up, ladies. We're going to Hell."

Then she sliced her own palm with casual aplomb.

Then all the girls around the circle held out their hands . . .

The Seal started to open.

Steeling her gaze, finding her center, Buffy started down.

In Robin's office, Willow sat on the floor, the scythe in front of her, her own athame and bowl at her side. Candles and incense; the trappings of witchery, as Kennedy watched her from the other side of the room.

"They should be in place," Willow said. "Okay, magic time." She gazed at Kennedy. "You ready to . . . heh, heh, . . . kill me?"

"Starting to be," Kennedy replied pointedly, but with warmth and love and all vibes good.

"Great. Fun. Right." She took a deep breath. "Brace yourself."

She shut her eyes, and Kennedy said softly, "Come on, Red. Make it happen."

* * *

Down among the dead men, into the cavern, Buffy and Faith and a few of the girls went as more followed.

And Spike, with the amulet around his neck.

"Not to be a buzzkill, love," he said, "but my fabulous accessory isn't exactly tingling with power."

"I'm not worried," Buffy told him.

"I'm getting zero juice here," he went on. "And I look like Elizabeth Taylor."

"Cheer up, Liz," Faith said to him. "Willow's big spell doesn't work, won't matter *what* you wear."

"I'm not worried," Buffy said again.

But her voice said otherwise, and the others gazed in horror as they moved to the precipice, which looked out over an endless cavern, and in that cavern . . . thousands of Turok-han.

Thousands.

"I'm not worried," Buffy said, practically catatonic.

"Really?" Rona whispered. "'Cause I'm flashing back to Xander's whole bathroom speech."

"Buffy?" Amanda asked shrilly.

Buffy closed her eyes. "Now Willow now Willow now."

"Buffy?" This time Amanda almost screamed.

"I'm not worried!" Buffy proclaimed. "As long as Willow can work the spell before they . . . see us."

As one, the vamps caught sight of the girls. Screaming, they charged.

"Willow," Buffy whispered.

The battle had begun.

* * *

*WordstotheGoddessprayerstotheGoddessprotectorof-
womanofwomenthepoweroftheGoddessQueenofthe-
MoonoftheEarthAirFireWateroftheAngelsofGuardians
andofSlayersofSlayersofSlayers*

"Willow?" Kennedy asked, alarmed.

Willow stabbed her a look and kept chanting.

*GoddessQueenoftheMoonoftheEarthAirFire-
WateroftheAngelsofGuardiansandofSlayersofSlayersof
SlayersofSISTERS*

Willow tensed up, eyes widening, as light began to fill the room, coursing through her, through everything: flowers in Paraguay and the coven back in England, all the Wicca, and there she was in Willow's soul, Jenny Calendar . . . and all who had fought for good, with magicks and with their souls and spirits. . . .

"Oh

my

Goddess!"

Willow cried.

Kennedy fell back, slammed by something unseen. She grunted, shouted . . . and was filled . . . filled as Buffy had dreamed she would be, when she had given each Potential her choice:

"What if all you could have that power? Now. All of you. In every generation one Slayer is born because a bunch of guys that died thousands of years ago made up that rule. They were powerful men."

And here she had pointed to Willow, and said the things that made Willow so uncertain:

"This woman is more powerful than all of them combined. So I saw we change the rules. I saw my power should be our power. Tomorrow Willow will use the essence of this scythe, that contains the energy and history of so many Slayers, to change our destiny.

"From now on, every girl in the world who might be a Slayer, will be a Slayer. Every girl who could have the power, will have the power. Who can stand up, will stand up.

"Every one of you, and girls we've never known, and generations to come . . . they will have strength they never dreamed of, and more than that, they will have each other.

"Slayers. Every one of us.

"Make your choice.

"Are you ready to be strong?"

Kennedy was ready. Her head reared back, her eyes sparkling with power.

As the Ubervamps swarmed to crush them, the Potentials were ready; the power was a rushing wind, a hammer blow, a slap and an embrace and true love and sure death. A fever dream . . . all, it was all, it was . . .

. . . appening everywhere;

In India, a girl fell to the floor as the power and knowledge coursed through her.

In an inner city school, a young girl fell against her locker, dazed . . . and new.

In a trailer park, a young girl blocked the ham fist of her drunken, abusive father.

On a baseball diamond, standing at the plate . . . a little girl straightened, grinning a wicked happy grin.

In Japan, a girl backed away from the dinner table, changed utterly and forever, trying to take it all in.

. . . take it all in, take it all in . . .

"Sweet fancy Moses," Amanda gasped.

Buffy and Faith beamed at each other.

"You feel that?" Faith asked the Slayer.

"I really do," Buffy told the Slayer.

Faith looked ahead; the Slayers steeled themselves—dozens of them, ready and uncertain, pumped and hanging on, hanging in, hanging tough.

"Everybody, hold the line," Faith said.

"These guys are dead," Vi said coolly.

The first wave of vampires hit, frenzied evil spilling over the girls in a blur of teeth and axes and spears, talons and muscles and no fear of pain or dying. They swarmed, enormous killing things . . .

. . . and the Slayers went into action.

Roundhouse kicks, uppercuts, sidekicks, leaps—punching and twirling in a jaw-dropping battle dance such as the world had never seen before. They were to the Power born. Each Slayer, cloaked and anointed in the Power, burning bright as they fought back the horde, slaying as if they had been doing it all their lives.

The Chosen, the valiant, heroes to a girl; the Champions of Good, beating them back.

Spike held off others, but there were so many—the army of darkness was endless. But he fought, waiting for the amulet to bestow power, not waiting to wade into the war and hold the line.

It was brutal and dark and bloody; it was why there were Slayers.

Why they were here, glimmering, shimmering with Power.

. . . Glimmering, shimmering . . .

Kennedy was still feeling it, still mesmerized by the Power as it worked inside her, coursing through her. It was like a drug, a high, and she was taken over by it.

Then she opened her eyes and gasped, "Willow?"

For Willow was more than Willow, too—she was the Power incarnate, blown by a force so powerful, so loving, that she was bathed in a pure white wind. Her hair was actually white, streaming out behind her, her smile a bowl to catch her tears.

Transcendent, forever altered . . . cleansed, forgiven, purified.

The loving wind sucked out of her and her appearance returned to normal. She was clearly completely spent.

Kennedy said wonderingly, "You are a Goddess."

And Willow replied, filled with joy, "And you're a Slayer."

She picked up the scythe and tossed it Kennedy.

"Get this to Buffy," she said.

Kennedy gazed at her one last moment, and then she raced away.

Collapsing to the ground, Willow giggled like a dope.

"That was nifty," she said to herself.

* * *

On the precipice, the Pride Rock of Doom in the endless cavern . . .

Buffy hovered near the edge, fighting every vampire she could touch: She tossed a Turok-han over the side, staked another, then took a couple of brutal hits.

A fearless warrior jumped through the Seal opening: Kennedy, shouting, "Buffy! Catch!"

She hurled the scythe at her; Buffy caught it in mid-fight, not even looking back, and dispatched two vamps immediately.

Kennedy was attacked and jumped high, kicking hard—pummeling the enemy with her newfound Power.

"Oh, I could get used to this!" she exulted.

Spike fought as he had never before; Amanda, Vi . . . everyone was pumped and armed and filled with it. War cries echoed over the frenzy: Faith and Buffy, vamps and Slayers, leaping at each other above the heads of the warring crowd. A sprawling, brawling mob: Armageddon.

Having breached the line, some of the vampires saw the Seal opening and scurried up it. More followed.

Robin and Giles heard them coming. Giles had rolled a cigarette—traditional last one before battle—and he offered it to his comrade in arms. Robin declined; one last drag for Giles, and then he stamped it out.

They hoisted their swords.

They were ready.

* * *

In the atrium, Xander and Dawn prepared.

She turned to Xander and said, "You were going to take me to *Oxnard*?"

He shrugged. "I know some people there." He added, "You're in my blind spot."

She gingerly and swiftly changed sides with him.

In the north hall, Andrew and Anya geared up for the fight.

"I think they're coming," Andrew said.

Anya nodded, swallowed. Her heart was pounding so hard she could barely hear her own voice.

"Oh, God," she said, "I'm terrified. I didn't think . . . I just figured *you* would be terrified and I would be sarcastic about it."

Terrified indeed, Andrew whispered, "Picture happy things. A lake. Candy canes. Bunnies."

Anya's eyes narrowed.

"Bunnies. Floppy, hoppy *bunnies*," she said.

Her sword came up, all her fear gone.

The Turok-han made it up and through the Seal; they came barreling down the hall toward Giles and Robin, whose blades were at the ready. *Vampires to the right of us, vampires to the left of us, volleyed and thundered . . .*

They were a matched pair of warriors; they fought expertly—Giles scoring a beheading—but they were only managing to hold them off, being driven slowly back. . . .

* * *

. . . while Anya and Andrew fought. Anya was a swordswoman, Andrew was Jerry Lewis, but they also managed to keep them at bay . . .

. . .as a group of five Bringers appeared in the hall behind them, all armed with knives and swords . . .

In the cavern, as Spike fought off in a corner, he was startled by a surge of power from the amulet on his chest.

"Uh, Buffy?" he called, but she was in the heat of battle. "Whatever this thing does, I think it's . . . *Ahh-hhh!*"

He dropped to his knees, stunned by pain.

The army of the bad was not getting smaller.

Buffy watched a Turok-han leap on a young Slayer, tear into her; the girl went down.

Faith battled her way over to Buffy's side, exhausted but game, as she said, "Think it's too late to talk this thing out?"

Buffy called out to the girls, "Keep the line together! Drive them to the edge! We can't let them—"

Pain.

Unbelievable pain.

She looked down to see the point of a sword extend from her belly, then retract. She had been run through.

Silence covered her thoughts; vaguely she realized that Faith was tackling the vampire who had stabbed her; the Buffy fell slowly to the ground, face first.

"Buffy?" Faith cried, running to her sister Slayer.

Buffy gazed up at her and rasped out, "Hold the line."

She held out the scythe—symbol of their Power—to Faith. There was a moment, then Faith took it. She stabbed the vampire behind her without looking at him.

Then she went crazy with battle frenzy, and started taking them out, one by one by one.

A vampire got her around the neck from behind; then more, dogpiling her. Her skin tore; the stench of the monsters assailed her. She tasted blood.

She looked around, saw Rona, and shouted, "Rona!"

As she was buried beneath the vampires, she tossed the scythe to Rona.

Who took it, and started hacking.

In the atrium, Xander swung his sword as he was driven back by vamps. Then Dawn yanked a rope, pulling a tarp off the skylight, sunlight pouring in and setting the three vampires ablaze.

"We call that the greenhouse effect," Xander explained. "Very dangerous."

Another leaped on Xander, tackling him, weaponless, as Dawn grabbed a sword and swung.

Three Bringers rushed behind Giles and Robin as the vampires pushed from the front. Robin turned and hurled a knife into one of their throats with perfect precision.

But another took its place; they fought hard; Robin

found himself thinking of his mother, imitating her moves; all right, she had died a Slayer, but she may have saved his life because he had been able to observe her, first-hand . . .

Then the Bringer's crescent-shaped knife sliced across his chest.

I'm out of the game, he thought in shock as he collapsed.

The Turok-han ran past him and Giles, free to escape into the next building.

Anya and Andrew . . .

They were here. They were driving them apart, Andrew toward the north hall, Anya down the adjacent hall that lead outside.

Okay with the dying, not with the pain, Andrew thought. *Okay with that . . . not so much, oh, God, I am so scared . . .*

Then a Bringer went down, holding out his sword like a limp . . . noodle, as a Bringer jumped onto him with a knife.

And Anya . . .

She slashed one.

Dropped it.

I'm winning!

I'm terrified!

And then another one came from the side.

She turned—

—*Mrs. Xander Harris, that is who I'll be . . .*

—*Aud.*

—*Anyanka.*

—*Anya.*

—and the Bringer gutted her.

He stabbed her repeatedly.

And she was dead.

—*Forever, Anya.*

Spike.

Searing pain wracked his body; he tossed away a vampire as confusion and pain contorted his body; he clutched his stomach.

He was burning from the inside out.

And Buffy . . .

As Amanda dropped right in front of her, eyes wide.

Amanda was dead.

Two more Slayers fell; Kennedy was backed against the wall, her weapon knocked from her head. She was steadying herself, preparing.

On the ground, her vision hazy with pain, Buffy looked up to see her own boots, her own legs . . . her own self . . .

But of course, it was The First.

"Oooh, ow, Mommy!" The First mocked her. "This mortal wound is all itchy!"

She leaned in and said to Buffy, "You pulled a nice trick." She smiled pleasantly and added, "Hey, you came pretty close to smacking me down. What more do you want?"

Buffy pulled herself up on her hands, shaking with

fury. She was not done, not yet.

"I want you . . . to get out of my *face*," Buffy told her.

Then she rose: Resurrection.

The First backed away, vanished.

Sweaty, bloodied, hair in her face, Buffy took a step forward; two, stumbling, hunched steps . . .

Rona saw her, and threw her the scythe. Buffy caught it, and stood a little straighter.

She screamed, swinging the back of the weapon like a bat, knocking five vamps back and over the edge in one blow.

And as if her power communicated itself to Faith, the Dark Slayer kicked her way out of the dogpile and rose as if from the dead—also bloodied, also unbroken.

The tide turned then: The Power surged in all the Slayers, and it used them to force the vamps back, may of them falling over the edge, and at least one Slayer going with them.

But they were on the offensive now; they were pushing and screaming as if reborn . . . *hallelujah*, as Caleb would have said . . . in the mighty throes of the Power, as they battled to save the world.

And Spike.

He staggered under the Seal opening, paused, and said, "Oh, bollocks."

Then energy shot up from within him, straight through, like a geyser, piercing the seal, and bursting through Robin Wood's office floor, narrowly missing where the still-prone Willow lay; she watched in astonishment as the brilliant plume crashed through the ceiling, bathing her in sunlight as she murmured, "I didn't do that."

And Spike:

The sun hit him hard; and he was pinned, pain and something else building inside him . . . he called out to his dearest love—

"—Buffy . . ."

She saw him, raced to him.

"Spike!" she shouted—and had to dive out of the way as a prismed ray of pure, soulful sunlight blasted out of the amulet and into the cavern.

In an instant, hundreds—thousands of vampires were incinerated.

Then the teeming cavern began to tear apart, walls crumbling, rocks tumbling like bombs; the ground shook and the foundations roared.

"Everybody out! Now!" Faith yelled.

The girls fought their way to the exit; everything was shaking.

Buffy came to Spike. He remained pinned in place, energy still blasting from him.

"I can feel it, Buffy," he murmured.

"What?" she asked, choking with emotion, fighting to keep present, stay present, be here for him, with him.

"My soul." He gazed at her with wonder. "It's really there." Grinned faintly. "Kinda stings."

The Slayers ran out of the Seal room and through the halls, footfalls clattering, racing from the collapsing building, staying on course.

Giles was helping Robin, who saw the girls and said to him, "The bus! Get 'em on the bus!"

"Everybody!" Giles yelled to them. "This way!"

Toward the buses, and final safety . . . Kennedy was helping Willow out, and Dawn was pulling on Xander, who was calling out, "Anya! Anya!"

Beneath the debris and fallen Bringers lay a still form, who would not be leaving . . . the fallen heroine, Anya.

And Andrew . . .

Completely dumbfounded as he stabbed his attacker and the Bringer fell down dead, Andrew's sword in his chest. Andrew was bloodied but alive . . . and completely astonished by that fact.

"Why . . . ?" he murmured.

A Slayer rushed to him, grabbed him, and hauled him out.

As the cavern fell . . .

Buffy stayed with Spike, who said to her, "Go on then!"

Buffy shook her head. "You've done enough, you can still—"

"No," he managed, burning, "you beat 'em back. It's for me to do the cleanup."

Faith called from the entrance of the cavern, "Buffy! Come on!"

Then Faith ducked some falling debris and disappeared from the entrance . . . leaving Buffy alone with Spike, as debris plummeted around them as well.

"Gotta move, lamb," Spike said tenderly to her. "I think it's fair to say school's out for bloody summer."

The cavern was collapsing at the top and bottom, the actual school falling in on the vampires.

"Spike," Buffy begged.

"I mean it," Spike told her. "I gotta do this."

His hand was held up, frozen in his rictus of revelatory pain. Buffy took her own hand, interlocked it with his. A moment . . . and both their hands burst into flames.

They ignored the fire, and looked at each other.

"I love you," she told him, shaking.

And there it is, then. That girl, Cassie, she told me she would say it. She didn't tell me how, or when . . . but it's been said.

Now I can go.

He smiled kindly. "No, you don't," he told her. "But thanks for saying it."

A quake rocked them, and Spike pushed her away.

"It's your world up there. Now *go!*"

She looked at him . . . and went, bolting for her life.

While Spike gazed at the destruction in front of him and smiled wickedly.

"I want to see how it ends," he said.

The bus, outside the high school as the structure collapse.

Robin shut the door—he was at the wheel—and peeled out.

At the very back, alone in the crush, Dawn searched for her sister.

"Buffy . . ." she murmured.

Buffy headed for the door out of the basement, but it was blocked. She moved quickly to the stairs.

While below, in the cavern, Spike smiled as he was eaten from the inside by the power, and the world fell away from beneath him as he died.

Died a hero.

Died a Champion.

Died good.

The bus rolled on, just ahead of the cracking earth. Faith crouched beside Robin, staunching his wound, as Giles wrapped a tourniquet around a wounded Rona, who was fading.

Vi was in her face, yelling at her, "Stay awake! Look at me! This is nothing!"

Andrew sat by himself, bewildered.

"Why didn't I die?" he murmured.

Xander tended a Slayer, lost in his fears for Anya.

Kennedy held Willow, who was still exhausted and drained.

And Dawn . . . Dawnie . . . worried that her sister had left her, as her mother had . . . that they were both gone . . .

Buffy?

And then she saw her sister running along the rooftops, jumping off a building as it collapsed, and onto another as the bus trundled down the street; windows and beams and girders smashing down beneath her feet as Buffy kept going, leaping like a freed captive. Then the bus pulled out ahead of the last building and Buffy jumped an impossible distance, directly in front of the crumbling Sun Cinema sign, and landed hard on top of the bus.

Buffy held on, looking over the back of the vehicle at the cracks chasing them.

The entire town was sinking into a smoking black crater, a tiny bus just making its way to the edge of the town ahead of the destruction.

Inside the bus, Faith looked out, and said to Robin, "Ease off. We're clear."

The bus screeched to a stop. Buffy jumped off and the occupants started piling out.

Dawn opened the back door and jumped out, ran to her sister, and they embraced. Warmth, solidity. *Buffy, oh, my Buffy . . .*

Xander knew.

The moment he saw Andrew, he knew.

Still, he asked him, "Did you see?"

Andrew was near tears. "I was scared. I'm sorry."

He pushed, harder than he had ever pushed for anything in his life." Did you see what happened?" He searched Andrew's face. "Was she . . . ?"

Andrew gazed at him. The tears were there . . . and so was the answer.

"She was incredible," Andrew told him. "She died saving my life."

God, no. Oh, God, no . . .

Xander put a hand on Andrew's shoulder. "That's my girl. Always doing the stupid thing."

The tears were there . . . and so was the answer: *I do, Anya.*

I do.

Then it was just Faith and the guy who figured he was some big hot surprise; she checked out his big hot wound and lied through her teeth as she said, "It's not bad. You just sit here."

"That's the plan," he gritted.

Faith said, "I'll get someone to—"

"Did we make it?" He looked at her. "Did we make it?"

She gave him the word.

"We made it. We won."

He smiled a little . . . and then he was just staring. And still.

Damn.

Faith took a moment to contemplate what had been, would could have been, and moved to close his eyes.

Then he coughed, spasming back to life; she drew back her hand, as startled as he was.

"Surprise," he whispered.

Sunnydale was a smoking black crater.

Buffy and Giles walked toward the edge of it, smoke rolling before them, as he said, "I don't understand. What did this?"

"Spike," she mourned. But oh, God, she was glad for him. Glad of him.

Spike.

Rest.

The sign that read WELCOME TO SUNNYDALE toppled backward into the crater; the fillip on the town's demise, as girls milled about, counting their losses, checking in, processing that they had not only survived, but prevailed.

Buffy and Dawn stood with Giles, Xander and Willow, a bit apart; then Faith came up to join them as they all gazed out at the end of Sunnydale.

"Looks like the Hellmouth is officially closed for business," Faith said.

"There is another one in Cleveland," Giles observed. "Not to spoil the moment . . ."

"We saved the world," Xander breathed.

"We *changed* the world," Willow corrected him. Her eyes were shining as she looked at her best friend. "I can feel them, Buffy. All over. There are Slayers awakening everywhere."

"We'll have to find them," Dawn said.

"We will," Willow agreed.

Giles sighed theatrically. "Yes, because the mall was actually in Sunnydale, so no hope of going there tomorrow . . ."

Dawn choked. "We destroyed the mall? I fought on the wrong side."

"All those stores gone," Xander said sadly. "The Gap, Starbucks, Toys 'R' Us . . . who will remember these landmarks unless we tell the world of them?"

"We have a lot of work ahead of us," Giles said.

Faith appealed to the group. "Can I push him in?"

"You got my vote," Willow said, grinning.

Faith yawned, stretched. "I just wanna sleep, yo. For like a week."

"I guess we all could," Dawn said. "If we wanted to."

"Yeah, The First is scrunched, so . . ." She looked at Buffy. "What do you think we should do, Buffy?"

Faith grinned at the Slayer. "Yeah, you're not the one and only Chosen anymore. Just gotta live like a person. How's that feel?"

Buffy looked at the Slayer.

"Buffy?" Dawn asked her big sister. "What *are* we going to do?"

Buffy Summers looked at her loved ones, then back at the crater, she considered the question. A small smile crept over her lips.

Cookie dough.

Season Seven Episodes

"Lessons" Written by Joss Whedon, Directed by David Solomon

"Beneath You" Written by Douglas Petrie, Directed by Nick Marck

"Same Time, Same Place" Written by Jane Espenson, Directed by James A. Contner

"Help" Written by Rebecca Rand Kirshner, Directed by Rick Rosenthal

"Selfless" Written by Drew Goddard, Directed by David Solomon

"Him" Written by Drew Z. Greenberg, Directed by Michael Gershman

"Conversations with Dead People" Written by Jane Espenson & Drew Goddard, Directed by Nick Marck

"Sleeper" Written by David Fury & Jane Espenson, Directed by Alan J. Levi

"Never Leave Me" Written by Drew Goddard, Directed by David Solomon

"Bring on the Night" Written by Marti Noxon & Douglas Petrie, Directed by David Grossman

"Showtime" Written by David Fury, Directed by Michael Grossman

"Potential" Written and Directed by Douglas Petrie

"The Killer in Me" Written by Drew Z. Greenberg, Directed by David Solomon

"First Date" Written by Jane Espenson, Directed by David Grossman

"Get It Done" Written and Directed by Douglas Petrie

"Storyteller" Written by Jane Espenson, Directed by Marita Grabiak

"Lies My Parents Told Me" Written by David Fury and Drew Goddard, Directed By David Fury

"Dirty Girls" Written by Drew Goddard, Directed by Michael Gershman

"Empty Places" Written by Drew Z. Greenberg, Directed by James A. Contner

"Touched" Written by Rebecca Rand Kirshner, Directed by David Solomon

"End of Days" Written by Douglas Petrie and Jane Espenson, Directed by Marita Grabiak

"Chosen" Written and Directed by Joss Whedon

"The mission continues"

An all-new original Buffy or Angel novel every month

As many as one in three
Americans with HIV...
DO NOT KNOW IT.

More than half of those
who will get HIV this year...
ARE UNDER 25.

HIV is preventable.
You can help fight AIDS.
Get informed. Get the facts.

www.knowhivaids.org
1-866-344-KNOW

ROSWELL™

ALIENATION DOESN'T END WITH GRADUATION

Everything changed the day Liz Parker died. Max Evans healed her, revealing his alien identity. But Max wasn't the only "Czechoslovakian" to crash down in Roswell. Before long Liz, her best friend Maria, and her ex-boyfriend Kyle are drawn into Max, his sister Isabel, and their friend Michael's life-threatening destiny.

Now high school is over, and the group has decided to leave Roswell to turn that destiny around. The six friends know they have changed history by leaving their home.

What they don't know is what lies in store…

SIMON PULSE
Published by Simon & Schuster

Aaron Corbet isn't a bad kid—he's just a little different.

On the eve of his eighteenth birthday, Aaron is dreaming of a darkly violent and landscape. He can hear the sounds of weapons clanging, the screams of the stricken, and another sound that he cannot quite decipher. But as he gazes upward to the sky, he suddenly understands. It is the sound of great wings beating the air unmercifully as hundreds of armored warriors descend on the battlefield.

The flapping of angels' wings.

Orphaned since birth, Aaron is suddenly discovering newfound—and sometimes supernatural—talents. But not until he is approached by two men does he learn the truth about his destiny—and his own role as a liason between angels, mortals, and Powers both good and evil—some of whom are bent on his own destruction....

the fallen

a new series by Thomas E. Snigoski

Book One available March 2003

From Simon Pulse

Published by Simon & Schuster